Fractured Storm

(Storm Series Book 4)

A. R. Vagnetti

Wicked Storm
PUBLISHING

Wicked Storm Publishing

First Edition

Edited by Sam Hendricks

Design by Les @ German Creatives

arvagnetti.com

Chapter 1

Viessa

An eerie mist surrounds me, amplifying my harsh breath. A pounding ache radiates through my knees pressed against the unforgiving stone floor. Tingles of unease dance across the nape of my neck and down my arms, quivering with fatigue after hours of maintaining them stretched wide in supplication.

I abhor this isolated, dank monastery built by monks in the late 1600s. It's an exquisite structure forged around the tiger lair cave in Paro Valley, Bhutan. Legend has it, a former wife of an emperor, known as Yeshe Tsogyal, transformed herself into a tigress and carried the Guru on her back from Tibet. The myth could be the first recorded sighting of a feline shifter, but who knows?

A constant fog shrouds the monastery. The structure hangs on a precarious cliff forged into the rock face. My father, Icarus, the High Priest Oracle, claims the mist aids during training, curbing the chaotic foresight of past, present, and future. But the humid vapor suffocates my senses, suppressing my ability to perceive the werewolf—no doubt, father's objective.

A sudden vision slams into my frontal lobe, forcing my spine to arch. I have yet to master how to keep the images at bay before easing them into my mind so I can evaluate each one to determine their relevance.

In this particular slide show, I recognize many of the participants. A tremendous battle ensues in a wide field hemmed in by towering woodlands. The vampire queen, Nicole Giordano, along with her mate, Logan, his brother, Sebastian, my twin, Lucretia, and a hundred Guardians, engage in open warfare with other vampires and white-winged fae.

My sister's prowess with a sword impresses me every time. She and Trezzo, her former mentor and lover—turned traitor—instructed me in combat on the rare occasions my mind was lucid enough to pick up on their cues. But I adopted the distant and quiet precision of the bow. There is enough chaos going on in my brain without the shrilling clamor of clashing swords.

My focus zeros in on a striking white wolf as he leaps into the fray. The majestic savagery of the two-hundred-pound predator is breathtaking to behold, and I would recognize my mate in any form.

When I spy King Dimitri Giordano brutally punch his fist through my mate's father's chest and yank the werewolf king's heart from his rib cage, my spirit aches hearing the agonized howl of my wolf.

This is the battle the prophecy foretold. Where the Halfling, Nicole, unselfishly plunged a silver dagger through her heart to end her father, Dimitri's life. Where my sire and mentor, Icarus, defied the gods to rescue the bringer of peace from purgatory with forbidden dark magic.

"What do you see, my child?" Icarus asks, kneeling in front of me, enduring the hardship right along with me.

"A frightful battle with King Giordano."

"Very good. And is this vision past, present, or future?"

It vexes me, he must ask, but I can't fault him. For 142 years, my mind could not resolve the answer to that very question. I resided in a perpetual hell state, never understanding when or where I was.

If it hadn't been for my sister, Lucretia, I would have perished a century ago. She is the reason I am a vampire, instead of just a shifter. In one of my more frenetic states, I slit my wrists down to the bone, repeating the process when the wounds mended. In my mind, I was someone else in another time and place, unable to separate myself from the visualizations, to be just the observer and not the participant.

When Lu found me, my pulse was non-existent. With mere seconds to decide, my twin, freshly turned herself by Dimitri, forced her blood down my throat to spare my life.

Since an immortal turning another is a rare occurrence, I suspect the sole reason it worked was that we are the offspring of an Oracle. Otherwise, I'd be six feet under, and my soul, God knows where.

"Let the images dissipate, child, and open yourself to the next one," Icarus demands in that gentle, even cadence that never fluctuates with emotion.

When I first discovered who my actual father was and my purpose in this world, I despised the little blue tattooed priest, assuming he deserted me as a youngster because I was a shifter twin instead of a mortal. All the Oracles over the millennia were born of human women and brought here as toddlers for tutoring. But I soon realized it wasn't Icarus's fault. Fate never allowed him to determine my whereabouts, so for over a century, I suffered from psychological chaos, presuming I was deranged.

A fresh vision slams to the forefront. My twin, chained to the wall, facing the Council of Unity for her transgressions. Crimes which she performed to shelter me, her mentally handicapped sister. Back then, I did not appreciate the lengths Lucretia underwent to protect me.

Our predicament forced her into prostitution at an impressionable young age to support us financially. She withstood years of vigorous and brutal training by Trezzo to become the first female vampire Guardian. And when King Giordano discovered my location, he used me as leverage to coerce my sister into betraying her queen. Lu survived three days of extreme torture by Trez just last year and willingly offered herself to the maniac to block him from raping me.

"Concentrate, Viessa. Communicate what you see."

"Lucretia is on trial," I say between clenched teeth, the agony in my limbs causing perspiration to pepper my upper lip. "I must get to her. Tell them why she did what she did. No. Wait. The vision is the past again."

"You are performing well. Two more and we will surrender for the night. Dawn approaches."

Icarus adapted with ease to teaching a sun-sensitive prodigy. Actually, I'm a Tri-bred. Part feline shifter—which has yet to declare itself, vampire, and Oracle. Because my bloodsucking side is prevalent, it compels us to train after the sun quits the sky. Although the deity component inside me only necessitates a few hours of sleep, instead of the expected six to eight forced on most nightwalkers. I can also go for extended periods between feedings. If pushed, a normal vampire can function without sustenance for several weeks, but any longer and they risk falling into a death-like coma or worse. My heritage allows me to abstain for a maximum of two months.

The press of the next scene clenches my fists tighter to keep them from dropping. It's the evening of Liam's vow, nearly two months ago, when the Watchers tried to execute the valkyrie princess, Alexandria Svaldana.

Heat infuses my frame, but not from exertion. Desire, pure and sharp, pebbles my nipples beneath the gauzy robe.

The second Icarus left Sebastian's Tuscan Villa, I launched myself at my wolf, desperate for his hardened muscles next to mine, the soft, dark tresses at his collar in my grip, and the lush fullness of his lips against my own. The werewolf king's addictive scent of summer rain and leather consumed and besieged me.

When his potent blood coated my throat, I realized I'd never partake of another ever again. But with no indication of the duration of my Oracle training, whether it took months or years, no way I could expect such a virile, sexual male to abstain and wait for me. Our conversation and the pledge

I manipulated from him in front of his friends, play out in my mind.

"It doesn't matter. I don't give a rat's ass how long it takes. When you're done, I will be waiting," the king declares.

"No."

"What do you mean, no? You violated your vow when you kissed me, drank from me. Now you're informing me not to wait for you?"

"Liam. I needed your strength. I'll require your potent blood every couple of months. Since I've sampled you, I can communicate to you when the craving becomes too extreme, and I have need of you."

"When you have need of me?" Bitterness edges into Liam's tone. "Is that all I am to you, a bag of blood?"

I laugh, reveling in his anger and glorying in the calmness of my mind in his presence. "You are so much more, wolf." I step closer before placing both palms on his cheeks. "Form a vow, Liam, in front of all your friends."

He contemplates me warily even as his gaze drops to my lips with hunger, and his fingers clutch my waist. "What vow?"

"Pledge to me, you will continue to flourish in your life, as you always have while I'm in training. Be happy, as if I never existed. Fuck as many females as you desire until my return. But, when I conclude with all this tedious study, and my mind is completely right, make no mistake, you'll be mine and mine alone."

"You wish me to fuck other women?" My remarks anger Liam, just as I hoped they would.

"What I want isn't relevant right now. It's cruel of me to demand you to abstain for so long." And while that is true, I'm hoping the bond will force him to state otherwise. Just the idea of his craving for me building to a breaking point excites me.

"And if I don't?" The Alpha's concentration narrows, his beast objecting to the command. His defiance produces butterflies of excitement in my belly. Liam's animal brings my spirit to life.

"I'll find another source of nourishment," I state with a shrug.

"The fuck you will," the king growls. The dark eyes flash blue as his wolf fights for control.

I grin. "Then, vow it, my king."

Liam regards me and I hold my breath, concerned I just screwed my chances. "When you return to feed, sweetness, how much time will we have together?"

Ah. My wolf is calculating if he will have sufficient time to fuck me. My heart rate spikes with a long-denied need.

"An hour, no more."

"Then I vow to be utterly faithful to my female, but hear me now, woman. Our time together will be more than just feeding. And when your training is complete, your flesh will bear the mark of my bite. Right here—" Liam glides a finger across the muscles between my neck and shoulder and I shiver — "for all to witness and know you belong to me." His smug grin has the males in the room chuckling softly in understanding.

I lick my lips. He's fallen right in line with my quickly formulated plan. "So be it. Your vow seals the contract. No matter what arises in that hour, you must abide by your promise."

Liam scowls, uncertain what he just conceded to honor. No doubt, when he discovers my genuine nature, his beast will balk. Viciously. The challenge sends a thrill through me.

I lean in close and brush my lips to his before whispering, "See you in two months, my king. Be ready for me." With a hasty wave to my twin, a new lightness in my spirit, I trace back to the monastery.

The fatigue in my arms bounces me to the present. My life was desolate, tragic, and the majority of the time, I didn't live in the present. Voices and imagery consumed every neuron in my mind. Until my stay at the mental institute where my twin reluctantly placed me. For a brief window of time, I discovered a means to reduce the constant assault on my sanity.

Control.

A beloved, crazed fellow inmate gave me a brief insight into sexual dominance. How controlling and directing a partner eases the barrage of images, and voices. I only experienced the elusive peace a few times before they ripped him from my life.

Whenever I'm in my mate's presence, the visions and voices subside even more than before. Like a softly muted TV. Still there in the background, seeking to intrude, but manageable. When I attempt to control his inner animal and dominate the man, that's when my mind goes mute, and I discover peace for the first time in my life.

I felt it at the castle when I first saw him, and again at Lu's trial, but it really hit home when I manipulated my wolf into agreeing to exactly what I wanted at the vampire's Italian villa.

Such euphoria is a drug for me, and I crave not merely the male in all his predatory sexiness, the dark whiskey irises devouring my body, but the submission of the Alpha beneath the beast.

Only through complete control does the chaos in my mind quiet. The problem? Liam is naturally dominant, the king of his people, so urging him to surrender to me sexually could be the most significant task of my life.

I have much to learn on that front as well, so at every dawn, alone in my room, I devoured every morsel of information I could find on the internet regarding what I now understand as BDSM. Most of it was frightening, but I cannot lie. The imagery of beautiful men bound with rope or shackles, their backsides reddened by a paddle or whip, excited me and I worked my swollen bundle to relieve the pulsing pressure.

If Liam and I are to obtain any future once this darn training is over, my mate must learn trust, love, and submission.

Soon I'll need nourishment, and my heart races with anticipation, but anxiety and dread cloud the thrill. Our first hour together will proceed much differently than my Liam expects, and I pray it won't be our last.

Chapter 2

"**J**oshua, take the side by side, and a couple of ranch hands out to the south pasture, drone images revealed a good section of fence down along that range," I instruct my younger brother, shoveling scrambled eggs and bacon down my gullet. "The vet is arriving later today to monitor the development of several pregnancies, and Eric's mare turned up lame yesterday."

"You got it, bro," my sibling answers around a mouthful of his own breakfast. "FYI. Cellica was out pretty late last night. Again. You should have a chat with our baby sister. She doesn't listen to me worth crap."

"Is her hair still the hue of sapphires?" I ask with a grimace. The second Cel hit twenty-five, she adopted a ridiculous goth phase. Her lipstick, fingernails, and attire changed to dark, usually pitch black, and now her gorgeous long curls are blue. Goddamn blue.

"Yup. Blue as the Montana sky in the summer," Joshua smirks as he shoves back from the kitchen table.

Even though thirty years separate my younger sibling and me, we are similar in looks. He sports a more clean-cut, all-American version, with a carefree, fun attitude and none of the tremendous responsibility weighing him down. Basically, he is me before our father died.

"Eli took the side by side out last, so you might need to fuel up before you take off."

The Wild Beast Ranch is an extensive cattle property with over 3,000 acres of lush rolling hills and woodland, requiring the operation of ATVs in addition to horses and drones. Even though we have a cook and several housekeepers for the 10,000-square-foot homestead, we both take our plates to the huge farm sink, as our momma taught us.

And that's when my zombie of a sister shuffles into the kitchen straight for the coffeepot. Joshua sneaks out the back door.

Coward.

Her inky skull pajamas brush the floor past fuzzy slippers, and the fucking blue hair sits haphazardly on top of her head. But her face is free of makeup, reminding me of the bewitching, innocent little girl I admire and worship.

"Good morning, sunshine," I say and stoop to her five-foot-three frame to kiss her cheek.

"Morning," she grumbles, rubbing the slumber from her eyes while pouring a generous cup of Joe.

"Late night again?" I ask, resting a hip on the granite counter and trying to appear not interested.

With both our parents gone, the safety of my siblings falls to me. But, since I have no fucking clue how to parent, especially a willful twenty-five-year-old who's close to shifting into full immortality, it's like galloping through a land mine on a raging bull.

"Don't start, Liam." She scowls up at me—the dark eyes, so similar to Dad's, hard as stone.

When did she go from the loving, hang on every word I uttered, little adolescent, to this sullen, can't stand to be in the same room with me, young woman? "What is going on with you, Cel?" I pour myself another cup. "You arrive home in the wee hours of the morning, you dress like some vamp wannabe, and now your damn hair is blue."

"Says the male whose fated one *is* a vampire."

"We are not discussing me." I scowl at the reminder.

The two-month mark came and went last week, and I'm fit to bolt out of my skin with need. Where the fuck is Viessa? She must be starving.

"Look," Cellica says with a sigh, fixing me with a strained smile that doesn't even come close to reaching her big eyes. "I appreciate the whole big brother/daddy routine, but I'm a grown woman who can take care of herself."

"Are you seeing someone?" If it were up to me, I'd never initiate this damn conversation, but as the sole parent figure in the household, it's my duty to probe.

"None of your goddamn business. Now stop prying in my personal life and deliver my fucking orders for the day."

"Watch your mouth," I growl, taking a menacing stride toward her. Cel has the foresight to retreat a step in the face of my beast's disapproving growl.

"Fine. I'm sorry," she sulks, and I back down, as always. I love both my siblings, but Cellica holds a special place in my heart. From the moment I held her tiny body in my arms, I vowed to protect my baby sister until my dying breath, and I would do anything she asked. Thank God she hasn't figured that out yet.

"Several cattle escaped the downed fence Joshua is repairing today. Why don't you saddle up and accompany him? Try to recover the lost cows."

"Yes, Sir," she mumbles before snatching a pastry off the counter. "But I have finals to study for this afternoon. I graduate this year, ya know." She pivots to head to her room.

I stop her before she disappears around the corner. "Cellica, you know I'm proud of you, right? Your wizardry with numbers astounds me. No matter which direction you decide to take, whether you utilize your skills here at the ranch or venture elsewhere, we are going to have the biggest damn party this county has ever seen the second that diploma touches your hand." She smiles and I step closer. "You can talk to me... um... about anything. I hope you know that. If you're in trouble, require anything, or just wish to unburden, I'm here for you."

She shoots me a somber glance over her shoulder. "I love you for asking, but as I said, I'm a big girl, Liam."

Something is going on with her, but with a shitload of my own problems piling up, I let her go, seize my Stetson by the door, and head out to the arena to break in a new mustang.

Maybe a few bumps and bruises will get my mind off Viessa. Every night, after a cold shower, I settle in my big empty bed and struggle not to dwell on her image, her honeysuckle scent, or those fangs sinking into my neck.

Her strength surprised me at the villa, but it shouldn't have. My female is the first recorded Tri-bred. The shifter side is currently inactive, but her power as an Oracle, even in the emerging stages of training, is extraordinary.

Thank goodness Lu's panther has remained dormant. If she could suddenly shift, I fear the Watchers would make an appearance once again. Since Viessa is an Oracle, the fallen angels would have no choice but to keep her alive.

Besides, the gods forbid Oracles to mate, so they have no concerns about an offspring with a werewolf. Any child conceived by Vi and I would be the first recorded Quad-bred. Part werewolf, shifter, vampire, and Oracle. The thought of what abilities it would possess staggers my mind.

If I have any hope of dominating my stubborn woman, I must unleash the beast. Conquer the determined resolve I witnessed the night at the villa. Even months before, at Lucretia's hearing, Viessa wished to control me. I will never allow that to develop.

I am an Alpha werewolf, king to my people, forceful and dominant by nature, demanding submission from my sexual partners. I've never relished the whole BDSM scene like Sebastian and Logan, or my shifter buddy Kurtis, but I require authority in how events play out, whether slow and tender or hard and aggressive. In the bedroom, what I say goes, not the other way around. My beast demands no less.

Viessa must come to heel. Submit to her male. The prospect of her kneeling before me, drawing my length between those luscious lips, has my dick pressing against my jeans. No matter how I work to ignore the visuals of my female, they bombard me every night. My dick becomes a painful, throbbing entity, compelling me to relieve the pressure just to earn some damn sleep.

If I don't possess her soon, I'll go mad. Once a wolf or shifter finds their mate, our sexual appetite becomes voracious, requiring our females daily, sometimes twice a day. I pledged to abstain during our two months apart, but shit, I didn't realize my dick would be permanently hard and throbbing the entire time.

Viessa better turn into a stellar student and complete this training soon, or I might ignore my vow and mark her as mine despite the consequences.

My woman has supernatural fortitude and healing ability, so no need to claim her while in human form. Unlike shifters, werewolves alter their shapes, growing into a cross between wolf and human. Our bodies enlarge to twice our stature, with the power and speed almost equivalent to a vampire, but our senses are more acute. The architecture of our face shifts, and the snout extends slightly, showcasing enormous canines. Our eyes deviate into the color of our animal and detect heat signatures of objects or people in absolute darkness.

Basically, we are upright wolves ready to rut our mates and mark their flesh. The metamorphosis can occur during mating if we allow it or when the moon is full. We gain ten times our traditional energy, can punch through solid metal, and leap eighteen feet into the air. Werewolves, in our beast form, are dangerous, but if we consume vampire blood, it triples our strength. We become the most feared creatures on the planet. Even the vampires steer clear of us during periods of change.

My female, powerful Oracle or not, will learn to submit.

Chapter 3

Liam

"Everythin' is set up in de dinin' room for yisser poker noight, me lord," my ever-faithful butler informs me with a bow, although I don't regard him as a servant. The Irish werewolf has been with my family for as far back as I can remember.

"Plenty of snacks for Ruse, Darath, and myself?" No need to set out a huge spread since the other players tonight are vampires.

After the wild evening with the Watchers at Sebastian's Tuscan Villa, I introduced a new tradition; guys-only poker night once a month to take my mind off Viessa and her lack of appearance beneath me. It allows the men a chance to catch up, minus the girls.

"Aye, me lord, an' cowl Guinness in de fridge or whiskey breathin' on de sidebar."

Translation: cold beer in the refrigerator and my best whiskey open on the bar in the dining room where we play.

"Thank you, Victor. What would I do without you?"

"'Ill de vampires be needin' anythin'?

"Yeah," I grin. "A healthy dose of luck to beat me."

Half an hour later, I'm cracking the top on a cold one when a streak of lightning illuminates the living area, and thunder rattles the windows. May is the rainy season for Montana, but by mid-June, the daily showers slow down to a weekly barrage of powerful storms sweeping through the valley. It appears we are in for a doozy tonight. A perfect backdrop to poker night.

My father, the infamous Werewolf King, Jimmy Scott, took the time to reflect and plan out the homestead when he and my mother built the extensive ranch house in the late 1800s. For the times, this structure was a modern, lavish marvel. Over the years, my parents made several modifications to keep the home updated.

The rear of the residence rests fifty feet from the banks of the Yellowstone River, which boasts some of the best fly-fishing in the country. A past-time Josh and I enjoy. Cellica mastered the skill as well, but since she is more of a fair-weather fisherwoman, preferring her love of numbers, she rarely wets a line with us anymore.

The main living area rests in the middle of the slant-ed L-shaped design, encased on either side with generous windows to experience the magnificent scenery from any-where. Five bedrooms, each with its own bathroom, rest on the far end of the two-story L. My brother and sister reside in that wing until they're mated. Plans to build their own homesteads on the vast holdings are in place when and if the time comes.

The shorter portion houses the Master suite, complete with a sunken jacuzzi tub, brick paver floors, rock and old timber accents, and a wood-burning fireplace. The chamber is over the top for me, but I anticipate sharing it with my female one day.

Next to the enormous walk-in closet is the door to my private recording studio, housing some of my most prized guitars; from a polished black Martin D-35 signed by the legendary Johnny Cash to a 1989 Fender Custom Telecaster, a gift from none other than country great Keith Urban.

At the LeLoo Bar in Newport, Oregon, I perform songs by other prominent artists, but occasionally, I throw in one of my creations to obtain the audience's reaction. If the feedback is positive, I'll include the song in my collection CD, which will never get produced. An immortal can't afford to be in the public eye. It raises too many forbidden questions. Like, why aren't you aging, Mr. Scott? And what big teeth you have, Mr. Scott.

As I peer around my home, it dawns on me. Since Viessa is a damn vampire, I'll need to implement extreme modifications to the house to protect my mate from the sun.

My dad would roll over in his grave if he realized a vamp was his son's fated one, although he carried a soft spot for Nicole and Logan.

I'm leaping way ahead of myself. Our High Priest Oracle, Viessa's father, warned us the gods forbid a divine seer to take a mate. So, the question remains; why did the powers that be pair me with a being I can't bond with?

With a heavy sigh, I wander into the living room. When Lucretia and King Ruse pop in next to the TV, I'm not surprised since I already invited the vampires into my home on previous occasions.

I grin when the big shifter takes a second to recover, still not comfortable with teleportation. Ruse is my closest friend and the sole individual I confide in about everything. Well, almost everything. We've been through serious shit together. The biggest test of our friendship came last year when I first met Lu. My beast responded to the Guardian in such a way, I assumed she was mine until Kurtis declared the warrior belonged to him.

Those were tense, crazy times for us, but we weathered the storm, and I love Lucretia like a sister. The twin vibe triggers my wolf's protective tendencies, and I would do any-thing for the tall, lethal beauty. Although, in human form, she could probably kick my ass.

While her mate recovers, I embrace the shifter warrior clad in leather with her trademark dark braid hanging over one shoulder. "Thanks for bringing the big lug over."

"Yes, well, you're welcome." Uncomfortable with easy dis-plays of affection, I'm startled when she leans up and kisses my cheek. "By the way, I heard from my twin."

My heart stops. "No, shit?"

Only relations or mated couples communicate telepathi-cally, although Nicole possesses the ability with anyone. For whatever reason, until this moment, Viessa was incapable of using telepathy. She *is* growing stronger.

"She asked me to inform you she'll arrive the night of the full moon."

"No. Absolutely not." *What the hell?* "As much as I crave to see her, I can't control myself during the lunar peak. The beast takes over."

"I warned her, but she insisted. My twin has become quite bossy."

"Yeah. I've noticed."

"Angel," Kurtis pipes in, recovered. "It's imperative you persuade her otherwise. Not much stops Liam when he's in beast form, and in the presence of his mate, nothing will prevent him from claiming her."

"I'll push the issue, but I make no promises." She twists to take off, but Kurtis's broad hand snakes out, fastens on her nape, and whirls her into his chest.

"You weren't about to disappear without offering me a proper goodbye, were you?" His low forceful tone lifts my eyebrow, and I stride back, allowing them space.

"You're a big boy, love," she purrs in the face of his aggression. "Have fun." Her saucy grin lingers in the air a brief second after she vanishes. I chuckle at the determined gleam in Kurtis's blue gaze.

"Uh oh. The little woman gettin' disciplined when you get home?"

The shifter turns to me with a smirk. "Indeed. The mischievous minx has been pressing my buttons all week, working to incite a spanking. It's quite amusing observing her shenanigans."

"Hmm, I bet." An image of the big shifter paddling the fierce warrior pops to the forefront, and I shove it aside, not needing that image in my brain since his mate is identical to mine. "Beer or whiskey?" I ask instead.

"Beer, if you have that local ale that tastes like maple syrup," he replies and accompanies me into the kitchen.

I chuckle at Kurtis's affinity for sweets. "You mean Fungus Shui from over in Sidney?"

"Yeah, that's the one. It still blows my mind they created a beer from mushrooms that tastes like syrup."

I open the fridge and grin. "Looks like Victor remembered you gushing on about it last time. He stocked up."

"God, I love that wolf. I seriously need to get myself a Victor. Lucretia is not much on the whole pampering her king thing."

"Yeah, I bet not." I laugh, handing him an ice-cold bottle. I clear my throat and pick at the label of my Guinness. "Can I ask you a personal question?"

"Liam, you're my best friend, you may ask me anything as long as you keep this ale in stock."

The six-eight mountain of a male causes the spacious kitchen to seem insignificant. Wait till the seven-foot demon king appears. At six and a half feet, the vampires and I appear small.

"Do you ever give Lu control sexually?" Shit. I can't believe I'm having this discussion with another dude. But if the Alpha shifter submits to his female, maybe I can too.

Kurtis regards me for several moments. "Depends on what you mean. Do I allow her to explore without direction? Yes. But if you're inquiring if I let her dominate me through

BDSM play?" He pops a potato chip from the bowl into his mouth. "Then no."

"And if she requested it of you?"

He contemplates the query. "If my mate required it, I would be amenable. On occasion." He takes a lengthy drink, nearly finishing the bottle, so I grab another from the fridge. "Why are you asking?"

"You recall the vow I made to Viessa at the villa?" When he nods, I continue. "I worry the unknown component to our arrangement is exactly that. The Tri-bred possesses a dominant side I fear could come between us." I swallow a huge swig of beer. This conversation is making my skin crawl. "My beast will never tolerate the control I suspect she's pursuing."

"At this stage, you're guessing, buddy. Viessa's mind is un-predictable right now. She's prepared to compromise. Are you?"

"Fuck. I have no clue." I shake my head in bewilderment. "I guess I'll wait and see, but she cannot come to me on the full moon. I'd have her pinned and mated by the end of the night."

He plants his huge palm the size of a dinner plate on my shoulder. "One fact I've learned about possessing a mate. Alpha male or not, we can surmount anything to bring them happiness."

"Well, here's hoping you're correct," I mutter, and we clink bottles.

"Are you two lovebirds ready to hand over your hard-earned cash?" The deep gruff voice of King Darath used to grate along my nerves, especially when I discovered his true identity—the one and only Lucifer, monarch of hell. But his sick sense of humor, adaptability to any situation, and devotion to the vampire queen, Nicole—whom I consider family—overrode my reservations.

"I still think you cheat, demon," Kurtis rumbles before they clasp hands in greeting.

"The devil doesn't cheat."

I'm taken off guard by his wicked smile. This scary creature definitely coined the term *devilish grin*. "Victor opened your favorite whiskey before he took off, Jag. It's on the sidebar in the dining room."

"Put tits and long blond hair on that Irish dog, and I would mate him," he snickers before withdrawing to locate his drink of choice.

"Sorry we are late," Logan mutters as he, Sebastian, and Christoph Nox materialize in the kitchen. "Nicole cornered us before we could escape."

"Messo alle strette? Abbiamo aspettato mentre facevi sesso," Bastian grumbles under his breath with an eye roll.

Christoph translates. "Cornered us? We waited while you had sex."

I laugh, spitting beer across the island.

"Do not take it out on me because your female does not live with you, brother," Logan counters back with a smirk, patting me on the back as I nearly cough up a lung.

"See. This is why you need to run as far as you can from a mate, be free as a bird, and fuck as many females as your little heart desires," Nox declares with a flourish.

Christoph, Sebastian's second in command of the queen's Guardians, and a veterinarian of all things, pipes in with humor even though it doesn't quite match the guilt in his striking mismatched eyes. The left is the color of the Caribbean ocean and the other is a cloudless sky at midday. While undercover as Dr. Warner, Nox had to wear dark contacts so as not to leave any distinguishing attributes for the mortals to remember.

Is the 100-year-old vamp speaking from experience? He's relatively youthful to have discovered his one true mate already.

"I've always been meaning to ask, why did you decide to become a veterinarian, Nox?"

"The medical field always fascinated me, and since restraining myself around human blood was impossible, I chose animals. It's similar enough it captured my interest, and actually it's more difficult." He shrugs. "The patient can't tell me what's wrong and we treat multiple species, not just one."

"His medical skill has come in handy in the field many times," Sebastian pipes in, bumping fists with his lieutenant.

As I peer at these immortal friends assembled in my home, it seems weird to see the vamps in jeans and t-shirts. Their leather uniforms are an intricate part of who they are--warriors, keepers of the peace.

"One day, a female will rock your world, Nox," I reply, slapping the vampire on the back as Jag walks in with a full tumbler of liquor.

Speaking of clothing. Anytime Jag's involved, it's a game of chance trying to guess the demon's attire from one moment to the next. Tonight, he's dressed in dark blue slacks and a crisp white button-down with the sleeves rolled up. Last month he showed up in frayed cut-off jeans and a pink t-shirt depicting the band Aerosmith.

"I hope I'm around to witness your demise, Christoph," I grin.

"Let's hope not," he mutters, and I frown at his strange reply.

"Yes, young vamp," Jag chimes in, settling a hip against the granite island. The eerie red eyes observe Nox over the rim of his glass. "You have much to learn."

With three vampires, a demon, a shifter, and a werewolf, my huge galley appears cramped, but I grin with contentment. A unique bond was forged between us after we joined together to rescue Lucretia from Dimitri's son, Zachariah, and I would die for any of them and they for me. Alpha males are instinctively mistrustful of other males, especially mated immortals. But our tribe of divergent species somehow works. We trust each other almost explicitly with our better halves. I say *almost* because our inner beasts might have different reasoning on the matter.

"Let's get this game rollin," I announce, capturing another beer for Ruse and me before glaring at Jag. "I feel lucky tonight."

"I told you, Liam, dogs are not my thing," the demon eyes me with mock regret before swinging a leering gaze at my best friend. "Although, I would make an exception for you, strapping shifter."

"Fuck off, Jag," Kurtis counters with a laugh.

Even though Jagorach lusts after the land nymph Priestess Kleora, he either finds Kurtis' size a challenge, or he enjoys saying the most outrageous comments to get a rise out of people.

"Tonight is cards, gentlemen. Keep them in your pants for the ladies." I chuckle before leading this group of sizable men into the dining room.

Chapter 4

Every full moon, I close the LeLoo Bar and invite packs from around the Newport region for an evening of drinking and dancing at my ranch in Montana before the beast takes over. They fly in, or caravan here from all over. This month, it was a tough call since it lands on the fourth of July—a high-profit night for the club. But as a king, my people come first.

My vast land provides them a place to run, hunt, and fuck to their heart's content, and I need not worry about any members of the pack instigating trouble and perhaps getting captured or killed by a vampire Guardian on patrol.

Sure, I surrender a few heads of cattle, but it's a paltry cost to pay to safeguard my wolves.

Since Oregon is a part of the Vampire Nation, the warriors patrol it regularly, but their numbers double, and no Guardian scouts alone, on the full moon.

When a werewolf is under the sway of the lunar cycle, a vampire is no match in a one-on-one fight. That's why I encourage all my territory leaders to follow my lead and secure an area where the werewolves can relax and grant their inner beast free rein.

The Werewolf Province encompasses Manitoba and Saskatchewan in Canada. North Dakota, Minnesota, Wisconsin, and Michigan in the United States, with our headquarters here in Montana.

Many of the commanders hesitated at first with the burden of finding one common space to gather the packs. But my father instigated this tradition for a solid reason and informed them, one night a month is not too much to ask to let loose and not have to deal with the repercussions.

My shoulders shift in agitation, the guitar strap irritating the hypersensitive skin under my shirt. I yearn to discard the human façade, bay at the moon, dart through the timbers with my fellow wolves, slay an elk, and feed on the magnificent gift of life. The escalating energy these individuals are projecting is becoming challenging to ignore.

I've set the band up along the perimeter of the patio, as usual, with the rushing river as our backdrop. Trucks, campers, and tents circle the front property and dozens of werewolves mill around the grounds, drinking, laughing, or dancing to the music.

The moment is approaching to deliver them on their way. The impulse to shift will become intolerable, and even though the change to beast is a smoother transition than the blast to wolf, I don't wish them anywhere near my home when it happens. With so many males gathered in one place with mates and potential conquests, rational thought disappears.

The group lingers in anticipation for the one song to transport them into their inner beasts' wild freedom—The Wolf by The Spencer Lee Band.

The lyrics force me to think of Viessa; how my dark tumultuous passions for her thrum through me, and how in a brief measure of time, the female became my addiction. Tonight, with my senses heightened and my lust raging, she's all I imagine when I sing. Every word applies to her. The beautiful amber eyes call to me. Her luscious lips beg to be plundered, and the agile body ignites a searing desire to caress it softly and pinken the surface with rough sex.

Fuck. It's time to get this show on the road.

When my brother gives me the salute, his irises shifting between brown and the green of his wolf, I stride to the mic.

"Okay, ladies and gents, drink up. The wolf reigns free tonight."

Loud cheering, shouts, and howls fill the night sky. I grin in anticipation. Most of the mob press around the makeshift stage, holding their cups up in excitement as I begin the send-off song.

At the chorus, the mated couples start gyrating against each other, aroused by the sexy lyrics, the beat, and the fevered call of the moon. Inhuman growls float across the ground.

"I wanna jack it, smack it. You know the shit that turns you on? I wanna lick it, kiss it. I'll give you everything you want. Howling out your name, run like champagne. You're gonna feel the vibes, when the wolf comes out tonight."

When I utter the last phrase, the crazed gathering of wolves throw their heads back and howl at the brilliant round ball in the black sky—my sight shifts between man and beast.

Before the final chord dissipates, my people head out in all directions. My hyperacute sight captures heat signatures disappearing in the timbers beyond the moon's silvery rays. The werewolves discard their clothes, placing them in neat piles to return to later. I nod toward the band, their signal to join the others. They promptly set aside their instruments and disperse.

As king, I only allow myself to change after I'm confident everyone is safely on their way, and none linger close to the grounds. My inner beast rages at me to award him freedom, but I ignore his incessant chuffs of impatience and take my usual course around the house.

A familiar scent hits my nostrils a millisecond before she materializes in front of me. Goddamnit. Fear, rage, and instant lust struggle for dominance.

"Viessa, get the fuck out of here!" I roar at her, spotting my reflection in the windows behind her. My irises are vivid blue, and my canines have dropped. The transition is upon me.

Instead of vanishing, she fucking steps closer. My claws extend, longing to shred the white robe from her body, force her to her hands and knees on the flagstone and rut her until the beast is content.

Mine. Claim her.

The echo of fabric ripping shoots terror through my heart. I've started the metamorphosis, gaining height and bulk, and my clothes struggle to contain the inevitable.

"This is who you are, Liam. I must witness it."

"Fuck, woman. If you don't leave, you'll do more than witness it, you'll experience it firsthand."

"Can you not manage your beast?" she asks, her head tipped with interest.

"No goddamnit. So, unless you wish to oppose the gods and become mine, I'm begging you to go home right now."

Viessa's bouquet is making me wild, fraying the thread of discipline fixed to snap. Just the notion of spreading her smooth thighs, lapping between her legs, mounting her like the beast I am, and fucking her rough and fast with my canines sunk into her shoulder, has my shaft pulsing, making it challenging to concentrate.

My jeans rip down the seam as my limbs enlarge. White fur springs up along my exposed skin. Dammit! I'm losing command over the wolf. "Now, Viessa." My tone is dark and guttural.

When the tattered shirt falls away, I dig my claws into my palms in a paltry attempt to stem the change. But the second my face alters, the snout lengthening slightly, the short white coat spreading across my cheeks and neck, and my ears elongating into a cross between human and wolf, I comprehend it's too late.

Viessa's lovely eyes expand, and she steps back, fear blazing in their depths. I raise a fur-covered hand to terminate her retreat. "Do not run, Vi." The structure of my face has evolved so much the words are barely distinguishable. "Make. It. Worse." If she were to take off, nothing would block me from hunting her down.

She nods, but instead of teleporting away to safety, the tenacious woman strides forward and boldly places her palm over the smooth fur on my chest.

At five-eleven, Vi is tall for a female, and normally only half a foot separates us, but in lunar beast form, my height reaches almost seven feet.

"You are magnificent, Liam."

Her tender voice and firm touch calm me considerably, but I am beyond the point of communication. Even though my breathing is heavy and ragged, and my hands clench and unclench with the urge to reach for her, I remain perfectly still.

"You need me, don't you?" she dares to ask.

Need is too paltry a word. Demand. Require. Claim or die are more accurate definitions of the chaos circling through my brain in her presence. I growl menacingly in a last-ditch effort to frighten her away.

"I'm starving, Liam. I can't wait another night to feed." She ogles my neck with hunger.

The remaining seams in my jeans rip apart, the tattered pieces drop to the ground, and my hardness springs forward. Viessa's eyes sink, and she gasps.

If Vi were a mere mortal, mating her in this form would kill her. But she's an immortal Tri-bred, able to handle my massive length and tremendous bite.

"During the full moon, do you… do you have sex with other werewolves?"

Why the hell is she talking about fucking at this moment? It expands the beast's demand for her flesh tenfold. I delve deep for strength and nod my response, but I'm powerless to halt my progress toward her when the beast inhales her intoxicating scent.

Her chest rises and plummets, and her harsh breath is loud to my sensitive ears. Jesus. Is she turned on by my appearance or the prospect of being fucked by the monster?

"Can you have sex without biting?"

The lithe minx wishes to fuck and feed. I can't believe I haven't thrown her to the stone ground and done that already.

With any other werewolf, tonight would result in several bouts of rough sex, but since Viessa is my mate, I'm uncertain if I'd be strong enough to hold back from claiming her with my bite. It's too big of a risk. I shake my head and brandish my hand in a gesture for her to leave.

She contemplates me for a second. "Listen to me, my king." Her manner is no longer the soft inquiry of before. The speech is rich with command, and my beast growls a stern warning. "You will not bite me. I forbid it. Do you understand?" She clutches my bicep in a sturdy hold.

I chuff, jerking my arm loose. Maybe this is my opportunity to teach this headstrong woman a lesson. Allow her to experience the full Alpha and force her to submit to us.

My claws extend before I clutch the front of her collar and rip the fabric in two with one violent jerk. Viessa gasps, stumbling back a step as the tattered remnants of her robe flutters around her feet.

The perfection of her pale breasts and puckered rosy nipples in the moonlight hardens my cock to painful proportions—saliva pools in my mouth at the vision of her glistening bare folds begging for my tongue.

"Liam," she barks out. "Stop."

Her command agitates the beast, and before I realize it, I'm reaching to heave her against my chest. Vi traces backward several feet, the worry visible in every line in her trembling frame.

I growl in warning and crouch in readiness of the hunt. Viessa's refusal to obey my order and leave sealed her fate. Tonight, my dick will plunge into her heat, my seed will fill her womb, and my teeth will mar that flawless skin.

"Ruuuuuuuun!"

The word comes out as an intimidating, gruff roar. My mate's mouth falls open and she freezes. She was warned. I leap for her. She squeaks in dismay, snaps out of her shocked revere, and spins, taking off at a dead run, bare-ass naked.

The sight of her pale, heart-shaped butt running from me boosts my adrenaline. I lift my head and howl my frenzy to the moon before sprinting after my prize.

Chapter 5

Viessa

Rough, angry growls chase me through the forest, gaining fast. Adrenaline surges through my veins. Excitement quickens my heart rate, and my breathing turns ragged. Not from exertion. From lust and fear.

I'm weak from over two months without blood, but the slight panic at what Liam's beast will perform once he catches me makes me swift as I traverse the uneven ground with increasing speed.

A mile in, I chance a glance over my shoulder. Don't see him. Did I lose him? It would be simple for me to trace back to the safety of the monastery, but the hunger cramping my gut for my mate's spicy, powerful essence outweighs the peril I willfully placed myself in tonight.

My sister warned me not to go to Liam on the full moon—twice—but I ignored her, desiring to see the transformation of my wolf for myself.

And my God, he was beautiful, spectacular, and savage. Furious determination burned in his pale blue eyes, and the size of his erection scared me more than anything. If he doesn't prepare me, he could do some grievous damage. I would mend, but the agony of the ordeal would linger.

The king is my mate. This monthly change is a part of who he is, and I need to experience it with him. Want it. Just the vision of the big hairy beast rutting between my thighs clenches my insides. Oh, yes. Liam and I will reach a compromise tonight in order to set the standard for every lunar cycle.

A vicious growl.

My eyes widen, but I don't dare look back as I sprint through the tall grass, leaping over fallen logs and small streams. The beast will capture me, of that I have no doubt. I'm too depleted to be much of a challenge, but the freedom of running naked, the luminous rays of the moon caressing my skin through the trees, heightens my desire, my thirst.

Claws sink into my ankle. I tumble into the soft grass, rolling with the momentum until I'm scooting backward across the meadow on my butt.

The beast watches me. He stalks with a scary focus. His enormous chest shifts with each inhale, and rough growls rumble with every exhale. The blue irises are radiant with feral intent. No one has ever studied me so... consumingly.

Why isn't he pouncing?

With slow, tentative movements, I push up to my knees, my palms outstretched in supplication. "I willingly surrender to your beast, Liam, but I need to feed first to withstand my... your size and strength," I whisper, hoping it infiltrates the primal urgings raging through him.

He grunts in response. Is that a yes? Shit.

He comes at me. I tense but maintain my ground. Huge hairy arms encircle my midriff as he picks me up before forcing my spine against a nearby oak. Oh crap. Our first time will be against a tree? Not how I imagined this moment going.

The creature lowers his head, sniffing my collarbone and neck. A warm tongue slides across my skin, and I shiver, coveting it between my thighs.

He hoists me against his chest, and the enticing fur rubs against my achy nipples. I wrap my legs around his thick waist, grinding my slick sex against the rock-hard abs covered in the smooth, silvery coat.

When his huge palm cradles the back of my skull, imploring me closer to his wide neck, I realize this is the beast's way of informing me he wishes me to feed.

After months of deprivation, I strike, penetrating through the thickened skin and luxurious fur, straight into the large jugular. Liam's blood is richer than before. It scalds my tongue and throat, warming me from the inside out, but the transformation in power jolts through me like a live wire.

I snake my arms around his colossal shoulders and wiggle closer, and for the first time in months, the visions and voices quiet, and energy courses through my system. Liam growls low before shifting somewhat to arrange his massive erection directly over my core.

Rough bark bites into my back as the fierce beast ruts against my slick folds, but the slight pain is nothing compared to the firestorm his prick is building against my sex. I gulp down pure summer rain as tiny explosions flare to life in my abdomen, advancing through my frame like a wildfire out of control.

His neck muffles my cry as I burst in a thousand different directions, a tornado of sensations spinning and spiraling as I continue to draw deep on his generous vein. My sex convulses, begging for his cock.

Wow. That was… the sensations were… a hundred times more enhanced than bringing myself off.

With Liam's animal grunts and low rumbles—his massive hardness sliding back and forth, slicked by the evidence of my passion—he strikes that swollen, achy bundle with every upward thrust, and I sense another explosion is imminent.

Gluttoned on his blood, I pull free, not bothering to lick the wounds closed. Within seconds, the punctures seal.

I lean back, peer into the altered face of my mate, and pump my hips in time with his. The piercing blue gaze devours me, lighting me up. "Liam!" I shriek, dropping my head against the timber as I let the orgasm overtake me. His howl joins me seconds later as his torrid seed sears my belly.

When his muzzle burrows against my neck, I freeze. I can't allow him to bite me. It would forfeit both our lives.

My strength fully restored, I stiffen, bracing to shove him away when he suddenly lets go. I plummet to the ground on my ass. Before I can recover, my mate has me flipped over on all fours. I tense, expecting his massive girth to spear into me at any moment. Desperate, I dig my nails into the earth and grip handfuls of grass, prepared to endure the pain and hold on for dear life.

I'm astonished when the beast kneels behind me and nuzzles my core. His low, needy whine melts any meager resistance, and I lower my chest to the cool ground, hiking my butt in the air, exposing my backside to the creature salivating for a taste.

The first lap of his rough tongue causes my knees to tremble, and when he sets in, lapping up the juices he created, my eyes roll back in my head as every revelation and voice constantly harassing me recedes into the background in the face of such pure fucking bliss.

His claws grip my hips as his fiery tongue licks me from clit to anus. This is deviant, naughty, and oh-so wicked, but I couldn't care less. Evident by my moaning his name repeatedly and spreading my thighs further to offer him better access.

Liam's low growls of dominance and grunts of pleasure against my ass shoot me over the proverbial edge once more, and I cry out, shoving my palms along the deep grass, gyrating my hips with urgent need against his face.

I'm so lost in my euphoric state; I don't hear the call of my name at first.

"Viessa!" the voice barks again, seizing my full attention, and the creature kneeling behind me.

The ground-shaking, predatory growl raises the hair on the back of my neck. I pop up on my hands and stare in horror at my father standing across the clearing.

Liam's protective instinct takes over. He grasps me by the waist, the thick claws gouging deep into muscle and bone, and tosses me behind him with such force my skull cracks against a nearby tree.

Pain skyrockets through my head, and I groan, clutching my cranium. Warm blood oozes down my hips from the gaping wounds he unintentionally inflicted. I endeavor to deliver healing energy to the wounds, but blackness creeps around the edges of my eyesight as nausea clogs the back of my throat.

"King Scott." Icarus's angry voice snags my awareness, and my focus sharpens. I've never seen him so livid. Ever. "You just sacrificed your connection to Viessa. She will no longer feed from you if this is the outcome."

Liam snarls at the Oracle, straining against an invisible shield encapsulating his body.

"I must sever your mate bond forthwith."

"No," I groan, wishing I sounded stronger. The mere notion of the link to Liam vanishing sends panic through my system. I battle to stay conscious for my king. "This is my fault, father. I came to him on a full moon. I... I didn't know." That's a lie. After my conversation with Lu, I realized it was a risk, but I did it anyway. "Please. I guarantee this won't happen again."

"I am sorry, child. You have no restraint with the werewolf," Icarus says, stalking toward me with purposeful strides, ignoring Liam's constant furious growls and the deadly blue eyes tracking his every move.

When he reaches me, he holds out a fresh robe I didn't even notice he was clutching and helps me to my feet. I sway, my sight blurring as I strive to focus on the beast who just presented me with such tremendous pleasure. The creature stares at the gaping wounds on my hips, extending a low mournful whine.

"I vow I will never surrender control again, father." I jerk the garment over my head. Embarrassment heats my cheeks at being caught in such a compromising position by my parent. Crimson immediately soaks the fabric, sticking to my skin even though the gashes healed. "I require my mate's blood to survive."

"Any immortal essence will satisfy; you are not Nicole."

"No!" I snarl, glowering at him. "Liam's blood, or I'm done. You can take this complete Oracle duty bullshit and shove it up your blue tattooed ass."

Oh my. This might be bad. But, dammit, don't threaten to hold my mate from me. My inner vampire will never allow it.

The powerful priest regards me for several seconds before twisting back to Liam, still straining against the invisible bonds.

"She will never come to you on the full moon again, my lord. When she requires feeding, you must submit to her control and provide her nourishment. Nothing more. Do you understand?" Icarus waves his palm, and the glorious beast fades, replaced by my proud, fierce, naked king.

I gasp at the true visage of Liam's body. Hard, bulging muscles stretch over his shoulders and biceps. The broad, chiseled chest, with a splendid exhibit of short ebony hair accentuating his virility, tapers to a trim waist before flaring to strong, sinewy thighs. My mouth waters, needing to claim every inch of my mate with my bite, hands, and lips.

Liam peers over the little priest's shoulder at me, his gaze still impregnated with lust. Will he obey, or could this be the last time I ever cast my eyes on my beautiful werewolf?

"Do you concede to the terms, King Scott?" Icarus asks.

"You're ordering me to submit?" Liam directs his question toward me, so I step around my father and face my mate.

"It is the only way, my king. For now."

Father has no inkling what he just instigated. He assumes submitting means I'll demand Liam offer his wrist with me controlling every element of the feeding. Little does he realize, our time together will involve the virile male's complete sexual submission, with me commanding his body, his responses, his desire, and granting us both great pleasures. While I'm in charge of every aspect, we won't need to worry about a mating. I hope.

"Vow it, Liam," I command softly, my eyes pleading with him not to end this.

He seems torn as he watches me with some fierce emotion. His fists clenched so tight the knuckles whiten. When his gaze falls to the crimson staining my gown, then the furious regard of the Oracle, fear tightens my chest. What the hell is going on in that brain of his?

"Sorry, sweetness. It's not in my nature to submit." He shrugs. "When you complete your training, look me up. I might be available."

Stunned by his cold rejection, a sharp pain shoots through my rib cage. "Liam," I whisper in disbelief, and I can't stay the quiver in my chin. My brain is powerless to fathom how he could end it after what just transpired between us.

"I'm taking you up on your earlier offer. I plan to live my life as if you never existed. Your future holds meaning. Purpose. I refuse to stand in the way of that. Goodbye, Viessa. Thank you for tonight."

With that, he turns and stalks into the woodland. I gape after him. My tears blur the sight of his muscular ass moving and flexing with each stride. What in God's name just happened?

The king gifted me the best sexual experience ever, and now he's running away as if he couldn't care less. All because the stubborn idiot refuses to let me have control sexually. I submitted to his beast tonight. Why won't he do the same for me?

"Come, child. The werewolf made his choice."

Yes, but he made the wrong one.

My jaw hardens, along with my determination, because the farther Liam advances away from me, the more a surge of fresh visions and voices work to intrude on my thoughts.

I need the peace only Liam can offer. If the stubborn ass needs time to come to terms with things, then fine, I'll grant him space. I have all the time in the world.

Chapter 6

The full moon is next week, and I barely eat or drink. I feel like I'm crawling out of my skin. Over the last several weeks, I've lamented my decision to walk away from Viessa. But the sight of the deep gashes marring her body inflicted by my beast horrified me.

I injured my female. We didn't mean to, our sole concern was protecting her, but the garish injuries, and the High Priest's fierce determination, sealed our fate.

Icarus will never allow us to be together. Oracles do not mate. I refuse to be an obstacle to Viessa's destiny. Her future is to develop into a primary deity. An emissary to the gods. Nor do I aspire to be on the wrong side of the priest. Vi's obstinacy and willful threat were the sole reasons he agreed to a controlled arrangement.

Controlled. Did the little blue powerhouse even fathom what that meant? I doubt it, or he would never have proposed it.

The best choice for both of us was to step away. End it. It stung more than I imagined. Doubts plagued my mind, like maggots devouring an infested wound, eating at my sanity.

Who will become her source of food? The sheer idea of her fangs and lips on anyone else's flesh makes my eye twitch, and my beast howls in a jealous rage. And what about her demand for dominance? Can she stifle the obsession, or is she seeking an alternate form? The image of such a scenario tightens a vice around my chest.

From where did this need for control stem? As far as I understand, Viessa was mentally unstable her entire life. Even institutionalized for a while. She must have experienced sex at some point. Either she lost all control and sought to gain it back, or she exerted control and enjoyed it.

Not your problem anymore, Liam.

When my horse stumbles, I let my worries go, and concentrate on my responsibilities—the three-dozen head of cattle in front of me.

The sweltering heat from the midday sun in August beats down on my shoulders, and my shirt fuses to my sweat-slicked skin. I remove my Stetson to mop my brow with my bandana.

"Joshua," I call out to my brother ahead of the herd. "Let's lead them to the river. I need a fucking break."

Over the last three and a half weeks, I picked up extra projects to drive myself into exhaustion at night, hoping to hold the images of Viessa at bay. But the vision of her kneeling in supplication before me, the addictive taste of her sex, the sweet melody of her moans, crying my name as she shattered apart, brands my soul.

Christ.

Each day I work my mind and body into a state of weakened fatigue, but it hasn't achieved the desired effect. I still drop into bed at midnight with a raging hard-on demanding release. After what seems like ages of tossing and turning, struggling to ignore the cursed thing, I succumb to my desires. As I stroke my length, I replay every second of that evening over and over until my muscles tighten with surrender and my brain finally shuts down, granting me a few blessed hours of sleep.

The small herd settles next to the stream, and I lead Tango over to the bank with a gentle nudge. The Buckskin Quarter horse is my favorite and ridden exclusively by me as he maintains a bit of an attitude even though he's a gelding.

It took extreme patience and a stern hand to tame him. From the moment I rescued him, he became my personal project, and because of all the time we spent together, we arrived at an accord and forged a special bond. I never work the ranch without Tango. He'd go ballistic if I went off on another horse and left him behind.

His big, majestic head lowers to the water to ease his thirst as I remove my canteen to do the same. Joshua crouches next to me at the water's edge, filling his own.

"You doing okay, big brother?" he asks casually before taking several deep swigs of the refreshing water.

I avoid the question for a minute to wash down the hot, dry dust clogging my throat before dipping my bandana in the river.

"I'm only askin' 'cause you've pushed yourself pretty hard these past few weeks, and Cellica and I are concerned."

"If you need a fucking break, Josh, just say so. Stop beating around the bush."

"Fuck you, Liam."

Shit.

"Hey. I'm sorry," I murmur and rise to my feet, rubbing my neck with the soaked bandana. Coolness trickles between my shoulder blades and down my chest. "I've got a load on my plate right now. I didn't mean to come down on you."

"Do you miss dad?" Josh asks quietly, his dark eyes staring across the river.

"Every damn day."

"I hate I wasn't there when he died. Maybe I could've…"

He breaks off, closing his eyes against the pain of the what-ifs. "I know. But there was nothing you could've done, Josh, and I needed you and Cel safe from Dimitri's or Syn's reach."

He nods, shifting his gaze from the open grasslands to me. "Cellica and I are both here to help, bro. If you require assistance with werewolf business or need us to accept more here at the ranch or hell, cover some shifts at the bar, just tell us. We're eager to pitch in anywhere."

Joshua and I haven't always seen eye to eye. He fought my authority for many years, hating having his big brother barking orders at him. But over the last two years, since the death of our father and king, he's matured, taking a more active part in the ranch and Providence business.

"Actually, I must attend a Council Meeting next week. Do you think you and Cellica could handle any issues around the homestead while I'm gone?"

"You got it. No problem," Josh grins.

"I might be there for the lunar cycle, so I'll need you to coordinate the pack's transformation party."

"You're not coming home to shift with the pack? Why?"

"We both know what will happen if I'm near any single werewolf. Even though I walked away from the Oracle, I'm not ready to fuck anyone else right now."

"Okay. Leave me all the contact info, and I'll take care of it."

"Get Cel involved. Her abrupt shift in attitude is worrying."

"Yeah, I agree. Her swing to full immortal is fast approaching and we need to watch her closely. But, how are *you* doing since the full moon? The next one is right around the corner, and you won't be with the pack or your mate."

"I no longer possess a mate, Josh. I refuse to side against Icarus. It would be suicide, and I value my existence. Even if I did, what kind of future could I possibly offer a Tri-bred deity? I'm a goddamn cowboy who rustles cattle and sings for a living."

"A damn fine one, *King* Scott," he frowns. "At some point, though, you're gonna need to choose a companion. A ruler needs a queen."

"I know," I sigh. "It's too fresh. I can't contemplate that now. This full moon, I will just run and hunt in the desolate wilds of Canada and fret about selecting a candidate another time."

"I recognize several right here in Forsythe who'd jump at the chance to wed the notorious ladies' man, Liam Scott."

"Yeah, with the added benefit of being queen." I sneer. "Icing on the cake, bro."

"I'm seeking a vote on the matter, Arra, not demanding it so." Nicki sighs in annoyance before lifting a full creamy mug of coffee to her lips.

We've been at this meeting for over an hour, and my head is pounding like a bass drum. Most of the representatives agreed to meet in person at the vampire castle: everyone but Syn Grayflame. The vampires and valkyries still consider him an enemy, even though he denied any awareness of Alexandria Svaldana's attempted kidnapping.

We all appreciate it's a load of horseshit, especially Nicole, the proverbial lie detector. But it comes down to "he said, she said."

That didn't halt the vampire queen from petitioning for a vote to abolish the bastard's seat on the Council of Unity.

"We can't establish a ballot without the Oracle present." Syn sneers from the monitor on the wall. "And what pray tell are your grounds for such a request? I already advised the members I had nothing to do with the valkyrie princess's kidnap attempt."

Nicole winces. "You are such a lying piece of shit, and we all know it."

"What we assume and the facts before us are two different matters entirely, Queen Giordano," King Darath interjects quietly. "You must produce valid evidence of any crime before the Council can vote to eliminate one of its members."

"Then I will uncover the proof, Demon," she growls back, her eyes flaring with gunmetal fury.

"Of that, I have no doubt, my beautiful Halfling." He grins in the face of her anger.

"Move on to the next order of business," Syn demands. "I have more urgent concerns requiring my attention."

"Yeah, I bet. Like whom to behead after dinner?" the queen counters, and a muscle pulses in Logan's jaw.

"I loathe to concur with the dark fae," Kurtis interjects, leaning forward with impatience, his blue gaze snapping to Nicole, "but we have one more addendum on the docket. Could we please get to it and wrap this up?"

"Fine," she snaps. "Moving on, but we will backtrack to this the second I gather the information you all require. So, stay frosty, Synie. Your sins will come to light, eventually." Before he can respond, she moves on to the last order of business.

Thank fuck. Twenty minutes until the full moon and my beast is roaring to let loose. Although, his need to savor our mate again keeps pounding through my dick. I arrived last night, thanks to Sebastian, and the inactivity is messing with my sanity. Too much downtime and all I think about is Viessa.

Fuck. Will this need for her ever subside?

Once the meeting breaks up, Kurtis slaps me on the back. "Need some company on your run?"

The shifter king's animal is a two-hundred-pound, lethal Alaskan Malamute, and I've hunted with him numerous times in wolf form, but never on the full moon.

"Unless you're a female werewolf, it's probably best if the beast runs alone."

"Oh. Yeah. I love you, buddy, but… not that much," he smirks.

I chuckle. "Ditto, my friend. Raincheck for another day."

I pivot to head for the exit when Viessa suddenly appears in my path. The sight of her stalls my heart. It's shocking to see her tall, lean body encased in jeans, a blue sweater, and brown cowboy boots instead of the customary white robe.

Fuck me. The woman is beautiful and seductive as hell. "What are you doing here?"

"I came…" she falters, scanning the others in the room with a delicate frown marring her forehead. Her lids flicker with nerves in the face of so many. "Do not run in the forest, King Scott. It is not safe."

"Viessa, there are very few immortals on this planet that can overpower me in beast form. I'll be fine." Does she believe I cannot defend myself? Pissed off, I move around her when she skips in front of me again. "Get out of my way, Vi," I growl low, my vision flickering. My beast is clamoring to rut and claim what is ours.

"Liam, I must forbid you…"

"You forbid me?" She uttered the one word to set my temper ablaze. I seize her biceps, lifting her with ease before thrusting her at Kurtis. "Go home, female, before I do something we both regret."

"Wait, Liam," Nicole orders. "Maybe we should discover what the all-seeing Oracle has to say?"

"I've heard enough."

"My king, I do not understand why you are angry with me." Is she fucking serious? "I don't doubt your strength. I came here to warn…"

"Viessa!"

We all start when Icarus appears next to Vi. It's obvious he's furious when he snatches her forearm and jerks her to his side. Against my will, the beast growls a warning at the rough treatment of our mate.

"I warned you about interfering unless granted permission."

Molten lava pins the priest, and she wrenches her arm free. "Do not presume to dictate to me when it comes to my mate's safety, *father*." She sneers at the title.

When those glowing ambers pivot in my direction, the beast trembles with the desire to dominate that look. I clench my fists to maintain control and swivel my gaze to Nicki.

"Get me out of here, Nic," I solicit, the deep gravel of my tone evident I'm on the brink.

'*This is an awful idea*,' she whispers in my mind but strides toward me and latches onto my wrist.

"Do not defy the Oracle, Nicole," Logan warns darkly, his brows drawn together.

"Which one?" she shoots back with an eye-roll. "Their opinions differ. We are just going right outside, kids. Nothing more. Viessa and Liam need a little distance."

When Vi steps forward, it's not the anger in her gaze that causes me to hesitate: it's the fear emanating from her in waves. A part of me yearns to soothe her agitation, but Nic and I are already disappearing. As long as I stay within the boundary, I'm safe.

Once we land outside the castle, I stride back from Nicki, the beast clawing for freedom. She's the one creature on this planet who could best me in a fight, but I have no wish to harm her.

"Why don't I take you home?" Nicole glances around before her troubled gaze lands on mine. "You can shift with your pack."

"I would love to, Nic, but the beast would have a female pack member beneath him in a heartbeat."

"And you wish to remain loyal to Viessa even though you are technically not together?"

"I realize it sounds stupid, but yes. I'm not ready to take that step away from her."

"It's not stupid, asshat. It's sweet, and now I want to gag."

I can't help but laugh at her sarcasm to avoid an intimate conversation.

"Just to be on the safe side, Liam, please stay within the shield."

A magical barrier Icarus erected guards the vampire compound, and the hundreds of acres surrounding the imposing structure, with its ten towers dominating the horizon. Those chosen, move in and out of it with fluency, but it prohibits anyone else from entering or exiting.

Only immortals see the shield. Otherwise, it is imperceptible to a mortal.

"I will try, but I'm not always in command during the full moon."

"Are you certain I can't run with you? You know I could kick your ass with ease," she teases.

She's right. If Viessa sensed or saw something, it might be prudent to have the most potent immortal by my side. "Okay, but don't follow too close and stay downwind."

"You got it. You won't even realize I'm here."

I doubt that since I visualize heat signatures from fifty miles away. "If at any point the beast scents you, trace inside. Promise me, Nicole."

"As long as you're not in any danger, I promise."

"Fair enough, now turn around."

She laughs as she pivots. "So fucking modest."

I undress quickly, folding my clothes and arranging them next to the stone wall, just as the moon peeks out behind a cloud. The metamorphosis is rapid, and I whirl and take off through the forest, a howl rising on the wind.

Chapter 7

Freedom exists in running and hunting as a wolf, but a primal joy fills my soul during a lunar shift when I am both wolf and man—my cravings peak. The male aspect reverts to my primitive impulses—self-preservation and survival. However, the beast, which is the prevailing force during the full moon, is driven by the three Fs. Fight. Fuck. Feed. And not necessarily in that order.

Tonight, fucking is off the table, unless some poor unsuspecting werewolf happens by, which deep in vampire territory is unlikely. At my ranch, that's a genuine possibility. Lone wolves join the fun for the sole purpose of being taken in beast form. But here in the vast, non-habitable acres surrounding the castle, hunting and feeding are my only options.

A deer darts from its protective brush. I veer off and the chase begins. With blazing speed, I vault over low shrubs and fallen logs, even using the timbers to my advantage, leaping from one to the other to maintain sight of my prey.

When the frantic animal sprints through the defensive boundary, I follow in hot pursuit, ignoring the tingle as I cross through the shield. My sole focus is the heat signature dashing through the shadowy forest.

I'm just about to pounce when an acute pain pierces my side. I stumble, falling to my hands and knees. I squint down in bewilderment at the arrow protruding from my ribcage, the deer forgotten in a second.

What the fuck?

Some part of my brain understands I should yank it from my body, but the beast doesn't always behave rationally when in full instinct mode. With an indignant rumble, I snap the rod in half and survey my surroundings.

"Liam!" Nicole shouts a warning, racing to me just as a large fae, fifty yards away, lets loose an arrow.

Nicki catches the projectile with ease, snapping it in two before flinging it to the ground. "You are so dead, winged motherfucker," she says with a low growl.

I gain my feet and surge at the huge immortal before it can nock another missile in its bow, landing on its shoulders. A sharp twist and pull rips its head from its body, his screams halting abruptly. Blood coats my fur-covered chest, staining the white crimson as the beast howls his satisfaction to the moon.

"Oh, shit."

I glance at Nic and detect more than a dozen fae warriors surrounding our position. What the fuck? I didn't even scent or hear their approach. No way they just flew in. I would've detected their heat signatures long before they landed.

They are a mix of male and female fighters, some carry swords, but the majority have bows drawn, sited on me. The beast lets out a sharp, ferocious growl and sinks low, fixed to take on the entire regiment of winged soldiers to protect my friend.

"Come peacefully, Queen Giordano, ur we will poison th' werewolf wi' our silver."

Right about now, I wish I could shout at her to teleport away.

'*Move closer to me, Liam,*' she commands telepathically, snatching a dagger from her boot and inching my direction. '*We are tracing out of here together.*'

The beast rages, yearning to burst more skulls from bodies. With extreme effort, I resist his control. Must. Protect. Queen. I shuffle a few feet toward her as menacing snarls emanate from my chest, blanketing the forest floor. The white-winged fae twitch with nervous anxiety, drawing their bows taut.

"You know, I would love a vacay in Scotland, but I think I'll wait until your king is dead." Nicole edges a few more steps closer, just as two female custodians loose their arrows.

I bat one aside, but the other plunges into my shoulder. Already feeling the effects of the poisoned tip protruding from my ribs, I tear it from my flesh and charge with an enraged roar.

"Liam, no!" Nicki shouts, sprinting to cover my six.

Instead of the lethal weapons sinking into my spine, I glance back and witness four arrows impale her in the torso. The force of the blows slams her into me, and I stumble.

Before I can react, she's on the archers, bursting a heart from a chest, while driving her fangs into the collar of another, shredding his jugular from his flesh.

By the time she pivots to confront another one to slash open his abdomen with her iron dagger, I've gained my feet and launched myself at the sizable black-skinned fae giving orders. A searing pain and an invading weakness spread through my body.

As my lethal claws rend bones and flesh, something catches my awareness. Long golden hair appears to flow from a tree about a hundred yards to the north.

What the hell?

I continue to battle several fae at once, slitting throats, hacking wings from shoulders, while retaining the bizarre anomaly in my periphery.

Where the fuck is Logan? Shouldn't he have sensed his mate's distress? My gaze bounces to my friend. The eerie gray eyes are lit with a perverse enjoyment as she slices through our enemy with velocity and fatal precision, I can't help but applaud. Even with several arrows protruding from her chest. But what is she doing? She could suspend them all in place with a single thought.

The silver invading my system is weakening my energy, and while I'm proficient in hand-to-hand combat as a mere male immortal, the toxin will progress and deplete my strength.

A stinging pain penetrates my back, the tip plunging deep. I reel, howling in frustration as I sink my massive canines into the neck of a fae, and clamp down hard.

Even as I sense the beast retreating, my powerful jaws crush vertebrae. Teeth macerate through muscles until his head falls to the ground with a wet thud.

Unable to remain vertical, I drop with the headless body. Pine needles and underbrush soften the hit. The wolf-like features alter, silvery fur recedes, and I crane my neck, seeking Nicki's position.

Fear tightens my gut as more fae land among the trees. They outnumber us ten to one. "Nicki, call for Logan," I implore, attempting to rise to my feet.

"I'm fucking trying," she grunts, beheading a female on her right. "Something is blocking me."

"Can you freeze them?"

"Don't you think I would've tried that already?" she pants. "I can't even trace."

"Then get the fuck out of here." I lurch in her direction when an arrow sinks into my gut.

She swivels toward me just as five arrows penetrate her torso, one running clean through her neck and out the other side.

"No!" With the last fragment of power, I leap for my friend, sheltering her body with my own as a half dozen more missiles pierce the muscles of my back.

With this much silver in my system, I'm not long for this world, and my thoughts immediately move to Vi. Fate doomed us from the outset, but I thrived on the slight flicker of hope we would be together after her training.

In hindsight, I understand this catastrophe is why she appeared. She foresaw my death. Nicole's capture. Why the hell didn't I follow her orders? My stubborn ass pride and outdated belief—that as the male, I should take the lead in all things—overrode my logic. The beast rejected the notion a female would govern our actions.

Stupid. Stupid. Stupid.

Blackness invades my sight as I lie prone over Nicole. "Nicki," I hiss in her ear. "As soon as they try to lift me, fight your way out of here."

"I'm not leaving you, dumbass," she growls, her irises sparking with irritation.

"They don't require me. Syn only wants you."

Rough fingers clutch my shoulders to drag me off Nic, but I tighten my arms around her and maintain my hold with every minuscule of strength left. I cannot allow them to take her. The odds of us getting her back alive from Scotland are slim to nothing.

A tremendous roar fills the forest, and the hands yanking on me tense.

"About damn time," the furious Halfling grumbles beneath me.

Relief floods through me as I lift my head and spy Logan and Sebastian charging full speed into the fray from my left while Christoph and Lucretia race around to the other side with Kurtis right on their heels.

The fae swivel to meet the additional threat. Nicki gently nudges me off her to stand over my prone, arrow riddled, naked outline.

"Tell that fucker, Syn Grayflame, he failed again," she sneers before splitting a wing from a fae's back as he screams bloody murder while attempting to stab her with his sword.

The others make swift work of the lingering dark fae, while the rest take flight in retreat. With the poison spreading through my system, I merely observe the silvery-white wings fluttering through the verdant treetops into the moonlit sky. I clench my jaw and strive to sit up, but the deadly effects of the toxin sapped my ability to move, and my eyesight continues to fail.

Through the hazy darkness, I watch Logan rush to his mate, yank the remaining weapons protruding from her chest, and urge her to drink from him.

"I'm fine for now, babe. Liam needs healing ay-sap. The arrowheads were silver."

"Oh shit," Kurtis breathes, kneeling to jerk arrows from my torso. Even through the gray haze, I recognize his fear. The amount of silver in my system is a death sentence for a werewolf, more so than any other species. "He's gonna need Viessa's blood."

"Are she and Icarus still inside?" Nicki asks as Sebastian plucks me off the ground.

"No. They disappeared right after you did. I've never seen my father so furious," Lucretia says.

"Let us get inside the castle," Logan directs. "We will figure the rest out later."

"He might not have a later if we can't summon Viessa back." Kurtis whispers exactly what I was pondering.

My energy and sight finally desert me. Soon my organs will shut down one by one until, eventually, my heart fails.

I ache for the burden my death places on my siblings, the effect on my friends. But chiefly, my delicate, damaged sweetness will mourn my passing. The grief could undo all she's accomplished mentally. My presence is her calming force to keep the chaos at bay. Can she learn to control her visions with training alone?

The beautiful female and I had a few stolen moments together, but our connection was undeniable. I treasured every second and wish now I'd conceded to her requirements.

If anything, it would have provided me the chance to understand the mysterious Tri-bred. To hold her and help drive away the demons plaguing her brain. It shouldn't have mattered if she sought a little control during sex.

All the "what ifs" dance around in my head while brawny arms carry me through a vacuum of nothingness as we teleport before I'm lowered to a bed. A soft wrist touches my lips and warm liquid pools in my mouth.

"Drink, Liam," Nicki urges, massaging my throat.

The second her potent blood invades my system, the very core of my soul catches fire. Flames rush through me, scorching me from the inside out, and my muscles seize.

"Shit! What's happening?"

Nicki's voice sounds muffled. Like she's yelling from an immense distance, and I've packed my ears with cotton. The intensity of her blood scorches every cell as it travels through my veins. The agony is so profound, I'm unable to catch my breath. Firm hands pin my frame to the mattress as I arch and roar in misery. What the fuck is in her blood that my body is rejecting?

I sense my consciousness slipping until her honeysuckle scent fills my nostrils. I strive to open my eyes, but they ignore my command. Strong arms lift my upper torso, and I groan as a renewed wave of flames sears through my extremities.

"Everyone out." The militant tone of my female tense muscles already straining to their maximum.

"Like hell," Nicki barks.

"My love, only the Oracle can aid him now," Logan rumbles.

"Fine. But if he dies, blessed deity or not, I'll finish you."

"If he perishes, I welcome death."

Well, I guess that answers my earlier question on how my woman will fair once I'm gone. The notion of her demise has the beast stirring for added strength.

"Okay, then. Excellent answer," Nic mutters.

Viessa holds me up from behind, whispering into my ear, her warm breath fanning across my cheek.

"Drink, my king."

The arm around my rib cage is like a vise. Unyielding. The fragrant bouquet of Vi's scent surrounds me, her shoulder cushions my head. Silken, wet skin touches my lips, and I rear back. Nicole's rich, powerful blood set me on fire. What the hell will an Oracle's blood do to me?

"It's okay, Liam. My life force will restore you. Trust me."

I push aside my uncertainties, willing to do anything at this point to squelch the inferno spreading through my veins. I latch onto her wrist, sucking hard on her open vein.

Her sweet essence hits my innards like a bucket of ice water, cooling the raging firestorm. The arm tightens, drawing me closer. Soft lips brush over my ear and along my cheek.

"Good, Liam. Take as much as you need."

A part of me never believed in the mate bond, even though I'd witnessed it various times in my century and a half of existence. Not until this very moment. The second the angry, reactive fire dissipates, Viessa's vibrant emotions sweep through me. Adrenaline surges through tissues and ligaments, supplying me with intense energy, unlike anything I've ever encountered.

A vampire's blood will enhance a werewolf's strength tenfold, but this, her essence, is so much more. Not only does it glide over my taste buds like a honeysuckle rainforest I long to drown in, but the assault of her desires, passions, fears, and insecurities electrifies our connection.

Does she experience my emotions this way every time she sips from me? And what about when and if we complete the bond? Am I prepared to deal with the psychological turmoil I sense lurking in the background, ready to consume me?

My mate's fractured mind could destroy us both.

Chapter 8

The glorious weight of my mate's torso against my chest, his head resting on my shoulder, his lips and tongue sucking and lapping at my vein forces the horror of his death into the background.

Someone threw a blanket over his hips and legs. But the outline of his heavy erection has me swallowing with hunger. Still, it doesn't eclipse the fury I held toward my father when he forced me to depart to the monastery with him, where he lectured me on the do's and don'ts of an Oracle's obligations while my heart sought to explode from my chest.

The longer he spoke, the more I craved to rip his tongue from his mouth just to shut him up so I could return to the castle. The constant image of Liam's body peppered with arrows caused my muscles to quiver with terror.

He only freed me a nanosecond before I appeared with a strict warning to provide the werewolf king my blood and nothing more—ordered me to vow it. I would've promised anything at that moment.

I smooth my free hand down his ribcage, and my fingertips bump against something protruding from his skin. Liam sucks in a sharp gasp at the contact. Glancing down at his sculpted torso, I scrutinize the object in question. A broken-off arrow juts out between two ribs.

I grip the metal and tug it from his body and toss it on the nightstand. His grunt has me soothing the injury by running my palm over his chest and kissing his temple.

This is what I live for, taking care of my mate's needs. I understand the gods created me to be an Oracle, to interpret the visions and voices in my head to aid the immortal world, but for me, the mighty werewolf king takes priority.

If anything were to happen to him, nothing else would matter. Not my twin, my father, or my duties. My inner vampire, the guiding force of my very existence, would gradually wither away.

Does my father understand how much this male means to me? How I longed for his presence before we even met? My brief revelations of Liam over the years were the sole reason I never walked into the sun and ended my miserable existence. The masculine beauty of his face warmed my soul. The deep timbre of his voice soothed my mind, and I craved to escape into my vision of him forever.

Satisfaction warms me when the damage in his chest and abdomen seals shut, and his pallor returns to the golden tan with each gulp. My mate's one weakness scares me like nothing else. If I could eradicate the world of silver to protect him, I would.

Unable to ignore the impressive girth twitching beneath the blanket any longer, I shove it aside and grip his firmness. The wolf groans low, bucking his hips.

"Remain still, Liam," I order. My breaths halt with apprehension as I await his response. Long black lashes close over the beautiful irises, but he settles back into the mattress. Joy fills my spirit, and the chaos nudging its way forward disappears altogether.

"Thank you, my king," I whisper against his ear, stroking his length in reward.

My mate growls low before clutching my wrist in both hands and penetrating my skin with his huge canines. I flinch at the slight pain, but it's soon forgotten as I pleasure my male with firm strokes, glorying in the wonder of his silken steel.

All the fantasies I've enjoyed over the years flitter through my mind. An idea forms and excitement tightens my stomach.

"Spread your legs, Liam." The king doesn't hesitate, and wetness floods my core even as a wave of peace settles on my shoulders at the authority he's allowing.

I skim my palm further and fondle his tight sac. My mate's grip on my wrist becomes almost painful, and I comprehend the valiant Alpha is employing it as a mechanism to remain still and not seize control of the situation and me.

"You are so beautiful," I murmur in his ear, licking along the rim. "I adore the hardness of your cock always ready for me, and I can't wait to sample and explore every inch of you."

His low groan vibrates against my breasts, hardening my nipples in anticipation of enjoying my mate.

I realize I promised only to offer him blood, but I'm assuming the "nothing more" meant sex. Numerous other gifts are available at my fingertips besides intercourse, and it's all spread out before me in the form of this vast expanse of tanned, sinewy flesh with the addictive aroma of leather and summer rain.

"Liam, do you trust me?" I inquire as I ease my wrist from his canines now that his body has regenerated. I lick the large punctures closed and scrutinize the werewolf as he sits forward before twisting to face me.

The male considers me for several long seconds, and my heart rate ramps into overdrive, scared to discover if he will forsake me once again.

"What is it you wish of me, sweetness?"

"Sexual control."

"Why?"

I suck in a sharp breath. He didn't say no, so that's progress. I take a risk and open myself to the possibility of rejection. "On the occasions when I've attempted to dominate your passion, the voices murmuring in my thoughts, and the images reflecting in my brain can't sway me." I caress the cheek, rough with stubble. "You are my sanctuary. Command over your body means the incessant wheedling and visions plaguing my every waking moment vanish. Our time together is my saving grace. It quells the nightmares flashing with sonic speed behind my lids, tames them even as it satiates them. You, King Scott, free my mind."

A muscle pulses in his jaw as he contemplates my words. Can the male let go of his innate Alpha tendencies and submit to my will? Or will this be a repeat of what transpired at his ranch? I swallow with nervous anticipation as I await his reply.

The warmth of his regard finds mine. "Then do with me what you will, sweetness. I am all yours."

I gasp. Flashes of fiery pleasure clench my insides. For months, I've craved his trust and submission. It angered and devastated me when he rebuffed me, but right now, simple joy pulses through my veins, dispelling the past hurt.

I lean forward and press my lips to his in thanks before easing back to peer into his devastatingly handsome face. "Thank you, my king. Remember, when we begin, if you desire me to stop, or you object to what I'm asking of you, please, please speak your mind."

He frowns before offering me a quick nod.

Liam's unease at the unknown plagues him. I sense it down to my bones.

"In order for Icarus to release me, I made a pledge. Sex is off-limits, but I'm putting everything else on the table."

"I refuse to engage here. Trace us back to my ranch."

"I have a better idea," I answer with a grin, and Liam regards me with a wariness I appreciate. It's not a comfortable task for the werewolf to follow my lead blindly. Yet he's willing to do so, and that gives me hope. "But first we must speak with the others, relieve their minds you are alright. The queen left your discarded clothes on the chair in the corner." I point to the royal blue wing-back against the far wall. Although I would prefer to keep him nude, it will be so much more entertaining to strip him of his clothes later.

Liam rises from the bed, and I can't help but marvel at his fit physique. The chiseled pectoral muscles, the ripped abdominals that arrow to a perfect V, exposing his mouth-watering hardness nestled in a groomed swath of dark hair. So unlike a vampire's hairless body, I find it strangely refreshing instead of appearing odd.

The powerful thighs flex as he kneels before me, uncaring of his nudity. "Viessa, it is my responsibility as your mate to take care of you, see to your needs, support you in any way I can. Tonight, you saved my life, for which I am eternally grateful. So, I surrender to your commands but do not expect my subjugation every time we're together. You must meet me halfway and oblige me authority over you as well."

I frown. "But, Liam…"

"No buts, Viessa," he interrupts with a determined note. "Agree to compromise, or I get dressed and walk away. Forever. I can concede to no less."

Panic spikes my heart rate, and I blink several times to check the burn of tears. What he's proposing is a reasonable request. I just pray my inner vampire will abide by it. "Okay. Fair enough."

"Good girl." His smile causes heat to engulf my body, and the praise lightens my soul. My mind may crave dominion during sex, but my spirit screams for the Alpha's love and acceptance.

Without another word, he saunters over to his clothes—my mouth waters at the splendor of his perfect ass.

Oh yeah. Tonight, I hope to shake his world to such an extent, he'll forget all about gaining control.

'Lu, tell the others they can return.'

I no sooner get the thought out to my twin when the thick wooden door swings wide and Liam's friends come barreling into the room, concern etched in their expressions.

While Liam embraces them one by one, assuring them he's fine, I once again struggle to ignore the voices and images clawing to intrude.

A particular image snags my attention. Purple irises, familiar but not, encased in a charred body, staring blankly up at me from a great distance. A dark-gray mist surrounds the carcass. I shiver at the oppression of black magic surrounding the body.

Kurtis' booming laugh jolts me from the dream and I shake my head, rubbing the goosebumps from my arms as if doing so will dispel the deep sense of foreboding.

I envy the camaraderie this group has developed over the past couple of years. I never had a *friend* as a child. Parents keep their kids as far away from the crazy girl as possible.

My sole confidant was my twin, and even then, we never had a close relationship. Half the time, no scratch that, the majority of the time, the swirl of chaos inside my brain consumed me. What I remember of our childhood was Lu's patience while attempting to train me during the intervals of peace.

She always stood up for me too. From other kids bullying me or even adults screaming at me to get away. When she institutionalized me, it nearly crushed my spirit. Gone was the one person I trusted and relied upon, replaced by cruel physicians and other inmates as insane as I was. All except one. Our time together was brief, but *he* opened my eyes to an alternative way to control my senseless life.

Suspecting my dark thoughts, Liam extracts himself from his friends and strides over, boldly wrapping an arm around my waist and tugging me to his chest.

"You okay, sweetness?"

"Yes, my king. Are you ready to depart?"

He inhales a deep breath before offering me a lopsided, sexy grin. "Let's get the fuck out of here."

Chapter 9

Viessa

The second we materialize, peace cradles my soul.

This rare slice of heaven is my getaway. The one place I turn to when I need to lay my burdens down and become absorbed in the tranquility of my secret home.

Drummond Island, dubbed the "Gem of the Huron," lies at Lake Huron's northern end and is the largest island in the Great Lakes. It boasts some of the most magnificent landscapes in Michigan.

For those who can't teleport, the sole transport on or off is a one-mile car ferry ride across the St. Mary's River. About 1,200 residents brave the cruel winters, but in the gorgeous summer months, that figure doubles and sometimes triples.

My little section of paradise, which my sister discovered over two decades ago, is eight acres with four hundred feet of lakefront on the island's Southside. Far enough away from the more popular North shore that I've always felt protected and hidden.

The dwelling itself is 1,800 square feet of wood floors, rock fireplaces, a modern kitchen, and a soaring wall of windows facing the water. The master bedroom is the only place in the house with metal shutters installed over the sliding glass doors that lead to the wrap-around deck. If I ever trace here during the day, I must sequester myself in the suite until the sun sinks below the horizon.

"Is this your home?" Liam asks, gazing out at the glittering water gently undulating in the sheltered cove.

I smile as a massive freighter—the lights illuminating its extended decking like a colossal horizontal Christmas tree—glides through the ocean-like waters with the stability of a giant through a windstorm, heading west toward the river.

"Yes. Lucretia stashed me here when Dimitri was hunting for me. I loved it so much, I've held onto it. My twin and I are the only individuals who know of this safe house. And now you."

"It's stunning. How's the fishing?"

I giggle. "Since that's a daylight pastime, I have no inkling."

"Oh, right." His blush warms my heart. "I sometimes fail to remember you are a vampire."

"Funny. I never forget you're a werewolf. Your beast is a part of you I crave."

His head tips scrutinizing me. "Each moment we are together, your mental improvements impress me. You've come a long way in a brief measure of time, sweetness."

I delight in his nickname for me. "That's because of you, Liam. I'm still a nut job on my own." I cringe at the admission.

"Even when training with Icarus?"

I tuck my hair behind my ear. "Even then, although I am getting much better."

My mate is stalling, his shoulders rigid with apprehension. "Liam." His gaze meets mine. "I wish to restrain you."

His heart rate spikes along with his breathing, and I'm giddy with anticipation. His jaw hardens, but when he presents an abrupt nod, I slip away into the bedroom, returning with an extended length of braided rope before he can change his mind. His eyebrow lifts as he contemplates the thing like it's a serpent about to strike.

I smile inwardly. One day, his cock will harden the instant he spies a restraint, recalling this night. "Remove your clothes."

He hesitates. I study him for several moments, holding my breath, waiting to learn if the Alpha will acquiesce. Back at the castle, he declared I could do with him what I wish. Was his promise just words? My skin tingles with the dark yearning for dominance, and my brain is alight with so many possibilities. Ones I've dreamed about and others I've researched. The enticement to bind him is as powerful as my need for blood, and I've practiced my knots until my fingertips were raw.

When he unbuttons his shirt, I relax the captured air from my lungs. Nervous energy swells through me. To experience complete authority over my male has played through my mind more times than I can count for decades. I've envisioned every scenario, down to the minute detail in my head.

Through the years, before I set eyes on Liam, and he was merely a dream I clung to, my fantasies were the sole means to shut off the tornado driving me insane. At first, they were sweet and loving, but I couldn't hold on to them for more than a few minutes. After the institution, the scenario altered. I become the aggressor, forcing the werewolf to submit. I could hold the chaos at bay and enjoy the scene for much longer, and I discovered a respite from the storm. Tonight is the first time a fragment of my inclinations will come to fruition.

I delve deep, quiet my breathing, and revel in the tantalizing display of my mate's chiseled perfection. I commanded him to undress, and he obeyed. My breasts are heavy with need, the nipples hard achy points begging for attention, and the manifestation of my long-awaited lust dampens my core.

"Fuck," he grunts, tossing his discarded garments to the side. "I scent your desire, Viessa, and it smells as sweet as it tastes."

Based on his massive erection, my womanly perfume is driving him wild. I lick my lips, and his gaze devours the movement. I thrust aside my raging appetite and focus on ramping up my king's passions. He may tout he detests being manipulated, but entombed in his subconscious, Liam gets off on this, although I fear he will never admit it. To himself or me.

I force an authority I am far from experiencing into my tone. "Do not speak until granted permission. Do not touch me unless I allow it and adhere to my every command. Can you do that?"

Liam's beautiful cock twitches as he inhales deeply before letting it out on a heavy exhale. "Yes."

I saunter toward him, the fat rope swinging from my fingertips. His bulging muscles tense as I draw near, but he doesn't move. Liam regards me with a wariness glimmering in his gaze.

"Place your arms behind you, your wrists crossed." When he complies, I walk around him and begin the process. By the time I'm done, I've bound his large forearms several times, encircled his elbows, crisscrossed the rope over his massive chest, up over his shoulders, and secured the ends with a carefully placed knot above his clenched fists.

I step back and admire my handiwork. It looks just like the picture on the internet and I smile with pride.

Liam is a dynamic werewolf; he could break these bindings with ease, so this is more about trust and submission than physical restraint. Seeing the brawny, dominant Alpha restrained, fixed to do my bidding, is the most erotic thing I've ever witnessed. By the engorged erection jutting up proud and strong, I'd estimate he's reveling in it as well. That notion pleases me to no end.

"I love the strength in your body, Liam." I pass my palm over his bulky shoulders as I prowl around him. "The way your muscles shift and flex. The delicious veins bulging in your forearms and biceps. But this is my favorite spot." I track my fingers down the defined V pointing a pathway to his groin. His eyes devour me, and a low sexy rumble vibrates his chest.

I stride back several steps, running a critical eye over the bindings once more before zeroing in on the heated regard of my male. I toe-off my boots and socks. The whiskey irises demand more of my flesh, so I slow my movements, prolonging his torture and ramping up his need. Just like he taught me.

After tossing my sweater on the couch, I shimmy enticingly out of my jeans. The vivid blue bra and thong reminded me of the beast's hypnotic irises, and I procured the set instantly.

A muscle pulses in his jaw. His spectacular body is tense with the need to devour me. Just taking this measure of control over such a vibrant creature is beyond anything I imagined. The thrill fuels my appetite.

I drift toward him, grazing my fingernails along his impressive length. It twitches in response, soliciting more of my touch, but I move away and brush past him. Liam inhales deeply, and his rough growl has me biting my cheek to keep from grinning like an overeager fool.

The high-top dining table rests in front of the U-shaped kitchen that looks out over the lovely sparkling bay. I nudge the armchair back from the head of the polished wood surface and hop up on the edge, my toes on the seat. King Scott watches me with such blazing intensity; it's practically a caress.

Perched on the threshold, I shove my dense hair off my nape and secure it in a messy bun with the elastic band from around my wrist. I reach behind and unclasp my bra, letting it slip down my arms with excruciating slowness. A rumble fills the great room.

"Come to me, Liam." He doesn't falter, approaching me in two strides. "Sit," I command, hoisting a leg so he can slide into the chair in front of me.

When he's settled between my open thighs, I bend forward and capture his lips in a feverish kiss. He angles his head, thrusts his tongue inside to duel with mine, and I suck it deep. He groans, straining toward me in his seat. The ropes creak as his muscles bunch against the bindings.

I lean back, our panting breaths loud in the silent house. The intense chocolate irises devour my breasts, and trail down my stomach before stalling on the soaked lace covering my sex. He licks his lips, and I nearly combust. Need to get these panties off and experience that mouth. I relished the beast lapping at my core before. Now, I demand the male.

I work the delicate thong over my hips, then plant my toes on his hard thighs, utilizing them as leverage to lift my butt enough to shove the cloth down my legs. When I reach my knees, I raise them straight up in the air to thrust the material up over my ankles and feet, giving him a bird's-eye view of my wet core aching for him.

"Fuck." His groan is absolute need. I cherish the tone. My toes drop back on top of his tense thighs, and I scoot to the edge of the table, spreading them wide.

"Not another word unless I demand an answer, Liam," I warn sternly. His gaze snaps to mine. "Do you understand?"

"Yes."

I grin. "Do you long to taste me, my king?"

"God, yes." The desperate rumble sends butterflies skittering through my tummy.

I clasp the back of his skull and drag him toward my aching breasts. "Soon, but first, these need your attention."

In a millisecond, his mouth locks on a throbbing nipple, causing my head to dip back as sharp pleasure skyrockets from his suckling lips straight to my clit. "Oh, yes."

When he lightly bites down, it's like an electrical current surging through every nerve, lighting me up from the inside. He turns to the other without direction, providing it equal consideration. A tightness builds in my core. I've read about women who can orgasm from this, and I wonder if I could be one of them. The sensations spiraling from my nipples to my sex and back again are extraordinary.

"Enough," I pant, letting go of his nape but not pushing him from me. A battle wages inside my mate. It's evident in his expressive regard glaring at me. I wait with bated breath to determine if he will comply with my demand or break his bonds and have his way. As tremendous as I suspect the sex would be, disappointment would darken the experience.

Liam eases away, and relief washes over me. It's strange, but the defiant fire in his eyes pleases me as much as his obedience.

I shimmy closer to the edge of the table and spread my thighs wider. His restless gaze falls to my bare, glistening folds, and I lean back on my elbows. My extremities tremble with increasing need.

"Are you hungry, mate?"

The irises flicker blue. "Starving." Bulky muscles tug against the stiff bonds, digging the rope deeper into his shoulders.

"One lick only," I instruct.

Liam eases forward, his gaze locked with mine. I sense his savage intent and willful disobedience a split second before my king sets in with abandonment. I groan in pure ecstasy, dropping back on the table, my spine arching as waves of extreme pleasure radiate through my sensitive flesh. Liam's growl of satisfaction stimulates me further and my breath hitches with every lap of his talented tongue. It penetrates and swirls with such expertise I'm soon shuddering for release.

The low guttural moans vibrate my swollen bundle, and when he latches onto it, sucking deep, I burst. Fire lances through my core, tightening every tendon. I grip fistfuls of his hair, crying out his name as I shamelessly gyrate against his eager lips. The rough stubble only adds to the experience, stimulating me beyond rational thought.

"God, Liam!" I shout, sailing over the brink a second time. He continues to feed on me with a zeal that seizes my breath.

When the tremors settle to a pleasant hum, I let go of his black locks and collapse back on the table. The wolf licks and sucks at my core as my heart rate returns to normal and my breathing deepens.

After several minutes, I brace up on my elbows and peer down my torso at the flickering blue regard. The bold gleam dares me to halt him as he thoroughly and possessively cleans my sex. It feels so damn good I could let him feast on me for hours, and I recognize he would covet that as well. But my mate disobeyed my command, and even though I reaped the benefit of his rebellion, punishment must be the outcome if I'm going to set a precedent for future sessions. A thrill zings up my spine as a plan forms in my brain.

"Stop." His eyes narrow, but he straightens, licking his lips for every last drop of my essence, pure male pride shining in his eyes. "Stand."

He obeys, shoving the chair with the back of his legs as he rises. His magnificent erection calls for my attention. But now is not the time for reward.

I hop off the table and circle my bound mate, grazing my fingertips over his heated flesh. "Spread your thighs," I whisper, kissing him between his shoulder blades. He takes a broader stance, holding his focus forward. He's clenched his enormous fists at his back so tight, the knuckles whiten.

"You willfully disobeyed me, my king." My tone is gentle, meant to lull him into a false sense of security. "Did you enjoy defying me?"

"I enjoyed your sweet pussy," he counters roughly. "Hearing you cry my name as you flew apart."

I bite my lip, reveling in his deep, insolent tone.

"When you misbehave, you incur consequences," I murmur, imploring his fingers to unfurl before facing him. "As much as I enjoyed the outcome of your defiance, you must learn to obey my commands during our time together."

He glowers, blinking several times. No doubt questions swirl through his brain, but they will have to wait until a later time. The true submission must begin.

Chapter 10

Any consequence pales compared to the feast I just enjoyed. If the price to suckle and devour my mate's incredible sex is restraint, then this cowboy is on board. The weak ropes are a reminder of who's in control, and while a part of me objects, my need for my woman's sensual perfume on my lips eclipses my reservations. I inhale deep, glorying in her fragrance on my lips. The binds creak, burrowing into my flesh, and my dick pulses in response.

Shit. Am I enjoying being tied up? No. It's Viessa I covet, nothing more. While she was trussing me up like a pig on a roast, I once again questioned how and when she learned, not only the intricate knots, but the steps she laid out tonight.

I regard her keenly as she escapes into the bedroom, salivating at the flawless beauty of her heart-shaped ass, the long, toned thighs. What is the woman up to now?

She returns with a riding crop gripped in her fist. I take a stride back, ready to snap the bindings and end this lunacy. But as she moves closer, I witness the immense desire flaring in the amber, hear her panting breaths, and rapid heartbeat. What captures my attention is the clarity and lucidity in her expression.

My woman requires this, and while the leather device could never cause me injury, the stinging pain nothing more than a nuisance, it's the indignity of submitting to her administrations that flares my uneasiness.

Then I recall her vow, and my agitation lessens somewhat. I may have to humble myself, tap down the beast for her on this occasion, but on the next opportunity we are together, I will enjoy full authority.

My sudden grin gives her pause, and she studies me. "I can't identify if you're content with what's about to develop or furious."

"Just remembering your oath and all the possibilities when it's my turn."

Her eyes widen as she walks forward before working the flap of the crop down my chest. The muscles in my abdomen tighten at the contact of the cool leather.

"You wish to restrain me, Liam? Brighten my flesh with your palm or a whip?"

Strangely enough, the images her words illicit cause my dick to pulse. Sure, I've bound women's wrists, smacked their asses as I rode them from behind, but I never ventured beyond that. Never had any inclination to delve into that side of kink. But gazing at my female's smooth expanse of skin, a hunger for all those things settles in my gut.

"Yes." My response is gruff with lust.

"Have you ever flogged a woman before?" she asks, roaming around me while passing the crop up and over my shoulder and along the rope's edges. My dick pulses with every stroke of the cool skin.

"No."

"It pleases me it will be a first for both of us then, and I look forward to experiencing it with you."

"How many men have you…" The sharp bite on my ass halts me mid-query. I clench my fists in response as a rough growl rumbles from my chest, even as my balls tighten.

"I cautioned you about speaking unless given permission or asked a question." The cold command in her voice raises my hackles, and I grit my teeth to hold my retort at bay. "I'm about to punish you. I will advise you again. Do not move. Two ways this finishes; either I stop it, or you demand it." She runs her nails across the spot the crop landed, and a tingling sensation trembles through my frame.

She strolls around to face me, and I glare down into the determined lava eyes resplendent with stunning transparency. In that second, I make a silent pledge; I'll endure whatever this female dishes out tonight to facilitate the lucidity I witness in her countenance.

"Do you understand?" she asks, scrutinizing me.

I lower my lids, gazing at her delicate feet, the toenails a bright red. "Yes, ma'am."

She gasps at my ready submission. "Oh, Liam. You have no concept of how much you thrill me. Thank you."

"Before you begin, may I make a request?" I propose, forcing my gaze to remain on the floor.

"Of course," she whispers before raising my chin with the crop.

"This remains between us. No one can know. Especially your twin."

If news leaked out, I submitted sexually to a female, my reputation as an Alpha king would take a severe dent. I would lose the respect of my commanders and people.

"Whatever passes between you and me *stays* between you and me, Liam. I would never betray your trust."

My lips twitch with relief. "Then, do what you must, sweetness."

Her saucy, resolute grin sets me on fire as she moves behind me once more, but instead of the sting of leather, capable fingers work the ropes at my wrists until the tight bindings fall away. I flex my hands as the circulation returns, perplexed as to why she set me free.

"Go place your hands on the table," she instructs. I do as commanded, even as the beast bristles at the order.

The polished wood structure is a high top, but I still need to stoop at the waist to flatten my palms on the smooth surface, and I inhale at the remembered sweet, musky scent and flavor of my mate.

"If your palms rise, our night ceases. You will find no sexual release with me, and I will leave you here to discover your own way home. Do you understand?"

Fuck. She'd desert me in the middle of nowhere with a raging hard-on? Not that it wouldn't take more than a phone call to Nic to retrieve me, but that would instigate too many questions I refuse to answer. Son of a bitch. Subjugation is more challenging than I guessed.

Your woman requires this for mental stability, Liam. You can do it.

"Yes," I mutter between clenched teeth.

"One day, you will address me as Mistress during our time together."

Not fucking likely.

The first strike of the crop jolts through my body. I squeeze my eyes shut to concentrate on not spinning around, snatching the damn thing from her, and snapping it like a twig before bending her over this table and fucking her into submission. That's who I am. Not this weak individual who's allowing his woman to spank him with a goddamn riding crop.

Blow after blow rain down on my ass, and it's all I can do to maintain my composure and the beast's growls in check. But when a slow burn spreads through my anus, I'm stunned at the ache pounding in my groin. With each hit, my balls draw tight, and moisture beads the tip of my rigid cock. If she touched me right now, I would detonate.

The overpowering demand to grip my dick and bring myself to release while she continues to rain stinging slaps on my backside is bewildering. What the fuck is happening to me? I should despise this with a passion. I am a fucking Alpha male. Why am I getting off on my female spanking me?

By the time the biting hits halt, my head hangs low between my shoulders, and my eyes squeeze tight to keep from ejaculating all over the kitchen floor. The sound of my harsh breath fills the room as I work to understand my responses.

"Step back, Liam."

Even her sharp command has my dick twitching. I suck in a deep calming breath before letting go of the slick surface and taking a stride back. What the hell happens now?

Viessa answers my question when she kneels before me, grasps my raging hard on in her fist, and peers up at me. The amber glow is dazzling in its severity, and I frown as a bizarre pride fills my chest. My submission delivered my female to this height of passion.

"I'm going to fuck you with my mouth, Liam. Keep your hands at your sides."

"Yes, ma'am," I rasp out, my ragged breathing making it challenging to communicate.

The second those soft lips contact my engorged cock. My lids close, and I groan in pure fucking rapture, fixed to combust. I clench my fists, staring down at my woman pleasuring me, and hold on, reveling in the ride as long as possible.

Her grip on my sac is a delicious punishment, while her other hand clamps down on the base of my shaft like a vice. At some point, she took out the messy bun, and I love watching her ebony hair swish back and forth across her shoulders as she works her lips along my length with increasing momentum.

The sensitive head hits her throat each time, and when she withdraws, she swirls her tongue around the tip before plunging deep again. My fingers flex with the need to dive them into her luxuriant tresses and seize control, fuck the exquisite mouth until I explode.

Instead, I clutch my thighs in a painful grip to maintain them at my sides. When Vi pops me free from the warm cocoon of her skilled mouth and sinks lower to lick and suckle my balls, I drop my chin to my chest and groan low.

She glances up, pure pleasure glowing in her eyes. "Do not come until given permission, Liam."

Fuck. The Oracle is crazy if she imagines I can last much longer, but I nod my compliance.

"Say it," she commands and tugs on my sac. Instead of the slight pain squelching the advancing inferno, it fans the flames.

"Yes, ma'am." The words are nearly incoherent, saturated with my beast's guttural tone. She smiles before setting back in on my throbbing length, one hand fondling my tightened balls and the other pumping my shaft in conjunction with her bobbing head.

This is sheer fucking ecstasy. My woman kneels before me, pleasuring me thoroughly. The burn on my ass from the crop radiates heat, escalating the seething inferno spreading through my frame, and the fact I'm not allowed to move somehow heightens my lust.

My mind takes a step back, viewing tonight from a spectral plane. I watch in sick fascination as my naked female strikes my ass repeatedly with that damn crop. And while my fingers dig into the wooden surface in objection, my hips lean back for more, my cock jumping with the need for release with every strike.

Fuck me. I got off on being spanked. Even now, instead of recoiling at the notion, just recalling it ramps up my desire and I fight to keep from exploding down her throat.

Just when I realize holding out a second longer is impossible, Viessa peers up at me, moderating her delicious manipulations. "Come, my beautiful king," she orders before setting in with vigor.

Her command lets loose the thin restraint, and I throw my head back, clutch my thighs harder so I don't reach for her, and shatter. "Fuck, Vi!" I shout as sensation upon sensation skyrockets through my frame. I lock my knees to keep them from buckling under the extraordinary pleasure washing through every muscle and tendon.

When the last of the tremors subside, I grasp my female's biceps and haul her to her feet, devouring her mouth with mine. My scent lingers on her lips and tongue as I delve deep, driving both hands into her luscious mane to hold her immobile. She groans low, clinging to my waist before dropping her palms down the heated flesh on my ass.

I pull away and settle my forehead on hers. Our panting breaths mingle. "That was fucking incredible, sweetness." My confession produces a beautiful, enchanting smile, and my heart melts. The slight humiliation and discomfort were worth it to witness her joy.

"Thank you, Liam. I... I can't convey how remarkable this hour was for me. Your cooperation and support affect me beyond words. I'm humbled by it."

A blush steals over her cheeks, and I'm stunned. Gone is the domineering Mistress of a few minutes ago, supplanted by my sweet, vulnerable, but courageous woman seeking my praise. Everything that just transpired, all my objections and concerns, my reluctant lust, fly out the window at this revelation into a buried chamber of Viessa's mind.

Yes, she struggles daily with the unrest in her psyche. Because of that, she vigorously demands her mate to submit sexually, but underneath all the stringent bravado lies a heart scarred by her past and insecurities.

For over a century, Viessa lived a reclusive existence, powerless to let anyone close, even her twin. Many shied away from her, judging her mad. At one point, Viessa's psychological instability forced Lucretia to institutionalize her for her own security and the safety of others.

By some phenomenon, my presence mitigates the chaos, and according to her, when she's working me over—like tonight—it subdues it all together. How she discovered this is something I repeatedly question in my mind. If the retelling involves a recount of her time with another man, my beast invariably shies away from the answers.

In some respects, I understand Icarus's reservations. What if something momentous took place in the world during one of our sessions? Would she even perceive it? Or could our time block a vision of the future?

If that were to happen, people could die, including my own friends. The burden of responsibility would land squarely on my shoulders because I was too weak to walk away from my fated female.

Maybe I should have the Oracle remove our bond. I couldn't live with myself if a catastrophe happened while Vi and I were otherwise engaged. And neither could she.

After what transpired tonight, I'm not positive I'm strong enough to renounce this precious, psychotic woman who just stole a chunk of my heart.

Chapter 11

Liam

"**T**his is utter bullshit," I rage at the delegates, many I consider close friends.

The second Viessa and I appeared back at the castle, she kissed my cheek and disappeared. Nic informed us she'd organized an emergency Council of Unity meeting to decide King Grayflame's fate. But since we are missing two representatives, Icarus and Jilaya, three if you include the topic of discussion, they are declining to vote on the issue.

"Agreed, young wolf," Jag nods in my direction, his crimson eyes smoldering with anger. "But the entire purpose of this council is that all members must be present to enact on such a pivotal matter."

"Where the fuck is Queen Oresha, anyway?" Nicki inquires. "She hasn't attended the last two meetings."

"I attempted to reach out to Jilaya for our monthly get together," Priestess Tanagra announces. "But she has yet to return my text or call."

"You strike up a friendship with the succubus, peach?" Darath asks with a smirk at the lovely, petite land nymph with beautiful jade eyes.

"It would amaze you how much we have in common," she counters back with an alluring grin.

"On the contrary, beautiful," the demon growls low. "I suspect you could teach Jilaya a thing or two."

"We have another dilemma," I grate out, snagging everyone's awareness. "While Nicole and I were battling the fae, I caught sight of something strange deep in the woods."

"The blonde woman?" Nicki interjects.

"Yes," I sigh, relieved she witnessed her, and it wasn't just the silver producing a hallucination. "She might be the reason your powers were nonexistent."

"Any idea who she was?" Kurtis asks.

"Not positive, but in wolf form, she didn't give off a heat signature, merely an odd purple glow that pulsed around her. After I shifted back, I recognized it was a woman."

"A purple light? Are you certain, King Scott?" Jagorach leans forward, his enormous body tense, his eerie stare direct.

"Yup. Pretty damn sure. Why?"

He shrugs. "I do not wish to create false concerns at this table. Allow me time to investigate a little further." The demon directs his remark to Nicki.

"Should we be worried, Darath?" she asks quietly, the gunmetal irises watching him closely.

"Not we, my young Halfling. You."

"What the fuck does that mean?" I demand. Enough of these games. "Just tell us now what you suspect, Jag."

He sighs heavily, and dread drops in my gut like a cannonball. Besides God, what else disturbs the devil?

"One creature with ample power to subdue Nicole's and who throws off an ethereal fog of magic in the form of a violet glow. Abigail Brevil."

"Who the fuck is she?" Nicki asks, taking a sip of the ever-present coffee at her elbow.

"She is a potent witch who has been around almost as long as I have, and a lethal beauty with the sting of a viper."

"Of course she is," the vampire queen sighs. "And now it appears she's working with public enemy number one. Syn Grayflame."

"Most witches exploit supernatural forces to varying degrees, with only their morality and skill level to define the borders. Abigail has no moral compass, and with the flexibility of magic, she essentially has limitless possibilities for what she can accomplish."

"Do you expect she's responsible for the barrier surrounding the Dark Fae Stronghold?" Queen Svaldana questions.

"Yes. It is simply a matter of time before Brevil figures out how to bring Icarus' shield down."

Son of a bitch. Without the border, the Vampire Nation and Nicole are defenseless, especially if this Abigail steals her powers. Throughout history, human and immortal, border walls and magical barriers were essential components to safety and security for the people within. That still holds true today.

"Can she possibly destroy an Oracle's shield?" I ask in disbelief.

"Anything is probable, Wolf. And we would be prudent not to underestimate the witch."

"Darath?" Nicki whispers, gazing into her coffee cup.

"Yes, my lady?"

Her lids slowly lift, pinning the demon king with her troubled regard. "Am I capable of defeating her?"

Silence meets her question. Bright ruby irises, laden with regret, stare down the table at the queen. "No."

Logan steps to Nicole, casting aside proper etiquette at the foreign threat to his mate. "Then tell us how we, as a collective, can destroy her."

"As of the here and now, I cannot answer that, commander." Darath's seven-foot frame unfolds from his chair. "Permit me an opportunity to investigate this further and perhaps return a fruitful course of action."

Will our lives ever settle down? Nicole has done a tremendous job of aligning many factions in the immortal world in a brief amount of time. The vampires, werewolves, and shifters are no longer at war. She brokered an accord with the Demon Realm, which no one conceived was achievable. Her brave, altruistic actions brought the land nymphs out of hiding to join the council, and she ended generations of carnage with the valkyries.

The species still on the fence are the notoriously hot-headed and extremely reclusive centaurs, the witches, golems, and the seldom seen dragon shifters. Even in human form, they stick to their Australian homeland.

The underlying deviousness of Syn Grayflame has simmered below the surface since the glorious battle with King Dimitri. The dark fae ruler possesses an irrational hostility not merely for vampires, but for Nicole specifically.

Little by little, Nicki has hacked away at the prophecy. Peace with these other creatures will grow in time. Of that, I have no misgiving, but two primary obstacles stand in her way-the bastard Grayflame and bearing a son. The future vampire king to walk in the sun, eat food, and produce the next generation of daywalkers.

Not too long ago, we rejoiced in her pregnancy. Proud she checked off another box on the list. But barely a month in, the gods demanded the life of her unborn child as payment for Icarus bringing her back from the dead.

"You have one week, Darath," Logan answers, his irises sparking green. "No matter the council's decision, the Vampire Nation cannot allow this offense to go unpunished. We guarantee retaliation with the full force of our Guardians. I will not rest until I have severed Syn Grayflame's head from his body."

"Understood, commander," Jag nods. His gaze lands briefly on Kleora. Her jade eyes peer up at him with curiosity.

"Stay well, peach." With a quick wink, he disappears.

"Just once, I would like things to go my fucking way." Nicole sighs. "We just solved the Watcher situation, and now a new threat pops to the forefront."

"What's your plan for retribution, Logan?" I probe. As a victim of the attack, I want in on whatever scheme the former commander is plotting. "You have the full support of my Wardens."

"Thank you, Scott. Maybe we could arrange a gathering here to formulate a strategy?"

"You got it. Whatever you need."

"The Sentinels are at your disposal," Kurtis chimes in, his blue eyes stone cold.

"I already have a beef to pick with the dark fae king," Arra interjects. "My Protectors, along with Alexandria and myself, are at the ready."

Several months ago, Grayflame attempted to abduct Alex to use as leverage against Nicki. Thankfully, Sebastian interceded, killing the Fae Custodian before he completed his task.

"While I have not brought my Storm Walkers into open combat in quite some time, this qualifies as a good enough reason to tighten our bows," Kleora pipes in with a wicked smile.

"Well, my lady," I stand and face the woman I consider a sister. "It seems you've united the majority of the immortal world in this quest. We have your back."

Gray irises slowly scan the rulers around the table. "The prudent response is while I appreciate your loyalty, and I do. This is my fight. You should not get involved." She shrugs. "But when have I ever been prudent? I need every one of you if we are to defeat Grayflame and this witch, Abigail." She runs an agitated hand through her auburn tresses. "In her presence, I am nothing more than a vampire with extreme combat skills. Your support means the world to me. You all command powerful, elite armies. Combined with my Guardians and the infamous Moretti brothers," she smiles up at her mate, and he snorts in reply, "we might stand a chance."

"Do we bring the Oracles in on this?" I question, hoping she responds in the positive. I will jump at any additional time I'm allowed with my female.

"Oh, when I inform Icarus his precious shield is in jeopardy of being hacked, you won't be able to stop him from being involved." The mischievous grin triggers chuckles around the room.

Hot damn. Even though we just had a fantastic hour, I crave my mate's presence once more. My skin tingles with an overwhelming desire to get my hands on her lithe body, my mouth on her tantalizing sweetness, and her complete submission. Another month seems like a lifetime.

"Hey, Liam," Sebastian signals, entering the conference room as the meeting disperses. "You need transport home?"

"Sure do." I nod, eager to head back to the ranch and solidify responsibilities with my siblings.

I also wish to pick Sebastian's brain on a few points. He's our local expert on all things BDSM, and if I'm gonna continue down this path with Viessa, I might require a heads up on what else to expect and how best to play my role. On either end.

The warrior grips my shoulder, and as the room darkens, my last image is of Logan gathering Nicole into his arms for a passionate kiss.

Chapter 12

Nicole

"Let's take a little trip to Scotland, Logan. We need to assess the situation," I mumble into the pillow, stretched out butt ass naked on my stomach, my sexual slave driver lounging next to me in our enormous bed. While the heat in my ass is fading, a lust-filled daze clouds my brain.

"Yesterday, I would have agreed, but now that we understand the actual threat, the answer is no."

The rough, commanding tone completely opposes the tenderness of his fingertips grazing the hypersensitive skin on my backside, prolonging the addictive tingle. A reasonable person would cower and obey an order from the legendary Moretti. I'm not reasonable or the cowering type.

I force heavy lids to open and scowl at him. "I am the queen, remember? My word is law."

I snort inwardly. Who am I fucking kidding?

In all our time together, I've never commandeered this magnificent hero. In public, my mate pretends to acquiesce to my orders. However, behind closed doors, if he deems my "tomfooleries"—his word, not mine—place my existence in peril, the provocative brute controls my mind and body with lust, shutting down my brain on any further deliberation on the matter.

My only weakness? The sexy as fuck Dom with a heart of gold. Correction. I've acquired another vulnerability—Abigail Brevil.

"Jag is paranoid. You know how protective of me he's become."

It's so bizarre to be on team Lucifer. The devil at my six, guarding my back. The words alone raise the fine hairs at my nape. It sounds wrong. Sooo wrong.

"I have never witnessed the big demon so intense. This witch has him tied up in knots, which ramps up my vigilance and escalates my demand to keep you safe. As it should you, my love."

"Yeah, yeah. I'll leave all the growling *"mine"* proclamations and pounding of the chest to you."

He barks out a laugh, smacking my bare ass. "Careful, baby. I may chain you in the dungeon and perform all sorts of deviant things to this exquisite body."

"Promises. Promises." I smirk and shift to stretch over his torso, gazing into the emeralds that captivated my dreams so long ago. "Seriously, though. I wish to identify what we're up against. I'm also concerned about Jilaya."

"The succubus queen? Why?"

I shrug. "A hunch, but I suspect Syn is holding her prisoner. Or the sex pot is back to fucking the disgusting fae. Either way, I need to determine what's up with her. And Icarus should get his little blue ass down here and travel to the land of greenness with us." I circle a nipple with my fingernail and watch in fascination when it pebbles in response. "I refuse to consider a mere witch can thwart me, you, and an Oracle."

"In my six centuries, I have encountered some pretty formidable witches, but none with enough magic to strip the abilities from a powerful being such as yourself."

"Ha! You admitted I'm powerful. So using your words against you later."

He chuckles, hoisting me up by the waist to straddle his hips and growing erection. Geez. The guy has the stamina of a herd of stallions. "Of that, I have no doubt, my love."

With slow sensual movements, he slides his huge palms, roughened by years of wielding a sword, along my ribs to cup my breasts, kneading them before rolling and tweaking the nipples. I lift my butt and position the enormous head at my wet, eager opening.

"Promise me we can go to Scotland," I demand in my best authoritative voice. "Or no sex for you, buddy." The irises spark right before he rears up, grips my hips in a punishing hold, and thrusts home. "Oh, God."

The exquisite pleasure-pain of his size invading and stretching already sensitive muscles nearly has me soaring into nirvana. I arch my neck and revel in the sensation for a second before brawny arms encircle my waist. Logan sets an unrelenting pace, and tremors convulse my insides, the forewarning of an impending eruption.

Right before I careen over the precipice, my mate halts, his enormous hands clamping down hard to inhibit any movement. I lift my gaze to his and glare into the stormy regard of the deadliest warrior in vampire history.

"Logan," I whine at being denied entrance into heaven.

"When it comes to your security, baby, *my* word is law. I will never permit anyone or anything to take you from me again. Including you. Do I make myself clear?"

As vampire queen, I outrank him, and with my long list of powers, I could defeat him in combat. It would be a lengthy affair with pain on both sides, though. I understand and respect his inclination to keep me safe, even from my own stupidity. And secretly, I love his dominance. Never in a million years would I admit such a thing out loud. A girl must safeguard her reputation, after all.

"Yes, Sir," I sigh with a saucy grin against his lips, clasping his face between my palms. He rewards my compliance by flipping me over onto all fours to demonstrate just how skillfully he rules my body.

Chapter 13

"You know, it would've been less conspicuous if it were just the three of us like I proposed, Icarus," Nicole laments for the second time as our group skulks around the perimeter of the dark fae shield on the Isle of Skye in Scotland.

"I required Viessa's power as well, and King Scott helps focus her mind."

"Whatever. Let's finish this and get the hell out of here. All this green dampness makes me nauseous."

Logan chuckles.

"This looks like a suitable spot," my werewolf interjects. "Icarus, you sure we're hidden beneath your spell?"

"Yes, my lord."

"If so, I agree. This is good enough a spot as any," Logan nods, scanning the surrounding area. "Nicole and I will scout around while you get started."

"What precisely are we working to accomplish here, father?" I ask as we kneel in front of the dark fae shield. Liam moves in behind me, and his warmth penetrates my thin sweater, causing a tingle of desire to advance up my spine.

My mind immediately rushes to what transpired at my lake house, and I totally miss what Icarus said. Shoot. I shrug mentally. I'll just follow his lead and hope I don't botch the entire thing.

The second my hand connects with the barrier; my brain explodes in a tirade of impressions. So many I can't ascertain their order. They whiz by, swirl in a funnel, and slam forward and back so fast I have no understanding of what's transpiring.

A scream permeates the night, and a part of me realizes it's emerging from me, but I'm so absorbed in the pandemonium in my mind, the savage images of war and death lancing pain through my torso, I cannot stop it.

A wide, warm hand covers my mouth, and I crave to yank it away so I can shriek against the agony infusing every synapse in my skull.

Lash after lash of a whip strikes my body, chained to a long table, splitting open my skin. I arch against the suffering, hitting a brick wall of warmth at my back. My muffled screams continue behind the palm over my lips, and I instinctively bite down, driving my fangs into the thick pad of flesh.

"Viessa! Goddammit, let go."

A part of my boiling brain perceives the deep rumble belongs to my mate, and I should heed his command, but I'm entrenched in the visual sensations bombarding me from all angles. They're laden with death, pain, rage, and anguish.

"Shut her up, or we're all dead." I recognize the furious tone of my queen, but instead of heeding the warning, her voice catapults me into another vision.

"Trace us out of here," my mate demands of my father.

"I cannot, my lord. To sever the link now would provoke severe damage."

I huddle under a bed in a shadowy room. Silent tears course down my cheeks, and I hold my hand over my mouth to remain quiet. My thin physique trembles with terror, hoping and praying he doesn't find me. But he always finds me.

The next second, the mattress and box spring go crashing against the far wall, and the frame splinters around me. I scramble backward into the corner and hug my knees to my chest, sobs shaking my body.

"Please, Dimitri. No more," I whimper, but the beast advances.

"I will never stop my beautiful daughter. You are mine for all eternity."

When those vile hands clutch my thin biceps in a vicious hold, I go ballistic, kicking, scratching, and biting anything I can reach. Over and over, I scream for my mom to save me. Massive forearms wrap around my torso, pinning my arms to my side. I fight harder, desperate to escape his evil touch.

"Holy shit. I know precisely where Viessa's mind has gone," Nicole exclaims, her tone laden with stunned disbelief. "Icarus, pull her out of there."

"Fuck, she's strong. Hold her damn legs, Nicki," Liam growls low.

"I'm sorry, my lady. I must drop the concealment to help Viessa," Icarus pleads to Nicole.

"Do it," she responds.

"We have company," the commander barks a few seconds later.

"Icarus, help Liam. Logan and I will hold off the fae as long as possible. Bring her back to the present ay-sap so we can get the hell out of here."

The voices become more evident. Or at least one voice does—my mate. The mighty werewolf holds me tight against his torso, his muscles bulging against the strain of keeping me immobile while trying not to hurt me. I sense my father at my feet, his cool hands gripping my jean-covered shins.

"Come back to me, sweetness." The deep gruff soothes the crashing tide of images until they are no more than gently lapping waves against the scalding shoreline of my mind.

His warm breath on my neck spreads heat down my chest, and I inhale deeply for the first time since the images invaded my brain. The influx of oxygen, scented with summer rain and leather, calms me and I suck in several deeper breaths.

"That's it, baby. Breathe. Shove the images aside and concentrate on me."

"Hurry the fuck up, Liam," Nicole yells from a short distance away. "She knows we are here. I've lost my damn powers."

"Viessa." Liam's manner alters, becoming more commanding as he shakes my torso. "Let them go, right now."

Somehow, I do as he commands and thrust the visions into the background. They still percolate, but I'm able to contain them and focus on Liam. Sweat dots my forehead, and my limbs tremble from fatigue like I just went ten rounds in a boxing ring.

The second I lift my lids; Icarus's anxious face fills my view. I notice movement all around, and when I peer up into the starlit sky, my heart stops. Over two dozen fae circle above us, their white wings reflecting in the half-moon's dim rays.

A quick glimpse into the surrounding area shows Nicole and Logan engaged in a grisly battle with many more.

"Viessa, can you stand?" Liam asks.

I'm beyond answering. My mind and body are complete mush. My werewolf gathers me into his embrace, climbing to his feet with ease. Unable to raise my arms, I rest my head against his shoulder and trust he will keep me safe.

"Logan. Nicki. Time to go!" he hollers, and in the next second, the two blood-soaked vampires join our group, and prevailing darkness envelops us.

"**C**an you explain what you witnessed, Viessa?" Liam asks tenderly, still holding me close. The heat from my mate's body soothes my muscles even as it ignites a tremor in my stomach.

Nicole traced us to her private office at the castle. She and Logan disappeared to shower and change while Liam eased into an armchair with me in his lap. Across the room, Icarus studies us, well, me in particular.

"I'm not sure. It... it was so chaotic. One minute I was in battle, the next I was being tortured, and finally, I believe I experienced Queen Giordano's abuse at the hands of Dimitri."

"Jesus," Liam whispers before brushing his lips across my temple. Shivers skate along my flesh at the contact.

"Break them out, child," Icarus commands. The Oracle is so still, he doesn't appear to breathe. His tattooed hands clasp at his waist as the icy cobalt irises observe and demand. "Who was being tormented?"

"I don't know. I watched through their eyes."

"Did you identify who was conducting the torture?" Liam asks softly, tucking a curl behind my ear.

"No. They remained out of my line of sight."

"Not you, sweetness."

"Right. Right. Of course. Not me." God. He must think I'm a basket-case. Tonight was *not* my finest hour.

"How about the battle you witnessed? Was it past or future?" my father inquires with a raised eyebrow.

"Did you not visualize what I did when you touched the shield?"

"Yes, my child, but you need to catalog the events in your mind. Place each scene in its appropriate order in time."

Everything is always a damn training moment with him.

I rub my temples to alleviate the pounding in my skull as I attempt to adhere to my father's mandate.

"I think she's had enough," Liam all but growls at the Oracle.

"You do not determine that, King Scott. Viessa's education is constant, and she must decipher the predictions while they are yet vivid in her mind. Please do not interfere."

Liam's expression tightens, but he suggests nothing further. Nicole and Logan pop back freshly showered and in clean clothes. The quote on the queen's t-shirt makes me smile. *"I'm not a bitch. I'm a teller of unfortunate truths."*

"Proceed, child. Place order among the chaos."

Says the Oracle with a couple of millennia of training under his belt. I sigh heavily and force my brain to cooperate. "The battle was in a forest, but all I saw were blood and arrows. The vision seems veiled in a purple mist."

"You cannot determine faces or species?" my father questions.

"No. Can you?" I retort. Liam smirks in my periphery.

The ever-stoic priest doesn't seem to take offense. "No. I cannot."

"What does that mean, Icarus?" Nicole asks from behind her desk. Logan perches on the corner next to her.

"I am uncertain, my lady. This has never happened to me before."

"Humph. You're informing me they stumped the great and powerful Oz?"

"I do not understand your meaning." His puzzled frown mirrors my own. "Who is this Oz person?"

"It's a movie about… oh, never mind." She waves it away before rounding on me. "Tell me about your last vision of Dimitri, Viessa. What did you see?"

My stomach clenches, recalling the horror in the darkness of her childhood room. I've gone through hell in my lifetime. But Queen Giordano suffered much at the hands of her father. I don't wish to reveal I experienced her suffering as my own, but the stormy gray irises demand an answer.

Since I've never learned the art of lying, I go with complete honesty and hope Nicole doesn't slaughter the messenger.

Chapter 14

Tonight's the full moon. Passion lights every nerve ending in my body. Hunger cramps my gut. I swore not to seek my mate, no matter how much I crave his beast and blood. Besides, Icarus hasn't left my side since the night in Scotland, watching me like a hawk to make certain I stay put in this fucking monastery.

"Father," I twist to him on the narrow, dirt path along the cliff. We've strolled down the ridge for the past hour and have finally descended below the blanketing mist. On such walks, I'm permitted to dispense with the stupid robe in favor of warmer apparel suitable for hiking. It's during these occasions, attired in jeans, a thick, knitted sweater, and my favorite buckskin cowboy boots, I'm most comfortable. Although the High Priest Oracle still dons the frock and sandals.

"Yes, my child?" Icarus responds, his head tilted as he eyes me curiously.

"Would it be possible to have my sister here for the engraving of my initial symbol?"

Not only is the full moon tugging at me to be with Liam, but tonight Icarus is inscribing a sacred emblem on my skin for passing my precognition test. Predicting the battle with the fae was the first coherent foresight I'd ever experienced. Most of the time, I still can't decipher the images into a semblance of order or even determine if it's a forthcoming event or some prior history.

But my foresight into Liam's death was as transparent as the full moon shining down on us and lighting our path. I perceived his pain, the poison invading his system and weakening his strength as if it were happening to me. His emotions tore through me like boiling water, blistering my veins with fear.

"I'm sorry. No. As much as I would treasure spending some time with my other offspring, this is a divine rite and forbidden to outsiders." He resumes his stroll down the trail, effectively ending the conversation.

Dammit.

"Well then, can I at least go visit her and share the news?" I reluctantly follow in his wake, my fists clenched in irritation at my sides.

Outside the mist, I'm finding concentration difficult. Voices attempt to encroach. Angry, petrified, menacing, pleading. They whirl in a chaotic circle, loud then soft. As much as I detest the fog, I must admit it aids in muffling them somewhat.

I halt abruptly. A voice slams to the forefront with such intensity my knees buckle, and I grip the sharp rocks protruding from the mountain to keep from tumbling over the rim and plummeting thousands of feet to my death.

"Go away!" My scream bounces off the cliff, strangled by the mist above.

"Viessa?" Icarus reverses his steps, clasping my wrists. "Ease your hold, child."

Confused, I peer up and realize I'm clutching fistfuls of my hair. "She needs help," I whisper as hot tears spill down my icy cheeks.

"Who, Viessa? Who requires aid? Concentrate."

"I... I don't know," I wail and sink to all fours as another scream rips through my brain. "Stop it! Leave her alone!" I shout in desperation.

In a blink, I am no longer crouched on the side of a bluff. Instead, I'm standing in the shadows of an elegant chamber. A magnificent four-poster bed with an intricately carved wooden headboard dominates one stone wall. On closer inspection, I realize the carvings depict dozens of creatures in the throes of various stages of copulation.

The floor is thick slabs of stone with soft, white throw rugs scattered about to ward off the chill. An immense fireplace dominates the surface opposite the bed.

I stride to arched windows and gaze out at the vibrant green landscape, startled to realize it's daytime. The warmth of the sun heats my skin through the glass, but it fails to set my flesh on fire. Strange.

A weak moan snags my awareness, and that's when I notice the woman chained in the center of the room. Her arms stretch wide, bound above her head from chains secured to the ceiling, and her lush nude body hangs limp, unable to support her own weight.

Deep gashes and angry red welts cover her torso and hips. The rich scarlet hair lays tangled, shrouding the face hanging between her shoulders.

Who is the woman? And where the hell am I?

I jolt when a door to my right slams opens, and I frantically search for a place to hide. Before I can dive under the bed, the towering dark fae strides past without a glance in my direction.

Good grief. He possesses no notion I'm here. Either I've cloaked myself, or this is a powerful vision. Since I do not understand how to camouflage from immortals yet, it must be the latter. Which means I cannot help this miserable woman, only observe.

"How is my favorite pet this evening?" the silver-eyed devil inquires, seizing a fistful of the scarlet locks and yanking her gaze to his. But more thick hair covers her face from view. "I felt the bitch's presence in Scotland this past week, and I am feeling a bit… randy. This is your lucky night." He drops her head and strides back, taking a strip of leather from the pocket of his dress slacks. The imposing fae shakes out his long white tresses before tying it at his nape in a low ponytail, highlighting his very pointed ears.

"Please, Syn," the woman pleads softly without raising her gaze. "No more."

So, this is the notorious King Grayflame and I'm in Scotland. I must say, the dark fae is quite beautiful and imposing. Icarus informed me the white-haired, six-and-a-half-foot creature was over nine hundred years old with a soulless, black heart. And by the looks of the woman, I'd estimate that was a valid description.

My heart goes out to her, and frustration burns in my lungs. I have no means of saving her right now.

Syn unbuttons his inky dress shirt with slow, unhurried movements. "Are you ready to confess? To help me?" he asks quietly, his gaze on the task of removing the silver cufflinks at his wrists as if he's not actually interested in her response.

"My answer is still the same. Besides, she hates me. How could I possibly draw her out?"

Who hates her? And who the hell is this female in chains?

"You are a remarkably persuasive woman. Conniving. I'm sure the sight of you after all these years should trigger a reaction in the young, pathetic Halfling." He discards his shirt on the bed, and I choke at the expanse of alabaster skin. Old scars crisscross the massive chest. At some point in his long life, someone whipped this creature brutally and often.

"It won't work, Syn. Please don't do this," she whispers brokenly.

"There was an occasion your heartfelt pleading would have softened my heart. But we both realize what a lying, cheating whore you are, and while you are in my grasp, I will punish you repeatedly for your treachery, my pet."

The silver eyes glimmer with malevolence as he takes his time circling the woman, defeat in every limp line of her tortured body.

My pulse races and shaky breaths tremble from my lips. I crave nothing more than to get the hell out of here, but the demand to identify the redhead glues my boots to the floor.

Syn is a dangerous threat to Nicole, and it seems he aspires to use this woman as a pawn to lure the vampire queen out of her castle. Before I retreat to the monastery's security and my father, I must know this woman's identity.

A shudder dances between my shoulder blades as the king runs his fingers over his previous handiwork on her skin with almost reverent care. She whimpers, and I mentally will her to lift her damn head.

"There was a time you relished my touch, pet. Craved it above all others. Harsh or tender, it did not matter." He towers over her from behind, and I swallow at the vengeful lust filling his gaze. "Until *he* turned you against me. All for that Halfling bitch."

"Please, Syn. I loved you. I did what I had to do."

"If only that were true, puppet." Without another word, he tears open his zipper and palms his enormous erection, running it over a deep cut on her ass before he captures her around the waist, viciously kicks her legs wider and impales her from behind.

The woman cries out, her head dropping back onto the fae's chest as he pounds into her with brutal force, rattling the chains. I'm astonished when his enormous hand gently brushes her long locks from her face to suckle her neck.

Disappointment rushes through me when I finally get a good look at her. I have no inkling who she is, but she plainly has some history with both Syn and Nicole. How and when is yet to be determined.

As the king maintains his relentless pace, I perceive two factors. Grayflame hates and loves this woman. She betrayed him. An offense severe enough, he's prepared to torture her for information. But underneath the vindictive spite, the fae still cares for her. It's evident in the soft suckling of his lips at her neck, the gentle caresses along her breasts before he delves his fingers between her folds, swirling her clit to bring her pleasure.

The woman moans, not with pain but with reluctant carnality, her body surrendering to the prowess of her captor. I can't help but respond to the erotic passion permeating the room. Dampness floods my core, and my nipples tighten as I imagine it's me chained to the ceiling, and Liam, in beast form, pounds into me from behind, his powerful jaws clamped tight at my neck.

"Syn," the female cries out as she orgasms, her muscles stiffening, her belly quivering.

"Yes!" he thunders in return, plunging deep, his fingers burrowing into her hips.

For a brief second in the aftermath, the feathered king settles his forehead on the back of his captive's head, breathes in her scent before tenderly kissing her temple. In the next instant, he's withdrawing, zipping his trousers, and stomping from the room without a backward glance.

The woman hangs limp once more. The low sobs crush my heart. If I don't discover who she is or a way to save her, this mortal will perish at the hands of her lover.

Chapter 15

Liam

"**S**orry we had to move poker night to the castle, Scott," Sebastian states as he shuffles the deck with such velocity it's challenging to track. "I enjoy the tranquility of your ranch, but until we neutralize the threat, none of us are safe outside the barrier. Nicole wants you all close."

"Yeah, I get it," I acknowledge, viewing my hand with disgust. A pair of twos. Really? "Running and hunting inside the shield wasn't as horrendous as I expected. Not to mention, you all hover'n in my periphery kept the beast from charging through it again."

"Anything we can do to help, my man," Kurtis interjects, requesting one card. One damn card.

I tip my Stetson back on my forehead and request three cards. I'm down five hundred bucks in this game. To the demon, of course. "I've mastered the art of video chat with my siblings and commanders around the globe, but this forced isolation is driving me to drink."

I raise my tumbler of GlenDronach 18, my favorite scotch whisky in salute. Tonight, with the throb in my chest matching the one in my groin, I'm on my third glass. Or is this the fourth? It doesn't matter. The slow, numbing burn is what I seek. With every sip, notes of raisins, sherry, and a bit of rum linger on my palate, much like my female. Viessa's flavor is a combination of honeysuckle with mouthwatering hints of woman. I sigh with discontent. It's a fucking nuisance getting myself off at night. I crave the soft, sultry vampire.

The previous lunar shift sucked. If anyone had gotten close, the beast wouldn't have given a fuck who they were. He'd have taken them down and rutted fiercely with images of Viessa in our mind.

The two-month mark since her last feeding is fast approaching. My aching dick is a perpetual reminder and as accurate as any calendar.

I do a double-take when Bastian's lids close. A slight smile lingers, his nostrils flare, and he tilts his head back, inhaling a sharp breath. A minute later, Alex comes prancing into the room, a black flouncy skirt swishing around her toned thighs.

"Sorry to interrupt your little game, boys," she smirks, not contrite in the slightest, and slips into Sebastian's lap. "Oooh, three aces. Is that good, babe?"

Groans circle the table, and the rest of us toss our cards down in disgust.

The commander chuckles. "You minx." His arms encircle her petite waist, and he nuzzles her neck. "You ruined my one winning hand, Red."

"I did?" She bats her eyelashes in mock innocence. "That's too bad. Maybe you should offer me a refresher on the *rules*."

His grin widens with intent. "I fucking love having you here," he growls before ascending from the chair, his mate clasped in his arms. "Later, guys."

Before he's taken two steps, Nicole strides into the conference room, with Icarus and Viessa in tow.

"We need a meeting," she announces with a stormy frown, and everyone jumps to clear the table of cards and chips.

"Darath, we will get to your report in a second," she nods to the demon once we are situated.

Lucretia materializes behind Kurtis's chair, dressed for battle, and lays her palm on his shoulder. I don't think I've ever encountered the warrior in anything but black leather.

"I realize we have other members of our task force now, but I prefer this to be just between us for the moment. If need be, we can include Kleora, Cipher, and Arra later. Understood?"

We all nod our agreement, my gaze fastened on my pale mate standing several feet away. She carries her head low, her fingers clinging to the necklace I gifted her in what seems a lifetime ago.

"What's on your mind, young Halfling?" Jag inquires with a raised eyebrow.

"Viessa endured another vision," Icarus announces and glides to the head of the table.

My gaze swivels to my mate. Oh shit. Now what?

When Vi remains stoic, her limbs trembling, I ache for her. "What did you discover, sweetness?" I probe gently.

She exhales sharply, and her muscles visibly relax at the sound of my voice. Pride swells my chest. I'm her calming force. Her amber gaze zeros in on mine, gratitude shining in the nervous depths.

My mate is such a dichotomy. On the one hand, she leans on my strength to help her weather the storms in her mind, clinging to me with an almost urgent need—a fact the beast and I both adore. Our sole purpose in life — protect, provide, and support our girl. On the other, this powerful Tri-bred mutates into this domineering, passionate Mistress with dark desires, demanding obedience.

The twists and turns of my female's psyche leave both of us in complete disarray.

"King Grayflame is holding a woman captive. She hangs by chains in his bed-chamber, and based on her appearance, he has mistreated her for a while," Viessa conveys, her direct stare never surrendering mine.

"Who is she?" Alex asks, perched on her mate's lap with her elbows on the wooden surface.

"I do not know," Vi replies, glancing briefly at the valkyrie. "She had red hair, but she never opened her eyes, so I'm uncertain what color they are."

"Could it be Queen Oresha?" Logan inquires with a frown.

When Viessa visibly shrinks under the vampire's direct question, Icarus responds for his daughter. "Nay, my lord. The woman was mortal."

"What?" I exclaim. "Syn is torturing a human? For what purpose?"

The council created our laws specifically to protect the fragile race. If we catch the dark fae mistreating one, he could face execution. We need to prove it somehow and get this ass out of our hair.

"He hopes to use her as bait, my king," Vi replies. "To draw Queen Giordano out from behind the shield."

Nicole shrugs, her expression full of confusion. "I don't know any human women. Certainly not an individual important enough to endanger everyone's safety for."

"Um... one further thing." Viessa straightens her shoulders, working to transmit a confidence she is far from experiencing with so many eyes focused on her. White-knuckled fists clenched around the fabric of her robe. "Syn has a love, hate relationship with this woman. She betrayed him, and he's punishing her for it, but I believe he also secretly loves her."

"What led you to that impression, sweetness?" I ask and am startled when her stare becomes heated. My neglected cock stirs in response.

"I observed him take her, but it wasn't brutal or ugly. It was... quite beautiful and tender. He brought her to orgasm before pursuing his own release."

Fuck me. I shift in my chair, adjusting my straining dick to a more comfortable position. Her comments, uttered in that smooth, seductive voice, delivered a spike of lust straight to my groin.

"Shit. That's a fucking visual I didn't need. Syn having sex. Gross," Nicki groans, and Alex snickers.

Discussion breaks out, but I no longer tune in to a damn thing. My gaze remains riveted on the soft amber glow holding mine. Based on her elevated heart rate, the swift little pants, and the sweet aroma of her desire, the retelling of her revelation sexed my mate up.

What did she picture while she examined the fae and this mysterious female? She mentioned he chained the woman's arms above her head. Did she imagine it was her in shackles or me? At this point, I would be fine with either scenario as long as I felt her skin against mine.

"I need to rack my brain for a bit to figure out who this woman is and what kind of threat she might be," Nicki plows her fingers through her auburn locks. "Do you think she was a genuine redhead, Viessa?"

"Based on the trimmed patch between her thighs, yes."

Nicole spits the coffee she just gulped, and Logan pats her on the back with a grin. "Well. Okay then," she grates out when the coughing subsides.

Jag laughs outright. "You are a delight, little Oracle." Vi blushes and tucks her dark locks behind her ear, ducking her head.

I pivot in my armchair to glare down the table at Darath. He raises both palms. "What?" he asks innocently. Yeah, not an innocent bone in the demon's body. "What did I say?"

"There's another matter we should discuss, Icarus," Nicki announces, taking the chair at the end and indicating the Oracles should take their seats. Much to my delight, Viessa takes the position across from me. I regard her intently as she nibbles her lip enticingly.

Fuck, I need this female beneath me.

"How may we be of service, my queen?" the priest asks, oblivious to the sexual tension careening over the surface of the table.

"In Scotland, something stripped my powers. Again. Do you think it was Abigail?"

"I assume she resides behind the shield and used black magic," Icarus responds, concern softening his expression. "You recovered fully?"

"Yes, but I gotta tell ya, it's a humbling experience. If I'm to be effective in this war, we must stop the witch from stealing my fucking abilities."

"Even as a mere vampire like the rest of us, you were lethal in the field, my love," Logan grins with pride at his mate.

She snorts. "Yeah, but I prefer when I can kick *your* ass. Not the other way around."

The dangerous warrior chuckles. "It reminds me of when I first appeared to you. Good times."

"Not sure I appreciate your newfound humor." Her attempt to keep a smile in check says otherwise.

A delicate foot slides up my shin, and I nearly jump out of my skin. The soft sole travels along the inside of my thigh, before settling on my crotch. I scoot closer to the table, not wanting anyone to witness whatever the little naughty Oracle has in mind.

Her bare toes wiggle on my rock-hard length, and I grit my teeth to restrain the groan, clutching the arms of my chair in a desperate attempt to remain in place.

In my periphery, Nicki's eyes roll, but I couldn't give a shit if she perceives what's going on under the table as long as Vi keeps grinding her foot against my aching cock and balls. I'm fixed to combust from my prolonged abstinence.

The vixen smiles, knowing precisely what she's doing to me. *'Do not come, my king.'*

Her sultry mental command hardens my jaw. The last thing I wish to do is to shoot my load prematurely while hemmed in by the individuals I consider family. I'd never hear the end of it.

Sensation after sensation spreads with each stroke, and I concentrate on keeping my expression passive to those around us. The rigid fabric of my jeans is an exquisite friction I never want to cease. When I'm confident I can't stand anymore, I capture her foot, imprisoning it against my pulsing dick. Her toes wiggle enticingly, but she allows me to hold her immobile.

My exchange with Bastian a few days ago surges through my brain. The commander provided several eye-opening tips and assisted in setting events in motion. My beautiful mate is in for an absolute treat at our next encounter. I grin wickedly and the Oracle's eyes widen with curiosity.

Chapter 16

Nicole

"What did you discover, Jag?" I ask quietly, strolling through the gardens, the tall male at my side. I peer over at Logan standing guard by the entrance, his penetrating gaze following my every move, and my insides tingle.

"It is as I feared, my lady. The woman in the forest was Abigail. And if she's paired up with Syn, we have much to prepare."

Shit.

"I notified the priest regarding your apprehensions with the shield. As predicted, he was rather indignant but insisted he and Viessa would work on reinforcing it further."

We roam the splendid gardens for a few minutes, each absorbed in our own thoughts. Finally, I break the silence. "Icarus seemed to know Abigail. Claimed he might provide assistance to help me counter her magic."

"Excellent. In the interim, I will dig a little further and see if I discover the witch's vulnerabilities—if any."

I halt and the red-eyed devil pivots to stare down at me from his imposing height. The long, black locks sway in the cool fall breeze. "Give it to me straight, demon. What am I up against?"

He sighs heavily. "Abigail is thousands of years old, little Halfling. She possesses all your abilities, except your internal lie detector skill. I don't believe there is another immortal on the planet who boasts that aptitude. In addition, she absorbs others' powers, virtually rendering her opponent helpless. She is likewise a master of illusion manipulation, causing her victims to see, hear, touch, smell, and taste things which do not exist, so beware."

"So basically, in her presence, what you visualize isn't always accurate?"

"Indeed. As of right now, her only flaw is her lack of combat skill. Abigail has never been a fighter, preferring to cast her spells from afar like a coward. So, if you manage to get close enough, I will enjoy watching you kick her ass." His grin is sheer wickedness.

I smirk, resuming our stroll. The weight of my Glock 19s, packed with iron slugs, shifting against the outside of my thighs, comforts me. As does old faithful, Annie, resting in the small of my back. She's loaded with silver bullets. Ya know, just in case.

"That's a load of 'what ifs', Jag."

"Yes. Commonplace for us nowadays. Do you not agree?"

I swing to the demon with the make-my-hackles-rise, crimson irises, plant my palm in the center of his impressive chest, and crane my neck to peer into his regard. He stills, his nostrils flaring as my energy warms his torso.

"We've come a long way since our conversation at your encampment outside my shield. You once schemed to murder me and lay siege to my castle. Manipulated my best friend's mind to assassinate me." His jaw tightens at the remembrance, and I step closer.

"Your point, young queen?" he counters, frowning down at me with wariness.

"We struck an accord those many months ago for reasons that benefited us both. Now, I trust you with my life, King Darath. I can't imagine anyone more perfect to guard my black soul than Lucifer himself."

He chuckles. With the sharp gaze of my mate watching on, Jag gently tucks my hair behind my ear and bends low, setting his scalding mouth over mine.

Logan's feral growl flows around us, but he doesn't interfere, and his trust warms my spirit.

"You have proven yourself worthy of my reverence, little one," he whispers against my lips and I tremble at the scent of sandalwood and fire. "I will undertake anything within my power to save your gorgeous ass and help you fulfill the prophecy."

When he straightens, I grin. "So, you think my ass is gorgeous, huh?"

"My original offer remains. Ditch the vampire, Halfling, and we could wreak havoc on the world together."

"And my answer is the same, demon. You couldn't handle me." I drop my hand and continue our walk. "Besides, I expect the beautiful Priestess Tanagra might have something to say about that."

A tender smile graces the sensuous lips, and his expression softens. I almost stumble. Wow. Lucifer has a heart and Kleora holds a privileged spot.

"You tap that yet?" I ask crudely, knowing he enjoys my unashamed bluntness.

His grin is pure determination. "All in due time, young vampire. All in due time."

Chapter 17

We eventually finish the relentless training, and my skin crawls with the demand to trace to my chamber and change out of this stupid robe so I can go to my Liam. Unfortunately, the mist hinders my ability to teleport.

When my father blocks my path, I almost let my fangs descend. "Look, Icarus," I sigh, going formal in my exasperation. "Whether you like it or not, I am a vampire with a mate, and I require his blood to survive."

Every two months, we engage in this same debate when it becomes time for me to seek Liam for sustenance. My insides quiver. It's grown more and more problematic to keep my vampire in check when I'm with the wolf. She demands to complete the bond and claim the sexy cowboy as ours.

"We could bag his blood, similar to what commander Moretti employed with Nicole before and after her transition."

"Yeah. How did that work out for her?"

According to what I've gathered, she couldn't keep his bagged blood down. Straight from the vein was her sole recourse, and exclusively from her mate.

"Yes, well, she is a Halfling and a unique case." He even argues in a composed demeanor. It's fucking irritating. Especially when my stomach is cramping with starvation, and my desire is ramping up alongside my anxiety imagining what Liam has prepared for tonight.

How will I submit when my consciousness screams for control over the werewolf's sexy, hard body? I made a vow, but constant reservations plague my mind. The insights and voices have steadily expanded in the last two days. So much so, I cannot step foot outside the mist without wailing and yanking my hair at the chaos violating my psyche, whirling me toward madness.

"I refuse to drink bagged blood, father. I am a vampire. Now please let me pass so I can change."

He sighs. "One day, daughter, I will not be here to aid and guide you. You must answer directly to the gods. As you are fully aware, they forbid an Oracle to mate." He grabs onto my arm with an urgency I've never witnessed in him before. "If you provoke them, they will destroy you."

"You defied them, and you're still standing," I remind him.

"Yes, but the cost of my rebellion was the life of Nicole's unborn child." His hand falls in defeat, and I realize I've won. It's a hollow victory in light of his warning. "Have you considered the repercussions of your actions, daughter? Who will pay the cost for your defiance? Maybe the ones you hold dear."

That's a sobering notion. Would the gods take my king from me if I mated him? Or perhaps my twin? The idea produces a spasm in my chest, solidifying my oath not to complete the bond.

"I understand, father. I have no intention of fully mating with Liam. No matter how extreme my vampire craves him. The consequences are too steep."

"As much as I detest to admit this, King Scott is useful for you. He calms you in ways the mist or I cannot. I will trouble you no more on this count and trust in your judgment. All I propose is while you are in his presence, tap into the connection. What specifically happens to your mind when you are with him? When he touches you? As you drink from him? Learn from it, and we will seek to incorporate it into our training."

"Yes, father. I never would've thought of that," I smile gently, satisfied he won't fight me anymore regarding my desire for Liam.

I pivot and head down the dim hallway, the slap of my sandals on the stone floor echoing down the passage.

"One more thing, child," Icarus announces just as I'm about to turn toward my room. I pause and peer at him over my shoulder. His hands rest serenely clasped at his waist. "Harness the changes when you dominate the wolf. It seems most dynamic during those occasions."

Holy hell.

A fiery blush steals over my face, and I duck my head, flying around the corner. I abhor the Oracle knows every damn moment in my life. Some things a father should *never* understand about his offspring. Chiefly my sexual control preferences.

I materialize inside the entrance to a dimly lit building. Where the hell am I? As an Oracle who has consumed her mate's blood, I'm able to track Liam anywhere. I merely close my eyes, visualize his rugged, handsome face, the smoldering whiskey irises, and in a second, I land within fifty feet of him. Usually.

Maybe my radar is off or something.

I wince as the low sexy thump of music pounds through my aching skull and squeeze my lids shut to concentrate on cramming the shouting, screaming, and gruesome images into a dark corner of my mind.

Once they are subdued, I gaze around, noting a moniker on the wall. *Dom's Place, NY.* Interesting. Does NY stand for New York?

I meander closer to the primary room, where the music emanates. The temperature in here is warm, and the spice of desire and sex permeates the space.

With the threat of the witch, Icarus insisted I dress for battle, but with the heat in this building, I'm seriously regretting the leather pants and black corset with short blades affixed to the front. I nervously adjust the strap across my chest, bearing my quiver and bows at my back.

I am nowhere near the proficient fighter my sister is, but I am deadly accurate with arrows or knife throwing. It's the style I prefer to fight—from a distance. Hand to hand is not my forte.

Shit. I hope this isn't a human business. If they observe me adorned with weapons, they will most likely signal the authorities.

Before walking the couple of steps down into the sunken room, I remain a minute to ponder the patrons and am reassured to detect the majority are immortals, with just a few humans scattered about and...

Wait. What is happening right now?

My eyes widen as I focus on the happenings in the chamber. Along one wall is a long bar, serving refreshments to customers. Typical. Nothing out of the ordinary there. But strategically located throughout the vast space, males, and females, in various stages of undress, are performing deviant sexual acts involving pain and pleasure.

Oh. My. God. This is a sex club. In all my research, I came across many organizations that cater to the BDSM society. Unsure what the acronyms actually meant; Google was kind enough to define it for me. B and D refer to Bondage and Discipline. D and S equal Dominance and Submission, while S and M signify Sadism and Masochism.

I beam in fascination as a petite female with striking features, dressed similar to my attire, with four-inch stiletto boots to her knees, whips a perfectly nude, athletic man with his neck and wrist trapped inside a primitive stockade type contraption.

Based on his raging hard-on and his moans of ecstasy, I'd estimate he is savoring the rough treatment, and my insides clench with lust, imagining it's me doling out such discipline to my wolf.

Holy shit. Just standing here, my body is a smoldering inferno in a millisecond, and my panties dampen with need as I greedily absorb the room.

Against the distant wall, a naked woman is belted to what looks like a narrow, miniature version of a padded picnic table. She straddles the scarlet center; her pelvis and torso lie on the cushioned leather, while her knees rest on the padded seats. Black, wide cuffs restrain her ankles and wrists, and a red ball gag covers her mouth.

The male with her takes my breath away. The werewolf is towering, with ebony hair, and a thick dark beard. A beautiful tattoo depicting a green-eyed, black wolf marks his upper chest. His expression is generous with intense concentration as he flogs the female writhing on the bench. His powerful strikes vary in strength, some causing instant welts on her skin, others offering a loving caress. He commands her body like a talented maestro.

Another female is on her knees; her bottom obviously spanked a rosy red. She's getting drilled from behind by an enormous black vampire while she works her mouth between the spread legs of a woman writhing in front of her.

Lord have mercy. This is sensory overload, and I'm about fit to combust. My nipples are hard, achy points rubbing against the inside of my stiff corset with each panting breath. The evidence of my desire soaks my thong. Every part of me is greedy to learn all I can to satisfy my king and myself further.

I glance briefly at the bar again, wondering if I should go sit down to enjoy the show before I fall flat on my face when I spy Liam leaning against the wooden top, analyzing me keenly.

My heart rate spikes at the sight of the werewolf king. Worn blue jeans hug his lean hips and muscular thighs. The deep navy t-shirt accentuates his chest and abdomen's sculpted muscles, and the black ball cap on backward is the hottest fucking thing I've ever encountered.

He makes my mouth water and my lips part—unable to curb my panting breath. My fangs descend, and based on the heat behind my irises, my amber light illuminates them.

I take my time letting my gaze traverse his body, from the dark cowboy boots to the substantial bulge straining against his zipper, up the splendid torso I crave to caress and nibble, to the steady beat of the pulse in his neck that calls to every part of me.

When I peer into the dark stare, my breath hitches at the lust darkening his expression, and I lick my lips in anticipation. He zeros in on the movement, but he doesn't budge an inch. And neither do I.

Finally, he raises a hand and waves around the room. "Choose," he commands softly, and I pick up his rich voice plain as day over the hypnotic pulse of the music and moans of ecstasy as if he were standing right next to me, whispering in my ear. My insides liquefy.

Oh, shit. Does he wish to discipline me publicly?

While watching the others get my juices flowing, I'm uncertain I'd be okay with putting our sexual interactions on exhibit.

He shakes his head as if reading my mind. "What transpires between us will be conducted in a private playroom. Now choose how you wish to proceed."

My shoulders relax somewhat as I skim the dimly lit arena crowded with gyrating bodies. If I were in control tonight, I would pick the spanking bench to harness my mighty werewolf. I inspect it reverently, watching for several minutes while a Domme paddles a male submissive strapped to the apparatus, his head hung low in complete abandonment.

Aware of my mate's focus, I force my scrutiny away and scour the room once more until I zero in on a gadget I actually researched—a suspension rack.

Basically, you stand between two wooden uprights, your arms suspended above your head by chains from the top with a spreader bar to maintain them apart. At the bottom, ankles are secured to each side, so you're stretched wide. The Dom can then flog front or back and between your thighs if so desired.

"Excellent choice, sweetness," he purrs, and my focus bounces to his once more. "Now, come to me."

The order in his tone spreads goosebumps across my skin, but I immediately comply, traversing the various stations, never lifting my regard from my scrumptious cowboy.

I halt in front of him and await his next action. The warm gaze scans my trembling frame from head to toe—his heart rate never fluctuates. I can't identify if he appreciates how I'm dressed or not, and it's disconcerting how relaxed he appears. This role reversal is messing with my equilibrium.

"The warrior outfit is enticing. Are you proficient with the bow?" he asks quietly, remaining absolutely still. If I couldn't hear his lungs expanding and contracting, I'd estimate he ceased breathing.

"Damn good," I reply in a throaty tone, finding it arduous to concentrate on the conversation when what I truly crave is to tear his clothes from his sculpted body and impale myself on that impressive bulge in his pants.

"I never would've pictured that about you."

"Why?" I ask with a raised eyebrow. "Did you presume I was the helpless damsel in distress, forever needing rescuing by her man?"

"Not at all, sweetness. I've always accepted your strength and power were extraordinary. I just never imagined you with a bow."

"Oh, well. I'm not efficient at hand to hand, and I prefer the silent precision over the obtrusive loudness of a gun or the unwieldy weight of a sword."

"I see," he smiles gently before straightening from the bar. "Hey, Bill," he hollers to the man serving drinks. "Is my room ready?"

"Yes sir, Mr. Scott," the bartender nods. "Master Moretti called earlier, and we have added the change you just requested."

I arch an eyebrow at my king. "Master Moretti?"

"Sebastian owns the club."

Ah. So, my amazing werewolf planned the evening. I wonder if the commander offered him any pointers for tonight? Instead of sifting my way through the numerous disturbing sites to research more about BDSM, I should have considered that.

"Are you ready for this, baby?" Liam asks, noting every shift in my expression.

"Yes."

"Yes, what?" he frowns, and I gulp at the authority in his tone.

"Yes, Sir." I amend swiftly and lower my gaze. I've played the submission role before. Dark thoughts threaten to intrude, but I shove them aside. Nothing will mar this experience.

Everything my mate expects of me tonight, I will perform and relish to the best of my ability because in two months, when it's my round, I'll demand the same of him.

When he turns without another word, I follow obediently in his wake. Nervous anticipation tingles through my body, even as extreme hunger for my mate's essence cramps my gut. I certainly hope Liam allows me to feed first, or this night could end in a vastly different direction than he is expecting.

Chapter 18

My eyes expand as I step into the room. A sensual beat softly strums from hidden speakers in the maroon walls. Candles flicker on every surface, and the subdued lighting gives a sense of intimacy. My heart nearly pounds out of my chest when I notice the suspension rack secured to the floor in the center of the chamber.

Holy shit. How did they get the contraption in here so quickly? That must have been the added feature the bartender mentioned to Liam.

In the far corner sits a king-size iron bed shrouded in blood-red sheets with steel cables at each end. Various whips, floggers, belts, and paddles hang from the walls, along with an assortment of restraints; rope, leather cuffs, satin for the more delicate touch, and silver handcuffs.

My male thought of everything, even the panty-wetting spanking bench I was inspecting for him earlier. I must speak with Sebastian and see about membership here because I will so have the wolf tied to that thing one day.

Having done my research, I kneel, sitting on my feet, my palms resting on my leather-clad thighs, and my eyes downcast as I await his guidance.

Silence reigns for several minutes and sweat beads my upper lip. I learned early on this could be part of the conditioning process—accelerating the anticipation and nerves. Even though I'm now proficient with knots and different restraint techniques, I recognize I have much to learn.

"Rise, sweetness."

Once I'm standing, he gently removes my quiver and bow, along with the two daggers sheathed below my breasts. Rough pads graze the swell of flesh above the tight corset. My lids lower at the perfection of his touch on my skin.

"So responsive," he whispers, and I fill my nostrils with his fresh minty breath. He clasps my hand and leads me over to a small couch in the corner. "You must be starving. Feed first, then we play."

Oh, how this male pleases me. He is forever setting my needs before his own.

When he relaxes into the cushions, he pulls on my arm, indicating I should straddle his hips. I don't hesitate, settling my heated core against his firmness, my gaze already zeroed in on the pulsing vein in his neck.

"Drink, baby. Let me nourish my mate."

I strike, burying my fangs into his artery with desperation. He grunts at the assault but gently wraps his tremendous arms around my torso, holding me tight. As his rich blood streams down my throat, I sigh in rapture, clutching his shoulders and pressing my needy sex against his groin.

"No. Don't move, Viessa." His sharp tone immediately freezes my gyrations. "Drink but hold still. Pleasure will occur later."

My inner vampire growls in revolt, clamping down harder on his neck. He greets my defiance with a firm smack on my ass. Sharp pain ripples through my flesh, and I attempt to turn away, but Liam clamps a palm on my nape to keep my fangs where they belong.

The swat was a reminder of who's in charge tonight, and a conflict arises within me. Buried deep, a long-forgotten side of me finds pleasure in my king's dominance. I once enjoyed fantasies of my werewolf controlling my sexual responses, secretly pleasuring myself while I imagined him spanking me or fucking me in beast form—until the first moment I exerted control over him in the dreams. It escalated my lust beyond anything I'd ever experienced and shut down the invading chaos. From that moment on, I was always the one in control in every mental fantasy of Liam.

I draw deep on his vein but remain immobile, proving to him I can obey. For now. Two months before it's my turn seems like a lifetime.

"Good girl," he praises and works the ties loose at the back of my corset. "This outfit is sexy as fuck. The perfect Dominatrix attire."

His words warm my skin. That's what I covet with everything I am. And not just any Dominatrix. Liam's Mistress. I yearn to hear his rough masculine tone calling me that title while I bring his body alive, drive him insane with lust, and command his mind into capitulation.

But will the proud werewolf allow that? It's one thing to roleplay as we did at my lake house. It was sensual fun. Nothing too intense or uncomfortable. A stepping stone for us both. And while I thoroughly enjoyed it, I require more—his complete sexual submission.

I have no inclination to humiliate or degrade my king as I watched in many videos online. Nor do I care to cause him undue pain beyond what he or I would enjoy. Some elements in those recordings were sick and warped, and I have no appetite to take either of us down that path.

But I do aspire to spank, flog, and whip him. Crave to see his skin redden under my ministrations. Desire to lead him to the brink while he's restrained, driving his lust into a fever before I unleash the beast and order him to pleasure me with his mouth and fuck me with that beautiful, wondrous cock. I need the fierce wolf at my mercy and begging for my touch.

The potent werewolf king's blood and my wicked thoughts have me so ramped I dig my nails into the couch to check my hips from gyrating along his length. If I hope for him to surrender to me, I must learn to do the same in return.

When the hunger pains recede, and I'm flush with Liam's strength and vitality, I gently soothe the punctures closed and lean back to stare into the lust-filled gaze of my mate.

"Thank you, Liam."

"My pleasure." The lopsided grin, the backward ball cap, and the generous, warm hands resting on my thighs produce a peculiar twinge in my chest. I frown at the odd sensation.

Before I can examine it further, the wolf stands abruptly and sets me on my feet. "I expect we should establish some ground rules before we begin."

"Okay."

"Do you have a safe word?"

Every site I ran across during my long journey into the dark web referred to a safe word. A term or phrase meant to terminate whatever was happening if it became too harsh. I reflected long and hard about what mine would be over the years, and I finally arrived at the perfect fit.

"Yes. Whiskey."

When I'd cast eyes on Liam, in real life during my captivity with Trezzo Massaro, it was the first thing I noticed about him. The beautiful whiskey-colored irises had more depth and color than my visions. Not to mention, he frequently carries a glass of the liquid in his hand.

He cocks his head in question.

"It reminds me of your eyes."

He considers me for several seconds, and I cannot decode his body language or his emotions. He's locked down tight.

"Do you have a safe word, Liam?" I think to ask.

"Why don't I follow your lead and use amber."

"Okay," I grin.

He sighs heavily. "Here's the deal, Viessa." Uh oh. Based on his tone and grim expression, this can't be positive. "We agreed you would permit me control every other visit, and that vow still applies. However, tonight I've elected to relinquish my turn and allow you to take the lead. My gift for accomplishing your first vision interpretation and saving my life."

I inhale sharply. "But you already thanked me for that at the lake, my king."

"To be honest," he mutters, hanging his head, his hands on his waist. "The dichotomy of your statements and actions tie me in knots."

I frown. "How so?"

"Your remarks are submissive, like the way you demurely lower your eyes and hail me as your king. It makes me want to shove you to the floor and fuck you just to hear you plead for more."

Oh, wow. The image sets my blood on fire.

"On the other hand, when your needs drive to the forefront, your tone and actions are all dominant."

"And... that troubles you? Me being in control?"

He glares at me for several long moments, his heated eyes clogged with conflict. "Yes, and no."

My heart stutters at his softly uttered confession. A part of him enjoys giving up command. Tingles break out over my skin at the mere prospect. If the male would just let go of his reservations and trust me, I would endeavor to be sure he never regrets it.

"I'd jump through fire for the chance to be with you, Viessa. And while this," his hand swings around the area, "fills me with lust, I despise the weakness you demand of me."

"Liam. Submitting to me doesn't make you weak," I whisper and step closer. "It shows courage. An inner authority that sets you above other males." His snort of disbelief tightens my belly. How do I convince him of the truth?

"You, the man, have the fortitude to control your beast's objections in order to satisfy and assuage your female's burden. Only a powerful individual with a pure spirit can surmount such resistance." I rest my palm on the center of his chest, straight over his heart. "Please. Trust me." He swallows, and I follow the bob of his Adam's apple in his strong throat.

At this juncture in our brief acquaintance, I am demanding a lot. But Liam doesn't appreciate the events I've seen, what I know. Right, wrong, or dangerous, I'm petitioning for his faith, imploring him to lower his barriers and provide me a measure of control. My chaotic brain calms when I employ complete authority over my great and mighty werewolf king.

He shoves the cap off his head, tossing it on the couch before shooting an agitated hand through his dark locks. The firm jaw hardens, and dread fills my gut. He's backing out, unable to subjugate himself to his female.

Shit.

Chapter 19

When my cowboy kneels at my feet and assumes the position of a sub, I stumble back in stunned disbelief. Holy Mother of God. I inhale a sharp breath at the sight of my brave king kneeling before me. Another picture of the beast doing the same bursts through my mind.

Oh, Yes.

Desire shoots through my system, pursued by delight and elation. My gaze rushes straight to the spanking bench, and I almost squeal with excitement. Once more, my mate supports me by fulfilling my ultimate fantasy and completely shutting off the voices controlling my thoughts.

Gently, I smooth my fingers through his soft tresses in gratitude before leaving him kneeling on the carpet. I mosey over to the remarkable array of toys displayed for my—and I hope Liam's—enjoyment. A hasty glance over my shoulder reveals Liam hasn't moved, his head still lowered, gaze on the floor. But instead of his palms resting easily on his thighs, they're clenched, the knuckles white.

My fierce warrior aspires to present me with what I require, relieving my turmoil, but his own mind and beast resist it tooth and nail. Somehow, I must conquer them both in such a way they will crave more. Nerves ramp up my heart rate. What if I fail? A few brief encounters long ago and research on the web limited my understanding of this world.

I snatch a broad paddle with small holes throughout and place it next to the apparatus and concentrate on the here and now, working on letting my anxiety go. Tonight, we embark on the next step in our relationship, and I refuse to screw it up.

I graze my fingers across the spanking bench. It's essentially two connected padded stools: one high, one low. The lower cushion is to kneel on with leather shackles dangling from the sides if you choose to cuff their ankles. The elevated pad is for the sub to settle their chest, effectively presenting their ass for discipline. At the bottom are restraints for the wrists if need be.

Bondage is not my purpose here. In truth, they wouldn't work on the wolf unless they were silver, and I would never shackle my mate with such poison. Obedience is the goal tonight. Liam will bow over the bench and remain there of his own volition. If he cannot, my alternatives are to either increase the punishment, which in Liam's case could backfire on me, or cease altogether and leave, showing him, I mean business. But shit, that could come back and smack me in the face as well.

"Liam, stand and discard your clothes," I instruct, and he rises smoothly, tossing his t-shirt over his head before toeing off his boots and jeans. When the boxer briefs join the rest, my mouth waters with the desire to savor my mate's spicy goodness, but I thrust it aside for later.

"Come here."

He strides over to me, his erection jutting proud and strong in front of him. His troubled irises dart to the bench briefly before he clenches his jaw and lowers his gaze to the floor. To transfer his focus from the coming spanking, I clasp his cock in my palm and tug him closer. His low groan sends a thrill straight to my clit. Whether or not he accepts it, King Scott likes a biting pain with his pleasure.

"You are such a fierce, noble warrior, Liam, but tonight you will surrender to me. Mind. Body. Soul. When I command you to do something, respond with yes, Mistress." A muscle pulses in his jaw and his eyes ignite with ire. "Do you understand?"

"Yes, Mistress." The words uttered in that defiant growl, stoke the fire in my belly. He's excited at the prospect of pain but loathes the submission.

"Good. Do you wish to find pleasure with me tonight, Liam?"

"Yes, Mistress."

No hesitation that time. I hold back a smile and stroke his length, loving the hard, silkiness of his size. "How do you envision us fucking, Liam?"

This erotic dialogue distracts him from what's coming and escalates his passions to the point he won't care what I ask of him as long as the reward is my taking. Although, I made a vow, and we both understand sex is off the table.

Will either of us be able to comply?

"With you on your hands and knees as I pound into you from behind." Liam's fists clench with the need to reach for me, but he obediently keeps them at his side.

I'm not sure who's more ramped up by our dirty talk, him or me.

"Hmmm. I like the sound of that," I purr before bending and sucking a nipple between my lips. Liam groans. His hand goes to reach for me but drops back at the last second. I sink a fang into the pebbled nipple. The werewolf inhales sharply at the slight pain, and his dick twitches in my palm.

I squeeze the enormous head, grab his balls in a tight hold, and suckle the delicious blood trickling across my tongue. "Do you enjoy a little pain with your pleasure, my king?" I ask between licks and strokes.

He hesitates, so I squeeze a little harder. "Yes, Mistress," Liam growls, pumping his erection into my fist.

I flick my fang once more across his sensitive nipple. His abs tighten at the sensation and I glory in the responses of his body. Reluctantly I let go of the steel rod I salivate for and step back. "Kneel on the bench with your chest resting on the top cushion."

When he complies—and I observe with glorious anticipation this magnificent male kneeling prone, ready for whatever I demand—a remarkable phenomenon develops: the incessant bombardment of imagery and speech in my brain ceases. My body stills, and I inhale at the utter tranquility. God, this is what it's like for ordinary people. Only your own thoughts in your mind, never worrying about whether this is reality or perception.

Tears clog my throat, and I brush my lips across Liam's bunched shoulder in gratitude, letting him perceive how much I appreciate the sacrifice he's making for me.

"I will not restrain you, Liam. This is about maintaining the position yourself. If you attempt to rise, without employing your safe word, then I will cuff you. Do you understand?" Not that it would do much good if he truly objected.

"Yes, Mistress," he snarls and clutches the legs of the bench in preparation.

I capture the paddle, but before I begin, I tenderly stroke his posterior, admiring the quality of solid muscles. I pass my finger between his cheeks and smirk as they clench in protest. One day, we'll explore this area further.

When I reach my target, I tease his balls, gripping and swirling them in my palm. Liam groans deep, his head dropping over the seat. Next, I clasp his raging erection, giving several vigorous strokes. His hips move in conjunction, and wetness floods my core at his rough, needy moan.

I straighten, releasing my hold. Before my mate can tense in anticipation, the paddle strikes his left butt cheek. He inhales sharply and clutches the bench tighter. I pause for a moment. When he doesn't rear up and snatch the instrument from my fingers in fury, I slide my palm over the pink mark, soothing and spreading the burn.

My king's grasp on the wood loosens, an indication he's ready for more. I set in, modifying my pace and the severity of my blows like I witnessed the Dom do in the other room. Euphoria rushes through my veins, lighting me up brighter than the fullest of moons. Dampness soaks my underwear, and my clit pulses in rhythm with my strikes.

Holy Mother of God. My soul is alive. Energized. Hot. But my intellect is at peace. This experience is like the ultimate high, and I'm hooked. If I had to choose between blood and being Liam's Mistress, I would so pick this and dismiss the consequences.

I open my senses, searching my mate's emotional state, never ceasing my hits. Some are soft, others hard enough to produce a grunt. I work the entire area, making certain no stretch of skin on his gorgeous butt goes untouched.

Soon my proud warrior's fine ass is vivid red. His ball sack drawn tight as if fixed to detonate. The dark head hangs low, and he no longer possesses a death hold on the wooden legs.

I slip past Liam's mental barriers and gasp at the lust raging through him. Even his beast is preening under my strikes, embracing every blow, and howling for more.

Elation saturates my mind, and I pant with my increasing desire. My mate is getting off on being spanked, and it's a magnificent, wondrous thing. But underneath his euphoria, lurking in the corner waiting to devour his enjoyment, is remorse, shame, and an iota of rage at his responses.

I toss the paddle on the carpet. "Stay put, Liam," I order, my tone husky with passion. He doesn't reply, and I'm okay with that because I realize he's lethargic with ecstasy and I need to keep his mind under control.

Quickly, I rip off the loose corset and leather pants before lightly kissing my king's shoulder. "Rise to your knees."

When he complies, I lower my ass on the seat in front of him. The irises devour my nakedness before stalling on my wet folds.

"You were incredible," I whisper, caressing his cheek. "Us like this is fucking amazing. And while my mind is at absolute peace, my body is bracing to splinter apart with need. Make me come with your mouth and fingers, my brave king."

I scarcely get the last word out when he latches onto my sex with a crazed ferocity, causing me to gasp and grip fistfuls of his hair. He adjusts to straddle the lower bench. Firm hands spread my legs wider, hoisting them to settle on his broad shoulders.

Liam makes me hunger in a manner I've never experienced before. Regardless of whether he comprehends it, he commands my body with the expert way his lips and tongue lap, suckle and ravage my sex—to the point where the churning sea of past, present, and future, along with the unpredictability in my growing abilities, fall away. I'm left with the myriad of passions he draws forth.

When the tip of his tongue brushes my anus, I keen with swift pleasure. In the next instant, Liam has me flipped over the bench on my stomach, and he's kneeling behind me, devouring my rear entrance. The sensations ignite my lust to a soaring pinnacle.

When he introduces two fingers into my core, I sob in bliss. "Yes, more." His other arm moves over my hips and begins circling my clit while his lips and tongue continue to perform devilish works on my sensitive, puckered opening.

In moments I erupt, shoving against his face and driving his massive digits deeper. My inner walls clamp down as I fracture into a thousand dancing sensations spreading through me like an erupting volcano.

Before the last of the tremors ease, Liam rears up, leans over my back, and thrusts his thick length into my convulsing core. I cry out, shocked immobile by the pain of his size breaking through where no man has been before.

Liam freezes. "Viessa?"

Somewhere in a dark corner of my mind, caution flags flutter a warning. I just broke my vow to my father. I'm appalled by my lack of control over the situation, but as the pain subsides, the delicious stretching in my core produces an achy, insistent urge to move my hips.

I grip the bench and push back, sinking him deeper. A moan of delight escapes my lips as I revel in the completeness of him stretching me. So large. So damn right.

A generous hand clamps around my throat, arching my neck backward. "Why the fuck didn't you tell me?" he demands roughly.

"It doesn't matter. I've always known you would be my first. And last." I pull away and shove back, gasping at the strange sensation of his cock gliding along my slick walls.

"Goddammit. You feel so fucking good. Stop moving," he demands, but I'm beyond listening. I crave his length pounding into my flesh.

I pull away and shove back again. "Oh, God, Liam," I keen, and it breaks his feeble restraint. All I can do is hold on to the bench and allow this powerful werewolf to ride me. It's rough and aggressive, laden with outrage and fear.

This taking is Liam's way of punishing me for forcing him to experience things he believes a male like him never should. He abhors the fact he got off on the pain, on playing the submissive, being spanked by his Mistress, and is livid with himself and me for craving more. He's also furious with me for not revealing the fact I'm still a virgin. The wolf's emotions pound into me with each plunge of his hips, the grip on my neck almost brutal.

I understand and accept this as his process. And who am I to lament? Shit. The slight tenderness of him stretching my insides is a pain I heartily embrace.

"One day, I'm going to fuck your sweet ass, Viessa," he pants roughly in my ear. "As hard and fast as my cock is pounding into your tight little pussy that now belongs to me."

"Oh, God," I whimper on the verge of shattering once more. "Harder. Make me explode."

"Yes, Mistress," he growls harshly and drives into me with such force in a millisecond my world cracks, and I reach back to dig my nails into his reddened ass.

"Come, Liam," I order. The beast roars as hot seed sears my innards, hurling me over the threshold once more.

When the support of Liam's palm slides away, I hang my head, unable to hold its weight. Shock wave after shock wave of pulsing sensations riddles my body.

"Oh, fuck. What have I done?"

Before I've even caught my breath, his thick length deserts me. I whine at the loss of his heat at my spine, grappling with the effort to lift my head. In my periphery, I notice Liam tugging on his jeans. I clutch the rim of the cushion and force myself to stand.

"What are you doing?" I ask with a frown. I can no longer read his emotions. He's shut them down tighter than an Oracle's shield. "We still have some time."

"No, we don't." Fully dressed, ball cap and all, he confronts me. The dark eyes swell with so many turbulent passions. His entire body appears to vibrate with it. "Why didn't you tell me?" Liam accuses. "I assumed, with your experience in this lifestyle, you'd had sex before."

Liam paces frantically, his movements jerky in his agitation. "Your first time should have been gentle, loving. Not this." His hand indicates the room, the bench. "I'm sorry, Viessa. For so many things. For forcing you to break your vow to Icarus. For giving you false hope. But mostly taking from you what I can never restore."

When angry, frustrated tears form in his eyes, my heart rate skyrockets, and dread settles in my gut like congealed blood.

"I realize you need to dominate me, and I want so much to ease your torment, but it's too extreme. I foolishly thought I could shove aside my innate instincts and become what you require, but my insides are being torn apart with all the wrongs and rights of the situation. The reality comes down to one fact—*this* is not who I am." He stalks to the door, and panic replaces the dread. "I thought I could submit to your demands. After tonight, it's become abundantly clear I cannot without the beast retaliating."

"Liam, wait." I stretch my arm out to him, beseeching him to stay and talk this out. My lips quiver with fear. "I craved for you to be my first for over a century. I don't care if it was rough. I'm immortal. The pain was temporary." I take a step forward. "You can't tell me you didn't enjoy what happened in this room. I felt your emotions."

The irises flicker blue as he battles the conflict inside him. "I enjoyed it. And that's the problem. I can't tell you how horrified I am at taking your innocence so brutely, no matter the fact you're immortal. But you want to know what disturbs me the most? Your demand for control brings out the wrath in the beast. He sought to punish you, and me, for forcing your dominance over his own, and I cannot allow him to hurt you again. First in the forest, now this. Goodbye, sweetness. Find what you're seeking with someone else. Someone who...." He swallows, struggling to get the words out. "Someone who can submit, give you what you need, and *not* hurt you."

Without a backward glance, King Scott strides out the door, fracturing my heart into a million slivers of agony.

Chapter 20

Hours stretch into endless days crammed with laborious duties. Days expand into weeks. Weeks into months.

Exhausted, I lean against a tree in the north pasture and close my lashes against the glare of the sun bouncing off the snow. It's been four long, torturous months since I stormed out of that playroom. The visual of my mate's beautiful nude body standing in the midst of her domain, her arm outstretched, the devastated ambers brimmed with tears, haunt my dreams.

I left her with the intention of never seeing her again. No more come-hither looks or sexual commands. No soft caresses or whiffs of her intoxicating scent. Those deadly fangs will never pierce my flesh, and my cock can never again fill the tight, warm sheath of my woman. I brutely took her virginity, and even though she is partially to blame for not revealing her inexperience with sex, I will never forgive myself or the beast.

My future is nothing but an interminable continuation of misery and pain. An avenue of my choosing and I despise myself. More so than the humiliation and shame I experienced at the lust slamming through my body as my female paddled my ass.

Goddammit.

The one visual that condemns my soul to purgatory was how I forced her over that bench and fucked her without worry or regard to her wants or wellbeing. Brutely plowed through her hymen, ripping it apart. The beast sought to hurt her. To wrap both hands around her throat and ruthlessly squeeze while pounding into her core. The crimson veil of rage clouded my sight, and I hungered to humiliate her as she had me.

For days after, a seething resentment, saturated with self–loathing, thrummed through my skull. My siblings avoided me after the first few weeks of snapping their heads off repeatedly. Two months in, I recognized I was more pissed at myself than at Viessa.

The vampire made no secret of her desires. I went into that night with my eyes wide open. In fact, it was my decision to relinquish control. She requested my trust, and I complied, only to hurl it back in her face when it was over. All because I was furious at violating her in such a brutal manner, but most importantly, at my response to submitting to the pleasure–pain offered me.

Over the following months, I flung myself into my obligations as king, training my Wardens to the point of exhaustion until my lieutenant braved my wrath and put his foot down.

"You're beating your troops into the ground, Sir. I don't begin to fathom what is going on with you, my liege, but you need to go solve it and stop punishing everyone around you."

His words struck a chord. But instead of working through the issue, I refocused my inner rage on booze and rutting on the full moon. I didn't give two shits what species as long as they handled the rough treatment. Submitted to the beast. There were no soft caresses or lingering kisses. I ripped clothes from their bodies, flipped them over on their stomachs to escape the apprehension in their expressions, and I plowed into them like there was no tomorrow.

I was callous. Vicious. My beast didn't care if the victim was male or female. He strived to fill the hole in our chest the size of a softball.

In my mind, they were all Viessa, and I was punishing her for what she forced out of me. Never in a million lifetimes would I have ever imagined something like that would excite me.

Even now, I yearn for the addictive burn of pain only my mate can provide. My cock hardens, thinking of the spanking bench, the paddle striking my flesh, spreading fire across my skin, causing my dick to pulse with the need to erupt with every burning swat. But my mind recoils, powerless to get past the terrible concept of submission.

After the last full moon, my pack refused to come out to the ranch, frightened of their king, and that shamed me even further.

The task force hasn't heard hide nor hair from the dark fae bastard, and we are all twitchy wondering when the next bomb will drop. Icarus and Viessa have made several improvements to the shield around the Vampire Stronghold and several clandestine trips to the fae castle in an attempt to figure out the witch's shield.

I'm aware of all this from Nicole, preferring to keep my distance from the castle to avoid a confrontation with Vi.

I crouch against the bark, burrowing inside my fleece-lined buckskin coat as I savor my favorite whiskey from my flask. Snow blankets the ground, and the cattle dig through the white powder to locate any morsel of surviving grass. They shift restlessly, anxious in my presence, sensing the beast clawing below the surface.

Not for the first time, I wonder how Viessa is coping without me. Who will provide her blood? I've been dying to ask Bastian if she joined one of his clubs, but the fear of how I will react to the knowledge keeps my mouth shut.

Christmas was a hellish affair. Even though family and friends surrounded me, having it at the castle instead of the ranch was a first for my siblings and me. When Icarus showed up, my heart nearly leaped from my ribcage until I realized he was alone.

"Where's Vi?" Lucretia asked her father with a frown.

Icarus's blue gaze flicked briefly in my direction. "Viessa sends her regrets, but she requested I deliver your gift, daughter."

Fuck. I'd hurt her severely enough that she'd forgo Christmas with her twin in order to avoid me? Her absence dampened my spirit.

As soon as I was able, I pulled Icarus aside. "I have no right to ask this, but will you give your daughter this for me?" I handed him a small, colorfully wrapped package. Nestled inside was an elegant gold chain with a pear-shaped, three-carat, orange diamond. The color reminded me of her eyes, and I purchased it on a whim.

After a brief hesitancy, the Oracle took the present. "Of course, my lord."

"How is she?"

"Viessa is excelling at containing her visions. She's earned three more sacred engravings." Icarus' voice soared with fatherly pride. "And her powers grow each day."

I nodded. "That's wonderful, priest. I knew she would do well."

I pivoted on my heel to head to the bar for a refill when a firm hand latched onto my elbow. I peered down at the diminutive deity with blue tattoos over every inch of his skin, my eyebrow raised in question.

"Sire, I sympathize with how much this separation disturbs you. And her. But it is for the best."

"The best for whom, Icarus?" I growled low and jerked my arm loose. "For you? For the gods?"

"For all humanity, my lord." His simple reply stunned me. "Viessa must remain focused on her obligations. Lives depend on it, as you fully realize."

When an immense nose nudges my shoulder, nipping on the lapel of my jacket, it bounces my mind to the present, and I rub Tango's jaw before grabbing my guitar strapped to the saddle. "One song, buddy, and then we will head home."

I relax against the tree once more and begin strumming the opening to Your Plan by Dustin Lynch. The lyrics match my mood perfectly.

With the cattle and my horse as my audience, my tone is somber, packed with doubt and uncertainty.

I've been swimming around

Trying hard not to drown

Waiting on my life calling to sound

And I'm hangin' on best as I can

Cause I know this whole crazy ride's in Your hands

It's your plan

The lyrics couldn't be more exact. Viessa has an obvious plan. She recognizes her needs, how to carry them to fruition, and patiently waits for me to get on board. What sets fear coalescing through my spirit? I'm not certain I'll ever be on board.

Am I prepared to wave a white flag and hand her the reigns as the song says?

When Tango nudges me again, I realize I'm no longer singing, just squatting in the snow, my ass freezing while softly strumming the melody, absorbed in the hurricane of my thoughts.

"Okay, okay, buddy. Let's bring this herd to the next pasture and get home before dark."

I pack the guitar away, slip on my riding gloves, and adjust my leather chaps before hoisting myself into the saddle. Dusk is fast approaching and based on the low-hanging clouds on the horizon, we might endure another blanket of snow by morning.

Two hours later, the cattle are in their new pasture with several bales of hay. Tango enjoyed a full rub down and feeding, and I've warmed my icy skin with a scalding shower.

I snatch a bottle of whiskey from the sidebar and head to the warmth of the crackling fire in the living room, thanks to Victor.

My steps falter somewhat when I discover Sebastian and Alexandria lounging on my couch. What the hell are they doing outside the shield?

"Does Nicki know you escaped the castle?" I ask, splashing a generous measure of liquor into my glass before dropping into the La-Z-Boy next to the fireplace. I hope Victor restocked my alcohol supply because I need to forget all the shit churning in my brain, and as an immortal, it takes mass quantities to get drunk.

"No, but she's pissed you left," Alex mutters, scrutinizing me.

"I have too many responsibilities to place my life on hold." I shake the bottle at her. "Care for a drink?"

"You bet," she grins, giving her mate a sideways glance. "I'll grab a cup." And with that, she bounds out of the room, her flaming curls bouncing with every stride.

I shift my gaze to the vampire, observing his female hungrily. "Tell me why you're really here, Sebastian?"

Those intense blue eyes rotate to mine. "A surprising membership form crossed my desk from my New York club, Dom's Place, last week. I felt it prudent to discuss it with you before I approved or rejected it."

Son of a bitch. She petitioned for membership. My lids lower. "Viessa?"

"Yes. She has requested to become a Domme` in training." Bastian leans forward, forearms on his thighs. "Is it safe to assume this is the reason you are no longer with her?"

"One of many," I grate out between clenched teeth. Just the notion of her controlling someone else has the beast raging in protest.

Sebastian sighs heavily. "Can I offer you some guidance?"

"You're the expert here."

"Trust me, I understand how problematic it is for an Alpha male to submit to his female and that you consider it a deficiency you cannot tolerate. Am I correct in that assumption?"

"Spot on." This conversation rubs me the wrong way, but who better to solicit information from than the Dom himself?

"Let me ask you this, is your mate prepared to compromise?"

I exhale loudly. "Somewhat."

"And did you enjoy your session at the club?"

My face heats, and I glance toward the kitchen. Thank goodness the little valkyrie is chatting it up with Victor. It's rough enough I'm delving into this conversation with the vampire commander, I would hate for Alex to learn of my weakness.

"Can you keep this between us?" I whisper, leaning forward and setting the tumbler on the coffee table.

"Of course. I would never forsake your trust, Wolf."

"A part of me enjoyed it, but I despised myself afterward." I pass an agitated hand through my damp hair. "I'm not positive I can move past years of convictions. My innate instincts."

"Fair enough," he acknowledges with a nod. "Viessa did not introduce you to this lifestyle properly, and that is on her. But in her defense, neither was she. If the Oracle seems amenable to switch up the roles, I think you should allow it a fighting chance. Honestly, I am in awe of you, Liam, for even contemplating it. It presents true bravery and fortitude."

I snort. "How the fuck is that?"

Sebastian relaxes into the cushions, draping an arm along the back of the couch. "If it were not for my history, I would embrace the flexibility to surrender to Alex occasionally. The euphoric high is unlike anything. But I possess some veritable demons from my childhood which prevent me from doing so."

Ah. Even in death, the mother still has a hold on the son. "I can't claim that as a reason. Only my beast's adamant objections."

"Grant me the opportunity to teach the Oracle. I can guide her with you in mind and keep her from straying to the more radical end of things."

"You wish to train my mate to be a Mistress?"

What in the holy fuck!

"Yes. There is nothing sexual in the practice. My fiery valkyrie would have my balls in a vice if there were," he smiles as if he might enjoy that. "You present me with your absolute hard limits, your soft limits, and I will direct her on the proper path. If you are amenable, I would prefer you to be her sub during tutoring. We can kill two birds with one stone. Train her. Train you."

"Are you fucking kidding me?" I choke out and surge to my feet. "No way. First off, I am NOT a goddamn submissive, and second, another individual will never bear witness to what transpires between Vi and me."

"Right now, my friend, nothing is going on between you." His steady regard irritates me, as does the reminder of my current circumstances.

"You want to instruct her, go ahead, Bastian. I have no voice in what or who she does any longer."

"She is your mate, Liam. You do have a say." The vampire stands gracefully to his feet. "If you do not wish for me to endorse her membership, I will not. Or if you are adamant about me not training her, I will bow out. *Tu sei mio amico.* You are my friend. Therefore, I abide by your wishes." Sebastian clamps a hand on my shoulder. "But fair warning, if she cannot achieve entry to *my* facilities, the determined Tri-bred will solicit entrance elsewhere, and I do not believe you want that."

Fuck. At least with Bastian, I know she's safe, and I can set some ground rules.

"If I agree, will you swear not to allow her to have sex with any of the subs?" No matter how fucked up the notion, Viessa belongs to me. I was her first, and if the fates allow it, her last.

"Male or female?"

"Yes."

He hesitates, and I grit my teeth. "Alright. I vow it. Her training will begin forthwith."

Fuck me.

Chapter 21

Liam

Alex and Sebastian stayed for another hour, drinking and chatting about life. I'd forgotten how much I enjoyed Alex's endearing sense of humor. Between her sharp wit, the amusing way she constantly pushed Bastian's buttons, and the five glasses of whiskey, I relaxed for the first time in months.

Alone once more, I toss several logs into the fireplace before grabbing my guitar and settling on the edge of the hearth. Music soothes my soul, helps me see past my barricades to dive further into my inner emotions. The ones I keep concealed in order to accomplish my day-to-day tasks.

As I strum softly, my gaze fixated on the snow drifting from the wintry sky outside the windows, I open that part of myself. The segment I'm reluctant to investigate for fear it will extinguish every other aspect.

I drag out my phone and promptly hit the record button as the words and melody swirl through my brain. I have a well-equipped studio off my bedroom, but sometimes you just have to create where you are while the juices are circulating.

You claim I'm your tower

That unbreakable rock that maintains your power

But every night, you demand my soul and I find I'm losing myself to your wicked desire.

Fear is a constant, unforgiving sin

Will I ever be myself again?

Your love holds my key

But what choice will you require?

Imprison my love forever or will you finally set me free?

The melody is soulful, matching the misery in my chest. How will Viessa and I conquer the hurdles in our path and find common ground? Happiness. Peace.

Even if I were to surmount my inherent objections, we still have the issue of Oracles being forbidden to mate. I'm prepared to surmount my qualms, but the gods or fate or whatever powers command an Oracle will never yield to our wants and needs.

As I mentally examine Viessa's troubled past, a part of me understands her need for control. Her whole existence, she never had authority over her mental faculties. The voices and visions ruled her, denying her laughter or love.

The vampire has never experienced a genuine relationship. Felt the joy of being cherished by another. For the first moment in her life, she's gaining the upper hand through training with Icarus and sovereignty over her desires.

Tonight, I granted Bastian permission to guide my mate on a journey to sexual control. And whether she utilizes these newfound skills on me or someone else is yet to be determined.

I set my guitar on its stand with a harsh sigh and pour another generous glass of whiskey. I'm about to tumble back down in my recliner when the windows facing the river suddenly implode. The tumbler crashes to the floor as I raise my arms to shield my face from the thousands of shards flying through the room and skittering along the wood planks.

What in holy hell?

Shaking the glass fragments from my hair, I peer over at the gaping hole letting in snow and a bitter icy blast, just as Joshua and Cellica come charging around the corner from the kitchen—each brandishing a rifle.

"What happened?" Josh yells over the howling of the gale, aiming his muzzle at the new entrance to our home.

"Not sure. It just exploded."

Not a second after I respond, a dozen dark fae descend on the veranda, and I leap for the old, repeater rifle above the mantle as my siblings open fire.

After the incident outside the vampire castle, I instructed my family to keep all weapons equipped with lead ammunition. Heads, torsos, and limbs explode on impact. Josh and Cel are both crack shots.

Fear seizes my lungs when a deadly wing slams into my sister's shoulder, knocking her to the floor. Josh jams the muzzle against the enormous creature's temple and pulls the trigger. Skull and brain matter burst through the room as my sister struggles to her feet, her face flushed with rage.

Unfortunately, the one weapon I didn't convert was the relic mounted over the fireplace. It's loaded with good old copper bullets. It will sting, but it won't kill them. With little alternative, I continue a steady trigger pull and work my way toward my siblings.

"Liam! Watch out!" Cellica shouts, just as a sharp pain slices my collar. I pivot to face off with three enormous fae, each brandishing a silver sword.

"Get her the fuck out of here!" I yell at my brother, knowing he will protect our baby sister with his life. I raise the rifle to deflect the middle one's strike, longing for a sword of my own. "Do not contact Nicki. That's just what these fuckers are after."

"But, Liam..." Cellica cries as Josh drags her from the room, discharging his rifle with one hand, swinging it in a circle to reload, daring any fae to pursue.

I leap sideways from another swipe of silver. "They want to use me as bait. Keep Nicole safe!" I yell, vaulting over the couch, and opening fire at the advancing winged creatures until I deplete my ammo.

Once I'm confident my family is out of harm's way, I let the beast's violent nature take hold, snapping necks, ripping wings from shoulders, and sinking my canines into flesh, ducking and evading their slashing swords and lethal wings. In a matter of minutes, my living room looks like a war zone. Blood and body parts litter every surface.

I howl at the carnage, glorying in the fight, and burst open another neck with my extended claws, spewing crimson gore across the recliner.

The silver from the initial hit weakened me somewhat, but not enough to preserve these fuckers. My wolf is wailing to be let loose, so I grant him free rein. The shift sends several of them crashing into walls, and before they can obtain their feet, I pounce, shredding their jugulars, crushing vertebrae with my powerful jaws, and slashing open their flesh with my wicked nails.

Before long, my white fur is stained red as I circle and lunge, shredding wings and tearing heads from bodies, making certain to steer clear of their weapons. If it were the full moon, this would have been over before it began. A dozen dark fae are no match for an enraged beast ramped up by the influence of the lunar cycle.

When the last head rolls out the busted window, I shift and drop my hands to my knees to catch my breath.

Just as I snag my cell phone from the hearth where I dropped it, Vi appears in the center of the carnage. The graceful, white-robed dream is out of place amidst the gore and body parts. My heart sours at her appearance after so long.

"You're a little late, Viessa," I mutter, scanning her nearly transparent garment, remembering her tightness milking my cock.

"Are you all right?" she asks, and there's something peculiar in her inflections. It must disturb her she didn't acquire the insight to intercept the invasion.

"I'm fine."

She crosses toward me, and I raise a scarlet-stained hand. "Don't come any closer. I'm covered in fae blood."

"I noticed," she whispers, contemplating my naked form as she maintains her route to me.

I regard her intently. Inhale deep and scent her desire in the air between us. My eyebrows lift in shock. Viessa wants me. The violence's aftermath jacked my heart rate into overdrive, and adrenaline rushes through my veins like the mighty Yellowstone River outside. I require a channel for all this aggression, and she's providing it with one glance.

In two strides, my fist clenches in her dark tresses and I jerk her body against mine, not caring that her clothing is getting steeped in red. She doesn't seem to care either as she runs her hands through the slick liquid, spreading it over my flanks.

When she clutches my hardened length between her firm fingers, I shove her back against a nearby wall, hike her robe to her midriff and hoist her upward. As soon as those long, gorgeous legs wrap around my waist, I plunge into her wet heat with a satisfied groan.

This is what I lacked. What I've been hungering for—my girl. Her scent surrounds me, her warmth engulfs me, and her sweet sighs of pleasure thrill me as I thrust fast and hard.

Soft fingers trail along my spine as she sucks and licks my neck. A sharp prick at my lower back, pursued by a dull burn, does nothing to distract me from the bliss of taking my mate.

I reach between us and pinch and roll a stiffened nipple over the gauzy material. Viessa keens low and I sense she's close, so I squeeze a little harder. Her head falls against the wall, and her cry as she explodes around me sends me over the brink with her.

Fuck, that was intense and exactly what I required in the aftermath of battle. Before I can ease away and ascertain if she's all right, Viessa lowers her legs to the floor and pushes against my chest.

With a glower, I explore her expression. What game is she playing? First, she's wanton, begging for a fucking, now her demeanor has altered a hundred and eighty degrees.

She lowers her garment and strides several feet away before swinging to face me. Ruby patches of blood stain the once white robe, but the beautiful ambers do not glow as they typically do when we are intimate.

"Are you all right?" I ask warily.

"Thank you, King Scott. I enjoyed that immensely."

What the fuck? The creature standing before me is not my mate.

"Who the hell are you?" Before my eyes, my female's image vanishes, and in her place is the blonde from the forest. "Abigail," I growl in revulsion.

"From the second I laid eyes on you in the woods, I sought you between my thighs, young wolf." A victorious grin spreads her lips. "And you did not disappoint. I've not been taken so thoroughly in quite some time." The violet irises sparkle with delight.

Bile swirls with the alcohol in my gut, threatening the back of my throat. "Why?" I hiss, glaring at her in disgust and horror.

She shrugs. "I had an itch that needed scratching." She pivots toward the gaping hole where windows used to be. "You might wish to keep this stupendous episode to yourself, King Scott. I foresee it generating a complete mental breakdown in your mate if she learned of your betrayal." The purple irises pin mine with such malevolence I cringe. "Not to mention your associates will see it as a treachery and turn from you."

"You bitch."

She steps through the window, her bare feet crunching over broken glass. The savage wind whips her blonde curls around her head. Snow pelts against her slim shape, but she doesn't even shiver. She wiggles her fingers in a wave before dissolving with the gale.

Christ. I fucked the witch—betrayed my mate. Shame and humiliation at being manipulated in such a way burns through my chest. How did I not perceive she wasn't Viessa? I sensed there was something off, but I rejected my instinct to satisfy my battle-induced lust.

I absently rub at the soreness in my lower back as I gaze around at the destruction of my home. It matches the havoc in my soul. How can I ever face my woman? She will discern my guilt. Dare I lie? She doesn't possess Nicki's truth detecting ability, so it's feasible she'd believe me. But could I live with myself knowing this hideous act stands between us?

I stoop, reaching for the phone I so readily abandoned to get my hands on my mate. No! Not my mate. The fucking witch.

'Fae destroyed. Grab me some pants and then help clean this shit up.' I text my brother.

'On our way.'

Next, I shoot a message to Nicole. 'Fae on the move. Tried to abduct me. I'm fine, but my living room isn't. Would u object to several house guests?'

'Son of a bitch! U shouldn't have left, goddammit. I'm sending Logan and Nox.'

The second I finish reading her reply, I glance up, and the warriors appear, dressed for battle as usual. "Quite the mess you created here, Wolf." Logan says before tensing and sniffing the air. My heart drops. "Was there someone here besides fae?"

"Just my siblings," I lie and begin picking body parts off the floor, hoping he abandons the subject. "And I wanted an excuse to redecorate anyway," I say with a shrug as Josh and Cellica come racing into the room.

"Good God, Liam," Cel mumbles, her eyes wide. "Are you okay?"

"Yes, go pack a bag. We are staying with the vampires."

Elation brightens my little sister's face. "Really?" She nearly bounces on her toes, ogling Christoph from head to shitkickers as he does his best to ignore her, a deep frown line between his brows. I slip into the jeans Josh tossed in my direction.

"Shall we repair the windows before we leave?" the commander asks, and I exhale at the respite. He's letting his suspicions go.

"Yeah. We have sizable pieces of plywood in the barn. I can..." Logan disappears and reappears by the window with six portions. "Shit," I remark with a smirk. "Wish you guys moved about during the day. We could benefit from your speed, running the ranch."

"Ranching is not my thing," the stoic warrior states, striding through the bare windows to lay the first board. That's when I notice my tool belt around his waist.

"Are you sure about that?" I chuckle, snatching the hammer and nails from the pouches. Logan holds the heavy wood in place while I tack it to the frame.

We work quickly and efficiently in the numbing cold while my siblings and Christoph attempt to clean up the interior as much as possible, tossing the smaller body parts in trash bags and chucking the larger ones out the window for the wildlife to ravage.

The stoic vampire quietly follows me around the house while I make certain everything else is secure. I rinse off in the shower before throwing on clean clothes and stuffing a small bag with essentials.

We meet up once more in the kitchen, and I conduct several quick phone calls to my foreman and trusted ranch hands. The cattle ranch is their responsibility for the next few days. Or weeks. I also communicate with my manager at the LeLoo, who assures me everything is running smoothly and not to worry.

With that out of the way, I nod to the vampires. Christoph hoists my sister into his arms, still avoiding looking her directly in the eyes. She squeals with delight, and Josh and I grasp Logan's bulging shoulders.

As I view my home fade to black, I question how long before I see it again. Days, weeks, or months? Living at the castle, the odds of seeing Viessa increase tenfold. My sin eats at my consciousness. I must steer clear of any encounters with her, or she will sense my remorse and treachery.

Chapter 22

"Make certain the strikes are differing in intensity and location."

My palm sweats with nervous anxiety, and I grip the flogger tighter, striving to follow Mr. Moretti's softly spoken commands. The handsome male in the center of the suspension rack eyes me with a greedy smile, bracing to weather my novice hand.

His protruding cock isn't as impressive as my mate's, but this vampire appears hungry for pain. If his twitching dick and drips of pre-cum are any indication.

"Even though you have restrained Peter, a Domme` does not need chains, cuffs, or ropes to subdue her sub. When she influences his mind, heart, and body, he will readily bind his soul to hers."

Wow. Such responsibility. I nervously adjust the leather corset constricting my breasts and continue my training under Sebastian's attentive eye. He's taught me much in mere weeks, but the sessions have magnified my lust for my mate.

It's been five months, two weeks, and three days since the playroom incident, and without Liam's presence and his blood, it's driving me insane. I've pushed myself hard during my lessons with Icarus, but it wasn't until I could funnel the energy I experience when performing the role of Dominatrix over the past month and a half that I achieved new breakthroughs. For the first time in over a century, I feel like a whole person. A whole person with a bleeding and broken heart.

My face still blazes with humiliation when I recall my confession to my father regarding my dark needs. It couldn't be helped. I had to inform him so he would allow me to leave the monastery regularly to meet with Sebastian. Not solely for training. The commander has become my blood pimp, furnishing me with willing donors to slake my hunger.

What I find fascinating? Icarus didn't seem surprised. He quietly accepted who I am. For that, he earned my love and devotion.

Unlike my mate.

Sebastian has aided me in understanding Liam's reasons for racing out of that room. This lifestyle isn't for everyone, notably for a proud Alpha male on the wrong end of the whip. What baffles me is he seemed willing and appeared to get off on the burn of pain, which set me on fire like nothing else.

Even working over these subs with Sebastian, while it soothes the voices and I bask in the euphoric drug of dominance, it doesn't heighten my lust. Only my king draws forth the craving to lick him all over or experience his mouth or hands on my body. None equal my appetite for my beautiful wolf.

Besides, Bastian said sex while in training was off-limits. So, when it came time to perform face sitting, I had to utilize a life-size sex dummy to establish proper placement so I don't suffocate my sub but receive the maximum benefit of their lips and tongue.

Yeah, quite embarrassing to squat on a prone dummy head while in full leathers. But I suppose it's better than the commander seeing me naked. Alex might have something to say about that—not to mention Liam. Maybe.

The wolf king and I didn't complete the bond, but I've drunk from him, so I get a sense of his emotions from time to time. They are most extreme during the full moon when his beast is unrestrained. My lover is just as miserable as I am, but his stubborn ass pride and bullheadedness keep us apart.

I refuse to pursue him. The werewolf must appear to me—prove he is amenable to accepting my needs and submitting. I already stated I would compromise and provide him with sexual control occasionally. On top of that, once a month, I would yield to his beast.

I exhale and work to refocus on the naked vampire's trembling frame before me. This male is a true passive, prepared to sacrifice anything for his Mistress or Master, no matter the cost. When the man strode into the playroom earlier, he immediately sank to his knees, lowered his regard, and awaited direction.

Sebastian gently touched the top of his head when he introduced him to me, and the male's dick jumped in response. This level of devotion spikes my appetite, but one element I covet most is the defiant gleam in Liam's eyes. The rebellious growl when he responds with 'yes, Mistress.' The way he took me roughly as punishment.

Even though I envisioned my first time with the wolf much differently, I wouldn't change a thing. Yes, it hurt like hell, but the pain vanished quickly, replaced by pure fucking bliss.

I have no desire to snuff his masculine spirit. His resistance, and reluctant submission, burn an intense passion through my core, and I crave nothing higher than the addictive stretching of my mate buried deep within me.

"Viessa. Stay in the here and now," Sebastian instructs, and I bounce back with a jerky nod. "You must remain in control. Remember, a Mistress is *always* respectful, guiding her sub, instructing him, spurring him, driving him to reach his maximum potential. In the bedroom as in life." The sexy commander steps to the array of toys spread out for today's session. "You become the most supportive person in his world. Each session, you challenge him and teach him facts about himself he never realized existed. It is your job to draw out the very best in him." He plucks a peculiarly shaped, stainless steel device from the shelf. "You did well escalating Peter's passion/pain receptors. It is time to arrange him over the bench. I will instruct you how to introduce a butt plug with minimal discomfort to the submissive."

"Butt plug?" I ask curiously. "For what purpose?"

"To enhance the experience during a spanking, but likewise when performing sex. During copulation, or if you are pleasuring him or vice versa, or simultaneously, he will encounter the erotic sensation of the plug shifting within him. In addition, he must focus on maintaining it in place."

"Oh," I blush slightly at such blatant talk with the commander. "And if he doesn't hold it there?"

"That will be up to you what punishment you dole out if any."

I nod and calmly unbuckle the horny vampire, ordering him to the bench. He eagerly complies.

"Make certain you reward and praise your sub before, during, and after each session of pain. What that reward is, a caress, a kiss, a kind word, or yourself, again, is up to you."

"I understand."

Sebastian points to the various shapes and sizes on the counter. "The smaller ones are more suitable for a novice like Liam, but for Peter here, he enjoys the stretching of a larger plug. Is that not correct, Peter?"

"Yes, Master."

"Oh. Okay."

I'm lubing the toy when a sudden pain shoots through my skull. I cry out, dropping the weighty device on the floor and clutch my head.

"Viessa? Are you all right?"

Sebastian's strong masculine voice, laden with concern, melts into the background as a compelling vision slams through my brain, churning with the velocity of a tornado. I vaguely recognize he's ordered Peter to his knees before he gently eases me onto the couch in the corner.

Blood. The deafening boom of rapid gunfire. Dead eyes staring into nothingness. A glint of silver. The horrendous cacophony of clashing swords. It all pounds through my head, inducing nausea to roll my stomach.

"Something is wrong with Viessa," Bastian says, and I risk the blinding light piercing my retina to discover he's speaking into a phone.

"I will grab Nicki and be right there, brother," Logan states from the other end, his manner brusque.

Another white, fiery flash of pain stabs through my cranium, and I whimper against the agony. "Need... Liam," I croak through the tears.

"Yes, Oracle," he whispers before disappearing, only to reappear moments later with the werewolf king in tow. He's wearing dusty chaps over blue jeans, scuffed cowboy boots, and a black, long-sleeved Levi button up. He takes in his surroundings in a second, but when his gaze lands on Peter, the whiskey irises flicker to the blue of his wolf and a low, threatening growl vibrates through the room.

Liam advances on the naked vampire kneeling in the corner, but Sebastian grabs his arm and orders the sub to trace away. "Liam. Viessa needs you now," the commander urges, spinning him to face me.

The fight melts from his expression and my mate bends down on one knee next to the lounge. "Sweetness?" His voice is tender as he brushes my sweat-slicked hair from my forehead. "What's happening?"

The scent of leather, rain, and wood smoke fills my nostrils, and I rear up, fold my arms around his broad shoulders, knocking his cowboy hat from his head, and bury my face in his neck. He gently lifts me before resting on the couch, my trembling frame tight against his chest.

Just his touch soothes the discomfort somewhat, and the gyrating mass of violent images, voices, and noise slows to a realistic speed.

I'm standing outside the entrance of what appears to be the vampire castle as dozens of fae stride past me into the bowels of the massive stronghold. Syn Grayflame and a blonde woman appear out of nowhere about twenty yards directly to my right.

I observe the scene play out, endeavoring to decipher if this is past, present, or future.

When Syn turns to Abigail, his question sends ice slithering through my veins. "How close do you need to be to detonate the chip in King Scott's spine?"

"About fifty feet," the witch answers with a shrug.

"Do not discharge unless the Halfling bitch refuses to cooperate. I would prefer her alive."

"I do not wish to slaughter the hunky werewolf after he fucked me so thoroughly." I gasp when the violet irises shift to leer directly at me.

A legion of questions bombards me. One, how can she see me if this is a foresight from another time and place? And two, if she genuinely sees me, were the comments a lie to upset me? Or were they real? Did Liam betray me with the witch? The notion fractures my soul.

No. I won't accept that. My noble king would never lower himself to rut this vile creature. She's the enemy. This eerie immortal knows I'm here and is endeavoring to deceive me.

Nicki appears before the duo with a sword, Logan on her heels. When Liam comes barreling out the entrance, I scream, attempting to reach for him and trace him from danger, but my hands pass right through him.

I stare in horror as the blonde raises her fist. Cradled inside is a small black device with a red button. Just as Nicole and Logan engage with numerous fae, Abigail grabs Syn's wrist. As they dissipate, the witch slowly presses the plunger with a malicious laugh.

I watch in terror as an explosion rips through my mate's powerful frame, blowing my friends to bits. When the sweet essence of my werewolf splatters across my face, the world fractures.

My body seizes in a multitude of shock waves, consumed in stunned disbelief and torment. Strong arms attempt to keep me immobile as I flounder about like a fish out of water, agony infusing every tendon and nerve.

"Icarus, do something," Liam grunts as the powerful convulsions shake me so hard my elbow fractures my mate's rib. "Help her," he groans.

"Hold her limbs, Commander," my father orders. Generous, warm hands clamp down on my shins.

I'm vaguely aware Logan and Nicole are in the room as icy palms that can only belong to the Oracle frame my face.

Potent magic seeps into my pores, lighting my flesh on fire. I shriek, even as the tremors lessen.

"Flee the vision, child. Focus on your mate," Icarus urges. Even through the chaos, his comment surprises me.

"Viessa," Liam murmurs. "Concentrate on my voice, sweetness. Come back to me."

Between the cold press of skin against my cheeks, the heated hands pressing on my legs, and Liam's rugged, seductive tone, I battle against the void attempting to drag me into the suffocating nothingness.

Increment by gradual increment, I process the scene, like an old-time movie projector set to slow motion. When the stunning blonde woman with strange violet eyes peers directly at me again, I hit pause.

Holy God. She sees me. How is that possible?

Pushing the oddity aside, for now, I endeavor to establish where in the timeline this event takes place. I squint at the dark sky. The moon is almost full. I maneuver my way over to Nicole and glimpse the watch on her wrist. Through every step, the creepy purple eyes follow me.

With a tremendous surge, I mentally leap from the vision back into my frame and the security and warmth of my king's embrace. My lashes flutter with the effort to lift them. I must caution the others.

"That's it, baby. Let me see those beautiful ambers."

But no matter how hard I struggle; my lids refuse to open. My brain feels encased in a cloud of darkness, and my body refuses to adhere to my mental commands.

Even my mate's soothing voice can't break me from this stasis, and panic builds. Did the witch somehow damage my mind? Will I never wake from this frightful void of nothingness—still cognizant of everything around me, but powerless to move or speak?

"Forge your path through the darkness, child," my father commands gently. Doesn't he understand I'm trying?

"Yes, Vi." Liam's rough fingers brush my hair from my face. "Come back to us."

"What's wrong with her, Icarus?" the queen asks from somewhere by my feet.

"The witch has trapped her mind."

"What the fuck does that mean?" Liam demands, his arms tightening around my waist in a protective gesture.

"It means Abigail is hatching a strategy to harness Viessa's volatile powers as we speak. Right now, my daughter's brain has gone into defensive mode, shutting down to block the witch. It is quite impressive, really." His cool fingers lift from my face. "I must take her to the monastery. Only within the mist am I able to recover her thoughts and interpret her revelation."

"How do…"

"Time is of the essence, my lord. Please, surrender her so I might save her."

Liam hesitates before his lips brush my temple, and I'm lifted into my father's chilly embrace.

I pray Icarus is correct, and he can restore my mind. I'd rather revert to being psychotic than suffer this void for all eternity.

No. I can't think like that. I will fight with everything I am to return to my mate, warn the others of the impending invasion, and the explosive device in Liam's spine. It doesn't matter how Abigail implanted the chip, or if her claim was legitimate. All that matters is transforming the future to save the people I love.

Chapter 23

"I will be in the yard training the men," Logan announces, stalking into my office shirtless with that sexy as fuck lethal prowl. I unashamedly ogle the chiseled perfection of my mate's torso, the black swirls of ink over his pec, shoulder, and bulging bicep. He smirks knowingly, perching on my desk.

"Where's Bastian?" The commander usually trains the Guardians.

"He is showing off his businesses to Alex."

I lean back in my chair, contemplating my beautiful vampire. "Were you ever a Dom at one of his clubs?"

Logan is the sexual dominant I crave, but I've never asked him how he acquired all those wonderfully talented skills.

His grin broadens. "Who do you think trained Sebastian?" The low purr causes my insides to clench with renewed need, even though we just had a marathon session a mere hour ago, and my backside still tingles.

"Hmm." It's about all I can manage at the moment as I eye the ever-expanding bulge beneath his leathers. The male is insatiable.

"As much as I would love to bend you over this desk and devour you, my men are waiting. But let me leave you with something to ponder. When I return, say two hours, I want you in our playroom, on your knees. Tonight, I hunger for your delectable ass, and every inch will enjoy my fingers, lips, and cock."

Fuck me.

"If you had horns and a spiked tail, I'd swear you were the devil, making me wait two hours?"

"It is your punishment for not accompanying me in the shower earlier. Besides, the devil does not appear with pointy horns and a barbed tail, my love. He arrives as everything you desire. Two hours."

I eye him defiantly. Oh, I could so fuck with his mind during training. Whisper naughty things while he attempts to clash swords with his men. A raging erection makes combat a little more complicated. Maybe he'll flog me as punishment.

"Yes, Sir," I reply, lowering my lids demurely even as I formulate my plan.

He growls low before shoving off the desk and heading for the exit. No doubt to put some distance between him and his greatest weakness—me.

"Do not leave the barrier, Nicole," he orders gruffly from the entrance, fixing me with those brilliant irises fringed with dark lashes that cause my insides to clench in response. "It is not safe."

"Duh," I counter with a saucy smile.

"Two hours," he warns with an unmistakable light in those beautiful eyes before disappearing.

Shit. He'll be back in thirty minutes if I have anything to say about it.

Just as I refocus on the never-ending paperwork in front of me, Liam pops his head around the corner. "My siblings and I are heading to the gym to spar with Kurtis and Lu. Care to join?"

Most of the task force resides at the castle now, each attempting to manage their vast holdings remotely. King Ruse and my former Guardian are used to this form of isolation, but the longer this confinement forces Liam and his brother to shift inside the barrier, the more agitated the werewolf king becomes. Not to mention his anxiety over Viessa's psychological condition.

"Wish I could. Would love the opportunity to kick your ass, but this fucking paperwork won't do itself, and my mate refuses to help me. I'll take a raincheck, though."

"You got it. And I know the feeling. Need to utilize your fax machine again. More documents require my signature. Any news from Icarus?"

The wolf asks the same question every day, and for once, I'm patient with my reply. I put myself in his shoes. If it were Logan, I'd be going ballistic. "No," I frown, his apprehension for his mate prickles along my skin. "She's in the best possible hands, Liam. No one I would trust more with such a precious package than the priest. He's like a father to everyone."

"I know. I just wish he would throw me an update."

"To quote the little blue weirdo, "Only so much one can reveal, my lord"," I smirk and am satisfied to see Liam's reluctant grin. "Now, go have fun and try not to let Lu kick your ass."

Twenty minutes in, I soon realize concentrating on this mind-numbing task is futile, so I prod the bear.

'*I already feel the warmth of your tongue on my pussy.*' I giggle as I imagine him floundering through a pivot or turn while training with his men when my husky voice penetrates his brain. '*My fingers are no substitute for your talented mouth, but I can't wait a second longer.*'

'*Goddammit, Nicole!*' The rough, sexy baritone growls in reply, causing my nipples to harden and my butt to clench in readiness. '*Nox nearly took my head off.*'

'*Well, come in here, and I'll suck another head till it explodes.*' Oh, this is getting fun. I lean back in my chair, prop my feet up on my desk and count down from ten as I anticipate Logan's appearance in my office.

A sudden blaring alarm pierces my eardrums, and I leap up just as my mate appears before me.

"What the hell is that?" I call out over the horrendous noise.

"Perimeter breach. Where are the others?"

"Gym."

He nods and hauls me against his chest. We arrive at the Training Center right before Sebastian and Alex. "How did you know?" I question Bastian.

He holds up his cell. "I linked the alarms to my phone. Plus, Logan barked in my head to get here."

"Have we determined who and how many?" Liam shouts. "And can we turn that damn thing off?"

Sebastian makes a couple of clicks on his screen, and the deafening noise shuts down. Thank fuck. It was giving me a headache.

"It looks like, surprise surprise, the fae have invaded. Abigail obviously cracked Icarus's shield," the commander informs us as he continues to scroll. "It appears to be several contingents. It is simply a matter of time before they discover our position." The worried blue gaze zeros in on mine. "We either join our fellow Guardians in the war, or we get you the hell out of here."

"I'm always down for option A," I declare with a low growl. "We can't leave my warriors to fight our battle for us."

"Agreed," Logan interjects, to my surprise. My mate is the first one to advocate getting me to safety. At all costs. "But these wooden practice swords are useless. We can get to the armory through the channels without being detected, grab weapons, and take back our home."

We all nod and follow my courageous consort to the super-secret James Bond type tunnels when Vi and Icarus halt our path. Oh, thank God! With them at our side, we are sure to win no matter the numbers.

"You must not engage the fae," the Oracle declares, and I scowl at him in annoyance. Just once I would love for him to agree with our plans.

"We are not running away with our tails between our legs, Priest," Kurtis growls, and we all nod.

"If you fight, Liam will lose his life," Viessa interjects with a boldness I've not seen from her before. She's obviously recovered.

"What the fuck are you talking about?" the werewolf king demands of his mate.

"In the base of your spine rests a detonation device, King Scott," Icarus announces, stepping slightly in front of Vi as if to shield her from Liam. "If the witch gets close enough, she can detonate it, effectively ending your life and those around you."

My jaw drops. *What in holy hell?* "How did that happen?" I whisper, shaken by the revelation.

"We do not have the time to analyze the reasons further," Icarus says, eyeing the werewolf.

Liam's pulled a complete turnaround. His head's lowered like he can't bring himself to look at Viessa. She appears stricken for a moment before her eyes harden.

"You all must disappear. Disperse in groups, anywhere you consider safe," Icarus instructs.

"You mean go on the run?" I scoff. "No fucking way." I spent most of my life on the road, hiding from my past.

"My love," Logan turns to me, worry etched in his expression. "Icarus has never steered us wrong. We should do as he proposes. Alert the Guardians mentally to stand down and teleport to our various safe houses around the globe." He caresses my cheek. "This time is different. We are hiding out together." The proud warrior reads me all too well. He pivots to the others before I can respond. "Kurtis and Lu?"

"We'll take refuge at my lake house. No one but this group knows its location."

"Alex and I will head to my villa. It is not in my name, so the fae cannot track us there."

"Is the mechanism in my spine a tracker by any chance?" the werewolf king asks Icarus, still not meeting Viessa's watchful stare.

"I do not believe so, my lord."

"Allow me to take Liam and his family to my house. Only you and Lu know it exists." Viessa suggests, her gaze glittering with potent emotion.

Hmmm. What's going on between the two of them? Her fury I sense loud and distinct, but with Liam, tremendous guilt flows from him.

"Agreed. Then return to the monastery."

"Not a problem, father."

The werewolf king's gaze lifts to the Tri-bred for the first time. "Icarus, please transport my siblings on ahead. Viessa and I need to make a quick stopover at my ranch."

"That is not wise, King Scott. The fae have already attacked your residence once."

"It's a risk I must take," he mutters, his expression grim. "I'm not going on the run without protective suits and weaponry for my family."

"Very well."

Just then, the door to the gym swings wide, and Nox comes barreling into the room. "Got your message. The others have taken off, but I wanted to check on you first." He eyes Liam's sister with a guarded glare. She tilts her head, blue hair tumbling down her shoulder, observing him with curiosity and fascination.

"Go with Icarus, Josh, and Cellica," I command. "Guard them with your life." When he doesn't respond, I poke him in the chest with my finger. "Christoph, did you hear me?"

"What?" His gaze jerks to mine. "Yes. Yes, of course, my lady."

"I've informed Cipher and Arra, and they are taking precautions," Bastian enlightens us as he types furiously on his phone. "Jag refuses to budge, declaring he can take care of himself but will safeguard Kleora."

Alex snickers. "I bet he will."

"Okay. Move out, people. First chance you have, acquire a burner phone. I'll communicate our new number when we get one. Keep your heads on a swivel and stay safe."

We all nod, our expressions grave before assembling in our groups and disappearing from my home overrun with winged fuckers.

Chapter 24

"**B**efore you gather your things, I'd like a minute," Viessa demands softly.

She teleported us into the center of my now pristine living room. Several pack members came over and replaced the shattered windows and swapped out the wrecked furniture with new. The walls gleam with fresh paint, and the floors are blood-free.

I stare at Viessa dressed in her sexy as fuck warrior outfit, and my dick twitches. Until I recall what was going on in that playroom under Bastian's watchful eye the last time I saw her.

Your choice, dumbass.

"Liam," she sighs and fidgets nervously with the buckles running down the front of the rigid corset showcasing the tops of her pale breasts. My Christmas gift rests between her enticing cleavage, twinkling in the overhead lights. She had it on the night of her vision too. Somehow the notion of her wearing it while working over that vampire asshole increases my annoyance.

"I can explain why I was in that playroom with Sebastian. Please don't be angry."

The way she yields so readily stuns me. The last time I was in her presence, she'd been the Mistress of some random sub. Now she stands rigid before me, fearful I'm furious and bracing to plead her case. She should be livid with me for taking off, leaving her standing naked amid a similar room, her eyes pleading with me to stay.

"Viessa, you need not justify anything to me. I walked away, remember?"

She flinches, and I loathe myself for it. "Yes," she murmurs, and her gaze hardens. "I recall all too well."

We glare at each other for several anxious moments while I struggle with what to say. Her expression is closed off, so I have no indication of what she might be thinking. And to make matters worse, the frigid indifference in her glare stiffens me further.

Dammit, Liam. You're one sick, fucked up individual.

"How is your training going?" I ask to end the stare-off, studying her expression as I work to bury my guilt and shame at what ensued in this very room over a month ago with Abigail.

Her smile is breathtaking and loaded with childlike wonder. "I've earned three sacred engravings so far." I'm so captivated, it takes a second to realize she's holding out her left arm. On the inside of her forearm is a long black emblem in the shape of a half-moon. A small circle drops from the center with a dot in the middle.

I caress the pad of my thumb over the symbol and notice with satisfaction the tremor my touch creates. "What does it mean?"

"Um... the translation is Perception."

The image of the other two mysterious tattoos somewhere on her body ignites my imagination, and I scan her from head to toe. Which only ramps up my hunger. Below the corset, tight black leather with a zipper that runs from her belly button, down over her crotch and up the back, showcases Vi's long shapely legs. I crave to unzip it and lick and suck to my heart's content at the gem hidden underneath. I imagine the inky low-heeled boots with buckles up the front digging into my spine, urging me deeper as I pump into her tightness.

Son of a bitch, Liam. Focus. You have a fucking detonator in your tailbone.

"Congratulations, sweetness, but that's not the training I meant." My desire roughens my speech.

Amber eyes widen. "He told you?"

"You are my mate, Viessa. Sebastian asked for my approval first."

All expression leaves her face. "News flash," she growls. "You walked away; I don't require your permission."

She pivots to head to the back porch, but I latch onto her elbow and spin her into my chest. "That's where you're wrong, darlin," I state calmly, glorying in her anger. It proves she still bears some emotion toward me. Granted, it's fury crammed with hurt and betrayal, but I'll take what I can get. "Everything you do concerns me."

"You have a funny way of showing it, Liam."

I inhale deeply for calm, absently caressing the inside of her elbow. "I know, love. If it's any consolation, I've missed you."

What a fucking understatement. The truth is, I'm miserable without her visits, the sexual commands, and the addictive flavor of her sex. And even though life has plodded along at a desolate snail's pace these past couple of months, I can't seem to utter the words she longs to hear.

"I am aware. Your blood runs through my system, Liam. I perceived your emotions."

Fuck.

"That's an unfair advantage," I mutter and drop her arm.

"Maybe, but it's who I am. You either accept me, or you don't." The remark, spoken in a soft, timid voice, contradicts the lava swirling in her irises.

She's speaking about more than her abilities as a bonded vampire. An unpleasant tingle skates across the back of my neck.

"Viessa, I…"

Deep down, where I refuse to investigate, I lust after a repeat of the night in the playroom. It was the most erotic encounter of my life, but the shame and humiliation at my weakness appalled me.

If I wish to be with my mate, I must discover a way around myself, let go of years of belief, my innate Alpha impulses, and my beast's dominance. Even after all these months apart, with only the brief interaction at Sebastian's club before her mind shut down, I'm uncertain I can—no matter how passionately a measure of me aches for what she's offering.

"Liam, we... we should talk about where you found me," she stammers, gazing at the floor.

"Not now, Vi," I step around her and head toward the bedroom. "I'm well aware of what goes on in those rooms, and I need to get changed."

"Can we discuss at the same time?" she persists, following in my wake.

We pass through the massive kitchen encompassed with granite and stainless steel and the eat-in breakfast alcove. Her heels offer a sharp staccato as the vampire scrambles to keep up with my long strides through the spacious dining room and sunroom.

I shove open enormous barn doors to reveal my relaxing oasis. Beautiful brick pavers in varying shapes and hues of tan make up the floor of the master suite. A stacked stone fireplace nestles in the corner to the right of a wall of massive glass sliders that step out to a secluded patio overlooking the Yellowstone River.

The huge four-poster bed dominating the opposite end of the big windows offers an incredible view of the starry night to fall asleep to and beautiful sunrises to embrace me every morning.

As I glance around the room, I realize this dwelling is a death trap for my female. She would have no place to evade the killing rays of the sun.

Just one more glaringly obvious reason the vampire and I shouldn't be together. And that's not even a close runner-up to the more compelling matters. Like the gods forbid an Oracle to take a mate. Or how about the fact she's a sadist, and I'm the farthest thing from a masochist. Ever. Or that's what I keep telling myself.

"Say what you need to, Viessa." I skirt the door to my private studio and amble to the walk-in closet, jerking my shirt over my head as I disappear through the doorway. Vi eagerly pursues.

When she doesn't blast me with questions, I peer over my shoulder. She paused in the archway, her gaze traversing my frame in boxer briefs as I plunge my legs into leather pants. I smirk. Her lust is evident on her expressive face. A rosy hue steals over her cheeks, and I chuckle.

"I love the way you study me with such hunger and then blush when caught."

"I didn't have sex with the submissive at the club," she blurts out and bites her lip when my smile evaporates.

"I know."

"How?"

"Do you honestly believe I would consent to Sebastian training you and allow you to have sex with someone else? It was one of my stipulations when I agreed to your instruction."

Her body stills and an amber glow permeates the closet. "Allow me?"

Probably not the best choice of words, but I hold my ground. "I may not provide you what you need; submission, but I'll make damn certain you don't fuck anyone else."

Do you mean like you did? My inner self reminds me and my jaw clenches.

The anger surging through me remains welcome, but shame drops hard into my blood. Her fangs descend as she strides into the closet. Her fury a glorious sight, but my eyes narrow menacingly in warning. She ignores it, and the low rumble emanating from my chest.

"Who the hell do you think you are?" She steps into my space, scowling at me, her breasts heaving against the tight corset. "Tell me, Liam, have *you* fucked anyone since walking away from me?"

Her palms thump against my torso, shoving me hard against the wall of drawers and cabinets at my back. *Shit, she's powerful.*

"And don't even think of lying, because I felt it." Tears of rage glisten. "Every. Damn. Time!" she shouts before slapping me hard across the cheek.

I deserve the sharp sting as I relive the remorse I experienced after Abigail revealed her true self. Not to mention, all the nameless werewolves I fucked during the full moon. Each one digs through my subconscious.

The impact of her strike threw my head to the side, splitting my lip. But instead of retaliating, I close my lashes and bow my face in dishonor. The fight evaporates.

"Forgive me, sweetness."

My whisper visibly deflates her rage in a second. "Why, Liam?" she asks quietly, and I gaze into her turbulent eyes, revealing the swirling emotions boiling below the surface. "Why would you have sex with that witch?"

"I thought Abigail was you." Her breath hitches. My gaze pleads for understanding even as my words inflict pain on her soul. I see it in the burning amber depths as she stumbles back a step. "She cast an illusion I should never have believed."

"She… she appeared as me?"

"Yes, but the speech was different somehow. I should have known."

"You ignored your instincts. Why?" she questions with a quiet resolve in her manner.

I can't answer for several seconds as I endeavor to curb my raging emotions enough to articulate my inner turmoil. "I'm lost, Viessa," I admit brokenly, my fist clenching.

The time to let these tempestuous feelings out on the table has arrived. She needs to understand what I've been going through. My internal conflict is not a pardon for what happened, but maybe an explanation.

"I need you. In ways my mind instructs me I shouldn't, and it's driving me insane. I crave to be *your* strength—the one you solicit to lean on for everything. When you compel me to submit, I feel less and less like a man, and I detest it. I hate *you* for making me fucking desire your sexual dominance."

Her beautiful eyes widen in shock, but the tremble in her chin is my damnation.

"How can I fight your beliefs and passions when they run bone-deep?" she whispers, and I'm uncertain if she's asking me or telling me. "What I've demanded of you is tearing my proud Alpha apart and my inner vampire rails against causing you such anguish." She steps closer. "But, my king, being a submissive has never been about being powerless or weak. It's about the informed decision to gift that authority to the individual you deem most worthy."

"Is that something Sebastian taught you?" The words resonate deep within me—a muscle pulses in my jaw beneath the fading imprint of her palm.

"No. Just an oath I believe."

If I don't salvage this, my beast will compel me to walk away again and pursue a submissive female for a companion and queen. Viessa's happiness means more to me than my desire for control, but I'm uncertain if I have the strength to submit completely, even understanding the serenity it provides her.

The alternative? Unless I have Icarus remove the mate bond, it's a wasteland of misery and pain for eternity. For both of us.

I watch in bewildered disbelief as Viessa lowers to her knees before me in the center of my wardrobe and bows her head.

"I am so sorry, Liam." Her words hiccup with chaotic emotions, affecting me to my very soul. "I never meant to cause you torment. Please. I'm the one who needs forgiveness. You are my strength in every way that matters. I love you, my king, with all that I am. I would willingly surrender control to be with you."

I hold perfectly still, gawking at this magnificent creature as I struggle to restrain the tears threatening. Sebastian asked me if Vi would compromise. Well, here's my answer.

This powerful, alluring female is attempting to put aside her own wants and needs for mine.

Her dark mane of hair shrouds her face, shielding me from witnessing her torment. If I lost this extraordinary woman, it would crush me. The last couple of months were merely the tip of the agony iceberg I'd endure if she hid from me forever. And without me, the pandemonium would consume Viessa's mind.

"Viessa," I sigh, and my abdomen constricts at the failure evident in my tone.

"Please don't give up on me," she pleads desperately.

My heart stutters. Lucretia was the only person in the world who never washed her hands of Vi, even though she had every reason and opportunity to do so. Everyone else in her life viewed her as a deranged psychotic, including the shifters who raised them till their thirteenth birthday. Individuals around her gave her a wide berth as if her mental unrest was contagious.

I can hardly imagine how deep the rejections cut, piling one on top of the other until her self-doubt became an impervious wall around her heart. Her mind probably whispered they were correct. Nobody could love a female who belonged in a looney bin.

It's time for me to grow a pair and protect my mate in whatever form that requires.

"Sweetness, what kind of man would I be if I demanded you give up the very element that offers you peace?"

Her head jerks up, gazing into my troubled countenance. I mark the candor in her expression, the vulnerability written in every tear that escapes. "*You* are my peace, Liam. From the moment I cast eyes on you, heard your voice for the first time in real life." She rises but makes no advance to touch me. "I've had dreams of you my entire existence. Your deep tone in my head soothed me even back then."

I'm astounded by her admission. This woman visualized our encounter eons before it even happened.

"That night at the castle, when you spoke to me through the shield, it shattered the dazed fog I'd been living in for a century. Your gaze set me on fire," her breath hitches, "and for the first time in my life, I felt alive." She sucks in a deep breath, and a lightness enters my soul. "People say love is blind. But I don't believe that's accurate. I think it's all-seeing. Especially because of the way you look at me, since the very beginning, and see what no one else sees."

"And what is that, sweetness?" I ask softly, taking a hesitant step toward her like she's a skittish colt in need of a delicate touch.

"Me."

My roughened hands cradle her face, and she lowers her lids briefly, exhaling an unsteady breath.

"I'm not proposing you let go of your desire for control, Viessa. I would never do that. It's a part of who you are. I'm just requesting we... we take things slow." I brush my lips gently across hers, and my need ignites in an instant. "I embraced what took place at your lake house, and I reluctantly enjoyed and detested what developed in that playroom. But that is my issue to work through. All I can tell you is I'll try if you meet me halfway."

She swallows, and brightness fills her irises, matching my soul for the first time in months. "Liam, I will only present you with what you truly desire deep down. We *will* start slow," she whispers with a timid smile. "Are you prepared to provide me your soft and hard limits, so I understand what you allow and what you don't?"

I grin as the warmth of a blush spreads across my cheeks. "I gave those to Sebastian. He's been training you accordingly."

Her eyebrows raise. "Oh. Wow. Liam, you're prepared to submit to all of that?"

"Yes." The confession heats my groin even as a weight lifts from my shoulders. "We have a little time before we must head to your lake house." I reverse our positions, backing her against the wall of cabinets. My heart rate spikes at the lust swirling in the golden depths.

"What's on your mind, cowboy?" she rasps out, panting like she ran fifty miles as her palms caress down my flanks.

"I crave a taste of my mate," I growl, dropping to one knee. I unzip the leather pants past her crotch and up the other side with excruciating slowness, leaving the two parts connected by a mere inch of zipper to reveal the red lace thong underneath. "So pretty," I utter before lifting her leg over my shoulder.

Proof of her desire dampens the silky barrier.

"Fuck, I love your fragrance," I growl before shoving the delicate material aside and licking the savory folds from wet opening to her swollen bundle of nerves. God. I'm addicted to her sweetness.

She groans in pleasure and leans her head back against the cabinets, gripping a fistful of my hair. Kneeling between her thighs, lapping at her core, sets me ablaze.

"Oh, yes, Liam. Fucking taste all of me."

I observe my mate with a possessive intensity as my tongue worships her. She grips my locks tighter. The sting only throws fuel on the fire in my cock, straining painfully against my zipper.

Viessa watches me pleasure her, her breathing rapid. My pulse hammers through my veins as I envision my arms bound with rope, my ass reddened from her whip.

In a matter of minutes, she shatters apart, grinding her sex against my face, moaning my name. I growl low, reveling in her abandonment as I continue to drive my tongue along her soft lips.

When I stand, ripping open my leathers, she reaches down to help, capturing my rock-hard length the second it's free and steering me to her opening. "Fuck me, my king. Don't hold back," she pants, her passion-filled gaze peering deep into my soul. "Let me complete my end of the bond. It will allow me an insight into your mind. I will perceive your wants and desires when we play."

She lifts a leg and wraps it around my hips, urging my erection deeper. I groan, gripping her ass. Against my better judgment, and the promise I made to myself that if we were ever at this juncture again to take things slow, I plunge forward, spearing her with my girth. She sucks in a sharp breath at the intrusion, and I pause a moment to savor the wonderful constriction of her walls as she works to accommodate my size.

She leans into me and suckles at my neck, drawing the vein closer to the surface. I don't move, holding utterly still inside her.

"Look at me, sweetness," I rumble, my body tense. When she eases back to obey, I cradle her face. "From this moment on, I will never seek another during the full moon, even if I have to lock myself in Nicki's dungeon. I vow it."

"Thank you, my love. I would hate to start a war because I slaughtered several of your people." She grins, and I chuckle, kissing her forehead. "If you agree to be my sexual submissive, Liam, I pledge to yield to your beast every lunar cycle, to surrender to your strength and guidance outside the bedroom, and *occasionally* grant you sexual control."

I smirk as she emphasizes occasionally.

My hips begin a slow, delicious glide. "Then drink from me, Viessa. I will be your sole source of nourishment from now on. Do you understand?" My tone is all authority, and she nods eagerly. "Fuck, you feel good," I groan, picking up the pace. "Feed, baby." I clutch her nape and guide her to my jugular.

"Yes, my king," she whispers before plunging those sexy canines into my flesh and drawing deep. Her fingernails dig into my shoulders as I pound into her with such force, she has no alternative but to lift her other leg, clutch my waist, and surrender herself in my ferocious taking.

The second I sense the mating bond connecting my spirit to hers, latching onto my soul like a steel vice, she plummets over the edge of oblivion. Tremors shake her core as she cries out, hurtling me into absolute ecstasy with her. I groan deep and shudder my release, even as joy and apprehension prickle my nape.

Viessa now possesses insight into my conscience, to the internal conflict of my emotions. My deepest, darkest desires. Will the vampire use them against me, or take me on a pilgrimage of such pleasure I'll gladly bow to her every command?

Chapter 25

Viessa

My link to this powerful werewolf affects me profoundly, and I'm stunned by the complexity of his mind. Liam's devotion to his siblings influences his decisions. As a pseudo-parent and as their king. But what surprises me the most is his utter loyalty to Nicole. He loves her like his brother and sister and would sacrifice a great deal to preserve her life and the legacy of the prophecy.

What I find fascinating is his emotions regarding me. His protective instinct is predominant, needing to ensure my safety and happiness above all others, even his own. Not surprising is the combined lust of beast and man. Liam's passion for me rules him. He craves my body like I require blood, but his inherent sense of honor and devote belief in the piety of the Oracles plagues his mind.

King Scott yearns to complete our bond, and claim me as his. Fights it every time we are together. Because of his stringent beliefs and values, his worry over the consequences impacting me, his friends, and his family. It forces him to maintain a firm hold on his beast in my presence.

The glimpse into his inner desires, the ones he fights tooth and nail for fear it will consume him, place a heavy burden on my shoulders. I crave to delve deep into those passions and fulfill every one of them, but I'm concerned by the war within this potent being.

He truly loves and hates the way I bring out the erotic fantasies he considers taboo for an Alpha male; how he gets off on being restrained. The utter thrill he receives with the burn of pain inflicted, even as his brain recoils at the mere notion.

But in the quiet moments during our life apart, late at night, alone in his enormous bed, my mate stroked himself to images of our time in the playroom. The second his release came, shame and humiliation stomped out the sexual stimulation as wrong and deviant.

I have a long and arduous road ahead to convince this proud warrior that what happens between us is beautiful, sensual, and oh-so-right. I must demonstrate the depth of my need for his strength. His submission.

"Liam?" I ask as I observe him pack weapons and clothing into several bags. "I want to show you something."

"What is it?" he responds, never looking up from his task.

"It's… a place, really." Something in my tone finally registers. The whiskey irises find mine. "We could make a quick stop before I take you to the island."

"Where to?" He zips the last bag closed, flings them over one shoulder, and holds out his other hand to me.

I step into his outstretched arm, hugging his waist. "A place that was once a huge part of my life. One I want to share with you."

My heart pounds a mile a minute, and my skin crawls with the thought of stepping foot in that horrible place again, but I wish for Liam to have an insight into my vulnerability. Show him I'm willing to let go of my reluctance and share a part of myself that only my twin understands, so maybe he'll find the courage to do the same.

"Of course," he murmurs, kissing my forehead. "Lead the way."

Instead of taking us directly inside the abandoned building, we touch down on the road leading to Awakening Hill Sanitorium. Thick storm clouds hover over the towering brick structure. A humid wind saturated with the souls of the deceased swirl around us.

"What is this place, sweetness?" Liam asks, gazing around with trepidation.

The entrance pathway is still somewhat discernible despite the many cracks and holes given to it by the elements. Dust and debris litter the circular drive while unkempt gardens lay cluttered with forsaken possessions.

"This was my home for many years," I whisper, afraid the ghosts from my past will strike out in rage at the sound of my voice. "Hundreds of immortals died here because of the cruel and vindictive owners."

"Your sister left you here?" He asks, astounded.

"An asylum should be a place of refuge from the storms that hurt the mind. A place of love and sanctuary, a place that welcomes you with open arms and becomes your anchor, the pillar in your hurricane." I wander closer, the darkness at the heart of this building calling to me as it did back then. "According to the brochure, anyway. On the surface, that's exactly how it seemed. But this asylum was no place to seek refuge."

Liam stays close to my side; his heat offers me comfort in a way I never understood here. I peek over at him to gauge his reaction to my former residence. Anger and sorrow swirl within my wolf. He's furious I suffered so greatly. Craves to avenge me by ripping apart anyone who caused me harm. A part of me wishes he could, but I'd taken care of my jailors in a way they'll never be found.

"Awakening Hill once bustled with people, but it was no life. I marked my time with the coming of blood, just enough to keep me alive, but not enough to heal any injuries unless Lucretia was visiting."

"You didn't tell her what was happening to you?"

"The owners of this asylum had far-reaching power across the globe. They warned me if I ever revealed what transpired here, everyone I loved and cared about would perish. It was an effective tool to keep my mouth shut." Especially since they threatened the one creature who kept me sane. My wolf.

"Trezzo is the one who actually hinted to Lu they weren't taking care of me properly." I laugh, but there's no humor in the sound. "Properly."

Liam touches my shoulder and I shake my head as my mind flashes to my room inside this hellhole. "The only freedom I received was at daybreak when they locked me in a padded cell and left me to the horror in my mind. For endless hours I went ballistic. I'd yank chunks of my hair out to silence the voices, screamed my lungs out, trapped in some brutal tragedy of the past, present, or future."

"Jesus." The wolf's agonized whisper jolts through me.

"Anyway, after the council cleared Lucretia of all charges, my warrior sister made a little surprise visit to avenge her crazy sister."

"Good," Liam growls. "I hope she made them suffer."

"She did not, for the place was already a tomb. When Trez-zo, or I guess I should call him by his legal name, Zachariah, when he freed me, he granted me a boon. If I came willingly, did everything he asked, he would help me take vengeance against those who wronged me." I close my eyes against the remembered carnage I inflicted. "My inner vampire took over, and I slaughtered everyone who hurt me. Zach burned the bodies."

I stare at this mental prison soaring six stories into the night sky with a bell tower jutting up another story in the middle. Bars cover every window, although most of the glass shattered long ago. Many of the doors have collapsed, ripped off the hinges by the desperate. The open doorways that were once inviting are now an eerie and unwelcoming sight. There are signs of the fires. Sometimes, it is merely a trail of soot and smoke above a windowpane.

The wind in the trees, and the creaking of wood, are the new dominant sounds in a community once rich with the screams of the damned. I wander through the busted front doors, Liam close on my heels. Even though the paint has peeled and dirt and trash litter the hallways, I know exactly where I'm going.

I descend the stone stairway to the basement level. No room with a view for this vampire. No. They kept me far below ground, on the same wing where they tortured so many. Their screams melded with my own until I couldn't tell where the sound was emanating from.

"Viessa," Liam latches onto my elbow, and I pause but keep my face lowered. "Look at me."

No. Making eye contact invites pain.

Without lifting my gaze, I squeeze my eyes shut to bolster my courage for my next confession. "Liam, so many suffered here, but amidst the horror, I found a soul whose affliction was similar to mine. He'd learned how to not only stop the visions but control them. Sedric was a powerful psychic, but he was also an incubus."

Liam stills. I open my lids, staring at his enormous boots.

Strong fingers grip my chin, lifting my face. "Baby, is he the one who taught you about dominance? Did he force you?"

Restrained fury rides his tone. Violence flickers in his irises. My heart plunges into my stomach as if I'm riding a roller coaster and just dropped down the other side. I'd scream if I didn't think he'd run for the hills.

"He… he disciplined his mind through sexual control. I became Sedric's mental escape, and he became mine. It helped somewhat, but when I pictured you in his place, obeying my commands, the turmoil eased even more." I place a tentative hand on his chest, willing him to understand. "We only had a few stolen moments, and as you are now aware, we never had intercourse. Even though it would have given him strength, he honored my wishes. The second the staff found out we were sneaking around, they separated us. I never saw him again."

"It makes sense now. Your knowledge of bindings, of being so sure of what you needed."

I can't tell if he's pissed off or resigned. Either emotion makes me anxious, and I glance around at the graffiti on the walls, remembering the sound of my own screams echoing down the halls.

"Hey," Liam commands, and I shift my gaze back to his. "You are here with me. Free from this place."

"I will never rid myself of this place, my king. It is who I am."

"No, Viessa. It's just a tragic piece of your past."

It is much more than that. And only a visual can showcase what I mean. "There's one more thing I need to show you. We are almost there."

He regards me for several minutes before nodding. I pivot and continue down the corridor, riddled with leaves, mold, and forgotten possessions. Several of the doors stand open in an eerie invitation. I keep my gaze forward, refusing to peer into the torture chambers. My skin tingles, remembering the doctor's *therapy* methods.

When we finally come to room 666, I hesitate, my heart in my throat, tears blurring my sight. "This was my room," I whisper, my fists clenched tight.

Liam strides around me but stops short as he takes in the small area.

The room is only eight feet in any dimension. Inside my cell is an eerie, grotesque, but beautiful testament to my headlong plunge into madness. Harsh lines of blood cover the cloth walls, forming a bizarre web of overlapping pictures and writing that is painful to look at.

It would take years to decipher the images blanketing every surface, but one word is unmistakable. Drawn in thick slashes of rusty red, it appears over and over, perhaps two dozen times in all.

LIAM.

"Sweetness," he whispers as he takes in the carnage, his gaze bouncing to every spot his name appears.

"Do you remember the night of Lucretia's trial?" I ask quietly, keeping my focus on my mate and not my horrendous surroundings of the past. As if acknowledging them might bring the deranged psychosis back.

Liam turns to face me, his eyes haunted. "Of course. You were very upset."

I smile sadly. "Upset. That's an extremely nice way of saying I was crazed. Unless you were touching me, I plunged back into the chaos in my mind. When you gave me your necklace, still warm from your body, it didn't clear my mind completely, but... it allowed me to be separate from you as long as I could see you." I touch the new yellow diamond on my chest. The other one I keep by my cot at the monastery. "How did you know it would help?"

"I didn't," he confesses, striding slowly in my direction as if careful not to spook me. "All I realized was when I touched you or spoke to you, your eyes focused." One foot from me, Liam runs his palm gently down my arm and I shiver at the contact. "I would've preferred you in my lap where I could wrap my arms around you, but Lu's life was on the line, so I thought something from me might help."

"Anything regarding you helps. Even just the thought of you kept me from losing myself completely. I lost count of how many times I craved to give up, to let them kill me. Then your face flashed behind my lids. Your image forced me to push on, to endure another night, another week. Because I knew one day, I would see you for real, and I would've endured anything for that to happen."

Liam gathers me in his arms, sheltering my head beneath his chin. "You'll never suffer again, Vi. I will eviscerate anyone who even looks at you wrong. I vow it." He gently tugs on my hair and I lift my face to his. "You are the bravest person I've ever met. And even though I can no longer slay the demons from your past, it warms my soul to realize the idea of me kept you alive so we could one day be together."

When my wolf's lips press against mine, the horror I lived through in this room washes away. Liam is no longer just an image I conjured to keep me sane. He's real. Flesh and blood. Nothing will keep us apart again. Not our enemies, my father, or even the gods themselves.

If anyone tries, I will rip them apart until nothing remains.

Chapter 26

"**L**iam, do you want more eggs? I can whip up some pancakes if you'd rather have that?"

"Cellica stop hovering," I demand with a frown when she keeps glancing at the sky and her watch. "And why are we eating breakfast for dinner, anyway?"

She shrugs. "Thought I'd change things up a bit." Another glance at the clock.

I know what she is waiting for—the setting sun. My sis has acquired a fascination with Nox that is pissing me off. I can't fault him. He's kept his distance and appears uninterested in my little sister. Best thing. If he touched her—I'd have to kill him.

The vampire Guardian has been sleeping in the walk-out basement during the day. It's slightly damp and noisy down there, but besides Vi's room, which as king and her mate I'm occupying, it's the only space completely protected from the sun.

I sigh and take my half-eaten *dinner* to the sink. Cellica eyes it with a disapproving frown. Since Viessa's revelation about the chip in my spine, my siblings haven't left my side.

Joshua broods and Cel mothers. I realize it's their way of coping with the possibility I could die with the push of a button, but they're suffocating me.

We've hashed out every plausible scenario on the best course of action to remove the damn thing, but without x-rays to show the tiny objects' exact location, it's just talk at this point. When we get back to the ranch, I'll have our veterinarian shoot some films and go from there.

We've been hiding out at Vi's lake house for two weeks, checking in with the rest of the team every couple of days through text messages, and I'm about to explode.

Fuck. Wrong choice of words.

Viessa came back once to give us the lay of the terrain, but I couldn't squeeze out a moment alone with her.

Our tour of that institute haunts my mind. My girl went through brutality at the hands of the so-called experts in that godforsaken place, and my beast raged, demanding a reckoning for our female. We hungered to sink our claws into their flesh and tear them apart. The pain and agony she endured shattered me. I never wish for her to be hurt in any manner ever again. She has experienced more anguish than most immortals could handle.

What sickened me was the sight of her padded cage. The fear, violence, and instability of Viessa's mind were clearly evident in the small space. Dark crimson smeared the walls. Shredded padding encased the room in several places, chunks of the stuffing scattered across the floor, caked with mold, and dried blood.

My heart stuttered at my name scrawled in rust over every surface. Amid the turbulence and horror, she clung to an idea of me. Inscribed it throughout the cell as a reminder to hold on and control her mind from surrendering to the pandemonium forever. Her yearning humbled me, but I grieved I wasn't there to protect her from such cruelty and despair.

Some unknown incubus tried to help ease her turmoil. And the fact he never bedded her speaks volumes about his character. Their kind has an unnaturally potent sexuality that's innately imprinted in all aspects of their physiology. It's biological, physical, mental, and even spiritual for them. Like a succubus, sex is how they survive. So the fact he was teaching her sexual control without ever consummating the deal is fucking rare.

The full moon is in one week, and my skin crawls with the fear of the unknown. My mate informed us that 68% of the island is state forest land, so we should have plenty of space to shift, hunt, and run without detection. Especially since it's mid–March and the winter season is still in full swing.

It makes me twitchy as hell being sequestered on an is-land, surrounded by water, and the sole means on or off is a car ferry ride on a set schedule.

Josh and I have kept ourselves busy scouting for the choic-est ice fishing spots around the bay. One of the ferryboat captains, a tall dude named Brad, provided me with a depth map of Pike Bay, what fish we could expect to catch, and even where to purchase the equipment to spear fish. He was a fascinating wealth of knowledge, if a bit rough around the edges.

In the interim, Josh, Nox, and I have split enough timber to last three winters, conducted some much-needed repairs around the house, and played so many hands of poker, I've won back the money I lost.   .

But every night, I lay in Viessa's enormous king bed, aching for my female, praying my friends stay safe, and we somehow get this shit resolved so we can move on with our everyday lives.

I still can't believe Vi forgave me for fucking Abigail. I assumed she was my mate in all fairness, but I'm not positive I would be as forgiving if the positions were reversed.

Cel grabs the deck for another round. Way too antsy for games, I snatch my jacket off the hook by the door. "I'm going for a walk. Alone." I bark out when my brother prepares to follow.

"Do you consider that wise, bro?" Josh asks with a frown.

"We're on a freaking island in the U.P. of Michigan in winter. If it's not secure here, it isn't safe anywhere." I grumble and yank open the front door.

Oranges and pinks streak across the sky as the sun performs its finale of the day. The bite in the air is bracing as I stroll down the lengthy dirt drive flanked by large cedars, birch, and poplars.

Viessa's secret retreat is undoubtedly beautiful, and while the winter beauty of the frozen bay is serene, I yearn for the wide-open territories of the Wild Beast Ranch. I miss my home. Over the previous weeks, I've kept in communication with my foreman. Besides a few hiccups here or there, the homestead is functioning smoothly. As is the LeLoo Bar in Newport.

I'm so absorbed in my thoughts; I don't even comprehend how far I've strolled or that the sun slipped below the horizon quite some time ago until a twig breaks to my left. Darkness surrounds me, but with my heightened eyesight, I scan the snowy terrain with no problem. A figure stealthily slithers through the timbers.

This whole scenario of being hunted instead of hunting makes my skin crawl with the urge to rend flesh and tear wings from backs so we can resume our lives.

When Viessa steps onto the path in full combat gear, I tense. Is this indeed my mate? Or has Abigail found me and is casting another illusion to coerce me into fucking her again?

"Liam, are you alright?"

The voice sounds like Vi. I raise my nose and sniff the air. Honeysuckle wafts in my direction, but I make no movement toward her.

"Liam?" she questions again when I continue to regard her suspiciously. "It's me."

"How do I know that?"

She smirks. "Ask me something only I would identify."

"Okay. What's my nickname for you?"

The luscious lips widen. "Sweetness," she whispers, and the knot between my shoulders loosens.

"Too obvious," I respond, and her smile falters. She glances around, and I can practically hear her mind whirling with ideas on how best to prove her identity. I bite the inside of my cheek to hold my grin in check.

Her eyes flicker with boldness, and my dick hardens. "You hail me by another name as well."

"Oh?" I draw a step closer. "And what is that?"

"Mistress."

In two strides, she's in my arms, and I'm devouring her mouth, growling in resentment at the thick layers between us—Viessa's tongue duels with mine in a dance that sets me on fire.

"Fuck, I've missed you," I groan, nipping and kissing my way down her neck. She moans softly, angling her head to allow me further access to the spot right behind her ear that causes her to shiver in response.

"And I you, my king, but I only have a few minutes. I needed to reassure myself you were safe."

"Spend the evening with me," I implore, backing her against a tree. "Let me devote hours to licking," I run my tongue across the top of her breasts above the corset, "sucking," reaching in I pop the exquisite flesh over the rim and latch onto a hardened nipple. Her low, needy groan urges me further, so I clutch her ass and lift her until my pulsing length rests against the crotch of her leathers. Her thighs tighten around my hips. "and fucking you until you can't recognize if it's day or night."

Viessa grabs my face with both hands, dragging my lips back to hers. She nips and sucks with fervor, and I'm lost, grinding against her core with a frenzied demand.

When her fang pierces my lip, drawing blood, the slight sting ramps up my desire. I crave those sharp canines in my dick, at the femoral artery in my thigh, and feasting on my jugular. I finally understand Kurtis's obsession with always feeding his mate. It's an addiction.

She leans away and I snarl in frustration, the beast struggling to take over. I wish her closer, not putting distance between us.

"Liam, as much as I crave to spend the night with you, I must return, or Icarus will come looking for me, and we both recall how that ended the last time."

"I can't get enough of you."

"Put me down, Liam. I have something for you."

The change in Vi's tone pulls me from my lust, and I lower her feet to the ground but keep her trapped in my arms. I frown in disappointment when she adjusts her bodice to cover those delectable breasts.

"What is it?"

"Follow the instructions to set this up, put it on when you climb into my bed tonight, then text me when you've accomplished the task."

I blink several times, apprehension skating up my spine when she hands me a plain brown package from a pocket in her leather duster. "What is it?" I ask again.

"You will see. Do as I command."

I scowl at the parcel for a few minutes, confident as the day is long, I will not like what's inside. I raise my lids and peer into the unwavering gaze of my female, watching me keenly.

Shit. Here we go. "Yes, Mistress," I growl.

She smiles triumphantly, sweeps her lips across mine, and disappears.

Fuck me. This is going to be a long night.

I avoided the dreaded task for as long as possible, but eventually, I mumbled goodnight to Nox lounging on the couch watching TV, my siblings having sought their own beds hours ago.

Now here I stand by the side of the bed, nude, gawking in dismay at the apparatus laid out on the comforter. It's called a Hummer—a hands-free blow job machine.

What the ever-livin' fuck?

I read through the directions like ten times. It promises me one of the best oral experiences o my life.

Not fucking likely.

With a harsh sigh, I plug the black box into the outlet, snatch the dark water bottle looking funnel with a tube running out the top into the box, and lay the remote with twenty-five fucking settings next to me on the bed.

I stare at my phone for like ten minutes, deliberating whether I should fling the thing in the drawer and go to sleep or do as Viessa requested. No, ordered. I imagine her, wherever she is, nibbling on her fingernails in apprehension, waiting for my text.

With another sigh, I deliver the message before I change my mind.

A second later, her soft, sultry voice is in my head. *"Are you in bed, Liam? Text your reply."*

'Yes.'

"Is the device set up?"

'Yup.'

"Excellent."

I'm startled when my phone buzzes, and I answer it immediately.

"I enjoyed the feel of your lips on my breasts tonight, Liam." Against my will, my dick responds to the seductive melody of my mate in my ear, stretching up my abdomen, growing thicker by the second. "Are you hard for me, my king?"

I press the phone against my ear. "As a rock," I mutter, panting like a teenager about to experience sex for the first time.

"I wish I was there to taste you. Run my tongue along your cock, devour you with my mouth."

Fuck me, this is erotic as hell.

"But since I'm not, you will allow this gift to pleasure you instead. I desire to hear your breathing turn harsh as you grow closer to orgasm."

"Fuck, Viessa. I need *you.*"

"I know, baby. Soon. Now, connect the earbuds to your phone, so you don't have to hold it and then lube your beautiful cock for me."

I snatch the earbuds from the package, my hands shaking with excitement. Once the pieces are in place, I drop the phone onto the mattress next to me and squirt a generous amount of lube into my palm.

The second I stroke myself, a grunt of pleasure escapes.

"I love the sounds you make, my king. They get me so wet."

"Vi," I moan with need.

"Is your cock glistening?"

"Yes."

"Yes, what, Liam?"

My length pulses in my hand at the command in her tone. "Yes, Mistress."

"Good, boy. Now arrange the masturbator over your hardness and choose the lowest setting to begin."

I proceed as instructed, still fucking amazed I'm doing this. The second the weird contraption starts a pulsating suction, sliding up and down on my dick, my eyes roll back in my head, and I groan deep. "Oh, fuck me."

"Quite correct, Liam," she purrs. "That's precisely what this beauty is going to do."

Chapter 27

Nicole

"**I** forgot how much I loathe being on the lam," I grumble, traipsing through darkened streets in some bum fuck town of nowhere.

"At least this time we are together," my helpful mate offers grimly, his eyes scanning the surrounding area.

I smile up at him. "Very true, my love."

"If you did not have to eat, we would not be out here at all," he gripes, his hand tightening in mine briefly.

"I can't help it if I have a sudden craving for Jack-in-the-box tacos." My gaze surveys every human wandering the boulevards, monitoring for bulges that shouldn't belong. Not that mortals are our biggest concern and being surrounded by them provides us with a thin layer of protection. Since the winged idiots stand out like a virgin on prom night, the dark fae would never risk being photographed or captured on video.

I chuckle mentally. I'd wager the fae, and all those who can't pass as human, abhor the technological age.

When my new burner phone dings, I slip my fingers from Logan's warm palm and dig it out of my back pocket.

Alex: 'Hey, sista, how's it hangin?'

Me: 'Vertical. Looking for a Jack in the box. U?'

Alex: 'Sounds delish. Bas and I r heading to the cottage for some of my shit. Want to meet for a quick pow-wow? I miss u.'

I peek at my vigilant warrior. "Alexandria and the commander are gonna trace to my old home for supplies. Can we manage a get together for just a couple of minutes?"

He frowns down at me. "Could be a trap."

I can't help the eye roll. "Communicate with Bastian and find out for certain," I suggest sweetly, tongue in cheek.

He smirks but conducts a mental convo with his brother, who confirms they will be at the cottage in twenty minutes.

Without waiting for him to respond, I text back. '*See you in twenty. I'll bring tacos.*'

"Eee!" Alex squeals the second we materialize in the living room of my former home, launching herself into my arms. "I've freaking missed you."

"Jesus. It's been two weeks," I grumble, hugging her back after dumping the bag of tacos on the coffee table.

The brothers embrace in the way manly men do. "Is my baby bro losing his influence?" Logan grins broadly. "I am amazed you do not have your mate tied up in bed to keep her protected."

Sebastian chuckles. "That is the pot calling the kettle, brother, since I learned my evil ways from you."

"Touché'."

"We're standing right here." I roll my eyes and fight a grin.

"Let's leave the boys to their "whose dick is bigger" debate and help me gather some things." Alex laughs, snatching my wrist and yanking me down the hall to her bedroom.

"Why haven't you moved into the master suite?" I ask curiously, perching on the unicorn bedspread.

She shrugs and retreats inside her closet. "I don't know. No time yet, I guess." Garments fly out the doorway as she sifts through the messy chaos of her wardrobe.

An uneasy awareness settles in the pit of my stomach, and I trek to the window, dodging a flying shoe. As I peer out into the darkened forest beyond, the knot of anxiety swells. Maybe coming here was a terrible idea.

"Hurry up, Alex." I swivel toward the closet. "We've been here too..." The windows behind me explode inward, shooting glass and splinters of wood into the bedroom.

Before the fragments settle into the carpet, my guns are in my hands, and Alexandria comes racing out with daggers in each fist. Within a second, Bastian and Logan appear, their swords drawn.

For several anxious moments, we wait, eyes plastered to the gaping void. From my vantage point, I don't see any movement outside. Something blasted the window. So, where the fuck are they?

"Boys. Perimeter check," I breathe, edging closer to the opening.

"I am not leaving you," my mate snarls, his irises on high beam.

"Damn straight," the commander chimes in with a menacing growl.

"Does the title queen not mean a damn thing?" I retort in a loud whisper. "Do as I fucking command."

"Goddammit," Logan growls and glances at Bastian.

"Fuck," he replies. His gaze bounces to his little mate briefly before they both vanish.

In all honesty, I'd feel a shit ton better with them in my sight, but I need to identify what's lurking in the dark before we consider the cottage compromised. The boys could trace, so the witch isn't close. Yet.

"Do you think it's the fae?" Alex hisses as she creeps to the other side of the gaping hole and squints into the night.

"I'd bet good money. If push comes to shove, and if you can shift, do it." I search the surrounding darkness. "How the hell did they discover we were here so quickly?"

"I have many resources."

At the heavy rumble behind us, we both spin to confront the silver-eyed devil leaning against the doorjamb, the witch perched on the headboard.

Son of a bitch!

'*Logan, haul ass back here.*' I shout mentally, just as I hear Alex call for her mate.

"They can't hear you," Abigail announces quietly, and my gaze zeroes in on her.

She's stunning in a Bonnie and Clyde evil type of way. Her long, blonde hair is a riot of loose curls tumbling to her waist. Pale skin and heavy inky eyeliner showcase the eerie violet eyes. The lush lips painted blood red, are a startling contrast.

Translucent black silk drapes her slim frame, exposing her curves with only a narrow leather strap covering her small breasts and sex.

What I find fascinating is the gray iron crown on her head. It sits mid-forehead with a crystal jewel hanging down between her thin, arched eyebrows. The top has several sharp peaks that appear deadly. She chose an interesting metal, considering she's aligned with the fae.

"You must be Abigail Brevil," I say, eyeing her with disdain. We need them distracted until Logan and Bastian return.

"Love the crown," Alex sneers.

The violet eyes widen. "You've heard of me?" She glances briefly to my right, and a malicious light enters her gaze before she focuses on Alexandria. "And you're the valkyrie princess."

"There isn't much I don't perceive." I step closer to Alex.

Keep your focus on me, bitch. I wonder if it will make a difference if I drop Jag's name.

"Ah," her smile hardens, and it chills the air in my lungs. "Lucifer informed you of who I am."

Shit on a shingle. She reads minds.

Grayflame steps forward, his silver eyes lively with vengeful delight. "We finally come face to face, little Halfling. I've dreamed of this day for years."

"What is your beef with me, Syn?" I stall, struggling to formulate a way out of this predicament. When I'm within reach of Alex, I clasp her forearm and attempt to trace the fuck out of the house.

Nothing. I glance at the witch, and she smirks. *Dammit.* If I can't teleport, then it's a good bet my other abilities are MIA.

Before she can determine my thoughts further, I slam thick metal walls around my mind, hopefully shielding my intentions from the wily bitch. Darath's remarks in the garden bounce through my brain. If I get close enough, Jag claimed she's no match for me in hand-to-hand combat.

"Your very existence bothers me." Syn sneers. "The day you were born, they stole something extremely precious from me. You will pay the price with your very flesh."

"Oh, right. It has to do with the woman chained in your room. The one you've been torturing and raping?"

Pleasure spirals through me at his shocked expression before he conceals it and strides forward, his huge wings unfurling behind him.

I must admit, if I didn't loathe this creature, I'd find him eerily beautiful. The gleaming silver eyes under the slash of dark eyebrows, along with the high cheekbones, straight nose, and generous lips, come together to create model-perfect features. And the long, white hair and pointed ears only add to his appeal. Ya know, if you're into psychotic, evil defiler of women types.

"As I stated, there isn't much I don't comprehend."

He grins, and my insides hiccup. "Including her identity?" he asks with deceptive calm.

Shit.

"Well, I didn't say I knew everything," I smirk before raising both Glocks with the intent of discharging the magazines into his skull.

Nothing happens—no loud boom. No bullets eject from the muzzle, even though I squeeze the triggers repeatedly.

Goddamn witch.

I toss the guns aside, reach under my coat, and draw out my sword, just as a savage roar from outside shatters the unholy silence.

"Run, Alex!" I shout and dip into a battle stance, thrusting the fear for Logan and Sebastian to the background.

Alex matches my posture. "No fucking way."

Syn sneers as if my abilities mean nothing. "Would it shock you to discover the woman I have been persecuting and driving my cock into is none other than... mommy dearest?"

I snort. "Nice try, douchebag. Bridget is dead." What the fuck game is he playing?

"No, my dear. She is very much alive, and if you don't come peacefully, mom will suffer the consequences, along with you and the little valkyrie here."

I swallow at the truth in his words and glance at Alex, still eyeing the large fae with fury. Since a beautiful tawny lioness isn't standing before me, I'm assuming the witch has bound her ability to shift.

Holy God! My mother is alive. The worst part of this whole reveal, according to Viessa, Syn Grayflame is in love with her. *Yuck*!

"Even if that were true, Synie," I grin when his eyes narrow at my nickname, "Bridget hated my guts, and frankly, the feeling is mutual. So as a leverage point, it sucks."

Every second Logan and Sebastian are a no show, it becomes apparent we are on our own. Fear boils in my gut for my mate and the commander, but I can no longer stall.

Sick of this chitchat, I spin and shove Alex out the window. She yelps, landing with a soft thump on the gravel several feet below. In the next second, I fall to my knees and slide under Syn's massive wing, slashing my blade into his thigh as I pass. I spring to my feet and launch myself at Abigail. If I can disable or kill her, Grayflame is no match for me.

Before I draw close, an enormous wing slams into my shoulder, sending me careening into the opposite wall. The pain is acute, and I quickly realize Syn and the bitch are cheating. He's employing his considerable power when mine is virtually non existent.

If that's the case, why hasn't he put Alex and me to sleep already?

I attempt to stand, just as the fierce valkyrie leaps through the remnants of the window, her eyes dazzling silver spheres, her vivid red hair showcased in the strobing effects of her lightning streaking across the sky. Fuck. I wish she could shift and blow these idiots against the wall.

We both leap straight for Syn, who's wielding deadly looking scythes in each fist, his grin pure hatred.

"Logan! Behind you!" Sebastian's shout sends terror through my soul, but I focus on the threat in front of me.

Alex and I have sparred many times together. She is the perfect complement to my more aggressive technique. Her petite body twirls, vaults, and strikes with such speed you don't see her until it's too late. While my attack is more of a direct approach. But without my full strength, I quickly fatigue. And doesn't that just chap my hide?

My best friend slashes and stabs at Syn, working to get close to the witch who traces around the room to avoid the battle. "Alex, get the fuck out of here!" I shout.

With a whoosh of wings, Syn's behind me, and before I can pivot, the tip of his sword rips down my back, cutting through leather to lance open my skin. Fire shoots through my spine. I gasp at the pain but thrust it aside even as I stumble forward, attempting to spin in his direction to block another blow.

"Abi, quell the valkyrie," Syn bellows, releasing one of his scythes to latch onto my wrist, holding my sword.

I rear back my other arm to slam my fist into his leering face when an intense, searing pain stabs my abdomen.

Alex screams.

White-hot agony spreads through my gut. I peer down in stunned disbelief at the massive blade buried deep in my stomach, blood oozing around the gleaming silver.

This is it. The end has finally arrived for me. The death of my unborn child wasn't sufficient for the selfish, vengeful gods. They demand it all.

"Logan!" I shriek with my last ounce of energy, even though every instinct firing through my shattered heart shouts he's already dead.

Chapter 28

My bare feet slap the stone floor, the sound ricocheting off the walls as I dash down the barren corridor—the heavy thump of my heart pounds against my temples. I press harder, desperation nipping at my heels. Need to get outside, away from the mist, so I can trace to Oregon. Time is of the essence.

Without breaking stride, I shove the massive wooden doors open with just a mental order, the fresh tattoo on my shoulder pulsing with an inner light. Sharp stones pierce the soles of my feet, my hair flies out behind me in a dark, fluttering curtain, but I don't slow. Must escape the mist. Lives depend on me.

The second I pass through the suffocating shroud, I skid to a halt. My father stands serenely at the trailhead leading down the mountain, the engravings over his face and arms shimmering with light.

He holds up a palm as if to block me. "We cannot interfere, child."

"Are you fucking kidding me?" I pant, disbelief widening my gaze. "This is Logan we're talking about, father."

"The gods will advise us on the best course of action. Until then, we wait."

"Fuck you and the unseen gods," I growl, the glow from my irises lighting up the cliff wall. Strange vibrations take hold in my gut. "You saved Nicole to preserve the prophecy. Now it's my turn to save the mighty warrior for the same damn reason."

"Remember the price of that defiance?"

"Yes. And as devastating as it was, everyone survived it. Whatever the cost this time, we will endure again."

"And if the price is your life or mine?" He questions calmly.

That gives me pause until I recall the image of Logan's extreme torment. The poison destroying his organs one by one, his mind fracturing, believing his mate dead. The inner vibration intensifies. Anything is worth it to soothe his agony.

"I would willingly sacrifice my existence for his, the preservation of the prophecy, and the future of the immortal race."

My father smiles. "Well answered, child. Now, let us go save Lord Moretti."

We arrive at a quaint cottage nestled among towering woodlands with trunks the size of some cars. As we stroll through the front door, the atmosphere inside the dwelling is anything but tranquil.

They've spread Logan's sizable frame on the kitchen table, his enormous shitkickers hanging off the end. His bare chest glistens with perspiration, and the powerful body convulses as the vampiric healing powers fight the invading poison. His brother, Liam, Kurtis, and Lu hold him down. Cipher and Arra stand helplessly off to the left, while King Darath holds a weeping Kleora.

Ignoring them all, I head straight for Logan, my father right beside me.

"Thank God," Liam whispers when I come up next to him. "Can you help him?"

"We are here to try."

"Nicole and… Alex were captured," Sebastian stammers, his blue irises blinding in his distress. "I witnessed Syn… impale the queen with his blade."

"We know, my lord," Icarus soothes. "One worry at a time." My father nods for me to stand on the other side of Logan's torso, and everyone shifts to accommodate us while still maintaining their palms on the mighty warrior so he doesn't convulse off the table.

"When we place our hands on him, you will need to step back," I command even though I don't know what the inferno I'm expected to do. If my father hadn't come with me, I was just going to wing it and hope the gods answered my pleading and intervened.

They all nod, fear and worry etched in every line of their expressions. I thrust my concerns aside and settle one palm over the intricate Moretti tattoo on his chest and the other on his neck, mirroring my father on the other side.

The second we touch his feverish skin, the others let go, and Logan's imposing frame stills, but his eyes dart back and forth beneath his lids, his breathing rapid.

"Imagine the venom," Icarus instructs, and I focus my gaze on the deep puncture marks in his collar and torso. "Draw it into you. We must gather every individual molecule."

"What did this?" I ask Bastian.

"Basilisks."

I shudder, visualizing the snake–like creatures with the head of a rooster. It's suggested they can induce death with a glance and are quite venomous. It will take Divine intervention to save the huge warrior.

I shove the distractions from my mind and concentrate. Magical energy, unlike anything I've ever experienced, discharges from my mid–section through every limb. The electrical current raises my hair around me as if I'm standing in the center of a funnel.

My sight alters. No longer do I see the anxious faces of Logan's family and friends. I envision the cells traversing his bloodstream, being devoured by my light.

Without guidance, I chant an ancient spell I had no previous knowledge of and soon hear my father's tone blend with mine. On and on, over and over, we recite the words until my mind and body fatigue, but I dig my nails into the soldier's flesh, refusing to halt or surrender him.

I will never let go, Logan, I silently vow, urging the warrior to come back to us. Without understanding how, I slide into Logan's mind and gasp at the pain, devastation, and agony saturating every thought.

"*Fight, damn you!*" I shout into his brain and witness a glimmer of green amidst the chaos.

Chapter 29

Well, this just fucking sucks. My powers are nonexistent—thanks to the bitch, Abigail. Although she was nice enough to repair the gaping wound in my gut. So at least there's that.

As soldiers haul me down a dimly lit, stone passageway, the influence of Syn's stupid sleep inducement ability presses on my intellect. I'm fighting it tooth and nail, but my lids are like lead, and I force one foot in front of the other.

My muddled brain is cognizant enough to understand they've taken me to the Dark Fae Stronghold in Scotland. Which means the odds of rescue are… slim to none.

I reach out mentally to Logan. Still no response. I refuse to consider my fierce mate isn't with me any longer. I paid the god's fucking price. If they take him from me, I will burn this world to the ground before joining him.

No. Stop thinking that way. It's just the witch blocking our link with the added restriction of Syn's shield. He's fine. Probably working on a plan to get to me right now.

The second the winged fuckers throw me into a silver barred cell, the lethargic pull on my brain lifts. I eye Syn with dispassion as he stalks to the rails.

"Don't bother trying to escape," he coos, and I itch to yank off a pointed ear. "The enclosure is coated with silver, and my beautiful Abigail has cast a spell to neutralize your powers. And let's not overlook the petite valkyrie. She will suffer if you misbehave." He steps closer, gripping the bars, his smile pure malevolence. "I look forward to our one-on-one time, Halfling."

Before he can turn away, I reach through the rods, clutch a fist full of his white locks, and yank, smashing his face into the metal. The resounding crunch of his nose breaking and the blood gushing from his nostrils temporarily satisfies my inner vampire.

"You fucking, bitch," he bellows and lurches back, his palm over his already swelling beak.

"You think I'm afraid of rape or torture, Syn? You forget who my father was. That's a Sunday afternoon for me."

The bright eyes glitter with violence as he plucks a handkerchief from his pocket, mopping the blood from his lips and chin, the cartilage already healed.

Pity.

"We shall see," he pivots, heading for the stone stairs his Custodians just dragged me down. "Rest up, vampire. We begin at daybreak."

"I look forward to it!" I shout after him.

Holy fuck. Now what?

I shove aside the panic for Logan, Sebastian, and Alex clawing up my vertebrae and examine my new prison. Since it's lined with silver, it's realistic to assume the jackass has no notion this girl is immune. If the witch can read minds, best to keep that secret locked down.

In one corner, tight to the rock ceiling, a small webcam follows me around the twelve-by-twelve space. Great.

They shoved a rickety-looking cot against the far wall, with a tattered blanket and a flat as a pancake pillow with no cover.

Under the camera sits a dingy metal pail with a roll of toilet paper lying next to it. Well, at least they were gracious enough to keep the makeshift commode out of view of prying eyes. I suppose I should be thankful for small favors.

As a Halfling, I eat and drink like a mortal, although not as frequently, and I still require blood to survive. Logan's blood. How long will I last without either and no powers to repair my organs when they shut down from lack of nourishment?

A low moan in the next cell catches my attention. A petite form, buried in the disgusting blanket, shifts on a cot similar to mine. I contemplate it warily, waiting to see who my new roomie is. A brilliant patch of red hair emerges, and I suck in a breath as Jilaya's battered face moves into view. The reason she's been MIA for the past month becomes clear.

I knew it.

"Oresha?" I whisper and traipse over to the bars separating us, mindful not to touch them in case the voyeur is observing.

Bright blue eyes circled by black and purple contusions zero in on mine, and she bolts upright. The long, tangled tresses stick up everywhere. Her leather skirt has a rip up one side showcasing pale legs sprinkled with lacerations and bruises. Generous breasts nearly spill out of the frayed, blood-stained tank top.

Shit. Even beat up, the succubus appears sexy as hell.

"Dammit, Nicole," she grumbles, leaning her arms on her thighs. "How the hell did he get to you?"

"Ambushed us. He must have been monitoring our safe houses." When she lifts a dark eyebrow in question, I explain. "They stormed the castle, so we went on the lam until I received a text from Alex wanting to meet for just a few minutes at our old house to pick up supplies. I arrogantly believed I was untouchable."

"Is she here?" Queen Oresha asks softly, shoving her thick, matted hair out of her face. She winces when her fingers brush her temple.

"Yeah. Somewhere."

"He will use her as leverage against you."

Fuck.

"For what?"

She shrugs. "I don't have the vaguest idea. All I know is he despises you with a passion and craves to make you suffer."

"Perfect."

"And let me guess, you can't connect with your hunky warrior?"

"Nope."

"So, we're basically screwed. Nice going."

"Not to worry, succubus. I can guarantee my team is working on a strategy as we speak. I just need to remain alive long enough for them to implement it."

"Well. If he kills you, I call dibs on Logan."

I almost reach out and grip the bars but remember the peeping eyes from the camera at the last second. "You touch him, and I will come back from the fiery depths and haunt your ass for all eternity. Trust me, I've done it before."

She shrugs. "It might be worth it." I'm mollified somewhat by the twinkling of humor in her gaze.

"Why the hell are you here? I assumed you and silver eyes were tight?"

"We were. Until I moved against him in the vote to keep you as queen," she gazes at me dispassionately. "Clearly a mistake."

"Imprisoning and torturing you seems a bit extreme, even for him."

"Yes, well. I also fucked his son, who promptly fell in love with me."

"You have a thing for winged men?" I ask curiously.

She lifts her brows. "They certainly know how to use them to maximum advantage, but I'm a succubus. I have a sexual thing for all creatures. It's how I survive."

"Oh, right. Sex is your fuel like blood is for vampires."

"Exactly." She leans back against the wall with a theatrical sigh, her lids lowering. "Unfortunately, if I don't slaughter them during sex, they fall madly in love with me and become annoyingly stalky."

"Ah, the burdens we must bear."

One eye opens, and she snorts at my sarcastic remark. "I'm starving. You wouldn't consent to a lengthy kiss and fondle through the bars to fuel me up, would you?"

"Sorry, Succubus. I don't bat for that team."

She sighs heavily. "I figured as much. Have you tried to speak telepathically with anybody besides your scrumptious mate?"

I nod my head for the camera. "Yes. I can't reach anyone." But I mouth the word, '*No.*'

'*Do you hear me? Blink once if you can.*' Maybe if we are in the same vicinity, it might work.

The queen blinks her open eye.

Whoopie. I can communicate secretly with my cellmate. I smell freedom already.

I peer at my watch and realize I have no inkling what time of day it is here, and since I don't suffer the vampire Spidey sense of the approaching dawn, and with no windows, it could be noon or midnight. My torture might be minutes away or hours. I'm not a patient woman. The not knowing is torment itself.

Sky blue irises follow me as I sit cross-legged on the cot with my back to the damp wall. I lower my lids and force my mind into a meditative state, which I've never been very good at, but desperate times and all that.

I concentrate on slowing my breathing and heart rate, clearing all the clutter from my brain, and fixating on a particular image—Logan. My mate's voice reached me in purgatory, here's hoping he can reach me through the witch's barrier.

'Logan. Please hear me.'

Chapter 30

"Where the fuck is Darath?" Logan growls, pacing the dining room at Bastian's Italian villa with restless agitation. And who could fault him? Syn has his mate, doing God knows what to her.

After an all-night séance-like event, the big Guardian bolted upright, shouting Nicole's name just as the first rays of dawn greeted the sky. Viessa collapsed in my arms, and Icarus was so weak he could barely stand.

Lu, Sebastian, and Darath traced everyone to this more secure location for the vampires.

What's strange is Sebastian's response to his mate being held prisoner. He's transformed into a stone-cold strategist, analyzing charts, flight plans, and maps to the ancient castle in Scotland. They depict schematics and vague architectural plans dating back to its construction.

Scattered along the opulent table are current satellite images of the dark fae's ancient fortification, including the Isle of Skye's rugged landscapes, which showcase the indented coastline of peninsulas and narrow lochs radiating out from a mountainous interior surrounded by the North

Sea. Unfortunately, spanning the vast area around the fae's castle is merely flat grassland. No coverage. Scotland is rich in green scenery with a violent history spanning centuries.

"He will be here in a few minutes," Sebastian responds, typing furiously on his laptop. "Claimed he needed to consult with another witch." The intense blue gaze flickers to Icarus briefly. "Do you think you can cloak our movements until we've breached the shield?"

"Yes, my lord," the Oracle acknowledges from his position on the floor. He's sat cross-legged in the corner meditating since we arrived several hours ago.

"That has to be our priority when we get through the shield; locate Abigail and put her down," I suggest. "If we don't, she'll suck our powers and render us useless against her and the fae."

"Leave Miss Brevil to Viessa and me," Icarus announces. "Your principal concern is rescuing the queen and young Alexandria."

"I camped my SEAL team in this mountainous range ten clicks from the Northwest perimeter of the shield awaiting orders," Kurtis states, pointing to the terrain surrounding the flatlands of the dark fae fortress. He's covered in the same combat gear of the SEALS, including Kevlar and a sick looking M4A1 Assault rifle hanging down his chest loaded with iron bullets. "Since they are human, if they're discovered, we hope they take no notice of them. It took some convincing, but the team is aware of the supernatural element of this mission. Your Guardians will need to wipe their memories when the operation is over. Also, a contingent of my best Sentinels watch their six two clicks north of their position."

We all nod in agreement as I adjust my MK18 at my chest. I clothed my upper body similar to Kurtis, but I went with leather pants for added protection against the elements. A SIG Sauer P226 rides my hip next to three spare magazines, with an Arming Sword strapped to my spine. Sebastian and Logan are bare-chested as usual, their sole weapons; two Long Swords sheathed on their backs.

Lucretia is in full leather combat attire, her Bastard Sword jutting above her shoulder, and her black duster laden with various daggers and throwing stars, all forged with iron.

Cipher and Arra arrived a few minutes ago, advising us they sent their teams, along with my Wardens, on ahead to Scotland in a private jet.

"Good," Bastian nods. "Have them standby at the airport. We do not send in any additional troops until we are ready to deploy. The less energy Icarus has to utilize in cloaking us, the better, but I do not wish to make the fae aware of our presence until the shield drops. The sun is about to ascend in Inverness, so we must wait until dusk before we take our battle stations. All Guardians will trace to the airport to help transport the shifters and valkyries when the time arrives."

"Agreed," I acknowledge, and Viessa clutches my hand.

A few minutes after we arrived, she disappeared, and returned clad in her warrior outfit from the night at the club before collapsing next to her father. After her rest, instead of meditating, she remains strong by my side.

Fear shoots through me the fae could harm my fragile mate with no combat skills during this siege, but I keep reminding myself every few minutes—my woman is a powerful Oracle and, according to her, deadly with a bow.

Heat spirals through my groin, recalling what transpired in my closet, not to mention our compromise. Now that she's linked to me, the vampire can detect all my emotions, not just the strong ones. It raises my hackles for an entirely different reason.

Buried deep in my soul, under a lifetime of lies I told myself, I get off on submitting to my female, and it terrifies me. I dread that part will engulf the beast, dismantle my confidence as a leader, and weaken me in the eyes of my peers.

No matter what develops between Vi and me, our murky desires must never see the light of day. Our sexual activity needs to remain concealed. Not that I've ever been one to kiss and tell, but men talk. Fuck, women are famous for prattling about sex with their friends. Shit. I have to warn her again not to confide in Lu or any of the others. It's bad enough the vampire commander is aware of our proclivities and even participated by training Vi.

"Icarus, as soon as the sun sets, you and Vi work on dismantling the cover." Sebastian orders with a brisk nod. "Kurtis, deploy your team. I need eyes inside that castle. Priest, once the mortal team is in position, teleport Kurtis and Liam. Ruse, arrange your Sentinels strategically around the shield, but keep them hidden. Scott, until I arrive, you direct the human team's movements within. No shifting. Either of you. And Wolf," The vivid blues flicker periodically. A definite sign Bastian is not as cool as he would like everyone to believe. "I cannot stress this enough. You are *not* to enter the castle until the witch is secure. You are a liability to us all with that chip in your spine."

Fuck. If Vi is in trouble, I'll be inside that structure in a heartbeat.

Sebastian sees it in my expression but doesn't press further. It wasn't too long ago he thought Alex was dead, murdered by his mother. The agony of her alleged death sent him spiraling until he eventually couldn't stand the torment and tethered himself in silver inside the Roman Colosseum to greet the sun. Both the Moretti brothers suffered the potential loss of their mates, and nothing would keep them from protecting them now. Even the loss of their own lives.

"Roger that," Kurtis responds, and I nod but utter no promise. The shifter pulls out his cell phone to start the ball rolling, and the Oracle saunters toward us.

Just as our trio sets to teleport, Jagorach materializes with a towering male dressed in a full-length midnight robe, his head covered with a hood. A dark beard, generous lips, and the tip of his nose are the only features peeking from underneath the darkened edge.

"This is Troy Tenebris," Jag introduces. "He's an impressive witch of black magic and has conceded to aid us on the condition we hand over Brevil to him."

"For what purpose?" I ask curiously. The male stands six and a half feet with the broad shoulders of a warrior. What could he possibly want with Abigail?

"Not your concern, King Scott." Troy's tone is such a heavy baritone; it's difficult to discern the separate pronunciations of each word.

"I do not give a fuck why you require the bitch as long as you help retrieve our mates," Logan growls. The emerald irises spark and dull in harmony with his clenching fists.

"Do we even know if your women are alive," the witch dares to inquire.

"Yes," Sebastian answers abruptly when his brother only provides a low, threatening growl and a display of deadly fangs. "Logan felt Nicole's presence earlier."

"Interesting."

"Do not perform your vile magic until requested, Tenebris," the priest commands. He gives Troy a malicious sideways glance, the blue irises swirling. Vi glances at her father, a frown marring her features.

"I'm not here to interfere, Oracle. I just want Abigail."

"If true, it would be a first," Icarus mutters before grabbing mine and Kurtis' wrists. From the sounds of it, the High Priest Oracle and Troy have a history and not a good one.

I peer at my beautiful female with an encouraging smile and a quick wink. "See you in a few hours, sweetness."

"Please be careful," she whispers, worry darkening her scrutiny. "There may be basilisks in the area."

I nod. Before the room darkens, I regard the Moretti brothers. "YODO." (You only die once)

"Not today, King Scott," Logan vows, his stare intense.

Moments later, we touchdown, and a group of men, ranging in age and size, have their weapons zeroed in on us.

A burly male separates himself from the contingent. "Sire?"

"Stand down, commander." Kurtis barks.

"Yes, Sir." The captain raises his palm, and the rest of the soldiers holster their firearms. The anxiety in my shoulders eases.

"As soon as the sun sets, you and your men will advance closer and provide cover for the Oracles to work the shield. Is that understood?"

"Roger that. We are here to assist in any way we can, Sir. Your human SEAL team progressed through the barrier several minutes ago. We have coms set up." He hands Kurtis a rugged tablet and earpiece. "That is a real group of pipe hitters for certain."

"The best," Kurtis acknowledges with pride.

"The shield is in place around your group to conceal your movements from the fae," the little priest mutters next to me.

"Thank you, priest. We'll meet up later."

The Oracle bows slightly before departing.

"My lord, will your Wardens be arriving soon?"

"Yes, they should land in Inverness within the hour. King Darath and his Warriors plan to greet them at the airport and transport them here when ready. The Guardians, Protectors, and Storm Walkers will converge at the designated time."

The commander rubs his golden beard. "I've never laid eyes on a Storm Walker before. Are they as beautiful as rumored?"

"Only met their ruler, Priestess Tanagra, and she is as gorgeous as she is deadly."

He grunts in response before giving his King and me a mission report of their time here in Scotland.

"Liam, since you've seen Abigail, why don't you handle coms for the SEALS, and I will organize my Sentinels," Kurtis says, passing me the earpiece and tablet showing live feeds of the team's movements.

As I observe and tune in to this group of men, it gets my adrenaline pumping. I understand now why Kurtis joined their team. They operate like a well-oiled machine-a solid unit, able to anticipate each other's moves and follow orders without question.

I stride over to a large tree and lean against the coarse bark while monitoring the developments inside the castle. The company already invaded the belly of the stone beast. They stay in the shadows to prevent detection as they advance with stealth through the structure.

"Master Chief, this is King Scott. Are you in a position to provide me a Sitrep?"

"Roger that," the hard tone whispers. "Breached interior, two mikes ago. Employing NVDs. (Night Vision Devices) Encountered no hostiles at this time. Confirmation on standard ROE, Sir?" (Rules of Engagement)

"Affirmative, Chief. Break off into two teams," I instruct. "Locate the Dungeon. Utilize silencers, but leave no evidence.

We do not want the fae aware of your location. This OP is ISR only." (Intelligence, surveillance, reconnaissance)

"Copy that. Bravo one will locate lower levels. Bravo two continue upward."

"Copy. Bravo one, proceeding to the second level."

I settle the pad on my thigh for a moment and focus on Kurtis directing his team with brisk efficiency. I nod to my best friend when he glances my way before squatting in the lush grass. The mortal military uses much of the same jargon the immortals do. It makes commanding this elite outfit a seamless endeavor.

I return my concentration to the live feed of the humans, risking their lives as they silently eliminate a lone Custodian here and there as they advance through the immense castle. The structure certainly isn't the magnitude of the Vampire Stronghold, which boasts a diameter of twelve acres and four stories. This ancient stone architecture is more condensed, soaring seven stories into the night sky but only spreading out two or three acres.

A flash of color in the video catches my eye. "Bravo two, take cover. HVT in sight." (High-value target) The men immediately blend into the surrounding shadows. "Maintain your position."

I recognize the blond curls bouncing down the corridor and hold my breath. Abigail is no more than thirty feet down a long, dark hallway, heading right for the squad. "Do not engage Bravo two," I instruct quietly. We have no notion if a bullet will take her out or not. The last thing we need is the SEAL team's cover blown.

Each step the blonde takes tightens my nerves. If she discovers them, they are as good as dead. But as I study the lethal female, I must admit, the witch is stunningly beautiful, even with the heavy eye makeup. The sinister-looking crown on her head gives me the heebie-jeebies.

She halts a mere ten feet from the SEALS. My heart nearly pounds out of my chest as I wait to learn if she'll spot them. She captures a long, platinum curl and toys with it for several seconds before pivoting and heading down a passage to the left.

My breath escapes in a whoosh at the near miss. "Charlie Mike (Continue mission) with extreme caution Bravo two," I direct, and the men slip from the shadows.

"*Liam*," Viessa's voice enters my head. "*Stay safe.*"

Her soft, loving tone soothes the knot between my shoulders. One day, I hope my female will bear my mark so I can respond in kind.

No matter what arises in the coming hours, rescuing Nicole and Alex is our top priority, but I must safeguard my fragile but resilient mate at all costs.

Chapter 31

While Jilaya naps, I welcome the opportunity to pee before my bladder ruptures and reassess my predicament. I have nothing to pick the lock with, and even if I did, the constant eyes from above guarantee a flock of feathered men would be on me in a millisecond.

Where are they keeping Alex? If anything happens to her, I'll tear this fucking castle apart, but not before Sebastian will fly into a rampage and slaughter every last fae. My commander has demonstrated he can't function without the little valkyrie—which is still somewhat of a shocker.

Not that I wouldn't be worthless if something happened to Logan or vice versa. No doubt he's going insane, trying to figure out a way to get to me. And while relief lessened the knot between my shoulders when I perceived his psychic presence earlier, we couldn't communicate directly.

I'm about to tackle another dreaded meditation session when four large fae stomp down the stairs. Jilaya bolts upright, her eyes wide with trepidation. How many times have they dragged her from her cell and beat the crap out of her?

But instead of approaching her cage, the quartet veers toward mine. Oh boy. It must be close to dawn. Which means no rescue until sunset.

Shit.

"Kin' Grayflame requests yer company." The big burly redhead states with a heavy Scottish accent and a vicious sneer.

"Perfect. I was just missing the pointy-eared fucker."

"Don't fight him, Nicole," Jilaya warns softly. "It simply makes it worse."

Before I can respond, the big, ugly redhead sucker punches me in the gut. I fold over, sinking to my knees, gasping for the oxygen forced from my lungs. Before I recover, he snaps my arms behind my back and slaps on silver cuffs.

I wince dramatically, even adding in a little whimper before they hoist me to my feet. I shoot my cellmate a sideways glance and wink. "Duly noted," I wheeze.

"You're a damn glutton for punishment." She shakes her head in disgust before flopping back down on her bunk.

"Haud yer wheesht," (Shut up.) the fella on my left spits. I gape at his mismatched eyes. One is black as night while the other is purple. Purple. "'En yoo're suin in fur a real treat, vampire."

I lean closer. "Doesn't fae society consider irises like yours a genetic defect? No wonder you're delegated to dungeon patrol."

I expect the punch, hell I egged him on, but the pain exploding through my cheek is excessive. The redhead behind me tightens his hold on my arms to keep me vertical.

My hair shrouds my face as I thrust the burn aside and snicker. "Wait, I was wrong." I lift my head and grin broadly. "It's because you hit like a girl."

When he raises his fist to have another go at me, I lean back, use carrot top as leverage, and strike out with my boot, nailing crazy eyes squarely in the nose. He staggers backward, clutching his face.

"Ye huir," he whines around the blood oozing from his nostrils. I don't speak Scot, but I think that means bitch.

I jerk forward and down, hurling the meaty fae up and over my shoulders and into the moron still bellowing more strange profanities from the floor. They go careening into the silver bars in a tangled mess as I leap up and draw my shackled wrists in front of me.

After a hasty breath, I vault over the two jackasses and slam into the third while kicking the fourth in the head. My vampiric powers may be dormant, but the best trained me in combat. And if I learned anything from Kurtis, it's to go on the offensive and always take your adversary by surprise.

"Grab 'er!" The redhead bellows from the opening to my cage. Before he can advance, I smash my fist into his jaw, battering him into his comrade, and slam the cell door shut. Thank God, it locks automatically.

I comprehend it's simply a matter of time before the watchful eyes from above send further troops, but I'm having too much fun to care. With only two fae to crush, one as substantial as Kurtis, I perform a running slide across the slick stone floor, knock the big guy's feet out from under him, and punch the other in the balls.

"Eww," I scold the idiot keening like a girl. "You guys don't wear underwear under those kilts?"

Before he can recover, I whirl and race toward the stairs. "I'll be back for you, Jilaya," I call out over my shoulder. "Just hang tight."

When I reach the top of the landing, the huge white-winged jerk on my heels, I'm astonished when the wooden exit swings wide. I skid into a cavernous space of mortar and stone, before spinning and slamming the door shut on the large fae's bulbous snout just as he reaches the landing. I can't help but snicker at the sound of curses and thuds as he goes careening back down the steep steps.

No latch. Dammit. I twist to pinpoint the next exit when a dozen or more winged fuckers spill into the chamber from multiple entrances.

Well, balls.

"Thank you for joining us, Nicole."

I twist to my right as Syn saunters into the room, barefoot and bare-chested with low-hung jeans hugging his hips.

"I aim to please," I mutter and try not to gape at the deep, brutal scars across his chest while covertly examining the space.

This isn't an ordinary entryway to the dungeon below. No, this is a bona fide torture chamber, equipped with iron and silver medieval tools that make my sphincter pucker. Oh boy. This might be slightly worse than I imagined.

"Even without your powers, you are resourceful."

"Yeah, I get that a lot. People always underestimate me." I inch away from Syn. I'd rather take my chances with his untrained Custodians than with the king himself.

Stall, Nicki. Fucking stall.

"Can I ask you a question?"

"Why not," he says with a wave of his hand and leans against a wooden table that looks like some sort of stretching machine. *Jesus.* "I'm feeling generous this morning. Even though you beat the crap out of four of my men."

"Yes, well. A girl's gotta do what a girl's gotta do." I advance a few inches to the left. If I can just get through one of the doors, I may be able to discover a fucking way out of this hell hole.

"Indeed."

As if on cue, the dungeon door slams open and the four idiots come flying into the room. The big redhead in the lead halts in his tracks when he spots his king, the others slam into him. I'd bust out laughing at their antics if my situation wasn't so dire. These buffoons are hilarious.

Syn straightens from the table. "You failed me for the last time." He signals several of the Custodians surrounding the room. "Take them. Cleave their wings from their backs and feed them to the basilisk."

Oh shit. That's rather harsh.

I'm about to say as much when those silver eyes refocus on mine and the white-haired king resumes his casual lean against the vile torture device. "Now, where were we?"

Wow. This guy is all kinds of scary.

"Why is it you don't have a Scottish accent like the rest of your heathens here?"

"I grew up in the states," he utters with a shrug.

"Seriously? How did you travel around without being spotted by humans?" With those pointed ears, silver eyes, and wings, he would never pass for a human.

"We lived in a very remote territory of Alaska. The state was not discovered until 1741, so in the early 1100s, it was easy never to encounter another individual for years. Just the occasional native now and again."

"Interesting." I honestly couldn't give a shit, but I need to keep him talking. The longer he's Chatty Cathy, the less time spent torturing me. "So that makes you how old?"

He crosses his arms over his chest with a sneer. "Let us just say over 900 and leave it at that."

"Yeah, I can imagine once you hit three centuries, you stop counting."

"Stall all you wish, little Halfling. I have all day."

Fuck.

"All right. You mind informing me why you despise me so much?"

He straightens from the table, his eyes flaring. Shit. Probably should've left that topic for last.

"It's a lengthy narrative," he begins, prowling toward me, but I hold my ground. "Your mother and I were lovers. We had intentions to spend the rest of our lives, well, the rest of her existence, together. But during a violent skirmish with the vampires, instead of killing me, your father took me captive. After weeks of torture, he demanded one thing."

Syn stops mere inches from me. Before I think it through, I boldly graze my fingers down a nasty groove along his pectoral. The king sucks in a breath.

"Did my father do this to you?" Whatever Dimitri beat him with, he must have laced with salt to leave a permanent scar on an immortal.

He seizes my wrist in a painful grip, and I peer into the vengeful face of my enemy.

"Yes," he grates out between clenched teeth.

"Why?"

"He required your mother's location."

I stare at him for several seconds, unable to extrapolate the words he just uttered. "Why?" My query is a mere whisper between us.

"Your father was already cognizant there was a prophecy, although not the details, and sought to slay mommy before you could be conceived."

"That doesn't make sense. He had sex with Bridget, or I wouldn't be here."

"Yes," he hisses in rage. "Apparently, she seduced Giordano with some dark magic spell, and he couldn't bear to kill her. Sentimental idiot."

"So why didn't he just slit my throat right after I was born? No one knew about the prophecy or our physical link until I was a teenager."

"Mommy dearest was a clever, conniving woman, but deep down, she couldn't allow Dimitri to harm you, so she went into hiding."

I wrench my hand away and step back. "That's bullshit," I growl. My fangs shoot from my gums, and a gray glow illuminates Syn's handsome face. "My mom stood by and did nothing while that bastard raped and tortured me for years."

After a deep contemplative inhale, the king strolls over to a long bench with silver shackles at each end. His white wings lay relaxed down his spine, gently undulating with each breath. "By the time he located Bridget, your father was fully aware of the consequences of destroying you, so he understood he must defile you in another way. Your mother allowed it to happen. She *claims* she had no choice."

He lovingly caresses the scarred, discolored wood, and I shudder, perceiving this is where he plans to exact his revenge.

"In her defense," he frowns. "And I cannot believe I am about to say this. She was just a pawn in a deity's sick games. A weak, pathetic human."

"Obviously, she didn't die after I fled. So, where has she been all this time?" And what deity is he talking about?

"Where she belongs." His silver gaze pins mine, and I swallow. "With me."

Holy crap. "You've been holding her prisoner and torturing her for almost ten years?" And he claimed Dimitri was a sentimental—albeit deranged—idiot.

He blinks several times. "Has it been that long?"

Good God. This creature is unbalanced.

"If my father did that to you," I point to the ruined flesh on his chest. "Why in God's name did you fight alongside him at the battle?"

"I needed you alive, young halfling. If I had killed your father, you would be dead and all this," he waves his hand around the room, "using you as a pawn in my revenge against Bri and the deity, would not be possible."

He's crackers. That's the only explanation. But let's get off the subject of killing me. "Don't you think Bridget's atoned already for whatever sin you suspect she committed?"

"You tell me, Nicole. Have I punished her enough for betraying her mate to the sick pervert you called father? I learned much too late it was your mother who gave up my location to Dimitri. He received an anonymous tip on where and when I was most vulnerable. She was wise enough to slip back into the shadows after her betrayal." He slams his fist against his chest. "For keeping her whereabouts safe, I will bear these scars for the rest of my days. Because of her treachery, her alliance with King Giordano, you suffered as well."

"But, why did she side with my father against you?" That's like jumping from the frying pan into the fire.

"Because your filthy tattooed Oracle orchestrated every pawn on the chessboard to ensure your birth. He is the reason we all suffered."

What. The. Ever. Living. Fuck.

Chapter 32

"Has the sun set yet?" I ask for the hundredth time, squirming restlessly. Over a hundred Guardians sleep on mats scattered around the house as we all wait for the enormous ball of fire to sink below the horizon in Scotland. Fatigue and anxiety ride my shoulders as I hunch over the dining room table. The schematics before me blur. I blink to clear my vision and refocus on the photographs I've stared at for hours.

My father sighs patiently next to me. "No, child. One mo re…"

Icarus arches, his fingers white knuckling the arms of his chair. All movement in the room stops. Logan and Sebastian, who were conversing quietly in the corner, stride toward the Oracle, their expressions filled with apprehension.

"Father?" I spread my palm over his to mitigate whatever is transpiring when a forceful vision slams into my frontal lobe at the touch. I gasp, seeing what Icarus foresees. Worse yet, my body feels every lash as if it were on my skin, and I moan in agony.

Nicole lies stretched out on a dull wooden table, her wrists and ankles shackled at each point. Strips of cloth and leather, I'm assuming were formerly her clothes, hang haphazardly from her frame, shredded by the lashes of the whip King Grayflame brandishes.

Various red, angry welts scatter her chest, abdomen, and thighs—several deep enough to seep blood. Nicki's livid stare appears frozen. Her jaw clamped tight. She doesn't cry out, scream, or even moan as the flashing point snaps across her skin. The sole indication she's in any pain is the slight jerk of her body.

Everything in me wants to rush to her aid, accept the lashes for her, free her from this nightmare. Since that's impossible, I peer around the place, noting the number of fae surrounding it and where each exit is situated. If nothing else, I can at least get intel back to Logan and Sebastian.

The woman from my previous vision sits chained against the far wall, amply clothed this time. Tears spill down her cheeks as she pleads with the king to stop.

"Please, Syn," she weeps. "I'm the one you are angry with. Take it out on me, not my daughter."

Ah, so the woman King Grayflame holds captive and possesses some dark affection for is Nicole's mother. I wasn't aware the queen had any family.

"No, my pet. I'm not angry." The bright silver irises turn on the female, his naked, scarred chest heaving from exertion. "I'm beyond angry. Since I can't take my wrath out on the Oracle for his duplicity, that leaves the two of you." He swings back to Nicole. "Now shut your lying, vicious mouth, or your offspring's suffering will escalate."

"You are a cowardly piece of shit, Synie," Nicki rasps. "Does it make you feel all manly to torture a restrained woman? Grow a pair of brass balls and fight me. Equal footing. No powers."

"While the notion appeals," he drones. "This is much more gratifying."

"Fuck you."

"We may get to that later."

Nicole struggles against her bonds. "I will die before I let you touch me."

"Oh, come now," he taunts, flipping the whip back and forth on the stone floor. "Just admit you enjoyed what Dimitri did to you."

"Syn!" Nicole's mother dares admonish, and I'm fascinated when a stain darkens the king's pale cheeks, and he lowers his head contritely.

But in the next second, he strikes out at the queen's mother. The shot is so precise; it hits her cheek but doesn't break the skin. She cringes, folding in on herself, as much as she can with her wrists shackled to the wall, as if preparing for more blows.

"You fucking bastard!" Nicki howls, yanking against her bonds. "I will eviscerate you; you piece of shit."

Just when he raises his arm to go at the queen again, the witch steps from the shadows. "Halt."

Syn immediately lowers the whip. "What is it, Abi?"

"We have visitors."

She shifts her bright, wicked gaze with pinpoint precision on Icarus and me. My insides clench and I peek at my father next to me. Surprised to see his face is a livid mask of fury.

"Troy is coming for you, Abigail. Fair warning," he announces in a deadly calm manner.

The witch's eyes expand. Why the hell is he warning her? And how can he communicate in the vision?

"Cease this, or your death is imminent."

"What's happening, Witch?" Syn barks, his gaze bouncing around the room, unable to see or hear us.

She ignores Grayflame, concentrating on my father and me. "Would you hand your daughter over to the devil?" she demands. I gasp in stunned disbelief. "Oh wait, I'm sorry, you did that already." Her eerie violet eyes snap to mine. "I see *Daddy* didn't educate you I was his flesh and blood? I suppose that makes you and I sisters."

Her irises darken when they rotate to Icarus. She clamps her palms together, producing a ball of purple light between her hands. "Tell Troy to come and get me. I'll be waiting."

When she raises the luminous sphere, as if to pitch it in our direction, my father clutches my wrist in a crushing hold. We slam back into our bodies hard enough to slosh my brain against my skull.

My eyes pop open. I wrench my hand off of my father's, leap to my feet, and send my chair careening into the wall.

"What the fuck did you witness?" Logan demands, his enormous hands planted on the table opposite me. "Where are Nicole and Alex?"

"I…" My mind is still in shock over what Abigail revealed. The witch is my sister.

"Is she alive?" The formidable warrior asks softly, his jaw clenching with his emotion.

"Yes." His lids lower on a sharp exhale. "But…" green fire snaps to mine with such intensity I swallow.

"But what?"

"Syn is…" I hesitate in fear. "He's torturing her."

Logan erupts in a furious storm, vaulting over the table for my throat. Instinctively, I raise my hand and suspend him mid-leap.

Holy shit! I stare at my palm in confusion. I didn't realize I had that skill.

I merely gawk at the crazed brute across the wooden surface. His mouth hangs open in a snarl, massive fangs craving to rip me apart hanging low. The magnificent green eyes glow bright, with a layer of tears threatening, and his muscles bulge, bracing to tear into anyone in his torment.

"Viessa, did you see Alex?" Sebastian asks, his hands in the air, worried I'll hold him in stasis.

"No, Commander. She was not in the room." I glance down at my father, still sitting in his chair, eerily silent.

"Step behind Christoph, young Oracle. When I have Logan secure, please release him." the Guardian instructs.

When I nod, Mr. Nox's powerful body strides in front of me. I peek around his massive shoulder. The second Bastian wraps his brother's heaving chest in his embrace; I revoke my influence, still amazed I could pinpoint my ability to just Logan.

Instead of fighting him, Logan deflates, turning in his brother's arms. "She suffers, Bastian, and I am once again powerless to protect her." His tone is guttural as he clutches Sebastian's shoulders in a death grip.

The commander holds on to his brother until the low rumbling growls cease. "We will get them back, brother. Focus on the task at hand."

Logan leans back, dropping his desperate hold. "How can you be so fucking calm?"

"Because, it's the only way to keep my sanity and ensure we get our women back." He clasps his brother's shoulder. "No matter what, those responsible will beg for death before we finish this. We will grant them zero mercy."

Logan's eyes bloom as the brothers clasp forearms. "They will wish for the bowels of hell. No. Fucking. Mercy."

As I watch these two warriors support and bolster each other, I'm envious of their relationship. With my mind scattered in every direction growing up, Lu and I never established such a bond. For years I loathed my sister after she placed me at Awakening Hills, blaming her for all I endured.

Under control once more, Logan turns his sharp glare on the occupants of the room. "Syn Grayflame is mine." They acknowledge his growled declaration with nods and yes sirs all around. The iridescent irises swivel my direction. "I apologize, Viessa. Please forgive me."

"I understand, my lord." I present a quick smile before I recount everything I observed and gathered in that cave-like chamber, skimming over the more extreme portrayals of Nicole's tortured body.

"How long before dusk?" Logan growls.

"Twenty minutes," Nox answers.

"You have anything you would like to contribute, Priest?" Sebastian asks, contemplating the Oracle with a frown.

"You cannot hand the witch over to Troy." My father rises, his eyes a blue torrent of emotions.

"He is the only one who can manage her magic, Icarus. What alternative do we have? We need Nicole at full strength." Logan demands.

"Please leave Abigail to Viessa and me. We will handle her."

I crave to disclose what I learned in that foresight, but it is not my truth to tell.

Well, damn. Now I *do* sound like my father.

Bastian's cell buzzes on the table, and he snatches it up. "The mortal team has completed their sweep and returned safely to Kurtis and Liam." He peers around the room at his Guardians, awaiting his command. "Suit up. We leave in ten."

Chapter 33

After two solid hours of enduring the drizzling rain, it has finally let up, but the dampness beneath my shirt is driving me insane.

I rub the back of my neck, working to dispel the trepidation bombarding me since the second my boots touched down in Scotland. This close to the shield, the land is just a vast expanse of green, flat with only the occasional outcropping of rocks for cover.

"Man, it seems like yesterday we camped outside the vampire shield working to rescue your fated female. Now here we are again, waiting on the Oracles to lower a barrier so we can storm a castle." I shake my head, running my fingers through my damp hair to keep it off my forehead, and glance briefly at the big shifter standing next to me before returning my focus to my mate and the priest kneeling at the edge of the boundary. They appear unaffected by the moisture in the air and ground.

Kurtis snorts. "On that occasion, I wanted to slaughter you, assuming you were in love with Lucretia." He twists to face me. "It took laying eyes on Viessa for the first time to recognize what you were going through. My beast's protective impulses toward her were strong, still are. We sensed the turmoil in her mind and her dependence and yearning for you."

"Yeah. My feelings for Lu tormented me. I didn't understand why I felt such fierce emotions for your mate." I nod to my woman. "I do now."

"How are matters progressing with you two?" He asks, turning his gaze to Lucretia speaking with the captain of his Sentinels. A slight smile of affection teases the edges of his lips. "How do you propose on getting around the whole, 'Oracles can't mate' decree?"

"Fuck if I know," I answer honestly. "Right now, my sole focus is on Nicole and Alex. I'll fret about the rest when we get them back safe and sound."

"Copy that."

"Are all the teams at the ready?"

"Yes. They're standing by in Inverness, under Logan and Sebastian's watchful eye. We don't want to blow our cover until the shield is down. As soon as we give the signal, they will teleport here, surround the castle, and engage." His blue gaze scrutinizes the castle. "While our armies distract the fae, the task force will infiltrate based on the intel the SEAL team acquired, in addition to what Viessa witnessed, rescue Nicole, and endeavor to locate Alex." He shakes his head. "I still can't believe Nicki's mother is alive or somehow entangled with Grayflame."

"Yeah, I'm curious to learn that complete story."

"King Scott?" Kurtis and I bump fists at the priest's summons before I stroll over to the two Oracles.

"How can I be of assistance?"

"Please place your hand on Viessa to help direct her energy."

I sink to my knees behind my mate in the damp grass, thankful I went with leather instead of Kurtis's cargo pants. Icarus's eyes swarm with the severity of an ocean amid a typhoon, his tattoos pulsing with fervent magic.

The second my palm contacts Vi's bare shoulder, the power flowing from her nearly knocks me over, but I tense my thighs to remain joined. The black ink on her forearm and the new design on her shoulder sparks to life at my touch. They pulsate in conjunction with the priest's numerous tattoos. Will Vi eventually have tattoos all over her body as Icarus does? I never imagined I would relish the thought of a tattooed woman, but on my mate, anything is sexy.

Unable to help myself, I brush my thumb across the silky skin over her scapula. "Focus, sweetness. You can do this," I murmur, and she sucks in a sharp breath, her engravings brightening.

Icarus sways, his fingers tightening on Viessa's forearm. "Give her more contact, my lord. The energy surge you provide is extraordinary."

Pride fills my chest as I sit back on my feet, spreading my knees and sliding them along the outside of hers before wrapping my free arm around her midriff. Painful magic stabs into my skin, but I embrace the pain and whisper words of encouragement into her ear.

"Unbelievable," Icarus murmurs, his tattoos almost blinding.

Within minutes, I see a slight shimmer in the air underneath their palms. "That's it, Viessa. Push harder." Her tense muscles vibrate with exertion, but she doesn't waver. If anything, the painful tingles intensify, and I grit my teeth.

A hasty glance around shows Kurtis and Lu stationed themselves right next to us—their Sentinels spread out in preparedness.

In a matter of minutes, warfare will begin. Not our first, but I pray to the gods our last. Fear for the safety of my mate, Nicki, Alex, and my friends weighs heavily on my mind. In the last major battle we engaged in, I lost my father.

As an immortal, centuries of war and death are part of our day-to-day life. After tonight, will that end? Could the prophecy come to pass, and Nicole's reign brings an abiding peace?

I certainly hope so. It's what we've all fought and suffered for decades to accomplish. Especially our females. They've taken the brunt of the torment along this journey.

Nicki endured atrocities at the hands of her father for too many seasons. Lived on the run like a fugitive, not understanding from who or why she was running. She willingly sacrificed her existence to defeat King Giordano and save us all.

Lucretia fought and struggled her entire life to keep her mentally unstable twin safe. She paid a steep price with her flesh to protect her queen and her sister.

Alex lost her memories for months, fighting the mental command to kill Nicole implanted by Jagorach. The fae attacked her. A Watcher, claiming to be in love with her, captured her and held her hostage for months. In the end, she extended the ultimate cost, giving up the prospect of motherhood to be with Bastian, and is once again being held captive against her will, along with Nicole.

Viessa suffered her entire life mentally. She lived in a perpetual psychological hell, battling the demons in her mind every second of every day. Was physically tortured at that fucking institute for who knows how long. The resilient Tri-bred was also kidnapped. Twice. Once by Dimitri and months later by his son, Zachariah.

The men have endured great hardships and trials as well—Logan and Sebastian, in particular. They endangered their lives, risking the possibility of execution night after night for years to deceive their king to keep Nicki hidden and protected.

We all sacrificed something or someone for this cause. My father surrendered his life for the woman he regarded as a daughter. The female suffering right now behind this shield. The one with a legacy to fulfill.

If anything happens to Nicole, we are all lost. She is the glue that holds us together—the bringer of peace to a species ravaged by wars, skirmishes, and power-hungry tyrants for generations.

We cannot fail. The powerful, tenacious, and stubborn Halfling's life has a purpose. Meaning. And every single immortal here tonight understands—she must survive at all costs.

A sudden surge of energy rips me from my musings, and I grip Viessa's waist tighter. The shield ripples like waves across a pond.

"Gather the troops, King Ruse," Icarus grates out, his face tight with strain.

"On it," Lu states before disappearing.

"Do not let go, King Scott."

"Not a chance," I reply, kissing my mate's temple in encouragement and fortifying my mind for the coming siege.

Chapter 34

Pain is familiar. Something I abhorred and feared as a teenager, but as an adult, I discovered a temperate amount of discomfort not only kept my demons at bay; it ignited my lust.

With my history, you'd think I'd shy away from anything remotely similar to what my father forced upon me. Instead, I seek it out, needing the submission, the letting go of control to the one individual I trust and love above all others, and the intense burn of pain.

Without those things and singing, I would dissolve into a melting pot of chaos and turmoil. The monster would win. I will never allow that to happen.

After hours of torture, the biting pain of Syn's whip striking my chest, stomach, and thighs, I allowed my mind to escape as I did as a child. While he subjects my body to horrendous pain, my mind is at peace, clouded with images and remembrances of Logan.

I almost smile, recalling the first occasion he became real. I was seventeen years old. I'd endured four years of abuse from Dimitri, and I'd reached my limit. A tremendous storm raged outside the window of my darkened room as I stood behind the door. My entire frame trembled with fear and determination, a knife clutched in my fingers as I waited for the bastard to "visit" me.

Logan suddenly appeared, and I froze in shock, but he lured me in a way I didn't understand. Logan lived in my dreams. He was my white knight—the one thing that kept me from going completely catatonic or Jeffery Dahmer insane.

Here I am again. At the mercy of a sick psychopath with his own demons guiding his actions.

What hurts worse than the burning lash of Syn's whip is Icarus's clandestine involvement in my birth. He blackmailed my mother away from Syn into the arms of Dimitri. Stood by and did nothing while my father coerced Lucretia into revealing my whereabouts. Allowed the fucker to abuse me sexually and then faked my mother's death.

If I get out of this, how will I ever trust him again? Besides Jimmy, Icarus is the only real father figure I've had. Even though he annoys the shit out of me sometimes, I love him deeply. This betrayal cuts deeper than a whip ever could.

"Nicole?"

The soft voice forces me back to my present predicament. Shackled to a table, my clothes shredded on the floor, and my body riddled with agony. Dammit. Who the hell brought me back to the living?

I slowly pivot my head to the right. Nope, it wasn't my mother. She's slumped against the wall, out cold.

"Nicki?"

I swivel my gaze to the left, the bones in my neck cracking in protest. My heart stutters in fear. Shackled like a prisoner from maximum security with a silver chain encircling her waist, her wrists and ankles handcuffed to the shiny links, is Alex. Two large fae grip her arms on each side.

Her cute face is a colorful array of bruises, one eye swollen completely shut. Her flaming red hair, while always crazy, is caked with dried blood.

Rage consumes me, and I glance around the room, seeking the source of my fury.

"He's not here," Alex whispers.

I peer at my best friend once more and try to keep my emotions in check. This is all my fucking fault. I didn't do a better job of protecting my friends. I should've insisted they all stay put. No coming and going. Period. And if they'd objected, locked them underground somewhere until this shit show was over.

"Are you alright?" I question, my voice thick with emotion.

"Yes. Are you?" A lone tear leaks from the slit of her puffy eye, and I want to scream in frustration.

"Yeah. I'll live," I whisper.

'Have you tried to communicate with Bastian?' I ask telepathically.

She nods.

'Any luck?'

A slight shake to the negative.

Dammit. 'Me either. But you know they're coming, right?'

The blue iris shines bright with hope as she nods.

'It will make it easier for them now that we are in the same room?'

Alex points her chin toward the woman chained to the wall with a questioning lift of her eyebrow.

'Believe it or not, my mother.'

Alex's eye widens.

'Yes. Quite the reunion you missed. Do you know what Syn and the witch have planned?'

Another shake to the negative.

Shit. 'Stay close to me if you can.'

She nods to her captors on either side. "Dumb and dumber here have become my new BFFs. Isn't that right, fellas?" When they scowl down at her, she smirks. "Well, it's a work in progress."

"Ah, good," Syn all but purrs as he saunters into the room. "You are all here."

Like we had a fucking choice?

He strolls over to my table, eyeing his handy work, before gently brushing a strand of hair from my face that's been driving me nuts. "We will soon have guests, so I thought I would let you have your choice of standing or sitting."

"Stand."

"Very well." He motions several fae forward, and they remove the shackles at my ankles and wrists. My poor stiff muscles refuse to obey my mental commands, just lay there like limp rags even though I'm shouting internally for them to fucking move.

"Allow me," Syn murmurs, and I eye him with confusion.

Why is he being so nice to me suddenly? This must be a trap. Or he's attempting to use reverse psychology. Either way, I'm on to him.

Once I'm in a seated position, I take a moment to shake out my tingling arms before I slowly lower my feet to the stone floor, beyond caring the few scraps of fabric do nothing to cover my girly bits.

"I brought you something to cover up with," he murmurs before dropping a black robe over my head as what's left of my tattered clothing drops at my feet.

"Who are you entertaining that you need to cover the evidence of your insanity?" I ask with a sarcastic smirk, trying to disguise how weak I truly am. It's all I can do to remain upright, so I casually lean against the table for support.

"Your mates, of course," he smiles, and I swallow at the malevolence in his silver gaze.

Oh no! As much as I want Logan and Sebastian to rescue us, I was hoping it would be a surprise attack. Syn appears eager and prepared.

I glance at Alex's wide eye, her fear shooting daggers into my already abused skin. Sometimes it really sucks being an empath.

Wait! I've regained that ability. What about my others?

Goosebumps scatter across my skin in excitement as I attempt to use telekinesis and lift one of the fae soldier's sword from his scabbard.

It raises an inch, and I nearly whoop out loud. I force a bored expression and lower the blade back into place. Just moving it one inch drained me. Sweat beads my forehead, and I clutch the table edge. Better to conserve my strength for when it's really needed.

"The new Oracle is resilient and powerful. Abigail doesn't know how much longer she can maintain the shield. So, I thought I should prepare us."

He motions to the two custodians holding Alex. They back her against the wall next to my wide-eyed mother, slap shackles on her wrist, and hoist them above her head until she's dangling off the floor.

I tense when they draw their swords, relieved at the energy surging through my veins, but they merely place the tips against her ribcage on either side and hold their position.

"You harm her, and I will drag you into the depths of hell with me to torment you for eternity," I growl. Heat blooms behind my irises, and my gums ache with the need to lower my fangs. I keep them both subdued—no need to give away my emerging strength just yet.

"This night will end with one or both of you dead and me the victor." He glances over at my mother kneeling on the floor. "I still have a great many plans in store."

"Father," a deep voice rumbles behind the wall of Custodians, who part in an instant to make way for a crazy handsome male with blue eyes so light they're almost translucent. Silver streaks through his dark hair, which falls to his collar. "The whole immortal world lays in wait outside the shield. Stop this madness," he urges, the inky eyebrows drawn tight in disapproval.

Hmmm. A potential ally?

"Keep out of this, Rordrick, or I will have you chained to the floor like your mother."

His mother? Wait. What? I do a double-take at the beautiful fae. He's a halfling? And my half-brother?

I peer over at my miracle of a mother. Not only did this mortal bear a child to a vampire, but apparently, she was fertile with a dark fae as well. Are there more humans like her; able to conceive with immortals?

Since I was the first halfling recorded in our history, my mother is either a phenomenon or no one has discovered the others yet. Vampires would treat such miracles with reverence. A viable path to continue our dwindling numbers. Full-term pregnancies in the Vampire Nation are scarce and sometimes fatal to both mother and child. Humans are an avenue we've never considered. Mostly because they are so delicate and sex with them is dangerous.

But my mother survived not only the brutal taking of my father, but Syn's as well. Is their rare resilience a part of who they are? A human breed meant for an immortal?

My new bro's pale gaze lands on me, and a muscle pulses in his jaw. Anger and regret wage war under the hard features and hypnotic irises.

"You're willing to destroy your entire race for revenge?"

I see the resemblance with Syn in his eyes, but also my mother in the shape of his nose and lips. And the fact he's not altogether on board with his father's insane plan grants him brownie points in my mind.

"She is mine!" Syn's calm demeanor shifts in an instant. White hair swirls around his shoulders as he pivots to his son. I slide down the table, putting some distance between me and the enraged fae.

"Is this how you treat your mate?" Rordrick shouts back, waving a hand at Bridget. "Don't you think you've tortured her and yourself long enough? Give up this madness, father. Hand these females over to their mates and end this war."

The more he talks, the more I like my new brother. If we could annihilate Syn, could I broker peace between Rordrick and the Vampire Nation?

"You're a fool if you believe the Moretti brothers will let this offense lie. Even if I hand them over, my head will bounce before you can blink."

Damn straight.

"Maybe I can help." All eyes turn my direction. "If you end this now, Syn, and agree to peace between our people, I will handle the wrath of Logan and Sebastian."

"Why would you agree to such an arrangement?" Syn questions, suspicion darkening the silver.

I shrug. "I understand the drive for revenge. It blocks out what's important. In this case, it's the extinction of your race. That atrocity rests squarely on your shoulders, Syn."

"I understand my responsibilities all too well, halfling. But why would you forgive what I've done? To you, the valkyrie, or your mother?"

A serious curiosity flows from him, and hope ignites in my heart. Can I persuade the dark fae king to end this without further bloodshed?

"There's one thing I've learned since becoming queen, everything is not always black and white. It's the gray areas that direct our actions toward one or the other. What Icarus and my father did to you, to Bridget, and to me was horrendous. I understand your desire for retribution. But maybe we should hear the complete story."

Listen to me, all philosophical and wise.

"Why would I believe *anything* the Oracle utters?" Syn says with a low growl, the silver eyes sparking.

"I'm not saying you have to believe him. Just hear him out. Once you have all the facts, then you can decide what's important. Is your revenge worth the cost of your species? Your life? Your son's life?"

Grayflame contemplates me for several moments, and it's all I can do not to fidget under his scrutiny. I would love nothing more than to rip his pointed ears from his head, grip a fistful of those shiny white locks, and slit his throat for what he put us through. But I must put aside my own craving for revenge if I wish for him to do the same and walk away from this alive.

I've never hated the phrase "practice what you preach" more than I do right now.

Logan's powerful presence suddenly flows through me like mana from heaven, and I inhale a quiet breath to disguise its effect.

'*Lower level, love, but hold outside the room,*' I whisper telepathically.

'*Fuck if I will,*' he growls back.

'*That's a direct order, Logan. I'm negotiating. If you come barreling in here, this shit storm will go up in flames.*'

'*Fine, but I make no promises for Bastian. Are you hurt?*'

'*Nope,*' I lie cheerfully.

'*You are a terrible liar, my love. You have five minutes, then I'm coming in.*'

'*Fair enough.*'

Before the king responds, Abigail suddenly appears by Syn's side. "They've breached the barrier. Kill her."

The second the witch entered the room, my newfound energy disappeared like a teenager's morals.

Damn her.

"Don't let her decide for you, Syn," I say, forced to grip the table once more to remain standing. "You are the king of your people, not her."

"Shut your filthy mouth," Abigail shouts, advancing on me with a raised palm filled with purple fire.

I brace for the impact, but Syn grabs the witch around the waist. "Enough, Abi. I cannot believe I am about to say this, but she's right. My need for revenge clouded my judgment. My people, my son, should come first."

She jerks out of his hold, stumbling back several steps, the violet eyes wide with shock. "What about our plan?" Her blonde brows draw together. "You kill her and Icarus will come running. You promised me the power of an Oracle."

"They outnumber us ten to one, Abi. I can't offer you any-thing if we are all dead," he hollers back.

He's not as dumb as he looks, I snicker internally just as the doors explode and my mate's bright green irises land on mine.

That sure as fuck wasn't five minutes.

Chapter 35

"Stay here until we forge a path to the castle," Liam instructs before pivoting and leaping into the fray of thousands of immortals battling. He's crazy if he believes I will stand by and let my father and the others battle without me. They will need my power for the coming confrontation.

I regard my mate for several minutes, marveling at his speed and accuracy with that wicked-looking rifle, the power in his punches and kicks, and his ruthlessness with his sword. His brutality on the battlefield speaks to my inner vampire on a visceral level, escalating my heart rate and clenching my core with desire.

Since close quarter combat is not my forte, I edge away from the conflict with a feeling of helplessness with every step. That's when I remember the bow and quiver full of arrows at my back and vault into a nearby outcropping of rock for better positioning. It's disconcerting to know I'm a powerful Oracle but can't focus my energy sufficiently without the worry of injuring our friends and allies.

I'd love nothing more than to freeze the fae in place but keep our allies mobile. It would undoubtedly save numerous lives. And while I employed such precision on Logan at the villa, I'm afraid to try it on so many. An individual is one thing—thousands might be beyond my scope.

Where the hell did my father go?

I shake my head and take focus on guarding my mate. While my arrows are not iron, my aim is true enough to slow them down.

When a colossal fae lands behind my king, I draw the bow taught just as the fighter raises his saber. Liam pivots in time to witness a well-placed arrow sink into the fae's eye socket. He finishes him with a bullet to the brain before scanning the area for me.

When he spots me perched on a large boulder above the clamor, he grins, offering a brisk nod before barreling back into the midst of the chaos, heading for the castle with the task force.

I guard their backs from above, dispelling the archers along the castle walls, making sure no silver penetrates my wolf's skin. Within minutes, they'll be out of range, but the carnage left behind leaves a clear path to follow.

I search once more for my father amidst all the fighting bodies, and that's when I notice him strolling casually through the chaos toward the entrance. The fae don't even engage him, sensible enough to give the powerful tattooed deity a wide berth. Will I one day command that kind of respect? I hope so.

When the task force is beyond my bow's limits, I trace to Icarus's side, hoping being near him will keep me protected.

I let go of my worry and trust in my mate's abilities to stay safe.

"Nice shooting, daughter," he comments with a grin.

"My sister taught me well."

At the mention of my twin, I peek over my shoulder and stare in awe as Lu battles beside Kurtis, spinning, twirling, slashing, and stabbing with her bloody sword. At the same time, King Ruse engages in hand to hand, tossing fae around like they were nothing, his blue irises shifting to the brown of his animal and back. When a soldier gets too close to his female, he lifts the deadly rifle and puts a slug between their eyes.

I've lost sight of Logan and Sebastian. They were the first into the fray, leaving a trail of blood and gore in their wake. Somewhere in the blend is Queen Arra and Cipher. Nox guards my back, pretty sure at the insistence of my mate. And even though I spot demons in the mix, I'm uncertain where the demon king and the mysterious witch disappeared.

'Please do not enter the castle Liam until the witch is subdued,' I instruct my wolf. 'She could have the detonator on her.' His fury pounding into my skull is my only response.

Once Icarus and I enter the castle, an eerie quiet settles around us, producing a shiver to waltz up my spine. "Where to, father?"

"Lower level, but we wait here."

"What?" He's lost his mind. "Why?"

"We arrive too soon, and it will disrupt the flow. Nicole needs to seize control. It's her destiny."

"Or is it you don't wish her to discover your secret?"

"All things come to light, my child."

His calm demeanor kindles my anger. "Why didn't you tell Lu, or me, we weren't your only children?"

"Abigail was conceived two millennia ago."

When he offers nothing further, I glare down at him. "And? What the hell happened to her? How could she go from a divine Oracle to an evil witch practicing black magic?"

"History will reveal itself in time, Viessa."

"Ugh. You're so frustrating," I huff and cross my arms over my chest.

"So Nicole keeps telling me," he smiles. "When this is over, I want you to link yourself to the vampire queen. She must always be your priority, above all else."

"Is that what you've done, father? Protected Nicole's destiny, no matter the cost or consequences? To you? To her? To her mother?"

"Yes," he answers without remorse or hesitation. "And you will do the same. Nicole is the future, and it is imperative she remains alive."

"Even if that means defying the gods?" I challenge with a curious lift of my eyebrow. Not that I don't already feel that way, but I need to hear the words.

He ponders, and I hold my breath, waiting. "Her life is precious, and when the occasion arrives for you to teach another Oracle, you must guide them to realize the same."

His remarks startle me. Why would I train the next Oracle? Another thought invades. Since I'm a female, how will

I conceive the new deity? It's not like I can impregnate some human woman to give birth.

I swing my head and dismiss those troubles for a later time. "What's the plan once we get in there, father?" I ask, instead.

"We must merge our powers. Imagine them as an impenetrable bubble, similar to the shield you designed for Zachariah Giordano." I cringe at the reminder. I've come a long way since that day. "Allow the energy to build in your palms."

"Like the purple ball of fire Abigail created?"

"Yes. I will identify the proper time to deploy it. Let nothing distract you from our task. Not Nicole, your friends, King Scott, or even me. Do you understand?" His swirling blue gaze pierces my soul.

"Yes, father."

But can I adhere to the promise if my Liam is in danger? How could I place Nicole's life above Liam's? This is precisely why it's forbidden for an Oracle to take a mate. They are a diversion from our true task.

"I will cloak us to enter the chamber. Keep silent and allow circumstances to play out. We only interfere if the queen fails."

At my nod, Icarus grabs my wrist, and in the next second, we are in the room from the vision. Nicole is standing—barely—draped in a black robe. They chained Alex and Bridget to the wall, and a dozen or more fae circle the place.

King Grayflame is quarreling with the witch under Nicole's watchful gaze when Logan and Sebastian come charging into the chamber.

Oh my. They are a fearsome sight to behold. Blood stains their massive torsos, creating a macabre artwork of their family tattoo. Green and blue light the walls, and ruby raindrops fall from their enormous swords to splatter on the stone floor.

The Moretti brother's fierce gazes land on their bruised and battered mates, causing the irises to brighten tenfold. A low, terrifying rumble saturates the atmosphere.

Grayflame grabs Nicole by the throat and drags her in front of him. "Are you a woman of your word, Halfling?" he whispers into her ear, and she nods.

When Logan advances, the queen raises her hand to impede him. His jaw clenches with violence, but he backs off a step, twirling his massive sword, his murderous gaze never leaving the fae holding his female.

"Release her now, Syn, and I might be merciful."

"Only a fool would believe that, Moretti," he replies.

I watch Abigail intently. She holds perfectly still, and no one in the room seems to give her any consideration. Why is that? She's the deadliest thing in this chamber. The witch slowly backs away from the Guardians, snaking in our direction.

Icarus's hold on my wrist tightens. Is that a signal to power up? I peek down at him, but his focus remains on his other daughter.

"Syn. Have your men stand down, and we can talk," Nicole whispers.

The dark fae king hesitates.

"Please, father," a smaller version of Syn implores, causing Bastian to peer at him with curiosity. "End this madness and negotiate a peace with the vampires."

"Your son Rordrick is wise, Syn. It's time to settle this vendetta and the war between our people," Nicki encourages softly.

Grayflame glances at Bridget as if seeking her guidance. She's up on her knees, straining against the chains, her concentration laser-focused on him.

"Please, love," she whispers brokenly. "Don't let it finish this way."

"Aaaabiiiigaaaail!" A rich, dark voice thunders from just outside an entrance, and the witch jerks in response, her wide gaze swiveling to Icarus and me.

Well, she knows we are here. So much for cloaking.

In the next second, all hell breaks loose. Syn tosses Nicki aside and dives for Bridget, sheltering her body with his own. His son guards them both with short daggers in each hand as he snarls at the Custodians to stand down.

Instead of pursuing the king, Logan traces to catch his mate before she collapses on her face. "Baby." I hear him whisper before placing the inside of his wrist to her lips.

Sebastian is at Alex's side, yanking the silver chains from the ceiling. I cringe at the sizzle of his flesh. He places her spine to his chest as her wee fangs embed in his wrist. The enraged warrior wields his sword with the other, daring anyone to get near his suckling mate.

The powerful male witch enters the chamber with Jag right on his heels. Before I realize what's happening, Abigail pounces on my back, ripping me from Icarus's hold. She shoves her palm in front of my face, and a frigid, purple flame dances amid her palm.

Something in the light catches my awareness. Its violet flickering captivates me, and I don't even acknowledge the freezing heat or the fact it is scorching my skin.

"Viessa! Snap out of it."

Liam's hard, commanding tone bounces through my skull. I blink rapidly, endeavoring to escape the hypnotic flame. Fear at his proximity to Abigail floods through me and ignites the low vibration down my spine I experienced before. The deadly flame somehow escalates the hum with each passing second.

The deafening crack of a firearm jolts me from whatever was tempting me away from reality. The large bullet discharged from Liam's rifle lodges in the purple ball before disintegrating into useless powder.

The buzzing spreads through every limb when the witch produces the detonator in her other hand. A foreign sensation takes hold, clawing to be let loose with painful intensity. With no alternative, I allow the pulsing phenomenon full control.

Abigail screams as the mighty explosion flings her across the room. The vampires shield their mates, taking the brunt of the shock wave.

Several seconds pass before I understand what transpired. When I move toward the fallen witch, I realize I'm no longer me. My dormant shifter side erupted the second Liam's existence was in jeopardy.

The sensations within me are primal and feral as I stalk toward the detonator flung under a nearby table. I sense the gazes of everyone in the room as they watch me with widened eyes. Lowering to my haunches, I ease under the table and carefully place the black tubular device in my mouth.

I snarl at the witch ogling me before pivoting to my mate. The werewolf king bends on one knee, his palm outstretched. The second I drop it into his palm, Kurtis kneels next to him and dismantles it with quick efficiency, then pulverizes it beneath his boot.

I prowl closer to Liam, the muscles in my body twitching, needing to assure myself he's okay.

He eyes me with wonder. "You are exquisite," he murmurs, running his palm down my sleek, black neck. With the emergence of my panther side, a new piece of the puzzle is finally in place. She is glorious. The power dancing in this majestic form is phenomenal, and I can't wait to explore this newfound identity. But right now, we have an evil scourge to annihilate.

Before I shift back, I ease closer to my mate and slowly lean in to lick his neck, needing his taste on my tongue—the king chuckles.

Icarus's power suddenly blooms beside me, driving its way into my skin. My body morphs once more, without pain this time, to leave me crouched in front of my mate bare ass naked.

In a heartbeat, Liam jerks his wet shirt off, shoving it over my head. I slip my arms through the armholes, shivering at the dampness, and stand to face the witch. I nod to Icarus, ready at my side. Liam's enormous shirt falls to mid-thigh, covering my intimate parts.

The second my mate touches my waist from behind; I envision my light merging with my father's. Within seconds, a basketball-sized orb builds before us. Brevil staggers to her feet to face off with our sphere of magic.

The Custodians scramble for the exits, instinctively understanding this magical showdown is far beyond them. Those left comprise our task force, the male witch, the dark fae king and his son, and Nicole's mother.

"Abigail. I order you to stand down," Syn barks at the witch encased in her purple radiance. He keeps Bridget locked behind him; the chains discarded at her feet. Nicki's mom clutches Syn's wings, allowing her captor to shield her.

Logan and Nicole hold at the ready on my left, while Bastian and a healed Alex do the same at our right. Liam remains steady at my back.

King Darath sidesteps away from Troy, gently urging Kleora, who has her bow trained on Abigail, to do the same.

In the next pulse, the witch throws her pulsating light, but before I can deflect, Icarus seizes my arm in a brutal grip, holding me immobile.

I watch in horror as Nicole steps in front of us, taking the full impact to her chest. She staggers back with a scream as the purple flame engulfs her.

Chapter 36

"**N**icole!" Logan's bellow is no match for the queen's shriek of agony as she arches, arms outstretched. Gunmetal irises ignite, expanding the glow across the stone ceiling.

Logan reaches for her, but I seize his wrist. "Do not, my lord, or you will be a mountain of ash in seconds." How I perceive such knowledge is beyond my understanding.

I swing to my father, putting Logan's tormented face aside. "What now?"

"Nicole!" Icarus barks at her, and I jolt, having never heard him raise his voice in such a manner. "Syphon the enveloping flames into yourself. Use its strength as your own."

Can she do that?

When Nicki doesn't move, suspended behind the shield of misery, her gaze locked on the ceiling; I question my father's sanity once again.

"Now, Viessa. Disperse our energy at Nicole," Icarus demands, his eyes swarming with bewitchment.

"What?" *He can't be serious?* "Won't that destroy her?" Actually, I'm stunned she's not dead already. I experienced the scalding heat of that flame. It was excruciating, and it didn't even touch my skin.

"Do it, daughter, or she *will* perish." Icarus's urgency overshadows my doubts. He would do nothing to harm the vampire queen.

Liam squeezes my waist, and that slight nudge from my mate gives me the extra boost to fling our magical ball at the powerful Halfling encased in purple flames.

The tormented scream pierces my spirit, just as Logan's roar causes my bones to tremble. The tattooed vampire flings his sword at Abigail in his helpless rage, but Troy shoots out a hand filled with inky gray magic, destroying the massive sword in seconds.

When those bright irises swivel to mine, I swallow in fear. If I've just killed his female, Oracle or not, the warrior will sever my head from my neck with his bare hands.

Logan draws his other sword, but instead of advancing on me, he moves in front of his mate, shielding Nicole from the livid witch. The others do the same, bracing to defend her with their lives. I'm so enthralled in the battle of violet versus amber flickering over the queen; I don't notice the priest has withdrawn until an azure spark catches my eye.

Icarus battles with Abigail and Troy. The male witch appears to be protecting the blonde while managing not to injure her or my father. I snatch one of my arrows scattered around the room and my bow, tracing to my father's side. I strike the black-robed male in the shoulder with a well-placed arrow.

The impact knocks his hood off, and I get my first proper look at the male witch. He's ruggedly handsome, with long mahogany hair streaked with blond highlights humans pay big bucks to produce. His scruffy goatee only adds to his bad boy sex appeal, and the black as night eyes mesmerize. They speak of carnality and promise eternal damnation.

He growls low, yanking the projectile from his shoulder. The inky irises spark with an inner fire, his grin full of menace.

Shit.

But instead of attacking me, he rushes Abigail, enclosing a muscular arm around her abdomen, pinning her back to his chest.

The witch appears taken off guard for a second, her body stone.

"Hurt her, and I will make certain your soul spends eternity in a special chamber of hell," my father threatens, his palms held in front of him, the tattoos pulsing wildly.

"No, father!" Abigail screams, her arms outstretched, beseeching Icarus to spare her. "Please don't let him take me."

"You must atone for the destruction you've caused, child." the priest declares, the anguish in his voice apparent as the stars in the sky. "The gods demand it."

The witch's expression turns livid. The blue eyes harden to ice. "You son of a bitch." From her waist, she draws a short dagger and stabs Troy's forearm braced around her midriff. He curses and releases her.

I watch in horror as the witch lights up the knife with her colorful fire. When it mixes with Troy's dark blood, the purple glow sparks, and before I can contemplate what that means, she's flung it at Icarus.

I raise my palm, not knowing what I can do to halt the blade since I extinguished most of my energy in the flames now engulfing Nicole. An inner power settles in my chest, building to a crescendo until it bursts out into the chamber.

I scan the room and realize I slowed time. Troy has encased his arm in a murky smoke to repair his injury, but his black eyes remain focused on Abigail.

King Darath's crimson irises blaze with a hellish fire, his enormous fangs blinding as he lunges for the soaring land nymph—his movement barely discernible.

Kleora hangs suspended about ten feet in the air; her bow stretched taut; an arrow aimed at Abigail. The priestess is a diminutive but formidable sight—her jade gaze blooms with determination.

I peer over at Nicole and am relieved to note the purple and amber flames consuming her have dimmed considerably. It flows and undulates between her outstretched arms. I glory in the team's fierce countenance as they surround her, keeping her protected.

I refocus on the flaming blade, moving with incredible slowness once more, and reach to pluck it from the air. When my arm progresses a mere centimeter, I almost shriek in frustration and failure.

In my fear, I inadvertently included myself in my power surge. All I can do is stare in horror as the fiery projectile sinks inch by torturous inch into Icarus's chest. Nicole shrieks in response, her pale gray eyes a garish light of despair.

Her shout breaks the suspension spell. My father's collapsing body slams into mine just as the vampire queen hurls the mostly amber ball of magic swirling between her palms straight at Abigail.

"No!" Troy bellows. Fire plows into her with the force of a locomotive, launching her in the air and across the room. My eyes widen in alarm when the sphere catches Kleora in the shoulder, inundating her petite frame in half a second before sending her careening into the wall with the witch.

King Darath erupts, discharging an outpouring of energy so potent it hurls every occupant within the room against the walls of the chamber. The back of my skull crashes into the rock with a loud crack. Blackness invades my sight, and I battle to remain conscious, to keep Icarus in my embrace. I shake my head to dissipate the murkiness, causing pain to shoot through my skull, but what appears before me makes me wish the darkness had sucked me into oblivion.

The once beautiful demon king morphed into… well, every scary version of Lucifer I've ever envisioned. Sinister ebony wings, the consistency of leather, extend out, crowding the room. Thick, lethal hooks that could render bones as efficiently as a knife through butter adorn the joints and tips. His once tan flesh is black as night, the muscles bulging to three times their volume. At each shoulder, two sharp bony protrusions stretch from the skin. The long luxurious mane of hair disappeared, and on top of the smooth rounded head, duel wicked-looking horns the same hue as the rest of him coil up from his forehead.

The terrifying monster reaches through the glowing magic, snarls against the pain, and gently clasps Kleora's nape. He growls deep, chanting in a harsh, guttural tone, his eerie crimson irises glowing bright with power.

Within seconds the flame dissipates, and the frightening beast kneels, cradling the priestess in his lap. An enormous hand, tipped with deadly black claws, tenderly brushes her hair from her cheek, tucking it behind a pointed ear.

When the devil's eyes lift to mine, I'm astounded by the torment in his malevolent gaze, at the raw, animalistic qualities of his face. I reach out my senses to the land nymph but detect no heartbeat. The fire meant for Abigail took the priestess's life. Sorrow floods my soul as tears slide down my cheeks.

"I'm so sorry, Darath," Nicki whispers brokenly, snagging the devil's attention.

The monster tilts his head back and roars, forcing me to cover my ears against the onslaught. The vast wings curve around Kleora in a loving caress, helping to cradle her body against his chest before they both vanish.

What will the demon king do? This is the second occasion he's suffered a considerable loss. First, his wife and child to Dimitri, and now Priestess Tanagra. Not to mention, the land nymphs have lost their ruler.

In his grief, will he retaliate against Nicki, or will he realize the fault lies in my lap and seek retribution? It was mine and Icarus' powerful magic that took her life. Nicki was just a pawn in the big prophecy scheme.

I peer over at Nicole on her hands and knees, working to recover from the immense energy surge of our combined power. Logan kneels next to her, dutifully guarding her in her exhausted state. One hand is on his sword as he eyes Syn. The other rubs up and down her back, offering comfort.

Liam fights to stand. His left femur broke in Darath's explosion, and blood trickles from a cut on his forehead. The wolf needs to shift to repair, but the occupants of the chamber couldn't endure another bomb. When his gaze settles on mine, I nod and offer a watery smile.

The second the demon's energy shot through the chamber, it tossed the torture contraptions not bolted down against the stone, smashing them apart. The odor of sulfur still lingers in the air, and the place appears as if it sustained a nuclear detonation. Chunks of brick and mortar are missing from the walls, while numerous stones split in half or crumbled to the ground. Chicory scorch marks splatter every surface.

"Abigail?"

I swivel my gaze to observe Troy running his palms, surrounded by black wizardry, over the witch laying crumpled on the floor, her mangled crown next to her. The charred skin smolders in the meager light, a startling contrast to the shining golden locks untouched by the fiery magic. Her pulse is so slow I barely discern it.

I remember a charred body with violet eyes from my vision. I foresaw this outcome but could not decipher the when, where, and who.

"Nicole." My father's raspy entreaty snags my attention. Abigail's blade still protrudes from his chest. Bright crimson saturates the fabric of his robe, seeping down his torso and onto my thighs.

Nicki's head swivels in our direction. Tears threaten as she takes in the damage to the one creature, besides Logan, whom she depends on and trusts. The queen scrambles on her hands and knees to our side—the troubled gray irises pin mine. "Do something," she demands in a fierce whisper.

The weight of the universe settles on my shoulders. I cannot perform the duties of Oracle without my father's guidance. Nicole will suffer significantly at his loss. We all will. Tears blur my sight as the reality of the situation sinks in into my shattered soul.

I have no damn clue how to save Icarus.

Chapter 37

The devastation in my mate's gaze tightens my chest. I overlook the radiating pain in my thigh and hobble over to her side while monitoring Syn and Troy tending to the downed witch.

The second I analyze the damage to Icarus, my heart drops in my gut. His pallor under all those tattoos is troublesome, as is the volume of blood coating the floor beneath him and Viessa.

The rest of the team gathers around the two divinities, staying vigilant but pushing the conflict with Syn aside for the moment to concentrate on the more urgent agenda; doing whatever is necessary to save the priest.

"How can we help, love?" I ask, lowering to my good knee next to her with the aid of my sword.

"I… I'm not sure." Her fear pierces my chest, and I gently grasp her shoulder to lend comfort.

It still boggles my mind the beauty of Vi's animal. A black panther. The quivering muscles beneath the inky coat were a testament to the power in her sleek frame. My woman's inner creature is an exact rendition of the female beneath.

Powerful beyond what she even realizes, but skittish amid so many. She sought a taste of her mate, my nearness, to calm her newfound raging emotions.

"Do something, Viessa," Nic demands, tears threatening. "He brought me back with Logan's blood. Maybe... maybe you and Lu can offer yours since you're related."

"It's worth a try," Lucretia volunteers, lowering to her knees across from Nicole. "Congrats on the emergence of your panther, sis." No jealousy rests in the golden depths as they gaze at her twin, even though Lu's shifter side has never made an appearance.

"Too... late... for me." Icarus's voice is so feeble it's barely discernible.

"Don't you say that, Priest," Nicki barks as one lone tear slips past her defenses. I've never seen Nic cry, and it melts my insides.

We're all surprised when the Oracle has the strength to raise his hand and tenderly wipes the moisture from Nicki's face. Her lids close as she leans into the caress, her body shaking with grief.

"Don't you leave me, Icarus. You've been more of a parent to me than I deserve." Her voice cracks as she bends over and brushes her lips over his forehead. "I need you," she admits quietly, and I'm stunned.

Nicole Giordano has never openly professed to need anyone except Logan. We all know her well enough to realize she loves each of us fiercely and would protect our ragtag bunch with her life, but her connection with Icarus goes beyond that. Her heartbreak opens a black void in my soul.

"Viessa." She glances up at the command in my tone, tears shimmering in her lovely irises. "Dig deep, baby. Plead with the gods. Make a deal with the devil. Do whatever you have to do to save your father's life."

She swallows but nods. "Let your beast's spirit flow into me, Liam. Your strength bolsters my own."

"What about mine?" Nicole asks.

"Or our shifter power?" Kurtis adds with a nod to Cipher across from him, Arra tucked into his side.

When Vi only blinks up at everyone's urgent appeals to help, I answer for her. "It can't hurt. Kneel, everyone. Touch Icarus wherever you can. Focus on pushing your immortal energy into his body." When I glance back at Viessa for verification, she offers a shaky smile before shifting her concentration to her father lying in her lap.

Lucretia and Viessa each wrap their fingers around the shaft of the glowing dagger in his torso. Lu winces against the discomfort of the magic but tightens her jaw and her grip. Nicole scooches closer and lays both palms on the blood-soaked chest.

"Help me, father," Vi whispers in the priest's ear.

Instead of responding, Icarus plants a palm over the twins clutching the hilt, then clasps Nicole's hand, joining it with theirs.

A soothing, gentle flutter of immense energy spikes from the Oracle. I stare in wonderment as the undulating flow travels to Nicole, Lu, and Viessa.

Lucretia's head drops forward. Her death grip on Kurtis's arm causes a wince in the mighty shifter. Instinctively, I imagine the strength of my beast flowing into my mate, besieging and impregnating her with its power. She cries out, arching against the invasion, and I withdraw, fearful of hurting her.

"No, Liam," she grates out. "Don't hold back. All of you shove your energy forward."

Even though uncertainty resides in my mind, I do as she directs and brazenly surge my power into her once more. I observe the others do the same, their brows drawn or their jaws clenched in concentration.

The extraordinary force sweeping over the Oracle's prone body suddenly alters, spiking into the air before slamming into Nicki's chest. She bows against the onslaught but maintains her connection with the twins over the hilt.

The mighty vampire Guardian reaches out to support her back, but I lean over, drawing a sharp breath against the pain in my thigh, and clamp onto his wrist a scant inch from touching her. "No, Logan. Keep your focus on Icarus."

He glances briefly at his mate fighting an unseen battle before presenting an abrupt nod and settling his enormous hands back on the priest's legs.

The energy surges again, but this time it strikes Viessa. She appears to absorb the charge like a sponge. Her eyes and tattoos spark brighter than the sun. The third spike hits Lu, and she sucks in a painful breath, letting it out with a low moan. Kurtis watches her with a concerned frown.

Within moments, the three females chant in an unknown dialect, their sockets filled with the Oracle's blue power. The surface of my skin tingles as electrical energy permeates the chamber.

"Holy shit," Alex breathes as her riot of flaming curls rised in the air, undulating like she's underwater. Nicole and Viessa's do the same, but the substance of Lu's thick braid keeps it plastered to her spine.

When the little valkyrie's knees rise from the stone floor, as if she might float away, Sebastian reaches over and clamps his free arm around her waist, arranging her between his thighs. Their hands never leave Icarus's frame.

I glance up just as Troy gathers Abigail's charred body in his arms and disappears. Is the witch dead? That bitch instigated this complete debacle from start to finish. If she hasn't perished, our team will hunt her down and make sure she answers for her crimes. I was astonished to hear her call Icarus, father. So many aspects regarding this little priest we do not fathom. At least I don't need to worry whether the chip in my back will explode anymore.

Rordrick and Syn ease toward our group. I tense. If the dark fae king wishes to attack, now would be a perfect time. We are all vulnerable with our energy and focus fixed on the Oracle.

But instead of attacking or fleeing to safety. The father and son gather the mortal woman off the floor. She wraps her arms around Syn's waist, kissing the brutal scars on his chest.

What the hell? Is this female suffering from Stockholm syndrome? The king held her captive, raped and tortured her for who knows how long, and she appears okay with it. But perhaps it wasn't rape after all. Vi said the women enjoyed Syn's taking in the bedchamber. Are they into such extreme play?

I shudder. Viessa and I will never venture that far down the rabbit hole. I relish a little pain with play, but I'm not into torture.

Syn lowers his head and kisses her forehead, murmuring something in her ear. She nods, and his arms draw her close before his gaze lands on the priest.

Syn's crimes against the Vampire Nation will not go unpunished, yet he seems ready to confront whatever sentence is in store for him. Interesting. Why the about-face? He spent years devising this plan to kidnap Nicole. Held her captive for hours, torturing her. He's fortunate Logan hasn't taken his head already.

When Nicole's mother embraces Rordrick, I'm stunned to recognize the resemblance in their features. This mortal not only mated with a vampire and produced the prophesied Halfling, but she also mated a fae and created another halfling.

I had no clue such a phenomenon was achievable. The immortal world has maintained over the centuries that humans didn't possess the biological link to mate with our kind, and therefore our seed contained no efficacy.

Well, standing before me is living proof that isn't true. This frail-looking woman gave birth to two hybrids: Rordrick and Nicole.

I let my worries go for now and refocus on my mate and saving the Oracle's life. This being has played an intricate role in our lives, guiding and directing our movements behind the scenes for centuries. If he perishes, it will shake the immortal realm down to its foundation.

Since we do not have a direct avenue to the gods, many of us rely on his divine wisdom to steer our actions on the appropriate path, but none more than the Vampire Nation. If Icarus dies tonight, my mate has big shoes to fill in a hurry. Is she ready? Or could the burden of not only her father's death but the magnitude of being the sole Oracle fracture her tenuous hold on reality?

Now more than ever, Viessa needs my strength. And the only means to boost that connection is a mating. The gods will have to see reason, if such a concept is possible, because I have no intention of letting her go. And this coming together every other month ceases after this night.

I've already advised my siblings to begin modifications on our home to prepare for a vampire queen and install the same precautions at the werewolf headquarters.

One way or another, Viessa will be mine. Body. Mind. Soul.

Chapter 38

The second the surge plowed into me, it drove me back to a period when I couldn't decipher who or where in time I resided. Voices and visions of the previous millennia bombard my brain, and I can't seem to tame the churning, uncontrollable mass.

A forceful rendering splits my spirit from my body. I hear myself chanting in a language I've never mastered, right along with Nicole and my twin. Every second that passes floats my soul higher. Past the towering castle, into the starlit sky.

The air becomes thinner, but I don't struggle to breathe. The temperature falls the farther I ascend, but the chill doesn't invade my skin. This weightless soaring is free-ing, euphoric even. I stretch my arms wide, reveling in the freedom of flying above the magnificent blue planet. Earth is stunning from space, with the contours of landmasses peeking under the swirls and dots of white clouds, and the striking azure of the vast oceans is beyond description.

My breath stalls in my lungs when a majestic, omniscient energy settles all around me, and my upward progression ceases. Somewhere in the back of my subconscious, I think it should terrify me. Instead, a cocoon of love and peace settles over me, warming my spirit form. I'm astounded to recognize I am in the presence of the Almighty.

Until this moment, I never believed He existed. Since the moment I met Icarus, I understood divine entities ruled the universe, but I rejected the notion of a one true God who oversaw everything.

"My child," a deep soothing voice booms from all directions. "Ye of little faith."

Wow. God just spoke to me directly as my spirit hovers somewhere in outer space. "Am I dead?"

"No, but your earthly father will soon join me. Your attempts to sustain his life are futile."

"Why, Lord? He means the world to so many."

"His time is at hand," the voice warns as a pleasant breeze skims over my hair like a loving caress. "The future belongs to you now."

"But I still have a great deal to learn. How can I assist the immortals without his guidance?"

"Believe in your inner self. Follow the instructions of the monks to complete your training. You possess more power than your predecessor, my child."

I sense my spirit drifting away from the divinity flooding me with tranquility, and I panic, requiring more one on one with God. "Wait. Will you be there to help steer my path?"

"I am forever with you. Draw on the strength of those around you. Complete the connection with your mate, brand him as yours, for it solidifies the authority over your capabilities." The loving atmosphere slides away and I want to grieve at the loss. "And remember, heed the voice in your mind, for I will never steer you falsely."

My spirit passes through the many layers of the earth's atmosphere, and with each one, a unique level of clarity takes hold. For the first time in my existence, I command the images that assault me upon entrance into the troposphere. With precise accuracy, I could never have obtained on my own; my intellect catalogs the predictions according to relevance, filing them away for later analysis.

Joy and elation flood through me. After over a century of turmoil and chaos, I'm finally in authority over my thoughts and emotions. Not because the mist is suppressing them, not because Liam's presence is dulling them, but because I obtain sufficient discipline of my faculties for the first time. I want to weep with exhilaration.

When my spirit eases back into my body, my father's impending loss strikes pain into my chest. I've only known this remarkable creature for a brief time, but he became a tremendous influence in my life, and in the lives of all the immortals kneeling around him.

His death will devastate our races—the impact felt for all eternity.

I peer at my twin and Nicole, reciting a spell they didn't have a snowball's chance in hell of understanding without divine intervention. Why give us this ability? All it accomplished was to offer false hope.

Warm fingers brush my hair behind my ear, and I glance up at my king crouched next to me. The agony of losing my father lightens somewhat. I may surrender my mentor, but I'm gaining my one true mate. The male who willingly submits to my wicked passions to keep me whole.

God blesses our mating, and I can't wait to share the news with him. Just the prospect sends a thrill through me, but I thrust it aside and concentrate on delivering the devastating news to my friends.

Before I let go of the blade, Icarus gazes up at me with a weak, encouraging smile. "*I foresaw my death for quite some time, Viessa,*" he whispers telepathically.

The gentle voice in my head brings fresh tears to my eyes. Even though the second I reentered earth, I recognized this was coming—an overwhelming pain crushes my heart.

'*I will miss you, father,*' I whisper brokenly in his mind.

'Guard Nicole with your life, child.'

"I vow it," I say before jerking the blade from his sternum, shattering the spell over my twin and the queen. They both rear back, swaying slightly until their mates steady them. When the gunmetal irises of the most powerful vampire on the planet zero in on mine, I can't disguise the grief from my expression or the tears sliding down my cheeks.

Nicki gasps in pain, shaking her head in denial even as acceptance fills her shimmering gaze.

"Nicole," my father beseeches in a shaky voice. She lifts his hand in hers, scooting closer.

"I'm here, Icarus."

"Do not lament, child. I am proud of you and all you have achieved in such a short time. Will you do something for me?"

"Anything, priest. Name it."

"Open your heart. Allow those around you inside. Your walls are your one weakness. Let them go."

"I promise, Icarus. I love you. You are the best part of all of us, and our lives are stronger for it. We will never forget you. You live right here." Nicole rubs her hand over her chest, struggling to keep the tears at bay. "Always."

"Please understand," he rasps. His light appears to diminish, and my soul fractures. "Every choice I made on your behalf was to guide you to this point in time. Forgive me. I ached along with you through all your suffering, but had I not intervened and changed the course of destiny; you would not be here to save them." His other hand rises, indicating the immortals grieving around him.

"I understand, Icarus. There is nothing to forgive."

A shimmer of tears enters the priest's fading irises. "Viessa, join hands with the queen," he directs. I'm amazed he can still communicate. His pulse is practically nonexistent.

Nicole and I immediately obey, and my father's palm covers ours. He murmurs a reverent prayer in the same dialect the three of us were chanting, causing Nicole's turbulent emotions to pour into me in an instant. I blink in stunned disbelief.

Underneath all the sarcasm and bravado lies a broken, vulnerable young woman. Her fears of the future come across as strong and distinct. To this day, it astounds the Halfling the gallant warrior by her side could love her, or the people surrounding her seem ready to sacrifice their lives for her. She still regards herself as the frightened teenager beaten and abused by her father. The responsibilities placed upon her shoulders petrify her.

My heart bleeds for the young immortal because, in a sense, I relate to her insecurities and fears. I struggle daily with similar self-doubt. I finally realize why my father adored and defended this damaged creature so fiercely, defying the gods to safeguard her survival.

Nicole meets so many challenges head-on with a reckless do or die attitude because a part of her still believes this isn't real. That any minute, someone will wrench the dream away, and she'll be back to life on the run, alone and scared.

As the last of Icarus's power flows into us both, I stare into the eyes of the female I would readily sacrifice my soul for and recite the words chanting through my brain.

"I pledge on my faith to devote my path in aiding you to fulfill the prophecy. Never will I cause you harm and will forever observe my allegiance to you completely against all individuals or gods in good faith and without deceit."

Nicole blinks at me, dumbfounded.

"Drink each other's blood to seal the covenant," Icarus whispers.

I am the first to present my wrist to the queen. She hesitates before gently nicking the vein and swallowing down several sips. When she offers hers, I do the same and am astounded by the power circulating in her essence. The woman is extraordinary and worthy of my fealty and devotion.

"It is accomplished, father," Icarus utters before the last breath sighs from his lungs, and his lids close over the beautiful cerulean irises forever.

Nicole collapses over his body and openly weeps.

Chapter 39

Liam

Shell-shocked doesn't do justice to what I'm experiencing. Icarus is dead. Viessa is the new High Priest Oracle and connected with Nic.

I glance around at my friend's stunned faces. As I did, they all expected that Vi, Lu, and Nicki would somehow save him. How could these three powerful females not?

Sebastian cradles a sobbing Alex as he stares at Icarus's body with wide-eyed disbelief. Logan's expression matches his brother's. He appears at a loss as he rubs his mate's back while she allows the grief free rein for the first time in her life.

I peer over at Lucretia, the ever-stoic warrior, as tears spill down her cheeks at the loss of her newfound father. Kurtis gathers her to his side, glancing at me. His bereavement mirrors everyone in the room.

When my palm trembles, I stare down in confusion until I realize it's not my hand that's shaking but the slender shoulder under it. Viessa's tears drop on the priest's forehead, and she gently wipes each one away.

A heaviness sits on my chest. Part of it is mourning for the little priest, but the majority understands my mate's new position. Her elevation puts an even bigger wedge between us. I never once imagined she would be the sole Oracle to lead the immortal world. Icarus has always been, and I assumed he would always be here.

The burdens and responsibilities on Vi's shoulders have increased tenfold. She's no longer the pupil being counseled. She is the real deal—a divine deity chosen by the gods.

Where the nightmare does that leave the two of us?

Shame saturates my conscience. How can I be so fucking selfish when I should offer solace and reassurance to her right now?

I'm about to help Vi stand when an unusual power pervades the area. I tense, and pain darts through my fractured leg. I need to shift, and soon.

The others leap to their feet, drawing their weapons as Ezekiel, Gadriel, Manakel, and Kalaziel appear on the other side of the room. The Watcher's black wings dominate the space. Their swords of death gleam in the meager light.

These beings are the leaders of the fallen angels—a group of entities who God cast out of heaven right alongside Lucifer. But instead of joining the devil or insinuating themselves into immortal society, they performed whatever they deemed necessary to earn favor back with God. They claim to be the wardens of the immortal realm, here to watch over the precious humans hell-bent on destroying themselves and on preserving the balance of power and nature.

Their directives forced Icarus to forfeit Alex's ability to bear children. Since she is a Hybrid, part shifter, part valkyrie, and mated to a vampire, they eliminated another Tri-bred possibility.

"Why are you here, E?" Alex demands, stepping forward. Not long ago, Ezekiel kidnapped the princess, hoping to keep her away from Sebastian. According to him, he did it to safeguard her against his brothers ending her life. Which we all know was a bullshit excuse. He was madly in love with the little valkyrie and sought to seduce her into marrying him.

"It is our sacred obligation to collect the Oracle's body," he answers in quiet reverence, his heated gaze skimming her curves like a starved man viewing a steak.

"Keep your eyes in your head, Watcher," Sebastian growls low, shoving Alex behind him as he steps aside to grant the angels room.

The others follow suit and produce a path for the Watchers. I maintain my place next to Viessa, contemplating the fallen with suspicion. I don't trust these fuckers. They slaughtered a contingent of my Wardens outside Bastian's villa to demonstrate a point.

The four beings kneel on either side of the priest's body and respectfully bow their heads. Manakel's soft melodic voice swells through the chamber.

"Incline thine ear, O Lord, unto our prayer, wherein we humbly pray thee to show thy mercy upon the soul of thy servant, Icarus Provanavich, whom thou hast commanded to pass out of this world, that thou wouldst place him in the region of peace and light and bid him a partaker with thy saints. Through Christ, our Lord. Amen."

Whether or not you believe, to witness four powerful angels kneeling in reverence and uttering a beautiful burial prayer is an inspiring sight.

"Viessa Bramen," Gadriel inquires softly before submitting a bow. "We pledge our allegiance to you, the new High Priest Oracle for the immortal world, and affirm to defend and honor you all the days of your life."

The tightness around my chest constricts further at the Watcher's oath. Fuck. A need to howl my anguish to the rafters engulfs me. Why can't I be a selfish jerk, claim my woman, and curse the consequences?

"I accept your fealty, Watchers," Viessa whispers before extracting herself from underneath Icarus's lifeless body.

The four beings gently scoop the priest into their arms and depart without a sound.

The second they vanish, Vi places her wrist at my lips. "Drink, love. You must heal, and you cannot shift in here."

A numbness settles over me as I glare into the translucent amber gaze of my mate. How could I pierce her flesh with my dirty canines? This exquisite creature communes with God, or gods, or whatever controls our destiny. I don't deserve even to touch her, let alone drink her celestial blood.

"My king?" She frowns.

"I'm fine, Viessa," I mutter and limp back with the support of my sword. "I'll just step outside to shift."

The worried gaze follows me as I shuffle toward the door, but she doesn't stop me.

"Wait, Liam," Nicole says, wiping the last residual moisture from her cheeks. "We have pressing matters to handle. Take a couple of sips to repair your leg."

I grit my teeth against Nicki's order, sick and tired of the women in my life barking orders at me. "Allow me five goddamn minutes."

I sense the scrutiny of everyone in the chamber, but it's the shimmering golden gaze I escape as I hobble out of the room with as much dignity as I can muster. My heart is a lead weight in my rib cage, and I require a few moments to collect myself and work through my chaotic thoughts.

Out in the corridor, I pause for a second to inhale deeply and thrust the pain in my leg aside. *What the fuck are you going to do now, King Scott?*

Icarus made it apparent from the outset. Oracles are forbidden to bond with a mate. Let's analyze where that order developed. From the gods. Or *the* God.

So, in essence, I'm fucked. If we oppose the higher beings and complete the link, we invite their wrath, and in doing so, someone pays a tremendous price. Lucretia is her twin; she could be at the top of the shortlist. Kurtis would never recover or would seek retribution. What if they took another child from Nicole and Logan? Would the couple survive another loss?

If I were to guess who tops their list, I'd have to say, me. As a lowly werewolf king with no real discernable purpose other than to lead my people—and any Alpha male can fill that role—it puts a big fat bullseye on my forehead.

My demise isn't what troubles me, though. It's Viessa's reaction to my death that's cause for concern. If they struck me down because of my selfish ambition to make Vi mine, I'm not confident she would recover. The immortals inside just lost their most trusted spiritual guide. I refuse to be the reason they lose another. Oracles are not born every day.

We, as a whole, need her. Her purpose, the meaning of her life, is more relevant than the two of us. But how do I let her go without crushing her? Or myself.

When she fell to her knees in supplication in my closet, she demonstrated she would give up everything to be with me. Would she throw away being an Oracle? I cannot allow it. She is too vital.

Decision made; I scan the vacant hallway. With no one in sight, I might as well shift here instead of enduring the long trek out of the castle.

I slip off my leather pants, wincing against the pain, and fold them in a tidy stack by the wall with my boots on top to scoop up in my jaws and take with me. I need to outrun the grief and misery in my heart.

The stones absorb the impact of my transformation without even a groan. The dynamic strength of my metamorphosis—the immediate restructuring of my frame, mends my injuries in a second. But it does nothing to alleviate the agony in my heart.

"Liam?"

Her gentle tone halts me halfway down the passageway, and I peek over my shoulder, my folded clothes clamped between my teeth.

God, she's a sight. Even in just my t-shirt, she's so damn beautiful, fragile, and lethal all at the same time.

"Where are you going?"

Obviously, I can't respond, so I stare at my woman, branding her beauty in my brain. It's a relief to be in wolf form for this goodbye. I'm not confident I'd be capable of remaining strong if forced to speak the words.

"Please, Liam. Don't do this. Choose me. Choose us."

The anguish in her remarks tears me apart. My heart chooses her. Always. It's the sole reason I turn from the hurt and betrayal in her gaze.

"If you leave me again, never come back."

Her comment freezes me mid-step. I promised never to forsake her, and here I am, bracing to desert her once more, perhaps when she needs me the most. What a fucking coward I've become.

But what choice do I have? Am I expected to spend the rest of my days pining for a female who can never be mine? Who answers to the Almighty? Whose concentration must remain absolute, or lives will perish?

With little alternative, I bow my head in shame and slowly trot away from the being who owns my heart and soul but belongs to God.

Chapter 40

Viessa

If there were a process to terminate my link to Liam, I would use it. Icarus mentioned it, but I have no clue how to perform such a ritual. The incessant onslaught of his emotions on top of mine is overwhelming.

My mate walked away because he presumed it was the noble thing to do, sacrificing his happiness for the betterment of the immortal race. And in a way, I applaud his unselfishness because I'm uncertain I would have been strong enough if the roles were reversed.

Every night when I awaken, my inner vampire shrieks to run to him, to reveal that God sanctioned our union, but something always holds me back. I relive the devastation I went through when he left me in the forest with Icarus, or the time he raced out of that playroom in New York. And even though I understood the monumental battle he was fighting internally, it nearly shattered me.

My king is an honorable male, forcing aside his wants and needs for what he trusts is right. What better champion could an Oracle ask for in a mate?

I snort as I traipse through the mist. That's the line of bullshit I continue to convince my brain into believing. The reality is I crave for him to commit to me, to place me first. To say, fuck it to the rest of the world and claim me as his. No matter how irrational that emotion seems, I can't help it.

I survived on the precipice of society. Shunned. Feared. Pitied. Besides my twin, Liam was the one being who looked past the chaos to the young woman beneath the insanity. The female who selfishly drew from his strength to steal tidbits of lucidity. The woman who would sacrifice anything to be his.

Now, my gift, my obligations as Oracle keep him away, and I secretly despise him for it. I require my Alpha male, but this ridiculous noble shit is tearing me apart. It makes me want to yank my hair and wail to the heavens, "Pick me!"

For once, choose me.

Clear of the mist, I shake my head, cram my concerns into a small corner to play with later, and run my fingers through my shorter locks. Last week, I begged one of the monks to give me a haircut. I desired a distinct look—a unique identity separate from my twin. I believed it would yield a fresh perspective.

It didn't. However, I'm getting used to the soft layers brushing my neck and collarbone and the dozen fresh tattoos across my spine. My father spread his symbols over his entire body. Other than the initial ones I received on my forearm, inner thigh, and shoulder—I kept the rest confined to my back.

The emblems of accomplishment begin in the middle and spiral out into an ever-expanding tight circle. When my training is complete, the full expanse of my back will be a magnificent exhibit of sacred designs the hue of amber and cobalt. The amber represents all I've endured to reach this point, and the blue is to honor my father's memory.

I dispensed with the whole toga garb. Instead, my uniform is a better representation of who I am—a Mistress. Tight leather pants with that convenient zipper running up the middle, backless halter tops in assorted shades highlight my sacred symbols, and thigh-high, black leather boots.

The monks nearly had a heart attack on the first occasion I sauntered into the common area in my new outfit, but they never questioned or admonished me. The robes epitomized my predecessor, and as much as I admired and loved him, I desired to wear something that represented me.

I can't wait for Liam to see me in my attire. My lips widen as I imagine his expression or the ever-expanding bulge in his pants in reaction.

But the smile evaporates. That will only arise if he gets the stick out of his ass and atones. Until then, I'm becoming more and more relaxed in my own skin with the support of the monks who took over my instruction, and Sebastian, who continues to refine my education, transforming me into a full-fledged Domme`.

Tonight, the council convenes to ascertain the fate of Syn Grayflame. My anxiety level spikes knowing I'm about to cast eyes on my mate for the first time in months. Will the wolf even acknowledge me or request to chat with me privately? I've fantasized about every likely scenario of him kneeling before me and pleading for my forgiveness before he tears my clothes from my body and stakes his claim.

As I teleport to the vampire castle, worry eats away at my gut, remembering the explosive chip still embedded in the small of Liam's back. With the detonator destroyed, he's safe for now, but we do not understand if Abigail is alive or dead. Troy disappeared with her charred body. I've gained several visions, but nothing that might help.

The second I materialize in the conference room, all conversation ceases. The members gape slack-jawed at my unfamiliar appearance. I inhale a fortifying breath but quickly realize Liam isn't physically here. The heated stare travels down my shape from a monitor on the wall.

Irritation hardens my jaw. The werewolf didn't trust himself to be in the same vicinity as me? Fine. If he prefers to maintain his distance? So be it.

I turn from his image. My lips lift at the collective gasp spreading the chamber as the immortals around the conference area view the intricate spiral. I've accomplished so much in a brief amount of time. My progress impressed even the monks who insisted that in another month, my education will be complete.

"How may I be of service, my lady?" I ask the vampire queen at the head of the table, her intimidating mate at her side.

"Wow, Oracle," Queen Oresha coos from her seat. "Love the outfit."

"And the new artwork," Nicole grins with a wink.

"Thank you. My training should conclude within the month."

"Holy shit. Really?" The Halfling exclaims.

"Yes. I have been working diligently."

"You have some pretty big shoes to fill, Viessa. I don't envy you the task." She waves to the chair at her left.

I nod before lowering into the comfy high back identical to those around the table and work to keep my gaze from bouncing to the monitor.

I'm confused when I see Alex sitting next to her mom. She rarely attends the council sessions. Or Sebastian, for that matter, unless required for I.T. concerns. Tonight, he stands stoically by the doors, his vivid blue stare riveted on Alexandria.

What doesn't surprise me is the other occupant in the room—Bridget, Nicole's mother. Her spine is ramrod straight as she perches on the edge of her seat against the wall. Her testimony tonight seals Syn's fate, and she doesn't appear too thrilled about it.

I follow her gaze to the second monitor mounted next to the handsome visage of my mate. Guards shackled the powerful fae to a wall with iron, his wings bound with thick bands of the same material.

After Liam left, I entered the torture room again just as Nicole ordered King Grayflame arrested. He went peacefully, but not before Logan slammed his fist into Syn's jaw, knocking the dark fae on his ass.

"That is for daring to touch what is mine. If it were up to me, it would be your head hitting the floor instead of your ass."

Syn calmly wiped the blood from his lip and ascended to his feet, only to have Sebastian's fist connect with his other cheek, slamming him against the wall. Cipher and Kurtis slapped iron handcuffs on his wrists, and Sebastian and Logan transported him to the Council of Unity prison to await his trial.

"What will become of him," Bridget asked, striding over to Nicole with cautious steps.

"The Council and your testimony will determine his fate." Nicole's gunmetal irises showcased her contempt as she contemplated her mother. "I will decide yours."

"Please take your seats." The vampire's harsh tone snags my attention away from that night in Scotland. The heart-breaking moment when Liam's wolf turned from me. "We have a full agenda tonight, so let's shoot through them as quickly as possible. It's not clear if King Darath will attend, and we still have no notion of the fate of Priestess Kleora, but we've delayed this as long as feasible. We must proceed without them. Does everybody agree?"

The five representatives, including myself, nod in agreement.

"First order, swearing in the new Oracle, Viessa Bramen, as a Council of Unity member." She shifts her bold stare to me. "Do you pledge to adhere to the bylaws presented to you?"

"Yes, my lady," I respond with sincerity. Even from hundreds of miles away, I sense the impassioned gaze of my mate from the monitor.

Nicole produces the parchment with bloody thumbprints, and I dutifully pierce mine with a fang and include my mark and signature below the others.

"Welcome aboard, Oracle Bramen," Nicki announces, and a chorus of hear hear rounds the table.

My commitment to the immortal realm and Queen Giordano has begun, as promised, to my father.

"Okay, next up, Arra would appreciate the floor. Please proceed, Queen Svaldana."

The petite monarch stands and Sebastian tenses. "I would like to announce to this body that I am officially stepping down as valkyrie ruler and am bequeathing my throne and seat on this cabinet to my offspring, Alexandria Svaldana."

I watch Alex intently. The little redhead doesn't appear too overjoyed with this development, but stands to accept her destiny with all the grace her five-foot frame can muster. She peers over at her mate, her expression clouded with apprehension. Bastian offers her a provocative grin and wink. The tension visibly leaves her shoulders at his support.

"Do you agree, Miss Svaldana?" Nicki asks, working to contain her smile.

"Yes, my lady."

"And do you vow to adhere to the bylaws presented to you?"

"I do."

Nicole slides the parchment down the table to her best friend, who repeats the process to secure her seat. Arra hugs her daughter and strolls over to settle into the chair next to Bridget.

The original four. Nicki, Kurtis, Alex, and Liam are all rulers of their people and occupy the majority vote on this council for the moment. The immortal race's future rests in their capable hands, and it's my duty to guide them in the proper direction without interfering on a grand scale, unless unavoidable.

No pressure.

"Welcome to the Council of Unity, Queen Alexandria Svaldana," Nicole announces with a huge grin and another round of hear hears.

The pride on Bastian's face fills my heart with envy. Not a virtuous emotion for an Oracle, but I'm only immortal after all, with all the passions and shortcomings of a vampire who craves to witness such an expression aimed at her from her stubborn ass mate.

"Now that we have the pleasantries out of the way, let's move on to Syn Grayflame." Nicole glances down at the tablet in her hand and whistles low. "Some pretty hefty charges against you, Synie. Attempted kidnapping of King Liam Scott. If it were up to me, I'd add attempted murder since an explosive chip rests at the base of his spine. Unfortunately, Abigail Brevil implanted it and not you directly. We also have no inkling where the witch and Troy Tenebris took off to, or if she's even alive, so the charge won't stand."

The Halfling grits her teeth, but Syn's silver gaze remains barren of expression.

"The other charges include capture and torture of two rulers and members of this council: Queen Oresha and myself. Kidnap and torture of formerly Princess Alexandria Svaldana. I would love nothing more than to charge you with conspiracy to murder a High Priest Oracle, but since that was once again Abi's doing, I can't prove you had anything to do with it."

"I would have never harmed Icarus," the silver-eyed fae states calmly.

The empath winces. "Shut your goddamn mouth, Syn," Nicki barks. "You don't get to utter his name."

"Abigail did state you promised her the power of an Oracle, Mr. Grayflame." I refuse to give him the title of Lord. Because of this bastard conniving with the witch, my father is deceased. "How exactly did you propose providing such a service?"

"Good fucking question," Nicole smirks.

"I had hoped Icarus and Abi would set aside their angst, reconcile, and he would accept her back under his wing as an Oracle. I never dreamed she planned on slaying him."

"You are a lying piece of shit," Nicki growls.

I lay a cautious hand on her fist, clenched on the table. "Unfortunately, my lady. We cannot prove or refute his statement." Am I presenting the best advice? I have no idea, but my father would hope to maintain peace during a meeting, and I must endeavor to do the same.

The queen sighs, closing her eyes briefly. "It's almost like he's here, channeling himself through you, Viessa."

"Perhaps he is, my lady," I smile, and she nods before proceeding.

"The last charge on your long list, and the one which carries a sentence of death; kidnap and torture of a human, for years, I might add. Also, revealing the immortal world to her. Let's start with that. If we find you guilty, none of the others matter, anyway."

Nicole rises and faces off with her mother. "Bridget Taylor, did Syn Grayflame take you against your will?"

The woman swallows, hazel eyes darting anxiously between Syn's chained image on the monitor and her daughter's. She climbs slowly to her feet, rubbing her palms down her jeans, before tucking a red curl behind her ear.

"Answer the question, *Mother*," Nicole sneers.

"No. I was with King Grayflame under my own volition."

Chapter 41

Viessa

"**A**re you fucking kidding me?" the queen's stunned tone reflects my own thoughts.

The occupants of the room gape at the human standing bravely before powerful immortals who could end her life in a matter of seconds. Her chin lifts in defiance. Now I realize where Nicole gets her stubborn streak.

A memory of her chained from the ceiling while Syn took her from behind flashes through my mind. The way she leaned against him, her moans of pleasure as the fae brought her to climax. Also, the tears and defeat in her frame when it was over and he departed without a backward glance.

Are we dealing with a Stockholm Syndrome case, or is there something darker going on here? A pang of underlying guilt she feels she must atone for, at any cost?

"My lady," I address Nicki as I rise from my seat. "May I question the mortal?"

Nicole eyeballs her parent with contempt for several more seconds before gesturing to me. "She's all yours, Oracle."

Syn jerks against his shackles. For the first time since I entered this room, the eerie silver eyes flicker with emotion. "Leave her out of this," he demands with a rough growl. "Interrogate me. I will confess to whatever you wish."

"Oh, your turn's coming, Synie," Nicole mocks, but regards him curiously.

"Bridget." Several inches taller than the frail mortal, I lift her gaze to mine with a gentle finger under her chin. "I witnessed you in chains in his chamber, welts and deep cuts from a whip covered your body. Are you claiming you consented to such cruel treatment?"

"Y... Yes," she stammers but holds my stare.

"Then why the breakdown in tears after he disappeared?"

She blinks several times, a clear sign she's about to lie. "I'm emotional. I usually shatter after an intense session."

"Pet," Grayflame growls from the monitor. "Why are you defending me after everything I put you through?"

I release the mortal's chin and shift to the side so the woman can direct her answer to the dark fae king on the screen. "You were once a wonderful male, Syn, a loving man, but my betrayal changed all that. I must pay for my sins and make it right. I hope one day you can forgive me once you learn why I did what I did and finally understand the reasons I couldn't confide in you."

"I will never be that naïve and stupid male again, Bri."

"Tell us, mortal," I encourage softly.

"Yeah." Nicole crosses her arms over her chest. "I can't wait to hear this."

"When Rordrick was born, we were so content. Happy. I loved you more than I believed a person could. You introduced me to a fantastical world I'd only read about in books, and I imagined living out the rest of my short life with you and my son by my side." She swallows, her fingers wringing in front of her. "That all changed when the blue tattooed man appeared in our bedroom at the castle."

"Icarus?" I question.

"Yes. He claimed the gods predetermined my destiny and outlined my future. He warned me if I didn't comply, fate would steal from me what I cherished most in the world. You and Rordrick."

"Why did you not come to me?" Syn implores. "We could have figured it out together."

"The monk commanded me not to divulge the truth to anyone, especially you, until after his death."

Oh, God. Icarus foresaw his demise even back then.

"What transpired next, Bridget?" Liam questions from the other screen.

His deep voice washes over me, causing goosebumps to skate over my skin. I lower my lids briefly to revel in the sensation before refocusing on the mortal before me.

"He instructed me to go to a specific club the king frequented at a precise time, and his spell would do the rest. As soon as I entered the bar, Dimitri's eyes were drawn to me." She peers up at Syn. "I did it to spare you and our son, and I would do it again if it meant you survived."

Pain and disbelief war with each other in Syn's expression, his silver gaze never faltering from the human.

"Did Icarus reveal what your future beheld?" I ask.

"Yes. He warned me it would be brutal, painful, and heartbreaking." She glances at Nicole, grief shimmering in the hazel irises. "But he forbade me to intervene. He said your destiny would ascend from the ashes of your hatred and thirst for revenge, and I was not to intrude."

Logan squeezes his lids shut briefly before zeroing his bright gaze on his mate standing ridged at the head of the table.

The queen's expression is a complete blank. I exert a slight mental pressure to determine her emotions, but her defense holds. Fascinated by her expertise to conceal her inner turmoil, I scrutinize her as she calmly reaches for her coffee mug that reads "Tears of My Enemies" and takes several sips.

I've finally discovered Queen Giordano's tells. Sarcasm and caffeine. Those are her shields.

"So," she begins after planting the cup back on the desk. "You forfeited your happiness to save your spouse and son by sacrificing your daughter. Interesting."

"The priest informed me of the prophecy. It nearly crushed me to look the other way and ultimately abandon everything I loved by faking my death. Still, it lessened the burden somewhat to realize you would one day defeat Dimitri, become a powerful vampire queen mated to the love of your life, and bring peace and incredible change to the immortal realm."

I can't count the laws my father violated to ensure Nicole's creation and direction. The mortal's narrative is living proof of his manipulation and subterfuge.

"Well. I'm glad it eased your mind, Mom."

On pure intuition, I stride to Nicki's side and lay my palm on her tense shoulder. When the gray eyes find mine, I force our connection to open. She inhales deeply against the invasion but doesn't shift away.

'Put aside your hurt and betrayal, my lady. Your mother did what she had to in order to protect her son and mate. Would you do no less?' The queen's jaw hardens, refusing to respond. *'Icarus defied the gods and our laws to ensure you fulfilled the prophecy. Without his intervention, you would never have been born. King Giordano would still be on the throne with Logan and Sebastian under his thumb or dead.'*

Her eyes tighten before she nods. *'I get it, but it doesn't make it any easier to swallow.'*

'Give it time, my lady. One day when you have a child of your own, you might understand.'

"Did the priest force you to betray me to Dimitri, pet?" Syn sneers and the focus returns to the matter at hand.

"Yes, my love. To achieve certain developments for the future and save your life."

"Mine, or your own?"

"I did not care what happened to me at that stage. Whether I survived or perished. All I knew was I had to secure my children's and your existence at any cost." Bridget's lip quivers, but she valiantly holds the tears at bay.

"Your revenge was the catalyst to bring out Abigail, whose presence drew Troy Tenebris from hiding."

"Why?" I ask curiously.

"I do not know, Oracle," she confesses. "The priest did not reveal everything."

"For clarification," I pivot to the council even though I address the mortal. "You're claiming the incidents which brought us all to this hearing, Icarus Provanavich, the High Priest Oracle, orchestrated the levies against Syn Grayflame to fulfill Nicole's prophecy?"

"Yes," she murmurs, and a stillness settles over the office.

"I have no further questions, Queen Giordano," I state before taking my seat, fully cognizant of every eye directed toward me. But it's the pair of smoldering irises following me across the room that ignites my blood.

Nicole sighs and shifts her focus back to the council. She glares up at Syn's image for several minutes, and I discern the feud within her. She's no doubt reliving what he put her through at the fae castle.

"In light of these recent discoveries, we should discuss our options. Please disconnect Grayflame's feed while we debate our next step."

With a few clicks from Sebastian's phone, the screen brightens to blue.

"How the fuck did a mere mortal not only mate with a dark fae and a vampire but conceive with both?" Liam demands.

"Yes," Nicole replies, "I wondered that myself." She twists to Bridget. "Are you the exception to the rule, or are there more humans in the world who can bond and procreate with immortals?"

"We are rare, but I've been told there are others. The priest informed me, once one of us drinks the blood of their mate, binding them to an immortal, and we continue to partake of their essence regularly, it enhances our lifespan."

"Are we talking several years?" Nicki asks with interest.

"No. By decades."

"Do you know how many exist?" Logan questions with a bewildered look.

"No, my lord. I never met another Breeder."

"Breeder?" Kurtis inquires, leaning forward, elbows on the table.

"That is what the blue priest called us," she explains with a shuttered expression.

"Humph," the queen turns to the members. "Let's pull back to the issue at hand. Thoughts?"

"I do not believe we should charge him. It sounds like the Oracle maneuvered him into this position. Who the fuck wants to dispute that?" Kurtis states.

"I will," Jilaya argues with a livid sparkle in her sapphires, her red-tipped fingernails tapping on her chin. "I'm curious. If you bonded with Syn and bore him a child, how could you conceive with King Giordano? It's abnormal for even an immortal to procreate with anyone other than their mate. Sebastian, and Alexandria's siblings being the exception to the rule."

Logan's mother was his father's one true mate, but after her death, he took Rowena as a companion, and they produced Bastian. A rarity for vampires. Hence the reason the population of the immortal world, vampires, in particular, has diminished.

Former Queen Arra Svaldana's fated one is Cipher Ruse, Kurtis's father. They created Alex, but before that, the valkyrie wed a berserker named Gadr. They had two children together. Not as extreme an oddity with valkyries and shifter breeds, but still sporadic in immortal history.

Wow. I guess that makes Alexandria and Kurtis half-siblings.

"Dimitri and I were never mated. Icarus performed some ritual with his seed, and I became pregnant. A Breeder's destiny is for one immortal in their lifetime."

What lengths wouldn't my father go to in order to fulfill that damn prophecy?

"I... I can't even begin to respond to that," Nicole states in stunned disbelief and spins back to the council.

"As much as it grieves me, I concur with King Ruse," Alexandria responds quietly, taking to her new role. "The Valkyrie Regency is unwilling to undermine the workings of an Oracle."

"How do you know it wasn't his design all along to have Syn executed?" Nicole mutters, the bitterness coming through loud and clear.

"We don't," Alex replies, her blue eyes alight with understanding, having suffered at Syn's hands as well. "But are you willing to take the chance it wasn't?"

She evades answering by turning to my wolf. "King Scott?"

"While it galls me he *manipulated* us in such a fashion, the Werewolf Province refuses to align against an Oracle. Dead or alive." His eyes harden as they settle on me.

My king is speaking about more than the deception instigated by my father, and my lips tighten. I've had about enough of this bullshit.

"Goddamnit," Nicole mutters. "Nor will the Vampire Nation. But I heartily recommend we expel him from his throne and this committee. Rordrick is young, but so was I when I took over. He seems wise beyond his years and more than competent to lead the Dark Fae Kingdom."

"I second the motion," Kurtis utters.

"All in favor?"

A resounding chorus of yea rounds through the diminished council, and we all feel the absence of King Darath and Priestess Tanagra.

"Bring Syn back online. It's time to reveal his fate."

Chapter 42

Viessa

The second Grayflame's restrained image pops on the screen, Nicki twists to her mother once more. "There's a little matter I need to handle before we sentence you, Syn."

Bridget swallows nervously but maintains her daughter's furious gaze, her fists clenched at her waist. "I don't expect you to forgive me, Nicole."

"Well, that's a relief," the queen sneers. "You had me worried you'd beg for forgiveness and it would get awkward."

"Nicole," Logan begins, but quickly shuts his mouth with a resigned sigh when his mate glares at him, daring him to proceed.

She swivels her livid glare, charged with hurt and betrayal, back to Bridget. "It doesn't matter your reasons. What you did, or should I say didn't do, was incomprehensible. I'll *never* absolve you. When this trial is over, one of my Guardians will escort you wherever you choose to go. If you ever attempt to contact me or any of my friends, I will have you imprisoned." She takes a threatening step toward her parent, her fangs lowered, the gray irises bright as day. "Are we clear?"

Bridget nods, tears cascading down her cheeks. "I'm so sorry. I merely did what I thought was best," she murmurs.

Nicole lunges for her mother, but Logan snatches her around the waist, holding her against his chest.

"Where were the tears and sympathy when Dimitri was torturing and raping me, *Mom*?" She struggles against Logan's grip, and the huge warrior clutches the desk behind him with his other hand to keep his mate in place. "You don't get to be sorry. You have to fucking live with what you did until you're old and wither to dust."

Syn's chains rattle as he strains against them, his glittering silver gaze on his mate.

My heart aches for the young Halfling. For all she suffered at the hands of fate. She didn't ask to be the prophesied bringer of peace. Despite all the hurt, betrayal, and suffering the title forced her to endure, she grabbed the challenge by the horns, gave it everything she had, and has prevailed in slowly chipping away at the check boxes of her legend.

When the fight finally drains from the queen, she spins in Logan's embrace and buries her face in his neck, granting herself a moment to gain composure. The fearless warrior holds her close, his atomic gaze fixated on Nicole's mother.

A hushed silence settles over the room as Bridget wipes her cheeks and eases back into her chair against the wall. I pity the human. A powerful being manipulated her beyond her capability to resist. Forced her to betray the love of her life and any prospect of a future with her son. She led a nightmare existence with the demented Dimitri and sacrificed her daughter's innocence and sanity, all in the hope

Nicki would blossom as my father declared and slay the crazed immortal who, in some ways, abused them both.

I don't blame Nicole for refusing to excuse her mother. That would be a tough pill to swallow. But maybe one day, she can look past all the pain and misery she endured and understand it from a mother's perspective.

A glint of silver catches my eye, and my gaze swivels toward Bridget. With her regard fixated on her mate's image on the screen, she raises a narrow dagger she must have had concealed in her sleeve and, without hesitation, swipes the blade across her neck.

"No!" Syn bellows, his wings busting the iron restraints and unfurling with a snap as he yanks against his bonds.

Arra jumps back as if the mortal's blood is contagious.

I scurry to her side, catch her before she crashes to the floor, and slap my palm over her wound to stem the flow. I peer over at Nicole. Her shocked gaze zeros in on the crimson tide oozing between my fingers.

"Nicole, give her your blood," I instruct with urgency. When she doesn't move, I bark her name once more. She jolts as if ripped from a trance, rushes to my side, and pierces the inside of her wrist, holding it to her mother's lips.

Bridget evades the offering, refusing to drink and save herself. "Logan, hold her head," I order, but his enormous palms remain clenched at his sides. He observes the mortal bleeding out with hatred and disgust.

"Please, Bri, take her vein," Syn begs from the screen while struggling for freedom. "I'm sorry. Don't leave me. I love you."

At the dark fae's declaration, Bridget's lips close around her daughter's wrist, swallowing down the gift of life. The Halfling's powerful blood closes the deep lesion in seconds, surging color into the pale cheeks.

"That's it, pet. Drink." Syn sags against the wall behind him, his battered wings tucked at his back once more.

"That was a cowardly, fucked up move, mother," Nicole growls and snatches her wrist away.

I disappear for a brief second and return with a moist washcloth and hand it to Bridget, who swabs at the blood on her neck. "I am a Breeder, daughter." She stands regally. The only sign she just slit her own throat is the stain of blood on her blouse. "A human who can mate and conceive with an immortal. By consuming your sacred essence, I've extended my life by centuries, not decades."

"Who informed you of this, mortal?" Logan asks with a furious glower.

"The priest assured me you would save me," she smiles tenderly at Nicki before glancing at the towering warrior at her side. "Icarus declared it and directed me to advise the council they must discover all the other Breeders and preserve their lives by drinking Nicole's blood."

"If it hadn't been for the Oracle here, your sorry ass would burn in hell for all eternity."

"I do not believe that. No matter how much you loathe me, I am still your mother."

"You were *never* a mother," Logan growls, his eyes sparking with green fire. "Get her out of here before I finish what she started."

Nox suddenly appears, bows to his queen, and escorts the mortal from the room.

Nicole returns to the conference table, and I'm flabbergasted by her apparent calm. Her authority over the turmoil buried beneath boggles my mind. I stride to my chair, mopping the blood from between my shaky fingers with the damp towel Bridget discarded.

Icarus never informed me certain human women could procreate with immortals. We must find these precious females and locate their mates. With the dwindling birth rate among immortals, this revelation could tip the scales.

Will I, as the sole Oracle, procure the foresight to locate these gifts? God, once word gets out, the unmated males will clamor for any aid in discovering their whereabouts.

Here's another tremendous question? Are these human women aware of their importance to the immortal realm? If not, the poor females are in for the shock of a lifetime when we find them.

"Syn Grayflame, we hereby absolve you of all charges," Nicole announces, jarring me from my internal conflict. "But based on your involvement in the aforementioned crimes, the council has deemed it judicious to discharge you from your duties as king and strip you of your seat on the Council of Unity. Your only surviving son, Rordrick, will assume leadership if he so desires. If not, we will vote in a high-ranking member of your society."

"Such power you wield, Halfling," the angry fae sneers even as armed guards remove his shackles.

"Oh, you don't know the half of it, Synie." She nods to Bastian, and the former king's visage dissipates.

"Has anyone heard from the Land Nymph Domain on what their intentions are concerning Kleora?" Nicole questions, reaching for her mug.

I chew my lip to keep from speaking. I've had several insights regarding Jagorach and the witch Troy, but nothing about Priestess Tanagra or Abigail, and I am forbidden to disclose anything until the relevant time. Although it seems my father had no such compulsion.

Being an Oracle really sucks sometimes.

As the discussion progresses, stripping Syn from his throne and council and appointing his son Rordrick in his place, I peer at my mate on the monitor. The stupid idiot craves me as much as I crave him. The blood I've consumed over the last few months pales compared to his rich, woodsy flavor.

I'm reminded again of our commitment to each other in his closet. I swore to only drink from him, and he vowed to always be faithful during the full moon. I sense every emotion that occurs through my proud king. I know the male has maintained his side of the bargain, but he failed in his vow never to leave me again, which compelled me to break my pledge to survive. The wolf is well aware since I haven't run to him for nourishment.

'My patience is at an end, my king,' I whisper in his mind. The whiskey irises blaze with emotion as they snap to mine.

Come the next full moon; if Liam has not sought me out through either Nicole or Lu, then I'll decide for him. His beast will submit, and before the night is through my neck will bear his mark, or there will be hell to pay.

Chapter 43

"**F**uck, Josh!" I grind out between clenched teeth, clutching the edge of the kitchen table I'm lying prone across. When I insisted my siblings surgically remove the chip next to my spine after no word from Troy, I didn't realize the pain would be so excessive.

"It's deep, brother. I'm sorry." Josh declares for the tenth time as he digs through muscle and tendons to locate the dormant explosive. The device is clearly visible on the x-ray clipped to the refrigerator, thanks to Doc Warfield, the ranch's personal veterinarian. The old-timer insisted I seek medical attention. I assured him I would, with no intention of having some human probing around and asking questions I'd refuse to answer. Plus, once they took my temperature, they'd hospitalize me immediately thinking I was ill.

Werewolves and shifter body temps run about 103 to 104, just resting. When we are near a shift or exerting ourselves, it spikes to 107–108. A temp that would fry a mortal's brain.

"You got this, Joshie," Cellica asserts from the opposite side as she dabs at the blood with a dishrag while gripping my shoulder with the other to hold me still. Thank God as immortals we don't have to worry about sepsis.

I bite down on the towel Cel handed me and distract my-self with thoughts of my mate. God, I couldn't get over the metamorphosis in not merely her appearance but her poise and calm demeanor at the hearing.

The shorter locks were stunning, framing her exquisite face and showcasing those incredible irises. And her outfit? Fuck. I'm addicted to the leather pants with the gold zipper meant for my enjoyment. The coil of blue and golden tattoos on her exposed back was staggering and beautiful. My mate has achieved so much in a brief measure of time. Pride filled my chest at her success as an Oracle and the healing of her spirit and psyche.

I witnessed her father in her as she questioned the mortal and telepathically communed with Nicole to help steer her decision in the appropriate direction. Every time those bril-liant eyes settled on mine, my muscles strained, and my dick hardened. I was never so happy the camera only presented me from the waist up.

"Ow, dammit, Josh!" He must have struck a nerve because an intense pain radiates down my hip and thigh, causing me to twitch. If I were a mere mortal, my brother would have just permanently paralyzed me.

"Almost got it."

"Well, hurry. I sense the drag of the moon and I don't need you shifting with your fingers embedded in my spine."

I used to glory in the lunar transformations. It was such a freeing experience to hunt and fuck in wild abandon. Now

I dread it. I promised Vi I would never seek another, but containing the beast is a perpetual battle the entire night. The second the rays of the sun peak over the horizon, my body and mind are so depleted from keeping him in check, I stumble through the doors naked, barely making it through a hasty shower before collapsing face-first into bed. Within moments, I've fallen into an exhausted sleep filled with dreams of Viessa.

After examining my mate, in all her splendid glory, I'm rethinking my noble idiocy. She declared she had another month of instruction left. I must hold out until she's finished. Then and only then can I seek her out, plead for her forgiveness, and hash out a plan to be together.

She has to make the gods understand I provide her strength. I'm not a distraction, but her peace in the storm, the balance to her chaos, and my powers bolster her own.

I just need to ride out this full moon and conceivably the next to provide her the chance to finish her education. After that, I don't give a fuck what the fates want, or the rest of the world. My female will become mine. Body. Mind. Soul.

"Got it!" Josh declares with a whoop.

"Careful," Cel admonishes. "Let's not blow up the house with your exuberance."

"Right," my brother whispers before depositing the little apparatus in my palm as my sister slaps a makeshift bandage over the wide gash. As soon as I shift, the wound will repair.

I gaze in fury at the metal object the diameter of a grain of rice, recalling the night the witch implanted it. So many sins I need to atone for with my mate. Resolve stiffens my sore spine as I climb off the wooden surface.

If I must devote the next century to proving to Viessa I am hers and hers alone, then so be it. She belongs to me, and I'm done running from a situation I can't control. Gods be damned. The Oracle and I will complete our bond by the next moon.

I twist to my brother. "Thanks, but never become a surgeon," I tease, clasping his forearm. I don't bother putting my shirt back on. In about thirty minutes the moon will be at its crest and the beast will make his appearance. "Is the band ready?"

"Yup. We set everything up and the pack is drinking and milling around as usual."

"Good. Let's get this over with."

"You may not look forward to the shifts anymore, but I damn well do. Couple of bitches I've got my eye on for tonight." He rubs his palms together in anticipation.

"You're such a man whore, Joshie," Cellica frowns. "Just pick one."

"What's the fun in that? When your time to shift is upon you, little sis, you'll finally understand."

"Whatever. I'm heading into town with my friends before you all turn into sexual sociopaths." She shifts to me. "I'm spending the night at Jessica's."

"Be careful."

"Always."

I snatch my guitar in the living room on my way out to the patio, impatient to get tonight over with, but at least I get to enjoy my genuine passion, performing in front of a live audience. They're a bunch of sex-starved, drunken werewolves devoted to me because I'm their king, but it doesn't matter.

The second I stride onto the platform overlooking the Yellowstone River and my home, my dread eases, and peace settles over my soul. Before I play The Wolf, the sendoff song, I strum the intro to Stronger Than Me by Garth Brooks.

The crowd quiets at the tender melody, or maybe it's the emotions I grant free rein as I sing. Either way, I've captured their undivided attention.

You know, I always thought I had to have the answers
Be her strength and take the lead
When it comes to everything that really matters
She's stronger than me

The words pierce through my soul. I've been such an idiot, dragging us into this solitary, torturous existence because I couldn't see past my inherent conviction that giving up control somehow made me weak. A stupid, self-righteous belief it was for the betterment of all immortals.

The reality relates more to the lyrics. Viessa lifts the world's weight off my shoulders, and when I surrender to her passions, it doesn't detract from who I am; it makes me proud to be her male. Everything in my life is hers, including my soul, till my last breath.

As I sing the last line; *And if I have a choice, I pray God takes me first 'cause she's stronger than me,* her addictive scent of honeysuckle and woman wash over me. I scan the crowd, swaying to the melody.

A familiar soft glow at the rear of the patio catches my eye and I rip the guitar over my head and thrust it at my brother.

"Take over."

I don't hear his response. The beast's hungry growls drown out everything but her, and it's all I can do to hold the shift at bay.

Once I'm clear of the crowd, I spy her slipping around the side of the house; the moonlight highlighting the engravings circling her back. If she wishes to play hard to get, she picked the wrong night.

When I round the corner, she's nowhere in sight. My canines extend. The beast's annoyance at having our mate just out of reach rides my every breath.

"Viessa!" I roar to the wind. "Come to me, woman."

My acute hearing catches the brief giggle. I smirk. If my female aspires to play with fire, so be it. I make quick work of my jeans and boots and let the transformation to beast form consume my body before tracking the little minx through the woods. The echo of my brother's rendition of The Wolf urges me to a brisk pace.

She must be tracing because I keep losing her scent before picking it up again a half-mile away. The beast detects a unique essence about my mate. Magic. Powerful magic. The energy signature is similar to Icarus's but more robust and complex. Like a fine whiskey.

I leap into the timbers for better advantage, and that's when I zero in on my mate's aura. She's waiting in the middle of a small open field about three hundred yards to my right. An amber glow surrounds her supple frame as she watches, her arms crossed casually at her chest over the blood-red halter top.

I bound through the trees, keeping her in sight as I advance on her position. The closer we become, the more her presence ramps up the beast. It salivates for a taste of its mate, fixed to make her ours.

When I drop from the pines a mere ten feet from the object I most covet, my breath is harsh. Not from exertion, from the lust and need coursing through my bloodstream, and the knowledge I'm about to take what's mine at last.

"Kneel, Liam."

She utters the command in a soft tone, but I rear back as if she shrieked it. What the ever livin' fuck? Does she expect the beast to submit? How the inferno will I rule him long enough to grant her request?

Son of a bitch.

The bright gaze holds my awareness. My frame quivers with the demand to force her to the ground and fuck her senseless while my jaws pin her in place. The growls rumbling from my chest intensify as the creature and I struggle for control.

"You wish to bite me, then do as I command and you will," she declares, seeming unaffected by the feral grunts and snarls dominating the space between us.

Mark her now.

No. Must obey.

Fuck obey. Claim.

The inner battle consumes me. When I consider I've gained the upper hand, the beast takes over and charges forward, ready to fuck, conquer, and mark her as ours.

Chapter 44

Liam

No! I bellow at the crazed animal inside me, suspending our progress a mere foot from Viessa. She didn't cower or retreat as I advanced. Her calm demeanor in the face of such savagery spoke to me. In those brief seconds, I dug deep for strength and terminated the beast's forward momentum just in time.

My torso heaves from the effort to hold him in check as I devour every inch of my mate. From the come fuck me boots, along the long, lean stretch of shapely legs, up the trim waist. My gaze stalls on the heaving breasts with the tight points of her nipples straining against the thin fabric of her top. I lick my lips, imagining the flavor of her skin on my tongue.

My woman has evolved since the first moment I laid eyes on her behind the shield, and not just in appearance. Her newfound self-confidence shines bright in her unflinching gaze. It's in the courageous lift of her chin. The way she carries herself, and the serenity in her expression.

It is sexy as fuck.

"Kneel, Liam," she commands again, and this time I sink to one knee even as my beast growls in displeasure.

The second her hand caresses my shoulder; a calmness seeps into my system. I bow my head in subjugation, astonished at this female's ability, not merely to calm the monster but force him to surrender.

I would give Viessa anything within my power, but all she's ever craved was my sexual submission.

Well, sweetness, your words finally penetrated my thick skull.

I'm capable of submitting sexually without being weak in other areas of my life.

"Look at me, my king," she whispers, and I obey, gazing into the brilliant amber depths. "I will ask this once. How you respond will either make or break us. The decision is in your hands."

Christ. Do the right thing, Liam. We can't lose her.

"Do you yield to being my sexual submissive?"

I scrutinize her gaze, searching for any sign she's uneasy about my response. I note the slow, steady heart rate, the even deep breathing. All indications she couldn't care one way or the other how I answer. Until I witness the smooth expanse of her throat move as she swallows.

I nod.

Her quick inhale says it all and wonder fills me.

"Oh, Liam. I love you, you stubborn idiot. I vow to you right here and now that I will bring your mind and body to pinnacles of ecstasy you've never encountered." She kneels with me on the verdant ground. I tense, aching to reach for her and yank her against my raging erection.

"In your true form," she confides, running a gentle caress over my fur-covered chest. My muscles twitch in response, "You are feral and beautiful. It makes me wet just thinking about submitting to you every full moon."

I grunt in approval, my insides swelling with pride at the devotion and lust swirling in her vivid gaze.

"I crave, down to my very soul, to dominate and worship the male, the king. But tonight, I wholly surrender to the beast."

She reaches up and releases the knot at her nape and low back. The crimson garment floats to the ground between us. My heart jacks into overdrive. The beast's focus pinpoints on one aim. Sink my cock deep inside this amazing woman and conclude our bond.

She rises. I tense to seize her when she unzips the sexy boots, tossing them to the side. My panting breath turns harsh, blended with short growls of need as she slides the perfectly placed zipper down her crotch to expose her bare, glistening sex to my enraptured gaze.

"Mark me. Make me yours forever."

In a heartbeat, I'm on her, knocking her to the grassy ground. She moans, knees bent; thighs spread. Toned arms reach over her head as she stretches like a cat in heat.

Unable to deny myself a second more, I drop between her legs and feast on my mate's sweet essence. She cries out at the first swipe of my tongue, her hips lifting to grind against my face.

I slap a claw-tipped palm over her hip to hold her immobile and shove one leg up to her chest, stretching her open like a scrumptious buffet. The second I lick at her puckered opening, Viessa jolts, burrowing her fingers into the grass, her neck arching in ecstasy.

Fuck, she tastes sweet and musky and so fucking perfect. I continue to tease her anus, saturating it with my saliva before retracting a claw on my finger. With slow care, not usually a characteristic in the beast, I rub the pinkness and gradually ease inside while proceeding to lick and suck her savory pussy.

"Oh, God. Yes, Liam."

Her cries and moans urge me on, and when the tight stricture eases, I press forward until my thick finger seats all the way. I hold it still as I swirl and suckle her swollen bundle of nerves. Within moments, her legs tense. I sense she's on the precipice, so I begin a slow thrusting and delve my tongue into her convulsing core.

Viessa screams my name. Her back arches as she digs her heels into my shoulders, gyrating her hips in abandon. I snarl with possessiveness, enjoying the sweet essence of my woman flaring across my taste buds, and guzzle pure fucking bliss. This powerful Oracle is mine forever.

Her limbs relax, and her arms flop to the side. I rear up, capture her around the waist and flip her to her hands and knees. The sacred engravings give me pause for a moment, but the hesitation vanishes when my female rubs her ass against the hardness aching for her.

I climb over her, planting one palm on the ground by hers while the other slides up her torso, tweaking a nipple along the way before closing around her throat and jaw.

The occasion has arrived to pierce my woman's flesh from both ends and claim her as mine.

With a sudden aggressive maneuver, I thrust inside her drenched core. Her muscles convulse, objecting to the harsh intrusion, but the beast is beyond gentleness at this point.

She stiffens when I stretch her neck to the side. Without her longer locks, it exposes her slender neck and shoulder for the taking.

"Liam?" she whimpers, her athletic frame taut with anxiety.

A werewolf's bite during mating is unpleasant. Glands behind our canines release toxins that inhibit the flesh from regenerating, like salt in a wound.

A part of me revels in her fear, the trembling of her body beneath me. But the man buried under the beast caresses her jaw and introduces a moderate, sensual pumping of my hips. The friction of her tightness sheathing my engorged length has the brute snarling to be let loose. But I keep him in check until my mate's beautiful ass pushes back for more.

With focused intent, I set a vigorous, unrelenting pace. Viessa meets me thrust for thrust, rubbing her spine against my chest. Christ, she's unbelievable. Emotions overwhelm my senses. Love. Lust. A savage protectiveness and sheer joy at taking my mate in beast form.

When she cries out, her insides clenching around my length like a delicious vice, I fling my head back, and howl to the moon, glorying in the raw intensity of this moment. As my roar echoes into the night, I strike, driving all four canines into the delicate flesh between her neck and shoulder.

Viessa screams, struggling to pull away from the extreme pain. I growl fiercely and clamp down tighter, ordering her without words to submit. She immediately stills, her fingers sunk deep into the earth.

Not letting go of my prize, I thrust once more. Slow and steady at first, until I feel her muscles unwind, and a small moan fills my ears. That's the beast's signal to take over. I offer him free rein, realizing my mate is strong enough to handle his primal aggression.

The second her savory blood flows over my taste buds and down my throat, the bond skyrockets through my system, and Viessa's emotions slam into me. The fear and anxiety of the mating ritual, her unconditional love, and support. The thrill of being a Mistress and finally gaining control over her life. The apprehension over her enormous responsibilities as Oracle but the elation of possessing a divine purpose, of making a difference. Her fierce protectiveness of our friends and family.

I allow it all to circulate through me, relishing the connection, and content to finally have an insight into this mysterious female that conquered my heart, dominates my passion, and soothes my spirit.

"Liam. Come with me."

My woman commands. I obey.

Chapter 45

The second our hearts and breaths slow—I withdraw from her warmth. Viessa flops over on her back to gaze up at me with such affection and contentment, I ache to deliver the words to complete the mating, but I cannot speak in beast form.

Her palm reaches up and caresses my cheek. "Liam James Scott, you are mine. From this moment forward, we are one. One mind. One heart. One soul. Forever."

I chuff in response, devouring the exposed flesh laid out before me in the grass, the porcelain skin glistening in the moonlight. The long, thin tattoo on her inner thigh, thickens my length once more. I imagine running my tongue across the black ink back to my favorite spot in the world.

Instead, I pass a claw gently along the edges of the design. Her muscles tense in response, contemplating me with wide-eyed wonder. Her fierce desire swirls with my animalistic lust, and I seize her wrist and haul her to her feet. The beast huffs in contentment at the raw wounds on her neck.

"Liam, what…"

Before she can finish, I toss her over my shoulder, smack her bare ass, pluck up her discarded clothes, and head off deeper into the woods. I picked up the scent of another pair of wolves headed in our direction. No way in hell will I allow them to observe my female naked. I'd have to kill them, and I don't relish murdering a member of my pack.

As my feet pound the ground, my mate grips the fur on my back, giggling like a schoolgirl, enjoying the adventure of being with the beast. Even though she's somewhat intimidated by this side of me, she also craves the raw, primal taking. Her emotions fill me with hope and trepidation. I may not have expressed the words yet, but my bite completed our mating. I've defied the gods to bind this female to me, and I have no doubt we will suffer the repercussions.

When I finally spy the hunting cabin, I let my apprehensions go with a grin. Before the sun ascends in the sky, my mate will be so thoroughly fucked and pleasured she won't care that we disobeyed the celestial deities. I'll hunt and nourish my body to provide sustenance for my woman. Just the prospect of her fangs sinking into my flesh escalates my need.

I leap onto the deck with my burden safely tucked against my shoulder, nudging open the door with my foot, and toss her clothes on the plaid couch facing the fireplace black with age.

My brother and I maintain the cabin for hunting trips, so it's well stocked with wood, canned goods, and propane.

"You can set me down now, Liam," Viessa murmurs lovingly, gliding her palms over my fur-clad backside.

In response, I smack her bare rump—hard—and proceed with building a fire to keep her warm and naked.

Once the onslaught of the full moon frenzy eases, I'm able to function as an ordinary man, somewhat. The beast is still quick to primal aggression and lust, and can't communicate, but I can achieve routine tasks with efficiency as long as I work to remain focused.

"I love the softness of your fur, Liam," she purrs as she continues to caress wherever her hands can reach. "I ache to rub it against my pussy."

My brain misfires.

Whatever task I was about to tackle flies out the window at her comment. In two strides, I'm across the cabin, tossing her on the queen bed set against the wall. She smirks and spreads her bent knees in invitation.

Saliva pools in my mouth, anticipating her flavor, but I bypass my craving and settle my frame between her thighs, grinding my leg against her glistening sex.

"Oh, God, Liam. You feel like the little teddy bear I would rub against when I was a freshly turned vampire and had visions of you."

Christ. Viessa masturbated with a stuffed animal while thinking of me? That's the hottest, goddamn thing I've ever heard.

I growl in approval.

"I would get wet just watching you rut and fuck other werewolves. I couldn't stop myself from climaxing, imagining the stuffed bear was you."

Her words inflame me. I grasp my cock, caressing the head along her soaked core.

"You wish to fuck me, beast?" she coos, smoothing her hands down my chest, over my abdomen until she grasps my balls. Her grip isn't gentle, but the creature doesn't crave gentleness. "Do you?" she demands, giving a harsh tug.

I growl low, baring my teeth at the slight discomfort, but nod in agreement.

She pouts enticingly. "But I prefer to suck your cock. Stand for me, my sexy wolf."

Apparently, the primal animal doesn't object to her sexual order because we are vaulting to our feet in a second, dick in hand and at the ready.

She scoots to the edge of the bed, licking her lips and inspecting my erection like it's a giant lollipop. I want nothing more than to grab her by her hair, guide that lush mouth to my pulsing cock, and fuck her till I explode, but the beast seems fascinated with this new development.

When she's perched between my thighs, she swats my hand away and replaces it with her own. My growl is ripe with longing as she glides both palms up and down my engorged length.

"You are so big," she murmurs every guy's dream of hearing. "Hard and silky at the same time." The dazzling gaze peers up at me as she licks the bead of moisture at the tip, and I'm lost. "Hmmm, and you taste so damn yummy."

When she sets in, enclosing those soft lips around the head, taking me down her throat, my eyes roll back at the exquisite bliss. I clutch a fistful of her silky locks and set the pace. She hums in approval, fondling my sac while stretching her free hand up my torso, loving the softness and texture of my fur.

Being able to discern and understand her emotions is fucking unreal. She literally gets off on experiencing my fur against her skin.

Viessa slows right before a sharp sting penetrates the side of my erection. I glance down and catch a trickle of blood escaping around her lips. Fuck. She's feeding on my cock. My balls tighten with the need to detonate.

'Come, my king. Give me all of it,' she demands in my mind. I'm powerless to resist it.

I arch my neck and roar as my seed blends with my blood gushing down her throat. Her irises brighten with pleasure as she sucks and swallows for more.

Holy Christ, my mate is fucking incredible.

Just as the spasms slow, Viessa raises a palm glowing with amber and slaps it over my right pectoral. Fire sears the fur and flesh beneath. I attempt to flee the pain, but my mate's teeth are still clamped down on my dick.

In seconds the heat expands, quelling the call of the moon and forcing the beast to withdraw. The pointed ears revert to normal, the canines recede, and the coat covering my body becomes smooth skin once more.

I peer down as my mate removes her fangs, suckling and licking at my length like she can't get enough. Her palm glides back down my abdomen, and I'm stunned to discover a symbol branded into my chest.

"What is this?" I ask, and the enigmatic Oracle rises, tracing the raised, tender flesh with her finger.

"My mark. God has sanctioned our mating, my king. Your immense strength sustains my own. Without your energy in the world, in my heart, I struggle to control my magic. My mind." She leans in and tenderly kisses the intricate symbol similar to the engravings on her back. "This binds you to me. Our life force is one. You will live as long as I do, so I may draw from your mighty power whenever I have need. If you perish, I do as well, and vice versa."

Exhilaration and pride warm my chest. This delicate, powerful creature requires me as much as I need her. I wrap my arms around her waist and drag her against my body, loving the smoothness of skin on skin.

"I gladly offer you my strength, protection, love, and life, sweetness."

"Say the words, my king."

"Viessa Vivian Bramen, you are mine. From this moment forward, we are one. One mind. One heart. One soul. Forever."

The happiness shining in her eyes melts every doubt. This fierce female with a divine purpose now belongs to me until my dying breath. Nothing will bar me from devoting the rest of my days to worshiping the beauty in any manner she desires.

"I love you, sweetness," I whisper, brushing my lips across hers.

"And I you." She clasps my face in her palms and the brand on my chest heats. "Do you vow to submit to me sexually?"

Without hesitation, I lower to one knee and bow my head. "Yes, Mistress."

The End

Epilogue

Nicole

"**I** understand your concerns, Jedidiah, and my team will look into the matter."

If I have to listen to one more whiny complaint from another stick up his ass aristocrat, I'll vomit the bile stewing in my gut. "Make sure my consort has your contact information. We will get in touch once I've investigated your claims."

"Yes, my queen. Thank you." The pompous idiot bows before turning to Logan on my right.

I gaze out over the dwindling crowd, and my irritation grows. The Moretti's and I have been at this for two hours already, and I'm so done. When I took on the responsibilities of the queen, I didn't comprehend it would morph into endless nights filled with the tedious task of listening to a tributary of vampires complaining about the most mundane, stupid details.

For fuck's sake, grow a pair and take care of it yourself. That's what I crave to holler to the rafters tonight. Normally, I grit my teeth and deal, but this evening my body aches, nausea rolls in my belly, and my vision blurs.

I peer over at my sex god of a mate as he finishes up with Jeb, the petulant, whiny fucker. *'Logan, you and Sebastian, please finish up. I've had enough. If I don't get my ass off this throne, I'll go postal.'* Telepathy is damn convenient.

'Are you alright, love? You look a little pale.'

'Yes,' I fib. If he knew I wasn't feeling up to par, his attempts to care for me would suffocate. I just need to vacate the premises and figure out what's amiss with my body. Alone. *'Alex wishes to get together for wine, so I'm gonna bop over to the cottage for a bit. I'll be back in a couple of hours.'*

God. Please buy it.

My perceptive mate regards me for several minutes. The iridescent gaze roams my face. No doubt he's probing my emotions, so I lock them down tight.

'When you return, how does a hot bubble bath sound?' he asks, and I breathe a sigh of relief.

'If you'll join me, I say it sounds perfect.' I force a smile as a fresh wave of nausea rises in my esophagus. If I don't get out of here soon, I'll soak the immortals milling around the throne room in yellow bile.

At any other time, the lopsided, seductive grin would trump anything else, but my demand to freak the fuck out in private overrides his effect on me.

I stand abruptly, and everyone halts their movements and discussions, shifting to face their queen. "Business elsewhere requires my attention. Logan and Sebastian will handle the remaining issues and report back to me later." Before anyone stops me, I disappear from the room.

The peace and tranquility of my previous home lull me for a second. In the next instant, I'm hauling ass down the hallway to the bathroom, sliding on my knees to the toilet. I barely get the lid up before my gut wretches, and the bile stewing for hours releases in a gush.

Dry heaves rack my body long after the contents have emptied. When the cramps in my stomach finally ease, I sit back on my butt, my spine against the tub.

Fuck. Fuck. Fuck.

This mass exodus means one thing. I'm pregnant. Again. Tears burn my eyes, but I blink them away. Losing my baby girl nearly ruined me. It almost destroyed my connection to Logan.

Three months later, my need for Icarus' guidance is glaringly obvious. I miss him so much. Right now, I'd give anything to have him kneel next to me and offer comfort because this woman can't deal with another loss.

"Please, Priest. I need you." My whisper echoes around the bathroom as I hug my knees to my chest. "I can't do this alone."

Yes, you can, Nicole.

My annoying inner bitch is the only response I receive. I'm uncertain what I was expecting—the priest's ethereal voice to surround me like a warm blanket, miraculously granting me the peace I seek? Or he'd somehow abandon his celestial home to appear to me?

Fat chance.

"Oh, shut the fuck up," I yell at myself and the walls.

I require a few minutes to wallow in my self-pity and fear. Sometimes the warrior needs to shatter in order to face the coming battle—the war with my emotions and past demons.

I've come a long way from the resentful, emotionless loner from two years ago. I still grapple with sharing my personal turmoil, even with my valiant, loving, and overly protective mate.

But the Oracle's last words instructed me to open up, to let the people I trust and care for inside. He claimed it was my one weakness, and I suspect he was correct. My inability to spew out my thoughts and feelings makes my lover gnash his teeth in frustration and anger.

My male is a fierce Alpha. Dominant and commanding. In the bedroom, I lust after the huge, muscle-bound Dom. The smack of his palm on my backside. The addictive burn of a flogger or whip. Restrained, blindfolded, or gagged with Logan governing my every reaction is the ultimate drug.

In our day-to-day life, or I guess I should state our night-to-night life, I make my own decisions. I am the queen of the Vampire Nation, the largest immortal species on the planet. My word is law.

Although I answer to the Council of Unity. All kings and queens must adhere to the laws created and agreed upon.

But even with all that authority and leadership, I'm still just a scared little Halfling struggling to live up to the prophecy of my life; to create and maintain peace in the immortal realm. Give birth to the first vampire king to walk in the sun and eat food. Now it appears the gods tasked the council members with locating the Breeders to gift them my blood and safeguard their lives, which in turn equals the preservation of the immortal races.

Just another day in my life.

I shove off the floor. Run a fresh toothbrush loaded with minty toothpaste over my teeth, gums, and tongue before rinsing the last of the nasty taste of my stomach contents from my mouth.

Only one thing helps me deal with my emotions, so I head toward the baby grand nestled in the center of the bay windows overlooking the moonlit Oregon forest beyond.

This cottage was once my sanctuary. The place I could escape from the anarchy in my mind. My history was a bitch of a tale packed with hurt, abuse, and fear. Music was the primary outlet I employed to bring those turbulent emotions simmering to the surface. A kind of purge and my only way to convey what I was going through.

Pain was another channel. Either through Krav Maga training with Kurtis or BDSM with an unknown Dom at some random club.

My mate offers me that release now, but I'm beyond the Krav Maga, and while being punched or stabbed hurts, it evaporates in a matter of seconds. No lingering burn to soothe my mind unless I haven't drunk in a while, but my overbearing warrior makes certain I am well fed, with both human food and his blood.

I slip onto the bench and rest my fingers on the cool keys for a moment. I know the song I wish to sing, but enjoying the ivory's smooth texture and reconnecting with my old friend must occur first.

The second the melodious notes permeate the room, my soul sighs, and my mind quiets, becoming lost in the words and melody of Control by Zoe Wees.

For me, the lyrics tell a story of survival, weathering past traumas, but still dreading the return of the loss of control I experienced back then. It unmasks the most intimate facets of myself, so closely, it's like Zoe wrote it specifically for me. It reveals my insecurity. How I leaned on Logan—in my mind, in my dreams, and physically to help me cope.

Tryin' to breathe in and then out but the air gets caught

'Cause even though I'm older now and I know how to shake off the past

I wouldn't have made it if I didn't have you holding my hand

I don't wanna lose control

As I sing, images rush at me with the force of a hurricane. But I ride it out, letting the pain, confusion, sorrow, and love permeate my voice, cleansing me of the demons.

I need you to know, I would never be this strong without you

You've seen how I've grown, you took all my doubts, 'cause you were home

My father; battered and bruised me. My mother; neglected and looked the other way. For reasons, I now understand, but as a child, it shattered me. I felt abandoned by Logan when he left me at that school, and later when he retreated from my dreams altogether. I assumed he was my salvation. At that point in my life, I needed him to be.

Circumstances compelled me into a life of loneliness because I couldn't remain in one location for very long. All of it caused my brain to shut down and suppress my past's hideousness in some dingy corner of my mind. For years, I had no remembrance of who I was or what I was running from.

Until my sexy knight came barreling into my soul. Logan. He possessed it. Owned it. The second I gazed into those beautiful, bright emeralds; the forgotten storm rushed to the forefront with the pressure of a tornado. It was only through my mate's aid that I developed a thicker skin. Became stronger than I'd ever been, which enabled me to grow into the warrior needed to conquer the monster under my bed and fulfill the prophecy.

Halfway through the song, I sense Logan's presence. He waits patiently, watching, granting me the space my spirit demands. This proud, courageous being is my rock. It should've been him I solicited for guidance. Not Icarus. He was always with me when it hurt. Calmed my mind. Chased away the demons. This male understood me from the very beginning, and our connection was absolute.

Before the last note rings through the room, my mate appears next to the piano. Still attired in leather, his shoulder-length tresses tied at his nape, the piercing gaze sparkles with concern.

"What is going on, baby? Why did you feel the need to lie to me?"

My shoulders slump. "You knew?"

"I may not have your expertise to detect lies, but I discern when my mate is hiding something from me."

My dress pants glide effortlessly along the polished bench as I slide out and head to the bar. If I had my druthers, I'd conduct all our meetings in jeans, sweatshirts, and boots. Logan insisted I wear a lengthy formal gown like some Victorian queen from the fucking turn of the century. When my response was "Not fucking likely" my backside enjoyed a fantastic spanking. After, we brokered a compromise. Dress slacks, blouses, and, of course, boots.

"If I must have this convo, I need alcohol."

Luckily, Alex keeps the cooler stocked even though she's seldom here anymore.

"Allow me." Logan's heat warms my spine as he comes up behind me, and my mind flashes back to the last time Logan poured me wine in this very room. It was a night filled with eye-opening revelations and hot, steamy foreplay.

Armed with a full glass of dark red yumminess, I head over to the couch and perch on one corner. My mate takes the coffee table, probably to analyze my expressions.

"Spill it."

I'm about to place my lips to the rim when it hits me. Holy fuck. I'm pregnant. I shouldn't be consuming liquor. Dammit. I needed the soothing influence of the wine.

With regret, and maybe a hiccup of a sob, I set the glass on the side table and face my mate. I stare into his handsome visage and panic bubbles. Dear God. We are going to be parents. The concept of being a mother scares the ever livin' shit out of me.

"I…" tears clog my throat.

Logan grabs me around the waist and hoists me onto his lap. I adjust my position, so my thighs straddle his hips. With unsteady fingers, I untie the leather strap holding his dark loose waves in check.

"Tell me what is vexing you, my love. And the truth better leave those luscious lips or your pretty ass will feel the heat of my palm."

"So bossy," I smirk, stalling.

"Nicole." His growl produces a shiver of desire to slither down my spine. How I love pushing this man's buttons, but now is probably not an ideal time.

"I think I'm pregnant," I blurt out. Better to just throw it out there.

The warrior stills, not even breathing as he studies my face. "Are you certain?"

"Just spent the last half hour puking my guts out, so pretty sure."

Logan glances down at my stomach, and I open my senses to him. The wonder and awe at my revelation humble me, but the worry for my life overshadows those sentiments. For this savage fighter, nothing in the world matters more than me. He would sacrifice anything or anyone to keep me safe.

"This is different, Logan. I believe this is the child the prophecy foretold. A boy."

When the mighty vampire lifts his lids to mine, I'm astonished by the tears illuminating the atomic green irises. "Baby, as much as the prospect of being a father thrills me, I am petrified."

Holy shit! The Legendary Moretti just admitted he's scared, and somehow his confession gives me the strength to be the strong one.

I cradle his face in my palms, wiping away the lone tear that escaped. "Logan, haven't you learned by now, nothing will keep us apart? Not war, kidnapping, loss, or death itself. Our love is infamous and infinite. They wrote a damn prophecy about it." The edges of his lips lift in a slight smile. "We've accomplished so much of the ancient foretelling already. This is the last piece. The next king."

He nods, running his fingers gently across my flat stomach. "I cannot wait to see your belly grow with my child."

"Let's not talk about me getting fat right now, shall we?"

He snorts, but immediately sobers. "I realize you are hesitant concerning your parenting skills, and who could blame you with your upbringing. But, Nicole, we are in this together. A united front to pick up each other's slack." He cradles my cheek with a warm palm, and I lean into the caress. "You and I will raise a magnificent king, one to extend your legacy of peace."

"*Our* legacy, my sweet, sexy man. I couldn't have accomplished anything without you by my side. I love you more than I imagined I was capable. Even though I'm paralyzed with fear too, a part of me is looking forward to raising our son. Us training him in combat together, eating dinner with him, listening to you offer him advice on women while I roll my eyes behind your back." My teasing produces the sexy, lopsided grin I was hoping to receive. "Most importantly, making sure he carries your moral standard and my badass, smart mouth."

Sex on a stick chuckles. "God help us all."

"We began this quest together, my warrior, and together we will see it through to the end."

"Yes, my queen," he murmurs before claiming my lips in a searing kiss. A promise of things to come.

Also By

Acknowledgements

My undying gratitude goes to the love of my life, my husband. Thanks, babe, for granting me the time to create my stories. For listening to me read out loud as my final proofreader. But mostly, for your patience and understanding. You're my rock.

Gratitude goes to my daughter, Racheal, for always reposting or sharing my marketing efforts.

Viessa and Liam's journey was a tough one for me to write about. Not merely because it takes me one step closer to the end of this series, but because their dynamic was unlike any of the other characters in the Storm series. In the end, I fell in love with Viessa and Liam, and I hope you do as well.

This book wouldn't be possible without my excellent editor, Sam Hendricks. Thank you for finalizing this fourth book with me.

I'd also like to thank my awesome, devoted beta readers! Dawn, Paul, Mia, and Jodi. You are amazing, and I'm incredibly grateful for your input. I couldn't do this without any of you.

A million thanks go to the extremely talented Les at German Creative for creating a fantastic book cover!

Most importantly, I'd like to thank you, my readers. My Stormsters. Without you or your wonderful reviews, my stories would sit on a shelf collecting dust. I hope you enjoy Fractured Storm as much as I enjoyed developing it.

Note From Author

Thank you, dear readers, for continuing to love my Storm series! Next up, Fatal Storm, featuring Jagorach, the demon king!

If you loved Fractured Storm, or any of the books in the Storm series, please consider reviewing it or recommending it to a friend—your reviews help indie authors so much.

Let's Connect: Join A.R.'s STORMSTER CLUB Newsletter! You will get exclusive previews, contests, and news of new releases. A.R. loves to connect with readers. Check out her website for all the information.

Website: www.arvagnetti.com
Email: ar@arvagnetti.com

Please follow her on:
Bookbub - Goodreads - Instagram - Facebook- TikTok